ROMANCE
IN THE
ROARING FORTIES
AND OTHER STORIES
BY DAMON RUNYON

ROMANCE IN THE ROARING FORTIES AND OTHER STORIES BY DAMON RUNYON

Introduction by Tom Clark,
author of
The World of Damon Runyon

BⱢB
BEECH TREE BOOKS
A QUILL EDITION
New York

Library of Congress Cataloging-in-Publication Data

Runyon, Damon, 1880–1946.
   Romance in the roaring forties and other stories.

   I. Title.
PS3535.U52R6   1985   813'.52   85-15788
ISBN 0-688-05421-8
ISBN 0-688-06148-6 (Quill ed.: pbk.)

Printed in the United States of America

First Beech Tree Books/Quill Edition

1 2 3 4 5 6 7 8 9 10

The word "book" is said to derive from *boka,* or beech.
The beech tree has been the patron tree of writers since ancient times and represents the flowering of literature and knowledge.

This book is dedicated to the memory of the late Damon Runyon, his son Damon Runyon, Jr., and their good friend the late Walter Winchell. We wish to give special acknowledgment to the following persons, whose cooperation, by way of research, permissions, interviews, and unswerving perseverance, made this book possible: Damon Runyon III and his sister D'Ann McKibben, the children of Damon Runyon, Jr.; David P. Faulkner, Esq., Guardian of the Person and Estate of Mary Runyon McCann, daughter of Damon Runyon, and his law associate, R. Edward Tepe, Esq.; Raoul Lionel Felder, Executor for Damon Runyon, Jr., who, along with the above-mentioned persons, devoted hundreds of hours of his time to help bring this volume to publication; Sheldon Abend, president of the American Play Company, Inc., New York City, the literary agent for the Guardian of Mary Runyon McCann and for the children of Damon Runyon, Jr., who "rode herd" on this entire project; and special thanks to Jane Meara, the editor at Beech Tree Books, whose knowledge of the literary works of Damon Runyon and determination to revive the Runyon stories brought about this book. Our gratitude to certain Runyon fans, who themselves are modern "Runyonesque" characters, for their suggestions. They are: Con "Scamp" Errico, New York, N.Y.; Skip Whitaker, Boulder, Col.; Al "the Brain" Rosenstein, Esq., New York, N.Y.; Stewart Wallach, Los Angeles, Cal.; Thomas F. Saullo, Jr., the original "Mr. T," Woodmere, N.Y.; "George Just," Miami, Florida; "Matty the Jeweler," Bronx, N.Y.; Stuart Whitman, Montecito, Cal.; Nick "AliBaba" the Greek, London and New York, N.Y.; Charlie Ha-Ha Celeste, Boston, Mass.; Rocky Graziano and Jake "the Raging Bull" LaMotta, former middleweight champions; Sarah "the Hat" Hospodar of New York and Switzerland; Diane "Nicely" Buccerio of New York; Nancy "the Pants" Bretzfield of Los Angeles and New York; Annie Simpson and Kathy Travis of New York; James P. and G. A. Browne of New York; Tommy "the Gun" Davey of New York; and lastly but very nicely, the doll Joan Loretta Hrubi of New York.

Contents

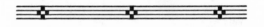

Introduction

Damon Runyon's tales are ironic mini-comedies based on the American outlaw code. It is the old Code of the West, transposed to Manhattan and the twentieth century. To live outside the law you must be honest, the saying used to go. Runyon rearranges it to read: To live outside the law you must be an interesting character, and anyway, no one is more honest than he has to be.

Runyon had outlaw roots. "My father was a product of the six-gun West," his son wrote in a memoir. "At one time somewhere in his prowls as a youth he actually packed a six-gun." That was in Denver at the turn of the century, where Runyon cut his writing teeth in the style of the Western pioneer reporter—on shot glasses and shotguns.

Referring to the family background, Runyon himself once confided to his son, "We come from a long line of Huguenot horse thieves who were run out of France by posses." Damon may have been stretching the tale a little, as he was accustomed to doing. But the spirit of his remark sums up the Runyon lineage accurately.

Damon's paternal grandfather, William Renoyan, an itinerant printer, led a band of gold-seeking adventurers in a cross-country boat expedition in 1852. His design was to discover an inland waterway to California, but the party wound up stranded on the dry Blue River of Kansas in August. There they founded the frontier village of Manhattan. Renoyan Americanized the family name to Runyan, and started a local newspaper. He taught the printer's trade to his son, Alfred. Alfred grew up to be a strong-minded character in his own right. Indian fighter, lover of the classics, gambler, drunkard, saloon orator, he was soon publishing and printing newspapers of his own—or, when his own papers collapsed, working for other people's.

Alfred's only son, Alfred Damon Runyan, was born in Manhattan in 1880. After a few more years of maverick newspapering around Kansas, Alfred, Sr., moved his wife, son and two daughters to Pueblo, Colorado. Elizabeth Damon Runyan was tubercular, a condition the high clear air of Colorado was expected to improve. It didn't, and she died before young Alfred Damon's eighth birthday. His sisters were sent back to live with their mother's family in Kansas.

The boy was thereafter a sort of newspaper and saloon orphan. ("He had the habit of silence, from the lonely early days when there was simply no one to listen to him," his son later observed.) According to most accounts, he left school in the fourth grade and spent his early years wandering barefoot on the streets of the steel-mill town of Pueblo, where there were plenty of bad habits to pick up. He was smoking cigarettes at age nine, drinking whiskey at fifteen, and not long afterward packing that six-gun his son mentions.

Young Al, as he was called, made his bed in his old man's flophouse room, learned about the world of high thought and letters from his old man's tavern monologues on Shakespeare, Buffalo Bill Cody and Billy the Kid, and soon, from the same source, was receiving an

on-the-spot journalistic education in everything from
how to handle hot type to how to handle a hot tip,
whether it be on a news story or on the nose of a
horse.

Apprenticed as printer's devil at the Pueblo *Evening
News*, where his father worked at the time, young Al
had his first reporting assignment at fourteen, to cover
a lynching. This would be rough stuff for most boys
of that tender age, but Al had already worked as a teleg-
rapher's messenger in the red-light district of "Little
Pittsburgh," as the wide-open town of Pueblo was
known. He did the job.

The next year he was made a full-fledged news reporter. Two years after that, he'd moved over to the
Pueblo *Evening Post*, where he received his first by-line.
The printer misspelled his name, with an *o* instead of
an *a*. Al became Alfred Damon Runyon on that day.
(Later, in New York, an equally arbitrary journalistic
"decision"—this time by an editor—resulted in the am-
putation of "Alfred" from Runyon's by-line.)

From his father, a philosophical individualist, young
Al Runyon had already inherited a great respect for
such independent types as gamblers and sportsmen and
outlaws, together with a great curiosity about their exploits, both of which would remain with him for the
rest of his life. So would his old man's cynicism about
such institutions as religion, politics, high finance and
so-called polite society, and also his old man's view of
women as a deeply untrustworthy species. But perhaps
the most important family legacy handed down from
father to son was a great loyalty to the profession and
life of newspapering.

Many years later, when "Damon Runyon" was a
household name wherever newspapers were sold in this
country, Damon's own son, Damon, Jr., wrote him a

letter expressing discouragement over the possibilities
of a journalistic career. "You say you don't know if
you will ever be more than a better than average reporter," Runyon wrote back. "Well, my boy, I think
that is better than being king."

From his early habit of long silences, young Al devel-
oped the skill of being a good listener. From the
fate-enforced loneliness of being a half-abandoned moth-
erless street-child he acquired the ability to make up
his mind for himself. Attention, curiosity, detachment
and a photographic memory—Runyon had all the reporter's tools from his teenage years on. Later, in New
York, the most famous editors of his era (Arthur Bris-
bane of the *Journal* and Herbert Bayard Swope of the
World) would call Runyon the greatest reporter in the
business. That, to Damon, was the second highest form
of praise, next to his paycheck. ("Get the Money" was
always his slogan.)

When Runyon was seventeen, the battleship *Maine*
was sunk in Havana harbor. Turned down because of
his age by a Colorado cavalry enlistment office, Al
headed north and talked his way into the Minnesota
volunteers, with whom he quickly found himself fighting as an infantryman in the Philippines. Apparently
he experienced combat against Moro insurgents, though
the details are lost in legends, Runyon's own later my-
thologizing and the heroic sentimentalities of his Kip-
lingesque camp verse of the period.

By the beginning of the new century he was back
in the States, free-riding the rails around Colorado between short-time newspaper jobs. His adventures as a
railroad hobo gave him plenty of material he later used
in newspaper vignettes and on such projects as ghost-
writing a serialized autobiography for heavyweight
champ Jack Dempsey, whose knockabout boy-

hood in the Rockies didn't differ too much from Run-yon's own.

Denver became young Runyon's base. He staffed on the Denver *Post*, went west for a while and got a job with the San Francisco *Post*, then returned to the Mile-High City and landed on the payroll of the *Rocky Mountain News* in 1906. It was his four-year stint with the *News* that established him as a notable reporter, famed for his "stunt"-oriented feature writing, his personal handle on news stories and his unusual powers of observation. He also won a small local reputation as a poet, as well as a large one for his drinking—no mean feat in a ripsnorting community where, in the words of one pioneer of the period, "Them swinging doors never stopped twenty-four hours a day!"

Only when knocked off his feet by the pretty society reporter of the *News*, Ellen Egan, did Runyon reform his ways, and subdue the alcoholism that had often caused him to lose whole stretches of time and memory in wild drinking binges. In order to win Ellen's hand, and also because, as he later told his son, "I wanted to go places," he gave up the bottle for good.

To many who knew him in later years, when he smoked three packs of cigarettes and drank sixty cups of coffee every day, Runyon seemed to have a sharp and sour disposition much of the time—a fact that may be attributed to his decision to swear off alcohol around 1910. Thereafter, as he once joked, he "became positively famous for hanging out with drunks and never touching a drop."

Runyon was thirty when he went off to New York to find his fortune as a writer. His first Big Town job was in the sports department at the Hearst morning paper, the New York *American*. His colorful reporting of the New York Giants' spring baseball camp in 1911 won him enthusiastic readers and, shortly, a raise. Soon he had his own Manhattan apartment. Ellen Egan moved east from Denver to marry him. She gave Damon a daughter in 1914 and a son in 1918, both births occurring when he was off covering baseball games. This was a regularity chez Runyon: Father was never at home.

By the early twenties, Runyon was earning the princely salary of $25,000 a year as the star feature writer, news reporter and sports columnist in the Hearst empire. He was able to put Ellen up in the expensive fashion she fancied and also to develop refined tastes of his own in dining and dressing. But his schedule as a morning newspaper employee and his predilections for the nocturnal life of the town, with its entertaining characters, had already conjoined by this time to create a lifestyle that was to keep Runyon permanently away from the family nest, on the move "around and about" (as he put it in his stories and in his expense account vouchers). The Upper West Side apartments where he kept his family were home to him in name only. He actually kept personal housekeeping in a series of bachelor scatters closer to the Broadway mainstream.

He usually rose late, and attended to a thorough first meal of the day at Lindy's restaurant (called "Mindy's" in the stories), where he mixed freely with a regular clientele made up not only of such big names as Arnold Rothstein—the famous "high shot" and free-lance bankroller—but also a miscellaneous crowd of show people, petty gamblers and hustlers. These were, in his view, highly innovative, inventive people, whose struggles to keep alive—by activities legal and illegal—made them worthy of interest. "What this fellow does," Runyon once said of such an acquaintance, "is the best he can, but the field, being slightly overcrowded, is none too well. It's a very crowded profession today."

More of the same types, particularly those of the betting persuasion, could be found of an afternoon, taking the sun on the pavement outside ticket agent Mike Jacobs's Broadway office—a stretch of concrete known locally as "Jacobs Beach." There Damon could be found rubbernecking, discussing odds on sporting events of the day or simply putting in time "on the Erie"—as he called the deliberate act of listening-in.

One of Runyon's most remarkable faculties was his gift for preserving (and often himself adopting) the speech patterns of others. Throughout the 1920s he was able to sit around in speakeasies and record in his head the syntax and vocabulary of Broadway night life and underworld characters, much of which made its way into that crowning reporting job of his career, the "guys and dolls" short stories. "He has caught with a high degree of insight the actual tone and phrase of the gangsters and racketeers of the town. Their talk is put down almost literally." So claimed one knowledgeable critic of the epoch, Heywood Broun. "To me the most impressive thing in *Guys and Dolls* is the sensitivity of the ear of Damon Runyon." That sensitive ear was the ear of a guy who was strictly asking for coffee at all times.

Some days in New York there was a ball game to cover, other days Runyon put in at the racetrack or doing the tour of the gyms, and evenings often found him alongside fight rings, pounding out his reports. There was always a story to file, and after that the night beat opened out into dining on the town and making the circuit of the card and dice games, then later, the drinking and dancing clubs. In the latter spots, Damon rubbed shoulders amiably with gangsters who were proven to have hearts by the fact that they kept losing them to the chorus dancers. These chorus "dolls" were outfitted, to quote one Runyon story, in barely enough costume "to make a pad for a crutch"—and were often in real life sophisticated gold diggers.

The association of sex and crime in the nightclub era was blatant enough. This was the period of the New Morality in America—a phenomenon that, many people suspected, was something the newspapers of the time invented in order to boost circulation. But in the nightclubs it was right there, out in the open. The half-naked dancing girls were wooed (and usually won) by men who had made their money in gambling, bootlegging and various rackets, including such "dodges" as banking and the stock market. From Runyon's highly educated and hardheaded viewpoint (he'd seen firsthand evidence of bank swindling and Wall Street "bucket shops"), these latter activities were, if anything, even *more* corrupt than the illicit operations of the bootleggers, gamblers, and such.

As for the New Morality, Damon Runyon had more opportunity to observe its violent fruits than most ordinary men, because of his position as the Hearst syndicate's number one trial reporter. No one could write a courtroom account with the swiftness, accuracy or descriptive color of Runyon, so every time some paramour or husband was bumped off in particularly sensational fashion, he was called into action. He became famous for his chilling portrait of Ruth Snyder, the "frosty blonde" who teamed up with a corset salesman to knock off her spouse. Reporting on this 1926 trial, Runyon compared the salesman's grip on the murder weapon—a sashweight—with the batting stance of Paul Waner, one of the most feared baseball hitters of the day. It was Runyon's somewhat cynical view that the public regarded murder as a very interesting kind of sport: "The Main Event," he called it.

Two years later Runyon's own marriage ended, not

quite as violently. The much-neglected Ellen Runyon had taken up drinking, while Damon had for years been carrying torches for a series of chorus dancers. The Runyons divorced in 1928. Ellen died in sad circumstances in 1931, the year before Damon married Patrice Amati, an attractive Spanish dancer at the Silver Slipper nightclub.

Between marriages, Runyon moved into the Hotel Forrest at Forty-ninth and Broadway, where for three years his penthouse suite and the hotel lobby became the classrooms of a sort of semipermanent floating Broadway seminar. In attendance were students from such fields as liquor distilling, betting commissions, race-track management, fight managing, wholesale clothing sales, boxing, acting and sportswriting. Professor Runyon, in residence, chaired the discussions. Between sessions, on his typewriter in the back room, he was working on a very important dissertation: a new kind of first-person narrative short story (five thousand words) with a classic twist ending, celebrating the guys and dolls of Broadway, describing their exploits in a purified present-tense tongue that was a very careful echo of their own, all to be carried off with a certain "half-boob air" (as the Professor called it) of humorous but knowing detachment.

These were the early days of the Depression, when Runyon's free-lancing acquaintances were having to hustle harder than ever to keep alive. The repeal of Prohibition put thousands of underworld citizens out of work, and times were also hard even for legitimate citizens. From 1929 on, Runyon recorded the new surge of gangsterism created by what his narrator in one story calls "the unemployment situation." He chronicles, with safely approximate veracity, the kidnapings, the shootings, the safe-crackings, the putting of people into sacks, the breaking and entering and the flinging of pineapples that explode.

The events in these stories reflect real life, such as it was lived on Damon Runyon's Broadway. Angie the Ox in "The Old Doll's House"—an "importer himself . . . besides enjoying a splendid trade in other lines, including artichokes and extortion"—is based on Ciro Terranova, a Jersey gangster who used a strong-arm squad to charge tribute on vegetables shipped into the New York metropolitan area, and to provide muscle and protection for his liquor-importing business. Bookie Bob, the affluent turf accountant snatched by Harry the Horse and friends in "The Snatching of Bookie Bob," was a character roughly drawn on the model of Billy Warren, a well-to-do Broadway bookmaker kidnaped in 1931 by Vincent "Mad Dog" Coll.

Miss Missouri Martin, hostess of the Sixteen Hundred Club in several Runyon stories, was Texas Guinan, the famous nightclub impresario who had once employed the second Mrs. Runyon as a dancer. Waldo Winchester, the scribe, was Runyon's close pal, gossip columnist Walter Winchell. For twelve years Winchell lived in the same building as Frank Costello, an underworld "don" whom he greatly admired. The columnist was slipped many a newsworthy item through the Costello pipeline. The two men knew each other well (they even resembled each other, down to the tilted gray hats), and often when Costello wanted to speak to his enemies or the law he did it through the medium of Winchell's column. One of Runyon's first Broadway tales—"Romance in the Roaring Forties," written in 1929 to help pay off debts incurred by an appendectomy and a bad bet on the Kentucky Derby—describes Waldo Winchester's fling with a mobster's doll. It was known on the Q.T. that Winchell himself had once had a brief, nervous

affair with a "private" doll of Frank Costello's—one of
Texas Guinan's hoofers.

Another familiar character is Regret the kindly horse-
player, who appears in several tales—including "Little
Miss Marker" and "Princess O'Hara" in this collection.
Abba Dabba Berman, the real-life character who inspired Runyon's fictional Regret, was no run-of-the-mill
thug; he was a man Damon had known well, and for
whom he had felt considerable affection. Otto Berman
(né Biderman) was a roly-poly follower of the nags and
a minor mathematical genius whose mind for systems,
handicapping ability and skill with numbers had at one
time earned him a tax-free $10,000 a week on the payroll
of bootlegger/racketeer Dutch Schultz. Berman went
down with the Dutchman in the bloodbath at the Palace
Chop House in Newark in 1935, a scene recently com-
memorated in the Francis Ford Coppola movie *The Cot-
ton Club*.

In Runyon's stories, Regret is always a helpful fellow,
ready to lend a hand to a friend in need—like the tight-
wad Sorrowful in "Little Miss Marker"—or even a
stranger in need, if she happens to be a doll. In "Princess
O'Hara," Regret's Robin Hood instincts lead him to
commit a horse theft—strictly on the Princess's behalf,
of course.

The illegal doings of his characters interest the narrator "more than somewhat," in Runyon's famous phrase;
in fact, the author was probably expressing his own
sentiments in the words of the slightly bemused narrator
in one of the stories: "It is only human nature to be
deeply interested in larceny."

The thinly veiled facts behind these fables were
known to most of Runyon's associates of the time. "I
recognize the characters concerned as real people," Heywood Broun said. The gangsters of Runyon's

tales are patterned on the great outlaw-individualists
of his era—the Buffalo Bills and Billy the Kids of the
Jazz Age.

Runyon soon began publishing his tales written in
the Hotel Forrest. *Cosmopolitan* took one, then demanded
more, and finally ran dozens, all at the previously un-
heard-of rate of a dollar a word. *Collier's* and the *Saturday
Evening Post* also ran many of the "guys and dolls"
stories, at the same price. Runyon, already Hearst's
best-paid reporter, now began to make some *real*
money.

The stories were also published in books, beginning
in 1931 with the collection called *Guys and Dolls*, and
then over and over again in paperback editions, some
of which sold into the millions of copies. By the mid-
thirties, Hollywood was buying up Runyon stories as
fuel for popular gangster pictures. The studios bought
sixteen tales in all, at increasingly higher prices, and
soon Runyon was traveling back and forth regularly
between New York and Hollywood, where he worked
at $2,000 a week and up, contributing ideas and scripts.
He maintained his column, which was now directed
to subjects of general interest and syndicated across the
country. He owned a stable of racehorses, a pack of
hunting dogs and a handful of heavyweight fighters,
all of which were famous for their expensive appetites.
Runyon now dressed like a Broadway high shot, ate
at the Colony and lived with his second wife at the
Parc Vendome, when they weren't in California or
Florida—where Runyon had built a $75,000 white villa
across Miami Bay from the villa of his friend Al "Scar-
face" Capone.

Capone's Florida place was vacant much of the time
after 1932, when the erstwhile gang boss went away
to prison. When he left he gave Runyon his prize

pair of whippets, as a keepsake. Capone knew Runyon liked dogs.

With the disappearance of Capone and many of the other underworld figures Runyon knew so well—theirs was a profession with a very high mortality rate—Runyon ceased to attempt more of his outlaw fictions. Eighteen of the twenty tales in this volume date from his period of greatest production, between 1929 and 1937. The exceptions are "Johnny One-Eye" (1941) and "The Melancholy Dane" (1944).

Ironically, it was at the height of his success, in the early forties, when his column was at its peak and his work in greater demand than ever at the movie studios, that Runyon contracted cancer of the throat. His larynx and trachea were surgically removed, leaving him with metal pipes for eating and breathing. His wife divorced him and married a younger man. Controlling an agony of remorse, Runyon awarded her a generous divorce settlement and eventually a large place in his will. He took a bachelor apartment in New York, spent much of his time at the Stork Club with old friends (he communicated on note pads, having lost his voice) and, despite his encroaching illness, went out every dawn to follow police calls in his friend Walter Winchell's automobile. The two columnists, who'd been chums since the twenties, drove all over the city to turn up unusual and interesting crimes. Runyon used the sights and sounds of these trips as material for his very moving final syndicated columns.

After a late and emotional reunion with his estranged son, Damon, Jr., Runyon grew gravely ill in late 1946. He died in December of that year. In his friend's memory, Winchell founded the Damon Runyon Cancer Fund, to which many notable mob figures immediately contributed (Frank Costello gave $25,000).

In accordance with Runyon's wish, his ashes were scattered over Broadway from an Eastern Airlines plane flown by Captain Eddie Rickenbacker, the World War I air ace, for whom, thirty years earlier, Runyon had ghostwritten some speeches. He'd also interviewed Rickenbacker a decade before *that*, when Eddie was in the race-car–driving game, and had written a sports page account of it. Those were only a few of the sixty million or so words that passed through the typewriter of reporter Runyon, who, to paraphrase one of his fellow Hearst columnists, Arthur J. "Bugs" Baer, would write you right out of the paper if you weren't careful.

For an earlier generation of readers, Runyon was an everyday experience. His newspaper columns and stories and his fictional tales were enjoyed by millions. One negative spin-off of this immense popularity was that it became a barrier to the acceptance of Runyon's fiction in "serious" literary circles, where in many cases the sheer success of a writer's work may be cited as an excuse for discriminating against it. At any rate, it would be no more fair to dismiss Runyon as a "popular writer" than it would be so to dismiss, say, Ring Lardner, who held an approximately equal position with Runyon in the public esteem, and who was an equally gifted writer—but who had for friends not gangsters but artistic people from Long Island, like F. Scott Fitzgerald, Dorothy Parker and Edmund Wilson. You don't get your work taught in college courses and printed in anthologies (as Lardner's stories are, and Runyon's are not) by hanging around with Al Capone or Arnold Rothstein. That's always been half of Runyon's problem in academic circles.

The other half, I think, relates to the trick of "indirection," or the "half-boob air," which Runyon said he used to conceal the fact that he was always "a rebel at heart." The irony in the stories continues to waft like smoke over the heads of many of his academic readers. Runyon's trick of role-reversal, placing criminals and "legitimate" people on unfamiliar sides of the sympathy-meter in his stories, seems to bother many professors.

Jimmy Cannon, one of Runyon's chief sportswriting disciples, spoke interestingly on this subject in a book called *No Cheering in the Press Box*. "One of the odd things about Damon," Cannon said, "was that he was a very cultured man. He pretended he wasn't. He concealed his culture and much of his knowledge. I have no idea why—but I think Damon wanted to get as close to the people he wanted to write about as he could. He wrote about mugs because they were interesting people. Damon did things that were extraordinary for those times, and for these times. They talk about guys doing daring things. Well, Runyon's heroes were pimps and prostitutes and murderers. He treated them as human beings. That is now the style. He was one of the forerunners."

On certain urban-bred writers of our day, such as Jimmy Breslin, Peter Maas, Mike Royko, George V. Higgins, or Jim Murray, the Runyon style has had an obvious influence.

Runyon's own view on the subject of acceptance by the "academic mob" was one he stated simply and frequently. "My measure of success is money," he wrote. "I have no interest in artistic triumphs that are financial losers. I would like to have an artistic success that also made money, of course, but if I had to make a choice between the two, I would take the dough."

A notably hard-boiled attitude, to be sure. But then, as his cartoonist-sportswriter colleague of the 1920s, Tad

Dorgan, often said, Damon was a "Ten Minute Egg"—as hard-boiled as they come. His tough demeanor, those who knew him best agreed, was calculated to conceal his feelings, which seemed to have been damaged beyond repair at some very early date, back in his half-mythological Wild West boyhood. Even his friends often complained that no one ever got to know Damon Runyon well. Runyon may or may not have preferred it that way. But no one who knew him disputes the fact that, as Bill Corum said, Runyon had "great character and the inner courage of a lion," and that, in the words of Runyon's own obit on the high-roller Rothstein, "he died game."

His reputation as a pioneering reporter is solid. His old columns can still be read for pleasure today. The *Dictionary of Slang* will tell you that Runyon, in his Broadway tales, nudged into the great common pool of spoken American a whole boatload of underworld expressions—the patois of Broadway. These expressions, to give only a token list, include such popular favorites as "cheaters" (for glasses), "cock-eyed" (for unconscious), "croak" (for die), "dukes" (for fists), "equalizer" (for gun), "hot spot" (for predicament), "kisser" (for mouth), "knock" (for criticism), "shill" (for pitch), "shiv" (for knife), "shoo-in" (for easy winner), "the shorts" (for lack of funds), and "monkey business" and "drop dead," which need no translation.

—TOM CLARK
Author of *The World of Damon Runyon*

ROMANCE
IN THE
ROARING FORTIES
AND OTHER STORIES
BY DAMON RUNYON

Romance in the Roaring Forties

ONLY A RANK SUCKER will think of taking two peeks at Dave the Dude's doll, because while Dave may stand for the first peek, figuring it is a mistake, it is a sure thing he will get sored up at the second peek, and Dave the Dude is certainly not a man to have sored up at you.

But this Waldo Winchester is one hundred per cent sucker, which is why he takes quite a number of peeks at Dave's doll. And what is more, she takes quite a number of peeks right back at him. And there you are. When a guy and a doll get to taking peeks back and forth at each other, why, there you are indeed.

This Waldo Winchester is a nice-looking young guy who writes pieces about Broadway for the *Morning Item*. He writes about the goings-on in night clubs, such as fights, and one thing and another, and also about who is running around with who, including guys and dolls.

Sometimes this is very embarrassing to people who may be married and are running around with people who are not married, but of course Waldo Winchester cannot be expected to ask one and all for their marriage certificates before he writes his pieces for the paper.

The chances are if Waldo Winchester knows Miss Billy Perry is Dave the Dude's doll, he will never take more than his first peek at her, but nobody tips him off until his second or third peek, and by this time Miss Billy Perry is taking her peeks back at him and Waldo Winchester is hooked.

In fact, he is plumb gone, and being a sucker, like I tell you, he does not care whose doll she is. Personally, I do not blame him much, for Miss Billy Perry is worth a few peeks, especially when she is out on the floor of Miss Missouri Martin's Sixteen Hundred Club doing her tap dance. Still, I do not think the best tap dancer that ever lives can make me take two peeks at her if I know she is Dave the Dude's doll, for Dave somehow thinks more than somewhat of his dolls.

He especially thinks plenty of Miss Billy Perry, and sends her fur coats, and diamond rings, and one thing and another, which she sends back to him at once, because it seems she does not take presents from guys. This is considered most surprising all along Broadway, but people figure the chances are she has some other angle.

Anyway, this does not keep Dave the Dude from liking her just the same, and so she is considered his doll by one and all, and is respected accordingly until this Waldo Winchester comes along.

It happens that he comes along while Dave the Dude is off in the Modoc on a little run-down to the Bahamas to get some goods for his business, such as Scotch and champagne, and by the time Dave gets back, Miss Billy

Perry and Waldo Winchester are at the stage where they sit in corners between her numbers and hold hands. Of course nobody tells Dave the Dude about this, because they do not wish to get him excited. Not even Miss Missouri Martin tells him, which is most unusual because Miss Missouri Martin, who is sometimes called "Mizzoo" for short, tells everything she knows as soon as she knows it, which is very often before it happens.

You see, the idea is when Dave the Dude is excited he may blow somebody's brains out, and the chances are it will be nobody's brains but Waldo Winchester's, although some claim that Waldo Winchester has no brains or he will not be hanging around Dave the Dude's doll.

I know Dave is very, very fond of Miss Billy Perry, because I hear him talk to her several times, and he is most polite to her and never gets out of line in her company by using cuss words, or anything like this. Furthermore, one night when One-eyed Solly Abrahams is a little stewed up he refers to Miss Billy Perry as a broad, meaning no harm whatever, for this is the way many of the boys speak of the dolls.

But right away Dave the Dude reaches across the table and bops One-eyed Solly right in the mouth, so everybody knows from then on that Dave thinks well of Miss Billy Perry. Of course Dave is always thinking fairly well of some doll as far as this goes, but it is seldom he gets to bopping guys in the mouth over them.

Well, one night what happens but Dave the Dude walks into the Sixteen Hundred Club, and there in the entrance, what does he see but this Waldo Winchester and Miss Billy Perry kissing each other back and forth friendly. Right away Dave reaches for the old equalizer to shoot Waldo Winchester, but it seems Dave does not happen to have the old equalizer with him, not expecting to have to shoot anybody this particular evening.

So Dave the Dude walks over and, as Waldo Winchester hears him coming and lets go his strangle hold on Miss Billy Perry, Dave nails him with a big right hand on the chin. I will say for Dave the Dude that he is a fair puncher with his right hand, though his left is not so good, and he knocks Waldo Winchester bowlegged. In fact, Waldo folds right up on the floor.

Well, Miss Billy Perry lets out a screech you can hear clear to the Battery and runs over to where Waldo Winchester lights, and falls on top of him squalling very loud. All anybody can make out of what she says is that Dave the Dude is a big bum, although Dave is not so big, at that, and that she loves Waldo Winchester.

Dave walks over and starts to give Waldo Winchester the leather, which is considered customary in such cases, but he seems to change his mind, and instead of booting Waldo around, Dave turns and walks out of the joint looking very black and mad, and the next anybody hears of him he is over in the Chicken Club doing plenty of drinking.

This is regarded as a very bad sign indeed, because while everybody goes to the Chicken Club now and then to give Tony Bertazzola, the owner, a friendly play, very few people care to do any drinking there, because Tony's liquor is not meant for anybody to drink except the customers.

Well, Miss Billy Perry gets Waldo Winchester on his pegs again, and wipes his chin off with her handkerchief, and by and by he is all okay except for a big lump on his chin. And all the time she is telling Waldo Winchester what a big bum Dave the Dude is, although afterwards Miss Missouri Martin gets hold of Miss Billy Perry and puts the blast on her plenty for chasing a two-handed spender such as Dave the Dude out of the joint.

"You are nothing but a little sap," Miss Missouri Martin tells Miss Billy Perry. "You cannot get the right time off this newspaper guy, while everybody knows Dave the Dude is a very fast man with a dollar."

"But I love Mr. Winchester," says Miss Billy Perry. "He's so romantic. He is not a bootlegger and a gunman like Dave the Dude. He puts lovely pieces in the paper about me, and he is a gentleman at all times."

Now of course Miss Missouri Martin is not in a position to argue about gentlemen, because she meets very few in the Sixteen Hundred Club and anyway, she does not wish to make Waldo Winchester mad as he is apt to turn around and put pieces in his paper that will be a knock to the joint, so she lets the matter drop.

Miss Billy Perry and Waldo Winchester go on holding hands between her numbers, and maybe kissing each other now and then, as young people are liable to do, and Dave the Dude plays the chill for the Sixteen Hundred Club and everything seems to be all right. Naturally we are all very glad there is no more trouble over the proposition, because the best Dave can get is the worst of it in a jam with a newspaper guy.

Personally, I figure Dave will soon find himself another doll and forget all about Miss Billy Perry, because now that I take another peek at her, I can see where she is just about the same as any other tap dancer, except that she is red-headed. Tap dancers are generally blackheads, but I do not know why.

Moosh, the doorman at the Sixteen Hundred Club, tells me Miss Missouri Martin keeps plugging for Dave the Dude with Miss Billy Perry in a quiet way, because he says he hears Miss Missouri Martin make the following crack one night to her: "Well, I do not see any Simple Simon on your lean and linger."

This is Miss Missouri Martin's way of saying she sees no diamond on Miss Billy Perry's finger, for Miss Missouri Martin is an old experienced doll, who figures if a guy loves a doll he will prove it with diamonds. Miss Missouri Martin has many diamonds herself, though how any guy can ever get himself heated up enough about Miss Missouri Martin to give her diamonds is more than I can see.

I am not a guy who goes around much, so I do not see Dave the Dude for a couple of weeks, but late one Sunday afternoon little Johnny McGowan, who is one of Dave's men, comes and says to me like this: "What do you think? Dave grabs the scribe a little while ago and is taking him out for an airing!"

Well, Johnny is so excited it is some time before I can get him cooled out enough to explain. It seems that Dave the Dude gets his biggest car out of the garage and sends his driver, Wop Joe, over to the *Item* office where Waldo Winchester works, with a message that Miss Billy Perry wishes to see Waldo right away at Miss Missouri Martin's apartment on Fifty-ninth Street.

Of course this message is nothing but the phonus bolonus, but Waldo drops in for it and gets in the car. Then Wop Joe drives him up to Miss Missouri Martin's apartment, and who gets in the car there but Dave the Dude. And away they go.

Now this is very bad news indeed, because when Dave the Dude takes a guy out for an airing the guy very often does not come back. What happens to him I never ask, because the best a guy can get by asking questions in this man's town is a bust in the nose.

But I am much worried over this proposition, because I like Dave the Dude, and I know that taking a newspaper guy like Waldo Winchester out for an airing is apt to cause talk, especially if he does not come back. The other guys that Dave the Dude takes out for airings do not mean much in particular, but here is a guy who may produce trouble, even if he is a sucker, on account of being connected with a newspaper.

I know enough about newspapers to know that by and by the editor or somebody will be around wishing to know where Waldo Winchester's pieces about Broadway are, and if there are no pieces from Waldo Winchester, the editor will wish to know why. Finally it will get around to where other people will wish to know, and after a while many people will be running around saying: "Where is Waldo Winchester?"

And if enough people in this town get to running around saying where is So-and-so, it becomes a great mystery and the newspapers hop on the cops and the cops hop on everybody, and by and by there is so much heat in town that it is no place for a guy to be.

But what is to be done about this situation I do not know. Personally, it strikes me as very bad indeed, and while Johnny goes away to do a little telephoning, I am trying to think up some place to go where people will see me, and remember afterwards that I am there in case it is necessary for them to remember.

Finally Johnny comes back, very excited, and says: "Hey, the Dude is up at the Woodcock Inn on the Pelham Parkway, and he is sending out the word for one and all to come at once. Good Time Charley Bernstein just gets the wire and tells me. Something is doing. The rest of the mob are on their way, so let us be moving."

But here is an invitation which does not strike me as a good thing at all. The way I look at it, Dave the Dude is no company for a guy like me at this time. The chances are he either does something to Waldo Winchester already, or is getting ready to do something to him which I wish no part of.

Personally, I have nothing against newspaper guys, not even the ones who write pieces about Broadway.

If Dave the Dude wishes to do something to Waldo Winchester, all right, but what is the sense of bringing outsiders into it? But the next thing I know, I am in Johnny McGowan's roadster, and he is zipping along very fast indeed, paying practically no attention to traffic lights or anything else.

As we go busting out the Concourse, I get to thinking the situation over, and I figure that Dave the Dude probably keeps thinking about Miss Billy Perry, and drinking liquor such as they sell in the Chicken Club, until finally he blows his topper. The way I look at it, only a guy who is off his nut will think of taking a newspaper guy out for an airing over a doll, when dolls are a dime a dozen in this man's town.

Still, I remember reading in the papers about a lot of different guys who are considered very sensible until they get tangled up with a doll, and maybe loving her, and the first thing anybody knows they hop out of windows, or shoot themselves, or somebody else, and I can see where even a guy like Dave the Dude may go daffy over a doll.

I can see that little Johnny McGowan is worried, too, but he does not say much, and we pull up in front of the Woodcock Inn in no time whatever, to find a lot of other cars there ahead of us, some of which I recognize as belonging to different parties.

The Woodcock Inn is what is called a roadhouse, and is run by Big Nig Skolsky, a very nice man indeed, and a friend of everybody's. It stands back a piece off the Pelham Parkway and is a very pleasant place to go to, what with Nig having a good band and a floor show with a lot of fair-looking dolls, and everything else a man can wish for a good time. It gets a nice play from nice people, although Nig's liquor is nothing extra.

Personally, I never go there much, because I do not

care for roadhouses, but it is a great spot for Dave the Dude when he is pitching parties, or even when he is only drinking single-handed. There is a lot of racket in the joint as we drive up, and who comes out to meet us but Dave the Dude himself with a big hello. His face is very red, and he seems heated up no little, but he does not look like a guy who is meaning any harm to anybody, especially a newspaper guy.

"Come in, guys!" Dave the Dude yells. "Come right in!"

So we go in, and the place is full of people sitting at tables, or out on the floor dancing, and I see Miss Missouri Martin with all her diamonds hanging from her in different places, and Good Time Charley Bernstein, and Feet Samuels, and Tony Bertazzola, and Skeets Boliver, and Nick the Greek, and Rochester Red, and a lot of other guys and dolls from around and about.

In fact, it looks as if everybody from all the joints on Broadway are present, including Miss Billy Perry, who is all dressed up in white and is lugging a big bundle of orchids and so forth, and who is giggling and smiling and shaking hands and going on generally. And finally I see Waldo Winchester, the scribe, sitting at a ringside table all by himself, but there is nothing wrong with him as far as I can see. I mean, he seems to be all in one piece so far.

"Dave," I say to Dave the Dude, very quiet, "what is coming off here? You know a guy cannot be too careful what he does around this town, and I will hate to see you tangled up in anything right now."

"Why," Dave says, "what are you talking about? Nothing is coming off here but a wedding, and it is going to be the best wedding anybody on Broadway ever sees. We are waiting for the preacher now."

"You mean somebody is going to be married?" I ask, being somewhat confused.

"Certainly," Dave the Dude says. "What do you think? What is the idea of a wedding, anyway?"

"Who is going to be married?" I ask.

"Nobody but Billy and the scribe," Dave says. "This is the greatest thing I ever do in my life. I run into Billy the other night and she is crying her eyes out because she loves this scribe and wishes to marry him, but it seems the scribe has nothing he can use for money. So I tell Billy to leave it to me, because you know I love her myself so much I wish to see her happy at all times, even if she has to marry to be that way.

"So I frame this wedding party, and after they are married I am going to stake them to a few G's so they can get a good running start," Dave says. "But I do not tell the scribe and I do not let Billy tell him as I wish it to be a big surprise to him. I kidnap him this afternoon and bring him out here and he is scared half to death thinking I am going to scrag him.

"In fact," Dave says, "I never see a guy so scared. He is still so scared nothing seems to cheer him up. Go over and tell him to shake himself together, because nothing but happiness for him is coming off here."

Well, I wish to say I am greatly relieved to think that Dave intends doing nothing worse to Waldo Winchester than getting him married up, so I go over to where Waldo is sitting. He certainly looks somewhat alarmed. He is all in a huddle with himself, and he has what you call a vacant stare in his eyes. I can see that he is indeed frightened, so I give him a jolly slap on the back and I say: "Congratulations, pal! Cheer up, the worst is yet to come!"

"You bet it is," Waldo Winchester says, his voice so solemn I am greatly surprised.

"You are a fine-looking bridegroom," I say. "You look

as if you are at a funeral instead of a wedding. Why
do you not laugh ha-ha, and maybe take a dram or two
and go to cutting up some?"

"Mister," says Waldo Winchester, "my wife is not
going to care for me getting married to Miss Billy
Perry."

"Your wife?" I say, much astonished. "What is this
you are speaking of? How can you have any wife except
Miss Billy Perry? This is great foolishness."

"I know," Waldo says, very sad. "I know. But I got
a wife just the same, and she is going to be very nervous
when she hears about this. My wife is very strict with
me. My wife does not allow me to go around marrying
people. My wife is Lola Sapola, of the Rolling Sapolas,
the acrobats, and I am married to her for five years.
She is the strong lady who juggles the other four people
in the act. My wife just gets back from a year's tour
of the Interstate time, and she is at the Marx Hotel
right this minute. I am upset by this proposition."

"Does Miss Billy Perry know about this wife?" I ask.

"No," he says. "No. She thinks I am single-o."

"But why do you not tell Dave the Dude you are
already married when he brings you out here to marry
you off to Miss Billy Perry?" I ask. "It seems to me a
newspaper guy must know it is against the law for a
guy to marry several different dolls unless he is a Turk,
or some such."

"Well," Waldo says, "if I tell Dave the Dude I am
married after taking his doll away from him, I am quite
sure Dave will be very much excited, and maybe do
something harmful to my health."

Now there is much in what the guy says, to be sure.
I am inclined to think, myself, that Dave will be somewhat disturbed when he learns of this situation, especially when Miss Billy Perry starts in being unhappy

about it. But what is to be done I do not know, except maybe to let the wedding go on, and then when Waldo is out of reach of Dave, to put in a claim that he is insane, and that the marriage does not count. It is a sure thing I do not wish to be around when Dave the Dude hears Waldo is already married.

I am thinking that maybe I better take it on the lam out of there, when there is a great row at the door and I hear Dave the Dude yelling that the preacher arrives. He is a very nice-looking preacher, at that, though he seems somewhat surprised by the goings-on, especially when Miss Missouri Martin steps up and takes charge of him. Miss Missouri Martin tells him she is fond of preachers, and is quite used to them, because she is twice married by preachers, and twice by justices of the peace, and once by a ship's captain at sea.

By this time one and all present, except maybe myself and Waldo Winchester, and the preacher and maybe Miss Billy Perry, are somewhat corned. Waldo is still sitting at his table looking very sad and saying "Yes" and "No" to Miss Billy Perry whenever she skips past him, for Miss Billy Perry is too much pleasured up with happiness to stay long in one spot.

Dave the Dude is more corned than anybody else, because he has two or three days' running start on everybody. And when Dave the Dude is corned I wish to say that he is a very unreliable guy as to temper, and he is apt to explode right in your face any minute. But he seems to be getting a great bang out of the doings.

Well, by and by Nig Skolsky has the dance floor cleared, and then he moves out on the floor a sort of arch of very beautiful flowers. The idea seems to be that Miss Billy Perry and Waldo Winchester are to be married under this arch. I can see that Dave the Dude

must put in several days planning this whole proposition, and it must cost him plenty of the old do-re-mi,
especially as I see him showing Miss Missouri Martin
a diamond ring as big as a cough drop.

"It is for the bride," Dave the Dude says. "The poor
loogan she is marrying will never have enough dough
to buy her such a rock, and she always wishes a big
one. I get it off a guy who brings it in from Los Angeles.
I am going to give the bride away myself in person,
so how do I act, Mizzoo? I want Billy to have everything
according to the book."

Well, while Miss Missouri Martin is trying to remember back to one of her weddings to tell him, I take another peek at Waldo Winchester to see how he is making
out. I once see two guys go to the old warm squativoo
up in Sing Sing, and I wish to say both are laughing
heartily compared to Waldo Winchester at this moment.

Miss Billy Perry is sitting with him and the orchestra
leader is calling his men dirty names because none of
them can think of how "Oh, Promise Me" goes, when
Dave the Dude yells: "Well, we are all set! Let the happy
couple step forward!"

Miss Billy Perry bounces up and grabs Waldo Winchester by the arm and pulls him up out of his chair.
After a peek at his face I am willing to lay six to five
he does not make the arch. But he finally gets there
with everybody laughing and clapping their hands, and
the preacher comes forward, and Dave the Dude looks
happier than I ever see him look before in his life as
they all get together under the arch of flowers.

Well, all of a sudden there is a terrible racket at the
front door of the Woodcock Inn, with some doll doing
a lot of hollering in a deep voice that sounds like a man's,
and naturally everybody turns and looks that way. The
doorman, a guy by the name of Slugsy Sachs, who is

a very hard man indeed, seems to be trying to keep somebody out, but pretty soon there is a heavy bump and Slugsy Sachs falls down, and in comes a doll about four feet high and five feet wide.

In fact, I never see such a wide doll. She looks all hammered down. Her face is almost as wide as her shoulders, and makes me think of a great big full moon. She comes in bounding-like, and I can see that she is all churned up about something. As she bounces in, I hear a gurgle, and I look around to see Waldo Winchester slumping down to the floor, almost dragging Miss Billy Perry with him.

Well, the wide doll walks right up to the bunch under the arch and says in a large bass voice: "Which one is Dave the Dude?"

"I am Dave the Dude," says Dave the Dude, stepping up. "What do you mean by busting in here like a walrus and gumming up our wedding?"

"So you are the guy who kidnaps my ever-loving husband to marry him off to this little red-headed pancake here, are you?" the wide doll says, looking at Dave the Dude, but pointing at Miss Billy Perry.

Well now, calling Miss Billy Perry a pancake to Dave the Dude is a very serious proposition, and Dave the Dude gets very angry. He is usually rather polite to dolls, but you can see he does not care for the wide doll's manner whatever.

"Say, listen here," Dave the Dude says, "you better take a walk before somebody clips you. You must be drunk," he says. "Or daffy," he says. "What are you talking about, anyway?"

"You will see what I am talking about," the wide doll yells. "The guy on the floor there is my lawful husband. You probably frighten him to death, the poor dear. You kidnap him to marry this red-headed thing, and I am going to get you arrested as sure as my name is Lola Sapola, you simple-looking tramp!"

Naturally, everybody is greatly horrified at a doll using such language to Dave the Dude, because Dave is known to shoot guys for much less, but instead of doing something to the wide doll at once, Dave says: "What is this talk I hear? Who is married to who? Get out of here!" Dave says, grabbing the wide doll's arm.

Well, she makes out as if she is going to slap Dave in the face with her left hand, and Dave naturally pulls his kisser out of the way. But instead of doing anything with her left, Lola Sapola suddenly drives her right fist smackdab into Dave the Dude's stomach, which naturally comes forward as his face goes back.

I wish to say I see many a body punch delivered in my life, but I never see a prettier one than this. What is more, Lola Sapola steps in with the punch, so there is plenty on it.

Now a guy who eats and drinks like Dave the Dude does cannot take them so good in the stomach, so Dave goes "oof," and sits down very hard on the dance floor, and as he is sitting there he is fumbling in his pants pockets for the old equalizer, so everybody around tears for cover except Lola Sapola, and Miss Billy Perry, and Waldo Winchester.

But before he can get his pistol out, Lola Sapola reaches down and grabs Dave by the collar and hoists him to his feet. She lets go her hold on him, leaving Dave standing on his pins, but teetering around somewhat, and then she drives her right hand to Dave's stomach a second time.

The punch drops Dave again, and Lola steps up to him as if she is going to give him the foot. But she only gathers up Waldo Winchester from off the floor and slings him across her shoulder like he is a sack of oats, and starts for the door. Dave the Dude sits up on the floor again and by this time he has the old equalizer in his duke.

"Only for me being a gentleman I will fill you full of slugs," he yells.

Lola Sapola never even looks back, because by this time she is petting Waldo Winchester's head and calling him loving names and saying what a shame it is for bad characters like Dave the Dude to be abusing her precious one. It all sounds to me as if Lola Sapola thinks well of Waldo Winchester.

Well, after she gets out of sight, Dave the Dude gets up off the floor and stands there looking at Miss Billy Perry, who is out to break all crying records. The rest of us come out from under cover, including the preacher, and we are wondering how mad Dave the Dude is going to be about the wedding being ruined. But Dave the Dude seems only disappointed and sad.

"Billy," he says to Miss Billy Perry, "I am mighty sorry you do not get your wedding. All I wish for is your happiness, but I do not believe you can ever be happy with this scribe if he also has to have his lion tamer around. As Cupid I am a total bust. This is the only nice thing I ever try to do in my whole life, and it is too bad it does not come off. Maybe if you wait until he can drown her, or something—"

"Dave," says Miss Billy Perry, dropping so many tears that she seems to finally wash herself right into Dave the Dude's arms, "I will never, never be happy with such a guy as Waldo Winchester. I can see now you are the only man for me."

"Well, well, well," Dave the Dude says, cheering right up. "Where is the preacher? Bring on the preacher and let us have our wedding anyway."

I see Mr. and Mrs. Dave the Dude the other day,

and they seem very happy. But you never can tell about married people, so of course I am never going to let on to Dave the Dude that I am the one who telephones Lola Sapola at the Marx Hotel, because maybe I do not do Dave any too much of a favor, at that.

Butch Minds the Baby

ONE EVENING along about seven o'clock I am sitting in
Mindy's restaurant putting on the gefillte fish, which
is a dish I am very fond of, when in comes three parties
from Brooklyn wearing caps as follows: Harry the
Horse, Little Isadore and Spanish John.

Now these parties are not such parties as I will care
to have much truck with, because I often hear rumors
about them that are very discreditable, even if the rumors are not true. In fact, I hear that many citizens
of Brooklyn will be very glad indeed to see Harry the
Horse, Little Isadore and Spanish John move away from
there, as they are always doing something that is considered a knock to the community, such as robbing people,
or maybe shooting or stabbing them, and throwing
pineapples, and carrying on generally.

I am really much surprised to see these parties on
Broadway, as it is well known that the Broadway coppers just naturally love to shove such parties around,

but here they are in Mindy's, and there I am, so of course I give them a very large hello, as I never wish to seem inhospitable, even to Brooklyn parties. Right away they come over to my table and sit down, and Little Isadore reaches out and spears himself a big hunk of my gefillte fish with his fingers, but I overlook this, as I am using the only knife on the table.

Then they all sit there looking at me without saying anything, and the way they look at me makes me very nervous indeed. Finally I figure that maybe they are a little embarrassed being in a high-class spot such as Mindy's, with legitimate people around and about, so I say to them, very polite: "It is a nice night."

"What is nice about it?" asks Harry the Horse, who is a thin man with a sharp face and sharp eyes.

Well, now that it is put up to me in this way, I can see there is nothing so nice about the night, at that, so I try to think of something else jolly to say, while Little Isadore keeps spearing at my gefillte fish with his fingers, and Spanish John nabs one of my potatoes.

"Where does Big Butch live?" Harry the Horse asks.

"Big Butch?" I say, as if I never hear the name before in my life, because in this man's town it is never a good idea to answer any question without thinking it over, as some time you may give the right answer to the wrong guy, or the wrong answer to the right guy. "Where does Big Butch live?" I ask them again.

"Yes, where does he live?" Harry the Horse says, very impatient. "We wish you to take us to him."

"Now wait a minute, Harry," I say, and I am now more nervous than somewhat. "I am not sure I remember the exact house Big Butch lives in, and furthermore I am not sure Big Butch will care to have me bringing people to see him, especially three at a time, and especially from Brooklyn. You know Big Butch has a very bad disposition, and there is no telling what he may say to me if he does not like the idea of me taking you to him."

"Everything is very kosher," Harry the Horse says. "You need not be afraid of anything whatever. We have a business proposition for Big Butch. It means a nice score for him, so you take us to him at once, or the chances are I will have to put the arm on somebody around here."

Well, as the only one around there for him to put the arm on at this time seems to be me, I can see where it will be good policy for me to take these parties to Big Butch, especially as the last of my gefillte fish is just going down Little Isadore's gullet, and Spanish John is finishing up my potatoes, and is dunking a piece of rye bread in my coffee, so there is nothing more for me to eat.

So I lead them over into West Forty-ninth Street, near Tenth Avenue, where Big Butch lives on the ground floor of an old brownstone-front house, and who is sitting out on the stoop but Big Butch himself. In fact, everybody in the neighborhood is sitting out on the front stoops over there, including women and children, because sitting out on the front stoops is quite a custom in this section.

Big Butch is peeled down to his undershirt and pants, and he has no shoes on his feet, as Big Butch is a guy who likes his comfort. Furthermore, he is smoking a cigar, and laid out on the stoop beside him on a blanket is a little baby with not much clothes on. This baby seems to be asleep, and every now and then Big Butch fans it with a folded newspaper to shoo away the mosquitoes that wish to nibble on the baby. These mosquitoes come across the river from the Jersey side on hot nights and they seem to be very fond of babies.

"Hello, Butch," I say, as we stop in front of the stoop. "Sh-h-h-h!" Butch says, pointing at the baby, and making more noise with his shush than an engine blowing off steam. Then he gets up and tiptoes down to the sidewalk where we are standing, and I am hoping that Butch feels all right, because when Butch does not feel so good he is apt to be very short with one and all. He is a guy of maybe six foot two and a couple of feet wide, and he has big hairy hands and a mean look.

In fact, Big Butch is known all over this man's town as a guy you must not monkey with in any respect, so it takes plenty of weight off of me when I see that he seems to know the parties from Brooklyn, and nods at them very friendly, especially at Harry the Horse. And right away Harry states a most surprising proposition to Big Butch.

It seems that there is a big coal company which has an office in an old building down in West Eighteenth Street, and in this office is a safe, and in this safe is the company payroll of twenty thousand dollars cash money. Harry the Horse knows the money is there because a personal friend of his who is the paymaster for the company puts it there late this very afternoon.

It seems that the paymaster enters into a dicker with Harry the Horse and Little Isadore and Spanish John for them to slug him while he is carrying the payroll from the bank to the office in the afternoon, but something happens that they miss connections on the exact spot, so the paymaster has to carry the sugar on to the office without being slugged, and there it is now in two fat bundles.

Personally it seems to me as I listen to Harry's story that the paymaster must be a very dishonest character to be making deals to hold still while he is being slugged and the company's sugar taken away from him, but of course it is none of my business, so I take no part in the conversation.

Well, it seems that Harry the Horse and Little Isadore and Spanish John wish to get the money out of the safe, but none of them knows anything about opening safes, and while they are standing around over in Brooklyn talking over what is to be done in this emergency Harry suddenly remembers that Big Butch is once in the business of opening safes for a living.

In fact, I hear afterwards that Big Butch is considered the best safe opener east of the Mississippi River in his day, but the law finally takes to sending him to Sing Sing for opening these safes, and after he is in and out of Sing Sing three different times for opening safes Butch gets sick and tired of the place, especially as they pass what is called the Baumes Law in New York, which is a law that says if a guy is sent to Sing Sing four times hand running, he must stay there the rest of his life, without any argument about it.

So Big Butch gives up opening safes for a living, and goes into business in a small way, such as running beer, and handling a little Scotch now and then, and becomes an honest citizen. Furthermore, he marries one of the neighbor's children over on the West Side by the name of Mary Murphy, and I judge the baby on this stoop comes of this marriage between Big Butch and Mary because I can see that it is a very homely baby, indeed. Still, I never see many babies that I consider rose geraniums for looks, anyway.

Well, it finally comes out that the idea of Harry the Horse and Little Isadore and Spanish John is to get Big Butch to open the coal company's safe and take the payroll money out, and they are willing to give him fifty per cent of the money for his bother, taking fifty per cent for themselves for finding the plant, and paying all the overhead, such as the paymaster, out of their bit, which strikes me as a pretty fair sort of deal for Big Butch. But Butch only shakes his head.

"It is old-fashioned stuff," Butch says. "Nobody opens pete boxes for a living any more. They make the boxes too good, and they are all wired up with alarms and are a lot of trouble generally. I am in a legitimate business now and going along. You boys know I cannot stand another fall, what with being away three times already, and in addition to this I must mind the baby. My old lady goes to Mrs. Clancy's wake tonight up in the Bronx, and the chances are she will be there all night, as she is very fond of wakes, so I must mind little John Ignatius Junior."

"Listen, Butch," Harry the Horse says, "this is a very soft pete. It is old-fashioned, and you can open it with a toothpick. There are no wires on it, because they never put more than a dime in it before in years. It just happens they have to put the twenty G's in it tonight because my pal the paymaster makes it a point not to get back from the jug with the scratch in time to pay off today, especially after he sees we miss out on him. It is the softest touch you will ever know, and where can a guy pick up ten G's like this?"

I can see that Big Butch is thinking the ten G's over very seriously, at that, because in these times nobody can afford to pass up ten G's, especially a guy in the beer business, which is very, very tough just now. But finally he shakes his head again and says like this:

"No," he says, "I must let it go, because I must mind the baby. My old lady is very, very particular about this, and I dast not leave little John Ignatius Junior for a minute. If Mary comes home and finds I am not minding the baby she will put the blast on me plenty. I like to turn a few honest bobs now and then as well as anybody, but," Butch says, "John Ignatius Junior comes first with me."

Then he turns away and goes back to the stoop as much as to say he is through arguing, and sits down beside John Ignatius Junior again just in time to keep a mosquito from carrying off one of John's legs. Anybody can see that Big Butch is very fond of this baby, though personally I will not give you a dime a dozen for babies, male and female.

Well, Harry the Horse and Little Isadore and Spanish John are very much disappointed, and stand around talking among themselves, and paying no attention to me, when all of a sudden Spanish John, who never has much to say up to this time, seems to have a bright idea. He talks to Harry and Isadore, and they get all pleasured up over what he has to say, and finally Harry goes to Big Butch.

"Sh-h-h-h!" Big Butch says, pointing to the baby as Harry opens his mouth.

"Listen, Butch," Harry says in a whisper, "we can take the baby with us, and you can mind it and work, too."

"Why," Big Butch whispers back, "this is quite an idea indeed. Let us go into the house and talk things over."

So he picks up the baby and leads us into his joint, and gets out some pretty fair beer, though it is needled a little, at that, and we sit around the kitchen chewing the fat in whispers. There is a crib in the kitchen, and Butch puts the baby in his crib, and it keeps on snoozing away first rate while we are talking. In fact, it is sleeping so sound that I am commencing to figure that Butch must give it some of the needled beer he is feeding us, because I am feeling a little dopey myself.

Finally Butch says that as long as he can take John

Ignatius Junior with him he sees no reason why he shall not go and open the safe for them, only he says he must have five per cent more to put in the baby's bank when he gets back, so as to round himself up with his ever-loving wife in case of a beef from her over keeping the baby out in the night air. Harry the Horse says he considers this extra five per cent a little strong, but Spanish John, who seems to be a very square guy, says that after all it is only fair to cut the baby in if it is to be with them when they are making the score, and Little Isadore seems to think this is all right, too. So Harry the Horse gives in, and says five per cent it is.

Well, as they do not wish to start out until after midnight, and as there is plenty of time, Big Butch gets out some more needled beer, and then he goes looking for the tools with which he opens safes, and which he says he does not see since the day John Ignatius Junior is born, and he gets them out to build the crib.

Now this is a good time for me to bid one and all farewell, and what keeps me there is something I cannot tell you to this day, because personally I never before have any idea of taking part in a safe opening, especially with a baby, as I consider such actions very dishonorable. When I come to think things over afterwards, the only thing I can figure is the needled beer, but I wish to say I am really very much surprised at myself when I find myself in a taxicab along about one o'clock in the morning with these Brooklyn parties and Big Butch and the baby.

Butch has John Ignatius Junior rolled up in a blanket, and John is still pounding his ear. Butch has a satchel of tools, and what looks to me like a big flat book, and just before we leave the house Butch hands me a package and tells me to be very careful with it. He gives Little

Isadore a smaller package, which Isadore shoves into his pistol pocket, and when Isadore sits down in the taxi something goes wa-wa, like a sheep, and Big Butch becomes very indignant because it seems Isadore is sitting on John Ignatius Junior's doll, which says "Mamma" when you squeeze it.

It seems Big Butch figures that John Ignatius Junior may wish something to play with in case he wakes up, and it is a good thing for Little Isadore that the mamma doll is not squashed so it cannot say "Mamma" any more, or the chances are Little Isadore will get a good bust in the snoot.

We let the taxicab go a block away from the spot we are headed for in West Eighteenth Street, between Seventh and Eighth Avenues, and walk the rest of the way two by two. I walk with Big Butch, carrying my package, and Butch is lugging the baby and his satchel and the flat thing that looks like a book. It is so quiet down in West Eighteenth Street at such an hour that you can hear yourself think, and in fact I hear myself thinking very plain that I am a big sap to be on a job like this, especially with a baby, but I keep going just the same, which shows you what a very big sap I am, indeed.

There are very few people in West Eighteenth Street when we get there, and one of them is a fat guy who is leaning against a building almost in the center of the block, and who takes a walk for himself as soon as he sees us. It seems that this fat guy is the watchman at the coal company's office and is also a personal friend of Harry the Horse, which is why he takes the walk when he sees us coming.

It is agreed before we leave Big Butch's house that Harry the Horse and Spanish John are to stay outside the place as lookouts, while Big Butch is inside opening the safe, and that Little Isadore is to go with Butch. Nothing whatever is said by anybody about where I am to be at any time, and I can see that, no matter where I am, I will still be an outsider, but, as Butch gives me the package to carry, I figure he wishes me to remain with him.

It is no bother at all getting into the office of the coal company, which is on the ground floor, because it seems the watchman leaves the front door open, this watchman being a most obliging guy, indeed. In fact he is so obliging that by and by he comes back and lets Harry the Horse and Spanish John tie him up good and tight, and stick a handkerchief in his mouth and chuck him in an areaway next to the office, so nobody will think he has anything to do with opening the safe in case anybody comes around asking.

The office looks out on the street, and the safe that Harry the Horse and Little Isadore and Spanish John wish Big Butch to open is standing up against the rear wall of the office facing the street windows. There is one little electric light burning very dim over the safe so that when anybody walks past the place outside, such as a watchman, they can look in through the window and see the safe at all times, unless they are blind. It is not a tall safe, and it is not a big safe, and I can see Big Butch grin when he sees it, so I figure this safe is not much of a safe, just as Harry the Horse claims.

Well, as soon as Big Butch and the baby and Little Isadore and me get into the office, Big Butch steps over to the safe and unfolds what I think is the big flat book, and what is it but a sort of screen painted on one side to look exactly like the front of a safe. Big Butch stands this screen up on the floor in front of the real safe, leaving plenty of space in between, the idea being that the screen will keep anyone passing in the street outside from seeing Butch while he is opening the safe, because when a man is opening a safe he needs all the privacy he can get.

Big Butch lays John Ignatius Junior down on the floor on the blanket behind the phony safe front and takes his tools out of the satchel and starts to work opening the safe, while Little Isadore and me get back in a corner where it is dark, because there is not room for all of us back of the screen. However, we can see what Big Butch is doing, and I wish to say while I never before see a professional safe opener at work, and never wish to see another, this Butch handles himself like a real artist.

He starts drilling into the safe around the combination lock, working very fast and very quiet, when all of a sudden what happens but John Ignatius Junior sits up on the blanket and lets out a squall. Naturally this is most disquieting to me, and personally I am in favor of beaning John Ignatius Junior with something to make him keep still, because I am nervous enough as it is. But the squalling does not seem to bother Big Butch. He lays down his tools and picks up John Ignatius Junior and starts whispering, "There, there, there, my itty oddleums. Da-dad is here."

Well, this sounds very nonsensical to me in such a situation, and it makes no impression whatever on John Ignatius Junior. He keeps on squalling, and I judge he is squalling pretty loud because I see Harry the Horse and Spanish John both walk past the window and look in very anxious. Big Butch jiggles John Ignatius Junior up and down and keeps whispering baby talk to him, which sounds very undignified coming from a high-class safe opener, and finally Butch whispers to me to hand him the package I am carrying.

He opens the package, and what is in it but a baby's

nursing bottle full of milk. Moreover, there is a little tin stew pan, and Butch hands the pan to me and whispers to me to find a water tap somewhere in the joint and fill the pan with water. So I go stumbling around in the dark in a room behind the office and bark my shins several times before I find a tap and fill the pan. I take it back to Big Butch, and he squats there with the baby on one arm, and gets a tin of what is called canned heat out of the package, and lights this canned heat with his cigar lighter, and starts heating the pan of water with the nursing bottle in it.

Big Butch keeps sticking his finger in the pan of water while it is heating, and by and by he puts the rubber nipple of the nursing bottle in his mouth and takes a pull at it to see if the milk is warm enough, just like I see dolls who have babies do. Apparently the milk is okay, as Butch hands the bottle to John Ignatius Junior, who grabs hold of it with both hands and starts sucking on the business end. Naturally he has to stop squalling, and Big Butch goes to work on the safe again, with John Ignatius Junior sitting on the blanket, pulling on the bottle and looking wiser than a treeful of owls.

It seems the safe is either a tougher job than anybody figures, or Big Butch's tools are not so good, what with being old and rusty and used for building baby cribs, because he breaks a couple of drills and works himself up into quite a sweat without getting anywhere. Butch afterwards explains to me that he is one of the first guys in this country to open safes without explosives, but he says to do this work properly you have to know the safes so as to drill to the tumblers of the lock just right, and it seems that this particular safe is a new type to him, even if it is old, and he is out of practice.

Well, in the meantime John Ignatius Junior finishes his bottle and starts mumbling again, and Big Butch gives him a tool to play with, and finally Butch needs this tool and tries to take it away from John Ignatius Junior, and the baby lets out such a squawk that Butch has to let him keep it until he can sneak it away from him, and this causes more delay.

Finally Big Butch gives up trying to drill the safe open, and he whispers to us that he will have to put a little shot in it to loosen up the lock, which is all right with us, because we are getting tired of hanging around and listening to John Ignatius Junior's glug-glugging. As far as I am personally concerned, I am wishing I am home in bed.

Well, Butch starts pawing through his satchel looking for something and it seems that what he is looking for is a little bottle of some kind of explosive with which to shake the lock on the safe up some, and at first he cannot find this bottle, but finally he discovers that John Ignatius Junior has it and is gnawing at the cork, and Butch has quite a battle making John Ignatius Junior give it up.

Anyway, he fixes the explosive in one of the holes he drills near the combination lock on the safe, and then he puts in a fuse, and just before he touches off the fuse Butch picks up John Ignatius Junior and hands him to Little Isadore, and tells us to go into the room behind the office. John Ignatius Junior does not seem to care for Little Isadore, and I do not blame him, at that, because he starts to squirm around quite some in Isadore's arms and lets out a squall, but all of a sudden he becomes very quiet indeed, and, while I am not able to prove it, something tells me that Little Isadore has his hand over John Ignatius Junior's mouth.

Well, Big Butch joins us right away in the back room, and sound comes out of John Ignatius Junior again as Butch takes him from Little Isadore, and I am thinking that it is a good thing for Isadore that the baby cannot tell Big Butch what Isadore does to him.

"I put in just a little bit of a shot," Big Butch says, "and it will not make any more noise than snapping your fingers."

But a second later there is a big whoom from the office, and the whole joint shakes, and John Ignatius Junior laughs right out loud. The chances are he thinks it is the Fourth of July.

"I guess maybe I put in too big a charge," Big Butch says, and then he rushes into the office with Little Isadore and me after him, and John Ignatius Junior still laughing very heartily for a small baby. The door of the safe is swinging loose, and the whole joint looks somewhat wrecked, but Big Butch loses no time in getting his dukes into the safe and grabbing out two big bundles of cash money, which he sticks inside his shirt.

As we go into the street Harry the Horse and Spanish John come running up much excited, and Harry says to Big Butch like this:

"What are you trying to do," he says, "wake up the whole town?"

"Well," Butch says, "I guess maybe the charge is too strong, at that, but nobody seems to be coming, so you and Spanish John walk over to Eighth Avenue, and the rest of us will walk to Seventh, and if you go along quiet, like people minding their own business, it will be all right."

But I judge Little Isadore is tired of John Ignatius Junior's company by this time, because he says he will go with Harry the Horse and Spanish John, and this leaves Big Butch and John Ignatius Junior and me to go the other way. So we start moving, and all of a sudden two cops come tearing around the corner toward which Harry and Isadore and Spanish John are going.

The chances are the cops hear the earthquake Big Butch lets off and are coming to investigate.

But the chances are, too, that if Harry the Horse and the other two keep on walking along very quietly like Butch tells them to, the coppers will pass them up entirely, because it is not likely that coppers will figure anybody to be opening safes with explosives in this neighborhood. But the minute Harry the Horse sees the coppers he loses his nut, and he outs with the old equalizer and starts blasting away, and what does Spanish John do but get his out, too, and open up.

The next thing anybody knows, the two coppers are down on the ground with slugs in them, but other coppers are coming from every which direction, blowing whistles and doing a little blasting themselves, and there is plenty of excitement, especially when the coppers who are not chasing Harry the Horse and Little Isadore and Spanish John start poking around the neighborhood and find Harry's pal, the watchman, all tied up nice and tight where Harry leaves him, and the watchman explains that some scoundrels blow open the safe he is watching.

All this time Big Butch and me are walking in the other direction toward Seventh Avenue, and Big Butch has John Ignatius in his arms, and John Ignatius is now squalling very loud, indeed. The chances are he is still thinking of the big whoom back there which tickles him so and is wishing to hear some more whooms. Anyway, he is beating his own best record for squalling, and as we go walking along Big Butch says to me like this:

"I dast not run," he says, "because if any coppers see me running they will start popping at me and maybe hit John Ignatius Junior, and besides running will joggle the milk up in him and make him sick. My old lady always warns me never to joggle John Ignatius Junior when he is full of milk."

"Well, Butch," I say, "there is no milk in me, and I do not care if I am joggled up, so if you do not mind, I will start doing a piece of running at the next corner."

But just then around the corner of Seventh Avenue toward which we are headed comes two or three coppers with a big fat sergeant with them, and one of the coppers, who is half out of breath as if he has been doing plenty of sprinting, is explaining to the sergeant that somebody blows a safe down the street and shoots a couple of coppers in the getaway.

And there is Big Butch, with John Ignatius Junior in his arms and twenty G's in his shirt front and a tough record behind him, walking right up to them.

I am feeling very sorry, indeed, for Big Butch, and very sorry for myself, too, and I am saying to myself that if I get out of this I will never associate with anyone but ministers of the gospel as long as I live. I can remember thinking that I am getting a better break than Butch, at that, because I will not have to go to Sing Sing for the rest of my life, like him, and I also remember wondering what they will give John Ignatius Junior, who is still tearing off these squalls, with Big Butch saying: "There, there, there, Daddy's itty woogleums." Then I hear one of the coppers say to the fat sergeant: "We better nail these guys. They may be in on this."

Well, I can see it is good-by to Butch and John Ignatius Junior and me, as the fat sergeant steps up to Big Butch, but instead of putting the arm on Butch, the fat sergeant only points at John Ignatius Junior and asks very sympathetic: "Teeth?"

"No," Big Butch says. "Not teeth. Colic. I just get the doctor here out of bed to do something for him, and we are going to a drug store to get some medicine."

Well, naturally I am very much surprised at this statement, because of course I am not a doctor, and if John
Ignatius Junior has colic it serves him right, but I am
only hoping they do not ask for my degree, when the
fat sergeant says: "Too bad. I know what it is. I got
three of them at home. But," he says, "it acts more like
it is teeth than colic."

Then as Big Butch and John Ignatius Junior and me
go on about our business I hear the fat sergeant say to
the copper, very sarcastic: "Yea, of course a guy is out
blowing safes with a baby in his arms! You will make
a great detective, you will!"

I do not see Big Butch for several days after I learn
that Harry the Horse and Little Isadore and Spanish
John get back to Brooklyn all right, except they are a
little nicked up here and there from the slugs the coppers
toss at them, while the coppers they clip are not damaged
so very much. Furthermore, the chances are I will not
see Big Butch for several years, if it is left to me, but
he comes looking for me one night, and he seems to
be all pleasured up about something.

"Say," Big Butch says to me, "you know I never give
a copper credit for knowing any too much about anything, but I wish to say that this fat sergeant we run
into the other night is a very, very smart duck. He is
right about it being teeth that is ailing John Ignatius
Junior, for what happens yesterday but John cuts in
his first tooth."

The Snatching of Bookie Bob

Now IT comes on the spring of 1931, after a long hard winter, and times are very tough indeed, what with the stock market going all to pieces, and banks busting right and left, and the law getting very nasty about this and that, and one thing and another, and many citizens of this town are compelled to do the best they can.

There is very little scratch anywhere and along Broadway many citizens are wearing their last year's clothes and have practically nothing to bet on the races or anything else, and it is a condition that will touch anybody's heart.

So I am not surprised to hear rumors that the snatching of certain parties is going on in spots, because while snatching is by no means a high-class business, and is even considered somewhat illegal, it is something to tide over the hard times.

Furthermore, I am not surprised to hear that this snatching is being done by a character by the name of

Harry the Horse, who comes from Brooklyn, and who
is a character who does not care much what sort of
business he is in, and who is mobbed up with other
characters from Brooklyn such as Spanish John and Little Isadore, who do not care what sort of business they
are in, either.

In fact, Harry the Horse and Spanish John and Little
Isadore are very hard characters in every respect, and
there is considerable indignation expressed around and
about when they move over from Brooklyn into Manhattan and start snatching, because the citizens of Manhattan feel that if there is any snatching done in their
territory, they are entitled to do it themselves.

But Harry the Horse and Spanish John and Little
Isadore pay no attention whatever to local sentiment
and go on the snatch on a pretty fair scale, and by and
by I am hearing rumors of some very nice scores. These
scores are not extra large scores, to be sure, but they
are enough to keep the wolf from the door, and in fact
from three different doors, and before long Harry the
Horse and Spanish John and Little Isadore are around
the race tracks betting on the horses, because if there
is one thing they are all very fond of, it is betting on
the horses.

Now many citizens have the wrong idea entirely of
the snatching business. Many citizens think that all there
is to snatching is to round up the party who is to be
snatched and then just snatch him, putting him away
somewhere until his family or friends dig up enough
scratch to pay whatever price the snatchers are asking.
Very few citizens understand that the snatching business must be well organized and very systematic.

In the first place, if you are going to do any snatching,
you cannot snatch just anybody. You must know who
you are snatching, because naturally it is no good snatch-

ing somebody who does not have any scratch to settle with. And you cannot tell by the way a party looks or how he lives in town if he has any scratch, because many a party who is around in automobiles, and wearing good clothes, and chucking quite a swell is nothing but the phonus bolonus and does not have any real scratch whatever.

So of course such a party is no good for snatching, and of course guys who are on the snatch cannot go around inquiring into bank accounts, or asking how much this and that party has in a safe-deposit vault, because such questions are apt to make citizens wonder why, and it is very dangerous to get citizens to wondering why about anything. So the only way guys who are on the snatch can find out about parties worth snatching is to make a connection with some guy who can put the finger on the right party.

The finger guy must know the party he fingers has plenty of ready scratch to begin with, and he must also know that this party is such a party as is not apt to make too much disturbance about being snatched, such as telling the gendarmes. The party may be a legitimate party, such as a business guy, but he will have reasons why he does not wish it to get out that he is snatched, and the finger must know these reasons. Maybe the party is not leading the right sort of life, such as running around with blondes when he has an ever-loving wife and seven children in Mamaroneck, but does not care to have his habits known, as is apt to happen if he is snatched, especially if he is snatched when he is with a blonde.

And sometimes the party is such a party as does not care to have matches run up and down the bottom of his feet, which often happens to parties who are snatched and who do not seem to wish to settle their bill promptly, because many parties are very ticklish on the bottom of the feet, especially if the matches are lit. On the other hand, maybe the party is not a legitimate guy, such as a party who is running a crap game or a swell speakeasy, or who has some other dodge he does not care to have come out, and who also does not care about having his feet tickled.

Such a party is very good indeed for the snatching business, because he is pretty apt to settle without any argument. And after a party settles one snatching, it will be considered very unethical for anybody else to snatch him again very soon, so he is not likely to make any fuss about the matter. The finger guy gets a commission of twenty-five per cent of the settlement, and one and all are satisfied and much fresh scratch comes into circulation, which is very good for the merchants. And while the party who is snatched may know who snatches him, one thing he never knows is who puts the finger on him, this being considered a trade secret.

I am talking to Waldo Winchester, the newspaper scribe, one night and something about the snatching business comes up, and Waldo Winchester is trying to tell me that it is one of the oldest dodges in the world, only Waldo calls it kidnaping, which is a title that will be very repulsive to guys who are on the snatch nowadays. Waldo Winchester claims that hundreds of years ago guys are around snatching parties, male and female, and holding them for ransom, and furthermore Waldo Winchester says they even snatch very little children and Waldo states that it is all a very, very wicked proposition.

Well, I can see where Waldo is right about it being wicked to snatch dolls and little children, but of course no guys who are on the snatch nowadays will ever think of such a thing, because who is going to settle for a doll in these times when you can scarcely even give them away? As for little children, they are apt to be a great nuisance, because their mammas are sure to go running around hollering bloody murder about them, and furthermore little children are very dangerous, indeed, what with being apt to break out with measles and mumps and one thing and another any minute and give it to everybody in the neighborhood.

Well, anyway, knowing that Harry the Horse and Spanish John and Little Isadore are now on the snatch, I am by no means pleased to see them come along one Tuesday evening when I am standing at the corner of Fiftieth and Broadway, although of course I give them a very jolly hello, and say I hope and trust they are feeling nicely.

They stand there talking to me a few minutes, and I am very glad indeed that Johnny Brannigan, the strong-arm cop, does not happen along and see us, because it will give Johnny a very bad impression of me to see me in such company, even though I am not responsible for the company. But naturally I cannot haul off and walk away from this company at once, because Harry the Horse and Spanish John and Little Isadore may get the idea that I am playing the chill for them, and will feel hurt.

"Well," I say to Harry the Horse, "how are things going, Harry?"

"They are going no good," Harry says. "We do not beat a race in four days. In fact," he says, "we go overboard today. We are washed out. We owe every bookmaker at the track that will trust us, and now we are out trying to raise some scratch to pay off. A guy must pay his bookmaker no matter what."

Well, of course this is very true, indeed, because if a guy does not pay his bookmaker it will lower his business standing quite some, as the bookmaker is sure to go around putting the blast on him, so I am pleased to hear Harry the Horse mention such honorable principles.

"By the way," Harry says, "do you know a guy by the name of Bookie Bob?"

Now I do not know Bookie Bob personally, but of course I know who Bookie Bob is, and so does everybody else in this town that ever goes to a race track, because Bookie Bob is the biggest bookmaker around and about, and has plenty of scratch. Furthermore, it is the opinion of one and all that Bookie Bob will die with this scratch, because he is considered a very close guy with his scratch. In fact, Bookie Bob is considered closer than a dead heat.

He is a short fat guy with a bald head, and his head is always shaking a little from side to side, which some say is a touch of palsy, but which most citizens believe comes of Bookie Bob shaking his head "No" to guys asking for credit in betting on the races. He has an ever-loving wife, who is a very quiet little old doll with gray hair and a very sad look in her eyes, but nobody can blame her for this when they figure that she lives with Bookie Bob for many years.

I often see Bookie Bob and his ever-loving wife eating in different joints along in the Forties, because they seem to have no home except a hotel, and many a time I hear Bookie Bob giving her a going-over about something or other, and generally it is about the price of something she orders to eat, so I judge Bookie Bob is as tough with his ever-loving wife about scratch as he is with everybody else. In fact, I hear him bawling her out one night because she has on a new hat which she says costs her six bucks, and Bookie Bob wishes to know if she is trying to ruin him with her extravagances.

But of course I am not criticizing Bookie Bob for squawking about the hat, because for all I know six bucks may be too much for a doll to pay for a hat, at that. And furthermore, maybe Bookie Bob has the right idea about keeping down his ever-loving wife's appetite, because I know many a guy in this town who is practically ruined by dolls eating too much on him.

"Well," I say to Harry the Horse, "if Bookie Bob is one of the bookmakers you owe, I am greatly surprised to see that you seem to have both eyes in your head, because I never before hear of Bookie Bob letting anybody owe him without giving him at least one of their eyes for security. In fact," I say, "Bookie Bob is such a guy as will not give you the right time if he has two watches."

"No," Harry the Horse says, "we do not owe Bookie Bob. But," he says, "he will be owing us before long. We are going to put the snatch on Bookie Bob."

Well, this is most disquieting news to me, not because I care if they snatch Bookie Bob or not, but because somebody may see me talking to them who will remember about it when Bookie Bob is snatched. But of course it will not be good policy for me to show Harry the Horse and Spanish John and Little Isadore that I am nervous, so I only speak as follows:

"Harry," I say, "every man knows his own business best, and I judge you know what you are doing. But," I say, "you are snatching a hard guy when you snatch Bookie Bob. A very hard guy, indeed. In fact," I say, "I hear the softest thing about him is his front teeth, so it may be very difficult for you to get him to settle after you snatch him."

"No," Harry the Horse says, "we will have no trouble about it. Our finger gives us Bookie Bob's hole card, and it is a most surprising thing, indeed. But," Harry the Horse says, "you come upon many surprising things in human nature when you are on the snatch. Bookie Bob's hole card is his ever-loving wife's opinion of him.

"You see," Harry the Horse says, "Bookie Bob has been putting himself away with his ever-loving wife for years as a very important guy in this town, with much power and influence, although of course Bookie Bob knows very well he stands about as good as a broken leg. In fact," Harry the Horse says, "Bookie Bob figures that his ever-loving wife is the only one in the world who looks on him as a big guy, and he will sacrifice even his scratch, or anyway some of it, rather than let her know that guys have such little respect for him as to put the snatch on him. It is what you call psychology," Harry the Horse says.

Well, this does not make good sense to me, and I am thinking to myself that the psychology that Harry the Horse really figures to work out nice on Bookie Bob is tickling his feet with matches, but I am not anxious to stand there arguing about it, and pretty soon I bid them all good evening, very polite, and take the wind, and I do not see Harry the Horse or Spanish John or Little Isadore again for a month.

In the meantime, I hear gossip here and there that Bookie Bob is missing for several days, and when he finally shows up again he gives it out that he is very sick during his absence, but I can put two and two together as well as anybody in this town and I figure that Bookie Bob is snatched by Harry the Horse and Spanish John and Little Isadore, and the chances are it costs him plenty.

So I am looking for Harry the Horse and Spanish John and Little Isadore to be around the race track with plenty of scratch and betting them higher than a cat's back, but they never show up, and what is more I hear they leave Manhattan and are back in Brooklyn working every day handling beer. Naturally this is very surprising to me, because the way things are running, beer is a tough dodge just now, and there is very little profit in same, and I figure that with the scratch they must make off Bookie Bob, Harry the Horse and Spanish John and Little Isadore have a right to be taking things easy.

Now one night I am in Good Time Charley Bernstein's little speak in Forty-eighth Street, talking of this and that with Charley, when in comes Harry the Horse looking very weary and by no means prosperous. Naturally I gave him a large hello, and by and by we get to gabbing together and I ask him whatever becomes of the Bookie Bob matter, and Harry the Horse tells me as follows:

Yes [Harry the Horse says], we snatch Bookie Bob all right. In fact, we snatch him the very next night after we are talking to you, or on a Wednesday night. Our finger tells us Bookie Bob is going to a wake over in his old neighborhood on Tenth Avenue, near Thirty-eighth Street, and this is where we pick him up.

He is leaving the place in his car along about midnight, and of course Bookie Bob is alone as he seldom lets anybody ride with him because of the wear and tear on his car cushions, and Little Isadore swings our flivver in front of him and makes him stop. Naturally Bookie Bob is greatly surprised when I poke my head into his car and tell him I wish the pleasure of his company for a short time, and at first he is inclined to argue the matter, saying I must make a mistake, but I put the old convincer on him by letting him peek down the snozzle of my John Roscoe.

We lock his car and throw the keys away, and then we take Bookie Bob in our car and go to a certain spot on Eighth Avenue where we have a nice little apartment all ready. When we get there I tell Bookie Bob that he can call up anybody he wishes and state that the snatch is on him and that it will require twenty-five G's, cash money, to take it off, but of course I also tell Bookie Bob that he is not to mention where he is or something may happen to him.

Well, I will say one thing for Bookie Bob, although everybody is always weighing in the sacks on him and saying he is no good—he takes it like a gentleman, and very calm and businesslike.

Furthermore, he does not seem alarmed, as many citizens are when they find themselves in such a situation. He recognizes the justice of our claim at once, saying as follows:

"I will telephone my partner, Sam Salt," he says. "He is the only one I can think of who is apt to have such a sum as twenty-five G's cash money. But," he says, "if you gentlemen will pardon the question, because this is a new experience to me, how do I know everything will be okay for me after you get the scratch?"

"Why," I say to Bookie Bob, somewhat indignant, "it is well known to one and all in this town that my word is my bond. There are two things I am bound to do," I say, "and one is to keep my word in such a situation as this, and the other is to pay anything I owe a bookmaker, no matter what, for these are obligations of honor with me."

"Well," Bookie Bob says, "of course I do not know you gentlemen, and, in fact, I do not remember ever seeing any of you, although your face is somewhat familiar, but if you pay your bookmaker you are an honest guy, and one in a million. In fact," Bookie Bob says, "if I have all the scratch that is owing to me around this town, I will not be telephoning anybody for such a sum as twenty-five G's. I will have such a sum in my pants pocket for change."

Now Bookie Bob calls a certain number and talks to somebody there but he does not get Sam Salt, and he seems much disappointed when he hangs up the receiver again.

"This is a very tough break for me," he says. "Sam Salt goes to Atlantic City an hour ago on very important business and will not be back until tomorrow evening, and they do not know where he is to stay in Atlantic City. And," Bookie Bob says, "I cannot think of anybody else to call to get this scratch, especially anybody I will care to have know I am in this situation."

"Why not call your ever-loving wife?" I say. "Maybe she can dig up this kind of scratch."

"Say," Bookie Bob says, "you do not suppose I am chump enough to give my ever-loving wife twenty-five G's, belonging to me, do you? I give my ever-loving wife ten bucks per week for spending money," Bookie Bob says, "and this is enough scratch for any doll, especially when you figure I pay for her meals."

Well, there seems to be nothing we can do except wait until Sam Salt gets back, but we let Bookie Bob call his ever-loving wife, as Bookie Bob says he does not wish to have her worrying about his absence, and tells her a big lie about having to go to Jersey City to sit up with a sick Brother Elk.

Well, it is now nearly four o'clock in the morning, so we put Bookie Bob in a room with Little Isadore to sleep, although, personally, I consider making a guy sleep with Little Isadore very cruel treatment, and Spanish John and I take turns keeping awake and watching out that Bookie Bob does not take the air on us before paying us off. To tell the truth, Little Isadore and Spanish John are somewhat disappointed that Bookie Bob agrees to settle so promptly, because they are looking forward to tickling his feet with great relish.

Now Bookie Bob turns out to be very good company

when he wakes up the next morning, because he knows a lot of race-track stories and plenty of scandal, and he keeps us much interested at breakfast. He talks along with us as if he knows us all his life, and he seems very nonchalant indeed, but the chances are he will not be so nonchalant if I tell him about Spanish John's thought.

Well, about noon Spanish John goes out of the apartment and comes back with a racing sheet, because he knows Little Isadore and I will be wishing to know what is running in different spots although we do not have anything to bet on these races, or any way of betting on them, because we are overboard with every bookmaker we know.

Now Bookie Bob is also much interested in the matter of what is running, especially at Belmont, and he is bending over the table with me and Spanish John and Little Isadore, looking at the sheet, when Spanish John speaks as follows:

"My goodness," Spanish John says, "a spot such as this fifth race with Questionnaire at four to five is like finding money in the street. I only wish I have a few bobs to bet on him at such a price," Spanish John says.

"Why," Bookie Bob says, very polite, "if you gentlemen wish to bet on these races I will gladly book to you. It is a good way to pass away the time while we are waiting for Sam Salt, unless you will rather play pinochle?"

"But," I say, "we have no scratch to play the races, at least not much."

"Well," Bookie Bob says, "I will take your markers, because I hear what you say about always paying your bookmaker, and you put yourself away with me as an honest guy, and these other gentlemen also impress me as honest guys."

Now what happens but we begin betting Bookie Bob on the different races, not only at Belmont, but at all the other tracks in the country, for Little Isadore and Spanish John and I are guys who like plenty of action when we start betting on the horses. We write out markers for whatever we wish to bet and hand them to Bookie Bob, and Bookie Bob sticks these markers in an inside pocket, and along in the late afternoon it looks as if he has a tumor on his chest.

We get the race results by phone off a poolroom downtown as fast as they come off, and also the prices, and it is a lot of fun, and Little Isadore and Spanish John and Bookie Bob and I are all little pals together until all the races are over and Bookie Bob takes out the markers and starts counting himself up.

It comes out then that I owe Bookie Bob ten G's, and Spanish John owes him six G's, and Little Isadore owes him four G's, as Little Isadore beats him a couple of races out west.

Well, about this time, Bookie Bob manages to get Sam Salt on the phone, and explains to Sam that he is to go to a certain safe-deposit box and get out twenty-five G's and then wait until midnight and hire himself a taxicab and start riding around the block between Fifty-first and Fifty-second, from Eighth to Ninth Avenues, and to keep riding until somebody flags the cab and takes the scratch off him.

Naturally Sam Salt understands right away that the snatch is on Bookie Bob, and he agrees to do as he is told, but he says he cannot do it until the following night because he knows there is not twenty-five G's in the box and he will have to get the difference at the track the next day. So there we are with another day in the apartment and Spanish John and Little Isadore and I are just as well pleased because Bookie Bob has us hooked and we naturally wish to wiggle off.

.But the next day is worse than ever. In all the years I am playing the horses I never have such a tough day, and Spanish John and Little Isadore are just as bad. In fact, we are all going so bad that Bookie Bob seems to feel sorry for us and often lays us a couple of points above the track prices, but it does no good. At the end of the day, I am in a total of twenty G's, while Spanish John owes fifteen, and Little Isadore fifteen, a total of fifty G's among the three of us. But we are never any hands to hold postmortems on bad days, so Little Isadore goes out to a delicatessen store and lugs in a lot of nice things to eat, and we have a fine dinner, and then we sit around with Bookie Bob telling stories, and even singing songs together until time to meet Sam Salt.

When it comes on midnight Spanish John goes off and lays for Sam, and gets a little valise off Sam Salt. Then Spanish John comes back to the apartment and we open the valise and the twenty-five G's are there okay, and we cut this scratch three ways.

Then I tell Bookie Bob he is free to go about his business, and good luck to him, at that, but Bookie Bob looks at me as if he is very much surprised, and hurt, and says to me like this:

"Well, gentlemen, thank you for your courtesy, but what about the scratch you owe me? What about these markers? Surely, gentlemen, you will pay your book-maker?"

Well, of course we owe Bookie these markers, all right, and of course a man must pay his bookmaker, no matter what, so I hand over my bit and Bookie Bob puts down something in a little notebook that he takes out of his kick.

Then Spanish John and Little Isadore hand over their dough, too, and Bookie Bob puts down something more in the little notebook.

"Now," Bookie Bob says, "I credit each of your accounts with these payments, but you gentlemen still owe me a matter of twenty-five G's over and above the twenty-five I credit you with, and I hope and trust you will make arrangements to settle this at once because," he says, "I do not care to extend such accommodations over any considerable period."

"But," I say, "we do not have any more scratch after paying you the twenty-five G's on account."

"Listen," Bookie Bob says, dropping his voice down to a whisper, "what about putting the snatch on my partner, Sam Salt, and I will wait over a couple of days with you and keep booking to you, and maybe you can pull yourselves out. But of course," Bookie Bob whispers, "I will be entitled to twenty-five per cent of the snatch for putting the finger on Sam for you."

But Spanish John and Little Isadore are sick and tired of Bookie Bob and will not listen to staying in the apartment any longer, because they say he is a jinx to them and they cannot beat him in any manner, shape or form. Furthermore, I am personally anxious to get away because something Bookie Bob says reminds me of something.

It reminds me that besides the scratch we owe him, we forget to take out six G's two-fifty for the party who puts the finger on Bookie Bob for us, and this is a very serious matter indeed, because everybody will tell you that failing to pay a finger is considered a very dirty trick. Furthermore, if it gets around that you fail to pay a finger, nobody else will ever finger for you.

So [Harry the Horse says] we quit the snatching business because there is no use continuing while this obligation is outstanding against us, and we go back to Brooklyn to earn enough scratch to pay our just debts.

We are paying off Bookie Bob's IOU a little at a time, because we do not wish to ever have anybody say we welsh on a bookmaker, and furthermore we are paying off the six G's two-fifty commission we owe our finger.

And while it is tough going, I am glad to say our honest effort is doing somebody a little good, because I see Bookie Bob's ever-loving wife the other night all dressed up in new clothes, very happy indeed.

And while a guy is telling me she is looking so happy because she gets a large legacy from an uncle who dies in Switzerland, and is now independent of Bookie Bob, I only hope and trust [Harry the Horse says] that it never gets out that our finger in this case is nobody but Bookie Bob's ever-loving wife.

Little Miss Marker

ONE EVENING along toward seven o'clock, many citizens are standing out on Broadway in front of Mindy's restaurant, speaking of one thing and another, and particularly about the tough luck they have playing the races in the afternoon, when who comes up the street with a little doll hanging onto his right thumb but a guy by the name of Sorrowful.

This guy is called Sorrowful because this is the way he always is about no matter what, and especially about the way things are with him when anybody tries to put the bite on him. In fact, if anybody who tries to put the bite on Sorrowful can listen to him for two minutes about how things are with him and not bust into tears, they must be very hard-hearted, indeed.

Regret, the horse player, is telling me that he once tries to put the bite on Sorrowful for a sawbuck, and by the time Sorrowful gets through explaining how things are with him, Regret feels so sorry for him that he goes out and puts the bite on somebody else for the saw and gives it to Sorrowful, although it is well known to one and all that Sorrowful has plenty of potatoes hid away somewhere.

He is a tall, skinny guy with a long, sad, mean-looking kisser, and a mournful voice. He is maybe sixty years old, give or take a couple of years, and for as long as I can remember he is running a handbook over in Forty-ninth Street next door to a chop-suey joint. In fact, Sorrowful is one of the largest handbook makers in this town.

Any time you see him he is generally by himself, because being by himself is not apt to cost him anything, and it is therefore a most surprising scene when he comes along Broadway with a little doll.

And there is much speculation among the citizens as to how this comes about, for no one ever hears of Sorrowful having any family, or relations of any kind, or even any friends.

The little doll is a very little doll indeed, the top of her noggin only coming up to Sorrowful's knee, although of course Sorrowful has very high knees, at that. Moreover, she is a very pretty little doll, with big blue eyes and fat pink cheeks, and a lot of yellow curls hanging down her back, and she has fat little legs and quite a large smile, although Sorrowful is lugging her along the street so fast that half the time her feet are dragging the sidewalk and she has a license to be bawling instead of smiling.

Sorrowful is looking sadder than somewhat, which makes his face practically heart-rending as he pulls up in front of Mindy's and motions us to follow him in. Anybody can see that he is worried about something very serious, and many citizens are figuring that maybe he suddenly discovers all his potatoes are counterfeit, because nobody can think of anything that will worry Sorrowful except money.

Anyway, four or five of us gather around the table where Sorrowful sits down with the little doll beside him, and he states a most surprising situation to us.

It seems that early in the afternoon a young guy who is playing the races with Sorrowful for several days pops into his place of business next door to the chop-suey joint, leading the little doll, and this guy wishes to know how much time he has before post in the first race at Empire.

Well, he only has about twenty-five minutes, and he seems very down-hearted about this, because he explains to Sorrowful that he has a sure thing in this race, which he gets the night before off a guy who is a pal of a close friend of Jockey Workman's valet.

The young guy says he is figuring to bet himself about a deuce on this sure thing, but he does not have such a sum as a deuce on him when he goes to bed, so he plans to get up bright and early in the morning and hop down to a spot on Fourteenth Street where he knows a guy who will let him have the deuce.

But it seems he oversleeps, and here it is almost post time, and it is too late for him to get to Fourteenth Street and back before the race is run off, and it is all quite a sad story indeed, although of course it does not make much impression on Sorrowful, as he is already sadder than somewhat himself just from thinking that somebody may beat him for a bet during the day, even though the races do not start anywhere as yet.

Well, the young guy tells Sorrowful he is going to try to get to Fourteenth Street and back in time to bet on the sure thing, because he says it will be nothing short of a crime if he has to miss such a wonderful opportunity.

"But," he says to Sorrowful, "to make sure I do not miss, you take my marker for a deuce, and I will leave the kid here with you as security until I get back."

Now, ordinarily, asking Sorrowful to take a marker will be considered great foolishness, as it is well known to one and all that Sorrowful will not take a marker from Andrew Mellon. In fact, Sorrowful can almost break your heart telling you about the poorhouses that are full of bookmakers who take markers in their time.

But it happens that business is just opening up for the day, and Sorrowful is pretty busy, and besides the young guy is a steady customer for several days, and has an honest pan, and Sorrowful figures a guy is bound to take a little doll out of hock for a deuce. Furthermore, while Sorrowful does not know much about kids, he can see the little doll must be worth a deuce, at least, and maybe more.

So he nods his head, and the young guy puts the little doll on a chair and goes tearing out of the joint to get the dough, while Sorrowful marks down a deuce bet on Cold Cuts, which is the name of the sure thing. Then he forgets all about the proposition for a while, and all the time the little doll is sitting on the chair as quiet as a mouse, smiling at Sorrowful's customers, including the Chinks from the chop-suey joint who come in now and then to play the races.

Well, Cold Cuts blows, and in fact is not even fifth, and along late in the afternoon Sorrowful suddenly realizes that the young guy never shows up again, and that the little doll is still sitting in the chair, although she is now playing with a butcher knife which one of the Chinks from the chop-suey joint gives her to keep her amused.

Finally it comes on Sorrowful's closing time, and the little doll is still there, so he can think of nothing else to do in this situation, but to bring her around to Mindy's and get a little advice from different citizens, as he does not care to leave her in his place of business alone, as Sorrowful will not trust anybody in there alone, not even himself.

"Now," Sorrowful says, after giving us this long spiel, "what are we to do about this proposition?"

Well, of course, up to this minute none of the rest of us know we are being cut in on any proposition, and personally I do not care for any part of it, but Big Nig, the craps shooter, speaks up as follows:

"If this little doll is sitting in your joint all afternoon," Nig says, "the best thing to do right now is to throw a feed into her, as the chances are her stomach thinks her throat is cut."

Now this seems to be a fair sort of an idea, so Sorrowful orders up a couple of portions of ham hocks and sauerkraut, which is a very tasty dish in Mindy's at all times, and the little doll tears into it very enthusiastically, using both hands, although a fat old doll who is sitting at the next table speaks up and says this is terrible fodder to be tossing into a child at such an hour and where is her mamma?

"Well," Big Nig says to the old doll, "I hear of many people getting a bust in the snoot for not minding their own business in this town, but you give off an idea, at that. Listen," Big Nig says to the little doll, "where is your mamma?"

But the little doll does not seem to know, or maybe she does not wish to make this information public, because she only shakes her head and smiles at Big Nig, as her mouth is too full of ham hocks and sauerkraut for her to talk.

"What is your name?" Big Nig asks, and she says something that Big Nig claims sounds like Marky, although personally I think she is trying to say Martha. Anyway, it is from this that she gets the name we always call her afterward, which is Marky.

"It is a good monicker," Big Nig says. "It is short for marker, and she is certainly a marker unless Sorrowful is telling us a large lie. Why," Big Nig says, "this is a very cute little doll, at that, and pretty smart. How old are you, Marky?"

She only shakes her head again, so Regret, the horse player, who claims he can tell how old a horse is by its teeth, reaches over and sticks his finger in her mouth to get a peek at her crockery, but she seems to think Regret's finger is a hunk of ham hock and shuts down on it so hard Regret lets out an awful squawk. But he says that before she tries to cripple him for life he sees enough of her teeth to convince him she is maybe three, rising four, and this seems reasonable, at that. Anyway, she cannot be much older.

Well, about this time a guinea with a hand organ stops out in front of Mindy's and begins grinding out a tune while his ever-loving wife is passing a tambourine around among the citizens on the sidewalk and, on hearing this music, Marky slides off of her chair with her mouth still full of ham hock and sauerkraut, which she swallows so fast she almost chokes, and then she speaks as follows:

"Marky dance," she says.

Then she begins hopping and skipping around among the tables, holding her little short skirt up in her hands and showing a pair of white panties underneath. Pretty soon Mindy himself comes along and starts putting up a beef about making a dance hall of his joint, but a guy by the name of Sleep-out, who is watching Marky with much interest, offers to bounce a sugar bowl off of Mindy's sconce if he does not mind his own business.

So Mindy goes away, but he keeps muttering about the white panties being a most immodest spectacle, which of course is great nonsense, as many dolls older than Marky are known to do dances in Mindy's, especially on the late watch, when they stop by for a snack on their way home from the night clubs and the speaks, and I hear some of them do not always wear white panties, either.

Personally, I like Marky's dancing very much, although of course she is no Pavlowa, and finally she trips over her own feet and falls on her snoot. But she gets up smiling and climbs back on her chair and pretty soon she is sound asleep with her head against Sorrowful.

Well, now there is much discussion about what Sorrowful ought to do with her. Some claim he ought to take her to a police station, and others say the best thing to do is to put an ad in the Lost and Found columns of the morning bladders, the same as people do when they find Angora cats, and Pekes, and other animals which they do not wish to keep, but none of these ideas seems to appeal to Sorrowful.

Finally he says he will take her to his own home and let her sleep there while he is deciding what is to be done about her, so Sorrowful takes Marky in his arms and lugs her over to a fleabag in West Forty-ninth Street where he has a room for many years, and afterwards a bellhop tells me Sorrowful sits up all night watching her while she is sleeping.

Now what happens but Sorrowful takes on a great fondness for the little doll, which is most surprising, as Sorrowful is never before fond of anybody or anything, and after he has her overnight he cannot bear the idea of giving her up.

Personally, I will just as soon have a three-year-old

baby wolf around me as a little doll such as this, but
Sorrowful thinks she is the greatest thing that ever happens. He has a few inquiries made around and about
to see if he can find out who she belongs to, and he is
tickled silly when nothing comes of these inquiries, although nobody else figures anything will come of them
anyway, as it is by no means uncommon in this town
for little kids to be left sitting in chairs, or on doorsteps,
to be chucked into orphan asylums by whoever finds
them.

Anyway, Sorrowful says he is going to keep Marky,
and his attitude causes great surprise, as keeping Marky
is bound to be an expense, and it does not seem reasonable that Sorrowful will go to any expense for anything.
When it commences to look as if he means what he
says, many citizens naturally figure there must be an
angle, and soon there are a great many rumors on the
subject.

Of course one of these rumors is that the chances
are Marky is Sorrowful's own offspring which is tossed
back on him by the wronged mamma, but this rumor
is started by a guy who does not know Sorrowful, and
after he gets a gander at Sorrowful, the guy apologizes,
saying he realizes that no wronged mamma will be daffy
enough to permit herself to be wronged by Sorrowful.
Personally, I always say that if Sorrowful wishes to keep
Marky it is his own business, and most of the citizens
around Mindy's agree with me.

But the trouble is Sorrowful at once cuts everybody
else in on the management of Marky, and the way he
talks to the citizens around Mindy's about her, you will
think we are all personally responsible for her. As most
of the citizens around Mindy's are bachelors, or are wishing they are bachelors, it is most inconvenient to them
to suddenly find themselves with a family.

Some of us try to explain to Sorrowful that if he is going to keep Marky it is up to him to handle all her play, but right away Sorrowful starts talking so sad about all his pals deserting him and Marky just when they need them most that it softens all hearts, although up to this time we are about as pally with Sorrowful as a burglar with a copper. Finally every night in Mindy's is meeting night for a committee to decide something or other about Marky.

The first thing we decide is that the fleabag where Sorrowful lives is no place for Marky, so Sorrowful hires a big apartment in one of the swellest joints on West Fifty-ninth Street, overlooking Central Park, and spends plenty of potatoes furnishing it, although up to this time Sorrowful never sets himself back more than about ten bobs per week for a place to live and considers it extravagance, at that. I hear it costs him five G's to fix up Marky's bedroom alone, not counting the solid gold toilet set that he buys for her.

Then he gets her an automobile and he has to hire a guy to drive it for her, and finally when we explain to Sorrowful that it does not look right for Marky to be living with nobody but him and a chauffeur, Sorrowful hires a French doll with bobbed hair and red cheeks by the name of Mam'selle Fifi as a nurse for Marky, and this seems to be quite a sensible move, as it insures Marky plenty of company.

In fact, up to the time that Sorrowful hires Mam'selle Fifi, many citizens are commencing to consider Marky something of a nuisance and are playing the duck for her and Sorrowful, but after Mam'selle Fifi comes along you can scarcely get in Sorrowful's joint of Fifty-ninth Street, or around his table in Mindy's when he brings Marky and Mam'selle Fifi in to eat. But one night Sorrowful goes home early and catches Sleep-out guzzling

Mam'selle Fifi, and Sorrowful makes Mam'selle Fifi take plenty of breeze, claiming she will set a bad example to Marky.

Then he gets an old tomato by the name of Mrs. Clancy to be Marky's nurse, and while there is no doubt Mrs. Clancy is a better nurse than Mam'selle Fifi and there is practically no danger of her setting Marky a bad example, the play at Sorrowful's joint is by no means as brisk as formerly.

You can see that from being closer than a dead heat with his potatoes, Sorrowful becomes as loose as ashes. He not only spends plenty on Marky, but he starts picking up checks in Mindy's and other spots, although up to this time picking up checks is something that is most repulsive to Sorrowful.

He gets so he will hold still for a bite, if the bite is not too savage and, what is more, a great change comes over his kisser. It is no longer so sad and mean-looking, and in fact it is almost a pleasant sight at times, especially as Sorrowful gets so he smiles now and then, and has a big hello for one and all, and everybody says the Mayor ought to give Marky a medal for bringing about such a wonderful change.

Now Sorrowful is so fond of Marky that he wants her with him all the time, and by and by there is much criticism of him for having her around his hand-book joint among the Chinks and the horse players, and especially the horse players, and for taking her around night clubs and keeping her out at all hours, as some people do not consider this a proper bringing-up for a little doll.

We hold a meeting in Mindy's on this proposition one night, and we get Sorrowful to agree to keep Marky out of his joint, but we know Marky is so fond of night clubs, especially where there is music, that it seems a

sin and a shame to deprive her of this pleasure altogether, so we finally compromise by letting Sorrowful
take her out one night a week to the Hot Box in Fifty-
fourth Street, which is only a few blocks from where
Marky lives, and Sorrowful can get her home fairly
early. In fact, after this Sorrowful seldom keeps her
out any later than 2 A.M.

The reason Marky likes night clubs where there is
music is because she can do her dance there, as Marky
is practically daffy on the subject of dancing, especially
by herself, even though she never seems to be able to
get over winding up by falling on her snoot, which
many citizens consider a very artistic finish, at that.

The Choo-Choo Boys' band in the Hot Box always
play a special number for Marky in between the regular
dances, and she gets plenty of applause, especially from
the Broadway citizens who know her, although Henri,
the manager of the Hot Box, once tells me he will just
as soon Marky does not do her dancing there, because
one night several of his best customers from Park Avenue, including two millionaires and two old dolls, who
do not understand Marky's dancing, bust out laughing
when she falls on her snoot, and Big Nig puts the slug
on the guys, and is trying to put the slug on the old
dolls, too, when he is finally headed off.

Now one cold, snowy night, many citizens are sitting
around the tables in the Hot Box, speaking of one thing
and another and having a few drams, when Sorrowful
drops in on his way home, for Sorrowful has now become a guy who is around and about, and in and out.
He does not have Marky with him, as it is not her night
out and she is home with Mrs. Clancy.

A few minutes after Sorrowful arrives, a party by
the name of Milk Ear Willie from the West Side comes
in, this Milk Ear Willie being a party who is once a

prize fighter and who has a milk ear, which is the reason he is called Milk Ear Willie, and who is known to carry a John Roscoe in his pants pocket. Furthermore, it is well known that he knocks off several guys in his time, so he is considered rather a suspicious character.

It seems that the reason he comes into the Hot Box is to shoot Sorrowful full of little holes, because he has a dispute with Sorrowful about a parlay on the races the day before, and the chances are Sorrowful will now be very dead if it does not happen that, just as Milk Ear outs with the old equalizer and starts taking dead aim at Sorrowful from a table across the room, who pops into the joint but Marky.

She is in a long nightgown that keeps getting tangled up in her bare feet as she runs across the dance floor and jumps into Sorrowful's arms, so if Milk Ear Willie lets go at this time he is apt to put a slug in Marky, and this is by no means Willie's intention. So Willie puts his rod back in his kick, but he is greatly disgusted and stops as he is going out and makes a large complaint to Henri about allowing children in a night club.

Well, Sorrowful does not learn until afterward how Marky saves his life, as he is too much horrified over her coming four or five blocks through the snow bare-footed to think of anything else, and everybody present is also horrified and wondering how Marky finds her way there. But Marky does not seem to have any good explanation for her conduct, except that she wakes up and discovers Mrs. Clancy asleep and gets to feeling lonesome for Sorrowful.

About this time, the Choo-Choo Boys start playing Marky's tune, and she slips out of Sorrowful's arms and runs out on the dance floor.

"Marky dance," she says.

Then she lifts her nightgown in her hands and starts

hopping and skipping about the floor until Sorrowful collects her in his arms again, and wraps her in an overcoat and takes her home.

Now what happens, but the next day Marky is sick from being out in the snow bare-footed and with nothing on but her nightgown, and by night she is very sick indeed, and it seems that she has pneumonia, so Sorrowful takes her to the Clinic hospital, and hires two nurses and two croakers, and wishes to hire more, only they tell him these will do for the present.

The next day Marky is no better, and the next night she is worse, and the management of the Clinic is very much upset because it has no place to put the baskets of fruit and candy and floral horseshoes and crates of dolls and toys that keep arriving every few minutes. Furthermore, the management by no means approves of the citizens who are tiptoeing along the hall on the floor where Marky has her room, especially such as Big Nig, and Sleep-out, and Wop Joey, and the Pale Face Kid and Guinea Mike and many other prominent characters, especially as these characters keep trying to date up the nurses.

Of course I can see the management's point of view, but I wish to say that no visitor to the Clinic ever brings more joy and cheer to the patients than Sleep-out, as he goes calling in all the private rooms and wards to say a pleasant word or two to the inmates, and I never take any stock in the rumor that he is looking around to see if there is anything worth picking up. In fact, an old doll from Rockville Center, who is suffering with yellow jaundice, puts up an awful holler when Sleep-out is heaved from her room, because she says he is right in the middle of a story about a traveling salesman and she wishes to learn what happens.

There are so many prominent characters in and

around the Clinic that the morning bladders finally get the idea that some well-known mob guy must be in the hospital full of slugs, and by and by the reporters come buzzing around to see what is what. Naturally they find out that all this interest is in nothing but a little doll, and while you will naturally think that such a little doll as Marky can scarcely be worth the attention of the reporters, it seems they get more heated up over her when they hear the story than if she is Jack Diamond.

In fact, the next day all the bladders have large stories about Marky, and also about Sorrowful and about how all these prominent characters of Broadway are hanging around the Clinic on her account. Moreover, one story tells about Sleep-out entertaining the other patients in the hospital, and it makes Sleep-out sound like a very large-hearted guy.

It is maybe three o'clock on the morning of the fourth day Marky is in the hospital that Sorrowful comes into Mindy's looking very sad, indeed. He orders a sturgeon sandwich on pumpernickel, and then he explains that Marky seems to be getting worse by the minute and that he does not think his doctors are doing her any good, and at this Big Nig, the crap shooter, speaks up and states as follows:

"Well," Big Nig says, "if we are only able to get Doc Beerfeldt, the great pneumonia specialist, the chances are he will cure Marky like breaking sticks. But of course," Nig says, "it is impossible to get Doc Beerfeldt unless you are somebody like John D. Rockefeller, or maybe the President."

Naturally, everybody knows that what Big Nig says is very true, for Doc Beerfeldt is the biggest croaker in this town, but no ordinary guy can get close enough to Doc Beerfeldt to hand him a ripe peach, let alone get him to go out on a case. He is an old guy, and he does not practice much any more, and then only among a few very rich and influential people. Furthermore, he has plenty of potatoes himself, so money does not interest him whatever, and anyway it is great foolishness to be talking of getting Doc Beerfeldt out at such an hour as this.

"Who do we know who knows Doc Beerfeldt?" Sorrowful says. "Who can we call up who may have influence enough with him to get him to just look at Marky? I will pay any price," he says. "Think of somebody," he says.

Well, while we are all trying to think, who comes in but Milk Ear Willie, and he comes in to toss a few slugs at Sorrowful, but before Milk Ear can start blasting Sleep-out sees him and jumps up and takes him off to a corner table, and starts whispering in Milk Ear's good ear.

As Sleep-out talks to him Milk Ear looks at Sorrowful in great surprise, and finally he begins nodding his head, and by and by he gets up and goes out of the joint in a hurry, while Sleep-out comes back to our table and says like this:

"Well," Sleep-out says, "let us stroll over to the Clinic. I just send Milk Ear Willie up to Doc Beerfeldt's house on Park Avenue to get the old Doc and bring him to the hospital. But, Sorrowful," Sleep-out says, "if he gets him, you must pay Willie the parlay you dispute with him, whatever it is. The chances are," Sleep-out says, "Willie is right. I remember once you out-argue me on a parlay when I know I am right."

Personally, I consider Sleep-out's talk about sending Milk Ear Willie after Doc Beerfeldt just so much nonsense, and so does everybody else, but we figure maybe Sleep-out is trying to raise Sorrowful's hopes, and anyway he keeps Milk Ear from tossing these slugs at Sorrowful, which everybody considers very thoughtful of Sleep-out, at least, especially as Sorrowful is under too great a strain to be dodging slugs just now.

About a dozen of us walk over to the Clinic, and most of us stand around the lobby on the ground floor, although Sorrowful goes up to Marky's floor to wait outside her door. He is waiting there from the time she is first taken to the hospital, never leaving except to go over to Mindy's once in a while to get something to eat, and occasionally they open the door a little to let him get a peek at Marky.

Well, it is maybe six o'clock when we hear a taxi stop outside the hospital and pretty soon in comes Milk Ear Willie with another character from the West Side by the name of Fats Finstein, who is well known to one and all as a great friend of Willie's, and in between them they have a little old guy with a Vandyke beard, who does not seem to have on anything much but a silk dressing gown and who seems somewhat agitated, especially as Milk Ear Willie and Fats Finstein keep prodding him from behind.

Now it comes out that this little old guy is nobody but Doc Beerfeldt, the great pneumonia specialist, and personally I never see a madder guy, although I wish to say I never blame him much for being mad when I learn how Milk Ear Willie and Fats Finstein boff his butler over the noggin when he answers their ring, and how they walk right into old Doc Beerfeldt's bedroom and haul him out of the hay at the point of their Roscoes and make him go with them.

In fact, I consider such treatment most discourteous to a prominent croaker, and if I am Doc Beerfeldt I will start hollering copper as soon as I hit the hospital, and for all I know maybe Doc Beerfeldt has just such an idea, but as Milk Ear Willie and Fats Finstein haul him into the lobby who comes downstairs but Sorrowful. And the minute Sorrowful sees Doc Beerfeldt he rushes up to him and says like this:

"Oh, Doc," Sorrowful says, "do something for my little girl. She is dying, Doc," Sorrowful says. "Just a little bit of a girl, Doc. Her name is Marky. I am only a gambler, Doc, and I do not mean anything to you or to anybody else, but please save the little girl."

Well, old Doc Beerfeldt sticks out his Vandyke beard and looks at Sorrowful a minute, and he can see there are large tears in old Sorrowful's eyes, and for all I know maybe the doc knows it has been many and many a year since there are tears in these eyes, at that. Then the doc looks at Milk Ear Willie and Fats Finstein and the rest of us, and at the nurses and internes who are commencing to come running up from every which way. Finally he speaks as follows:

"What is this?" he says. "A child? A little child? Why," he says, "I am under the impression that these gorillas are kidnapping me to attend to some other sick or wounded gorilla. A child? This is quite different. Why do you not say so in the first place? Where is the child?" Doc Beerfeldt says, "and," he says, "somebody get me some pants."

We all follow him upstairs to the door of Marky's room and we wait outside when he goes in, and we wait there for hours, because it seems that even old Doc Beerfeldt cannot think of anything to do in this situation no matter how he tries. And along toward ten-thirty in the morning he opens the door very quietly and motions Sorrowful to come in, and then he motions all the rest of us to follow, shaking his head very sad.

There are so many of us that we fill the room around

a little high narrow bed on which Marky is lying like a flower against a white wall, her yellow curls spread out over her pillow. Old Sorrowful drops on his knees beside the bed and his shoulders heave quite some as he kneels there, and I hear Sleep-out sniffing as if he has a cold in his head. Marky seems to be asleep when we go in, but while we are standing around the bed looking down at her, she opens her eyes and seems to see us and, what is more, she seems to know us, because she smiles at each guy in turn and then tries to hold out one of her little hands to Sorrowful.

Now very faint, like from far away, comes a sound of music through a half-open window in the room, from a jazz band that is rehearsing in a hall just up the street from the hospital, and Marky hears this music because she holds her head in such a way that anybody can see she is listening, and then she smiles again at us and whispers very plain, as follows: "Marky dance."

And she tries to reach down as if to pick up her skirt as she always does when she dances, but her hands fall across her breast as soft and white and light as snowflakes, and Marky never again dances in this world.

Well, old Doc Beerfeldt and the nurses make us go outside at once, and while we are standing there in the hall outside the door, saying nothing whatever, a young guy and two dolls, one of them old, and the other not so old, come along the hall, much excited. The young guy seems to know Sorrowful, who is sitting down again in his chair just outside the door, because he rushes up to Sorrowful and says to him like this:

"Where is she?" he says. "Where is my darling child? You remember me?" he says. "I leave my little girl with you one day while I go on an errand, and while I am on this errand everything goes blank, and I wind up back in my home in Indianapolis with my mother and sister here, and recall nothing about where I leave my child, or anything else."

"The poor boy has amnesia," the old doll says. "The stories that he deliberately abandons his wife in Paris and his child in New York are untrue."

"Yes," the doll who is not old puts in. "If we do not see the stories in the newspapers about how you have the child in this hospital we may never learn where she is. But everything is all right now. Of course we never approve of Harold's marriage to a person of the stage, and we only recently learn of her death in Paris soon after their separation there and are very sorry. But everything is all right now. We will take full charge of the child."

Now while all this gab is going on, Sorrowful never glances at them. He is just sitting there looking at Marky's door. And now as he is looking at the door a very strange thing seems to happen to his kisser, for all of a sudden it becomes the sad, mean-looking kisser that it is in the days before he ever sees Marky, and furthermore it is never again anything else.

"We will be rich," the young guy says. "We just learn that my darling child will be sole heiress to her maternal grandpapa's fortune, and the old guy is only a hop ahead of the undertaker right now. I suppose," he says, "I owe you something?"

And then Sorrowful gets up off his chair, and looks at the young guy and at the two dolls, and speaks as follows:

"Yes," he says, "you owe me a two-dollar marker for the bet you blow on Cold Cuts, and," he says, "I will trouble you to send it to me at once, so I can wipe you off my books."

Now he walks down the hall and out of the hospital, never looking back again, and there is a very great silence behind him that is broken only by the sniffing of Sleep-out, and by some first-class sobbing from some of the rest of us, and I remember now that the guy who is doing the best job of sobbing of all is nobody but Milk Ear Willie.

The Idyll of Miss Sarah Brown

OF ALL THE high players this country ever sees, there is no doubt but that the guy they call The Sky is the highest. In fact, the reason he is called The Sky is because he goes so high when it comes to betting on any proposition whatever. He will bet all he has, and nobody can bet any more than this.

His right name is Obadiah Masterson, and he is originally out of a little town in southern Colorado where he learns to shoot craps, and play cards, and one thing and another, and where his old man is a very well-known citizen, and something of a sport himself. In fact, The Sky tells me that when he finally cleans up all the loose scratch around his home town and decides he needs more room, his old man has a little private talk with him and says to him like this:

"Son," the old guy says, "you are now going out into the wide, wide world to make your own way, and it is a very good thing to do, as there are no more opportu-

·nities for you in this burg. I am only sorry," he says,
"that I am not able to bank-roll you to a very large
start, but," he says, "not having any potatoes to give
you, I am now going to stake you to some very valuable
advice, which I personally collect in my years of experience around and about, and I hope and trust you will
always bear this advice in mind.

"Son," the old guy says, "no matter how far you travel,
or how smart you get, always remember this: Some day,
somewhere," he says, "a guy is going to come to you
and show you a nice brand-new deck of cards on which
the seal is never broken, and this guy is going to offer
to bet you that the jack of spades will jump out of this
deck and squirt cider in your ear. But, son," the old
guy says, "do not bet him, for as sure as you do you
are going to get an ear full of cider."

Well, The Sky remembers what his old man says, and
he is always very cautious about betting on such propositions as the jack of spades jumping out of a sealed deck
of cards and squirting cider in his ear, and so he makes
few mistakes as he goes along. In fact, the only real
mistake The Sky makes is when he hits St. Louis after
leaving his old home town, and loses all his potatoes
betting a guy St. Louis is the biggest town in the world.

Now of course this is before The Sky ever sees any
bigger towns, and he is never much of a hand for reading
up on matters such as this. In fact, the only reading
The Sky ever does as he goes along through life is in
these Gideon Bibles such as he finds in the hotel rooms
where he lives, for The Sky never lives anywhere else
but in hotel rooms for years.

He tells me that he reads many items of great interest
in these Gideon Bibles, and furthermore The Sky says
that several times these Gideon Bibles keep him from
getting out of line, such as the time he finds himself

pretty much frozen-in over in Cincinnati, what with owing everybody in town except maybe the mayor from playing games of chance of one kind and another.

Well, The Sky says he sees no way of meeting these obligations and he is figuring the only thing he can do is to take a run-out powder, when he happens to read in one of these Gideon Bibles where it says like this:

"Better is it," the Gideon Bible says, "that thou shouldest not vow, than that thou shouldest vow and not pay."

Well, The Sky says he can see that there is no doubt whatever but that this means a guy shall not welsh, so he remains in Cincinnati until he manages to wiggle himself out of the situation, and from that day to this, The Sky never thinks of welshing.

He is maybe thirty years old, and is a tall guy with a round kisser, and big blue eyes, and he always looks as innocent as a little baby. But The Sky is by no means as innocent as he looks. In fact, The Sky is smarter than three Philadelphia lawyers, which makes him very smart, indeed, and he is well established as a high player in New Orleans, and Chicago, and Los Angeles, and wherever else there is any action in the way of card-playing, or crap-shooting, or horse-racing, or betting on the baseball games, for The Sky is always moving around the country following the action.

But while The Sky will bet on anything whatever, he is more of a short-card player and a crap shooter than anything else, and furthermore he is a great hand for propositions, such as are always coming up among citizens who follow games of chance for a living. Many citizens prefer betting on propositions to anything you can think of, because they figure a proposition gives them a chance to out-smart somebody, and in fact I know citizens who will sit up all night making up propositions to offer other citizens the next day.

A proposition may be only a problem in cards, such as what is the price against a guy getting aces back-to-back, or how often a pair of deuces will win a hand in stud, and then again it may be some very daffy proposition, indeed, although the daffier any proposition seems to be, the more some citizens like it. And no one ever sees The Sky when he does not have some proposition of his own.

The first time he ever shows up around this town, he goes to a baseball game at the Polo Grounds with several prominent citizens, and while he is at the ball game, he buys himself a sack of Harry Stevens' peanuts, which he dumps in a side pocket of his coat. He is eating these peanuts all through the game, and after the game is over and he is walking across the field with the citizens, he says to them like this:

"What price," The Sky says, "I cannot throw a peanut from second base to the home plate?"

Well, everybody knows that a peanut is too light for anybody to throw it this far, so Big Nig, the crap shooter, who always likes to have a little the best of it running for him, speaks as follows:

"You can have 3 to 1 from me, stranger," Big Nig says.

"Two C's against six," The Sky says, and then he stands on second base, and takes a peanut out of his pocket, and not only whips it to the home plate, but on into the lap of a fat guy who is still sitting in the grand stand putting the zing on Bill Terry for not taking Walker out of the box when Walker is getting a pasting from the other club.

Well, naturally, this is a most astonishing throw, indeed, but afterwards it comes out that The Sky throws a peanut loaded with lead, and of course it is not one of Harry Stevens' peanuts, either, as Harry is not selling peanuts full of lead at a dime a bag, with the price of lead what it is.

It is only a few nights after this that The Sky states another most unusual proposition to a group of citizens sitting in Mindy's restaurant when he offers to bet a C note that he can go down into Mindy's cellar and catch a live rat with his bare hands and everybody is greatly astonished when Mindy himself steps up and takes the bet, for ordinarily Mindy will not bet you a nickel he is alive.

But it seems that Mindy knows that The Sky plants a tame rat in the cellar, and this rat knows The Sky and loves him dearly, and will let him catch it any time he wishes, and it also seems that Mindy knows that one of his dish washers happens upon this rat, and not knowing it is tame, knocks it flatter than a pancake. So when The Sky goes down into the cellar and starts trying to catch a rat with his bare hands, he is greatly surprised how inhospitable the rat turns out to be, because it is one of Mindy's personal rats, and Mindy is around afterwards saying he will lay plenty of 7 to 5 against even Strangler Lewis being able to catch one of his rats with his bare hands, or with boxing gloves on.

I am only telling you all this to show you what a smart guy The Sky is, and I am only sorry I do not have time to tell you about many other very remarkable propositions that he thinks up outside of his regular business.

It is well-known to one and all that he is very honest in every respect, and that he hates and despises cheaters at cards, or dice, and furthermore The Sky never wishes to play with any the best of it himself, or anyway not much. He will never take the inside of any situation, as many gamblers love to do, such as owning a gambling house, and having the percentage run for him instead of against him, for always The Sky is strictly a player, because he says he will never care to settle down in one spot long enough to become the owner of anything.

In fact, in all the years The Sky is drifting around the country, nobody ever knows him to own anything except maybe a bank roll, and when he comes to Broadway the last time, which is the time I am now speaking of, he has a hundred G's in cash money, and an extra suit of clothes, and this is all he has in the world. He never owns such a thing as a house, or an automobile, or a piece of jewelry. He never owns a watch, because The Sky says time means nothing to him.

Of course some guys will figure a hundred G's comes under the head of owning something, but as far as The Sky is concerned, money is nothing but just something for him to play with and the dollars may as well be doughnuts as far as value goes with him. The only time The Sky ever thinks of money as money is when he is broke, and the only way he can tell he is broke is when he reaches into his pocket and finds nothing there but his fingers.

Then it is necessary for The Sky to go out and dig up some fresh scratch somewhere, and when it comes to digging up scratch, The Sky is practically supernatural. He can get more potatoes on the strength of a telegram to some place or other than John D. Rockefeller can get on collateral, for everybody knows The Sky's word is as good as wheat in the bin.

Now one Sunday evening The Sky is walking along Broadway, and at the corner of Forty-ninth Street he comes upon a little bunch of mission workers who are holding a religious meeting, such as mission workers love to do of a Sunday evening, the idea being that they may round up a few sinners here and there, although personally I always claim the mission workers come out too early to catch any sinners on this part of Broadway. At such an hour the sinners are still in bed resting up from their sinning of the night before, so they will be in good shape for more sinning a little later on.

There are only four of these mission workers, and two of them are old guys, and one is an old doll, while the other is a young doll who is tootling on a cornet. And after a couple of ganders at this young doll, The Sky is a goner, for this is one of the most beautiful young dolls anybody ever sees on Broadway, and especially as a mission worker. Her name is Miss Sarah Brown.

She is tall, and thin, and has a first-class shape, and her hair is a light brown, going on blond, and her eyes are like I do not know what, except that they are one-hundred-per-cent eyes in every respect. Furthermore, she is not a bad cornet player, if you like cornet players, although at this spot on Broadway she has to play against a scat band in a chop-suey joint near by, and this is tough competition, although at that many citizens believe Miss Sarah Brown will win by a large score if she only gets a little more support from one of the old guys with her who has a big bass drum, but does not pound it hearty enough.

Well, The Sky stands there listening to Miss Sarah Brown tootling on the cornet for quite a spell, and then he hears her make a speech in which she puts the blast on sin very good, and boosts religion quite some, and says if there are any souls around that need saving the owners of same may step forward at once. But no one steps forward, so The Sky comes over to Mindy's restaurant where many citizens are congregated, and starts telling us about Miss Sarah Brown. But of course we already know about Miss Sarah Brown, because she is so beautiful, and so good.

Furthermore, everybody feels somewhat sorry for Miss Sarah Brown, for while she is always tootling the cornet, and making speeches, and looking to save any souls that need saving, she never seems to find any souls to save, or at least her bunch of mission workers never gets any bigger. In fact, it gets smaller, as she starts out with a guy who plays a very fair sort of trombone, but this guy takes it on the lam one night with the trombone, which one and all consider a dirty trick.

Now from this time on, The Sky does not take any interest in anything but Miss Sarah Brown, and any night she is out on the corner with the other mission workers, you will see The Sky standing around looking at her, and naturally after a few weeks of this, Miss Sarah Brown must know The Sky is looking at her, or she is dumber than seems possible. And nobody ever figures Miss Sarah Brown dumb, as she is always on her toes, and seems plenty able to take care of herself, even on Broadway.

Sometimes after the street meeting is over, The Sky follows the mission workers to their headquarters in an old storeroom around in Forty-eighth Street where they generally hold an indoor session, and I hear The Sky drops many a large coarse note in the collection box while looking at Miss Sarah Brown, and there is no doubt these notes come in handy around the mission, as I hear business is by no means so good there.

It is called the Save-a-Soul Mission, and it is run mainly by Miss Sarah Brown's grandfather, an old guy with whiskers, by the name of Arvide Abernathy, but Miss Sarah Brown seems to do most of the work, including tootling the cornet, and visiting the poor people around and about, and all this and that, and many citizens claim it is a great shame that such a beautiful doll is wasting her time being good.

How The Sky ever becomes acquainted with Miss Sarah Brown is a very great mystery, but the next thing anybody knows, he is saying hello to her, and she is smiling at him out of her one-hundred-per-cent eyes, and one evening when I happen to be with The Sky we run into her walking along Forty-ninth Street, and The Sky hauls off and stops her, and says it is a nice evening, which it is, at that. Then The Sky says to Miss Sarah Brown like this:

"Well," The Sky says, "how is the mission dodge going these days? Are you saving any souls?" he says.

Well, it seems from what Miss Sarah Brown says the soul-saving is very slow, indeed, these days.

"In fact," Miss Sarah Brown says, "I worry greatly about how few souls we seem to save. Sometimes I wonder if we are lacking in grace."

She goes on up the street, and The Sky stands looking after her, and he says to me like this:

"I wish I can think of some way to help this little doll," he says, "especially," he says, "in saving a few souls to build up her mob at the mission. I must speak to her again, and see if I can figure something out."

But The Sky does not get to speak to Miss Sarah Brown again, because somebody weighs in the sacks on him by telling her he is nothing but a professional gambler, and that he is a very undesirable character, and that his only interest in hanging around the mission is because she is a good-looking doll. So all of a sudden Miss Sarah Brown plays plenty of chill for The Sky. Furthermore, she sends him word that she does not care to accept any more of his potatoes in the collection box, because his potatoes are nothing but ill-gotten gains.

Well, naturally, this hurts The Sky's feelings no little,

so he quits standing around looking at Miss Sarah Brown, and going to the mission, and takes to mingling again with the citizens in Mindy's, and showing some interest in the affairs of the community, especially the crap games.

Of course the crap games that are going on at this time are nothing much, because practically everybody in the world is broke, but there is a head-and-head game run by Nathan Detroit over a garage in Fifty-second Street where there is occasionally some action, and who shows up at this crap game early one evening but The Sky, although it seems he shows up there more to find company than anything else.

In fact, he only stands around watching the play, and talking with other guys who are also standing around and watching, and many of these guys are very high shots during the gold rush, although most of them are now as clean as a jaybird, and maybe cleaner. One of these guys is a guy by the name of Brandy Bottle Bates, who is known from coast to coast as a high player when he has anything to play with, and who is called Brandy Bottle Bates because it seems that years ago he is a great hand for belting a brandy bottle around.

This Brandy Bottle Bates is a big, black-looking guy, with a large beezer, and a head shaped like a pear, and he is considered a very immoral and wicked character, but he is a pretty slick gambler, and a fast man with a dollar when he is in the money.

Well, finally The Sky asks Brandy Bottle why he is not playing and Brandy laughs, and states as follows:

"Why," he says, "in the first place I have no potatoes, and in the second place I doubt if it will do me much good if I do have any potatoes the way I am going the past year. Why," Brandy Bottle says, "I cannot win a bet to save my soul."

Now this crack seems to give The Sky an idea, as he stands looking at Brandy Bottle very strangely, and while he is looking, Big Nig, the crap shooter, picks up the dice and hits three times hand-running, bing, bing, bing. Then Big Nig comes out on a six and Brandy Bottle Bates speaks as follows:

"You see how my luck is," he says. "Here is Big Nig hotter than a stove, and here I am without a bob to follow him with, especially," Brandy says, "when he is looking for nothing but a six. Why," he says, "Nig can make sixes all night when he is hot. If he does not make this six, the way he is, I will be willing to turn square and quit gambling forever."

"Well, Brandy," The Sky says, "I will make you a proposition. I will lay you a G note Big Nig does not get his six. I will lay you a G note against nothing but your soul," he says. "I mean if Big Nig does not get his six, you are to turn square and join Miss Sarah Brown's mission for six months."

"Bet!" Brandy Bottle Bates says right away, meaning the proposition is on, although the chances are he does not quite understand the proposition. All Brandy understands is The Sky wishes to wager that Big Nig does not make his six, and Brandy Bottle Bates will be willing to bet his soul a couple of times over on Big Nig making his six, and figure he is getting the best of it, at that, as Brandy has great confidence in Nig.

Well, sure enough, Big Nig makes the six, so The Sky weeds Brandy Bottle Bates a G note, although everybody around is saying The Sky makes a terrible overlay of the natural price in giving Brandy Bottle a G against his soul. Furthermore, everybody around figures the chances are The Sky only wishes to give Brandy an opportunity to get in action, and nobody figures The Sky is on the level about trying to win Brandy Bottle

Bates' soul, especially as The Sky does not seem to wish to go any further after paying the bet.

He only stands there looking on and seeming somewhat depressed as Brandy Bottle goes into action on his own account with the G note, fading other guys around the table with cash money. But Brandy Bottle Bates seems to figure what is in The Sky's mind pretty well, because Brandy Bottle is a crafty old guy.

It finally comes his turn to handle the dice, and he hits a couple of times, and then he comes out on a four, and anybody will tell you that a four is a very tough point to make, even with a lead pencil. Then Brandy Bottle turns to The Sky and speaks to him as follows:

"Well, Sky," he says, "I will take the odds off you on this one. I know you do not want my dough," he says. "I know you only want my soul for Miss Sarah Brown, and," he says, "without wishing to be fresh about it, I know why you want it for her. I am young once myself," Brandy Bottle says. "And you know if I lose to you, I will be over there in Forty-eighth Street in an hour pounding on the door, for Brandy always settles.

"But, Sky," he says, "now I am in the money, and my price goes up. Will you lay me ten G's against my soul I do not make this four?"

"Bet!" The Sky says, and right away Brandy Bottle hits with a four.

Well, when word goes around that The Sky is up at Nathan Detroit's crap game trying to win Brandy Bottle Bates' soul for Miss Sarah Brown, the excitement is practically intense. Somebody telephones Mindy's, where a large number of citizens are sitting around arguing about this and that, and telling one another how much they will bet in support of their arguments, if only they have something to bet, and Mindy himself is almost killed in the rush for the door.

One of the first guys out of Mindy's and up to the crap game is Regret, the horse player, and as he comes in Brandy Bottle is looking for a nine, and The Sky is laying him twelve G's against his soul that he does not make this nine, for it seems Brandy Bottle's soul keeps getting more and more expensive.

Well, Regret wishes to bet his soul against a G that Brandy Bottle gets his nine, and is greatly insulted when The Sky cannot figure his price any better than a double saw, but finally Regret accepts this price, and Brandy Bottle hits again.

Now many other citizens request a little action from The Sky, and if there is one thing The Sky cannot deny a citizen it is action, so he says he will lay them according to how he figures their word to join Miss Sarah Brown's mission if Brandy Bottle misses out, but about this time The Sky finds he has no more potatoes on him, being now around thirty-five G's loser, and he wishes to give markers.

But Brandy Bottle says that while ordinarily he will be pleased to extend The Sky this accommodation, he does not care to accept markers against his soul, so then The Sky has to leave the joint and go over to his hotel two or three blocks away, and get the night clerk to open his damper so The Sky can get the rest of his bank roll. In the meantime the crap game continues at Nathan Detroit's among the small operators, while the other citizens stand around and say that while they hear of many a daffy proposition in their time, this is the daffiest that ever comes to their attention, although Big Nig claims he hears of a daffier one, but cannot think what it is.

Big Nig claims that all gamblers are daffy anyway, and in fact he says if they are not daffy they will not be gamblers, and while he is arguing this matter back comes The Sky with fresh scratch, and Brandy Bottle

Bates takes up where he leaves off, although Brandy says he is accepting the worst of it, as the dice have a chance to cool off.

Now the upshot of the whole business is that Brandy Bottle hits thirteen licks in a row, and the last lick he makes is on a ten, and it is for twenty G's against his soul, with about a dozen other citizens getting anywhere from one to five C's against their souls, and complaining bitterly of the price.

And as Brandy Bottle makes his ten, I happen to look at The Sky and I see him watching Brandy with a very peculiar expression on his face, and furthermore I see The Sky's right hand creeping inside his coat where I know he always packs a Betsy in a shoulder holster, so I can see something is wrong somewhere.

But before I can figure out what it is, there is quite a fuss at the door, and loud talking, and a doll's voice, and all of a sudden in bobs nobody else but Miss Sarah Brown. It is plain to be seen that she is all steamed up about something.

She marches right up to the crap table where Brandy Bottle Bates and The Sky and the other citizens are standing, and one and all are feeling sorry for Dobber, the doorman, thinking of what Nathan Detroit is bound to say to him for letting her in. The dice are still lying on the table showing Brandy Bottle Bates' last throw, which cleans The Sky and gives many citizens the first means they enjoy in several months.

Well, Miss Sarah Brown looks at The Sky, and The Sky looks at Miss Sarah Brown, and Miss Sarah Brown looks at the citizens around and about, and one and all are somewhat dumfounded, and nobody seems to be able to think of much to say, although The Sky finally speaks up as follows:

"Good evening," The Sky says. "It is a nice evening,"

he says. "I am trying to win a few souls for you around here, but," he says, "I seem to be about half out of luck."

"Well," Miss Sarah Brown says, looking at The Sky most severely out of her hundred-per-cent eyes, "you are taking too much upon yourself. I can win any souls I need myself. You better be thinking of your own soul. By the way," she says, "are you risking your own soul, or just your money?"

Well, of course up to this time The Sky is not risking anything but his potatoes, so he only shakes his head to Miss Sarah Brown's question, and looks somewhat disorganized.

"I know something about gambling," Miss Sarah Brown says, "especially about crap games. I ought to," she says. "It ruins my poor papa and my brother Joe. If you wish to gamble for souls, Mister Sky, gamble for your own soul."

Now Miss Sarah Brown opens a small black leather pocketbook she is carrying in one hand, and pulls out a two-dollar bill, and it is such a two-dollar bill as seems to have seen much service in its time, and holding up this deuce, Miss Sarah Brown speaks as follows:

"I will gamble with you, Mister Sky," she says. "I will gamble with you," she says, "on the same terms you gamble with these parties here. This two dollars against your soul, Mister Sky. It is all I have, but," she says, "it is more than your soul is worth."

Well, of course anybody can see that Miss Sarah Brown is doing this because she is very angry, and wishes to make The Sky look small, but right away The Sky's duke comes from inside his coat, and he picks up the dice and hands them to her and speaks as follows:

"Roll them," The Sky says, and Miss Sarah Brown snatches the dice out of his hand and gives them a quick sling on the table in such a way that anybody can see she is not a professional crap shooter, and not even an amateur crap shooter, for all amateur crap shooters first breathe on the dice, and rattle them good, and make remarks to them, such as "Come on, baby!"

In fact, there is some criticism of Miss Sarah Brown afterwards on account of her haste, as many citizens are eager to string with her to hit, while others are just as anxious to bet she misses, and she does not give them a chance to get down.

Well, Scranton Slim is the stick guy, and he takes a gander at the dice as they hit up against the side of the table and bounce back, and then Slim hollers, "Winner, winner, winner," as stick guys love to do, and what is showing on the dice as big as life, but a six and a five, which makes eleven, no matter how you figure, so The Sky's soul belongs to Miss Sarah Brown.

She turns at once and pushes through the citizens around the table without even waiting to pick up the deuce she lays down when she grabs the dice. Afterwards a most obnoxious character by the name of Red Nose Regan tries to claim the deuce as a sleeper and gets the heave-o from Nathan Detroit, who becomes very indignant about this, stating that Red Nose is trying to give his joint a wrong rap.

Naturally, The Sky follows Miss Brown, and Dobber, the doorman, tells me that as they are waiting for him to unlock the door and let them out, Miss Sarah Brown turns on The Sky and speaks to him as follows:

"You are a fool," Miss Sarah Brown says.

Well, at this Dobber figures The Sky is bound to let one go, as this seems to be most insulting language, but instead of letting one go, The Sky only smiles at Miss Sarah Brown and says to her like this:

"Why," The Sky says, "Paul says 'If any man among you seemeth to be wise in this world, let him become a fool, that he may be wise.' I love you, Miss Sarah Brown," The Sky says.

Well, now, Dobber has a pretty fair sort of memory, and he says that Miss Sarah Brown tells The Sky that since he seems to know so much about the Bible, maybe he remembers the second verse of the Song of Solomon, but the chances are Dobber muffs the number of the verse, because I look the matter up in one of these Gideon Bibles, and the verse seems a little too much for Miss Sarah Brown, although of course you never can tell.

Anyway, this is about all there is to the story, except that Brandy Bottle Bates slides out during the confusion so quietly even Dobber scarcely remembers letting him out, and he takes most of The Sky's potatoes with him, but he soon gets batted in against the faro bank out in Chicago, and the last anybody hears of him he gets religion all over again, and is preaching out in San Jose, so The Sky always claims he beats Brandy for his soul, at that.

I see The Sky the other night at Forty-ninth Street and Broadway, and he is with quite a raft of mission workers, including Mrs. Sky, for it seems that the soul-saving business picks up wonderfully, and The Sky is giving a big bass drum such a first-class whacking that the scat band in the chop-suey joint can scarcely be heard. Furthermore, The Sky is hollering between whacks, and I never see a guy look happier, especially when Mrs. Sky smiles at him out of her hundred-percent eyes. But I do not linger long, because The Sky gets a gander at me, and right away he begins hollering:

"I see before me a sinner of deepest dye," he hollers. "Oh, sinner, repent before it is too late. Join with us, sinner," he hollers, "and let us save your soul."

Naturally, this crack about me being a sinner embarrasses me no little, as it is by no means true, and it is a good thing for The Sky there is no copper in me, or I will go to Mrs. Sky, who is always bragging about how she wins The Sky's soul by outplaying him at his own game, and tell her the truth.

And the truth is that the dice with which she wins The Sky's soul, and which are the same dice with which Brandy Bottle Bates wins all his potatoes, are strictly phony, and that she gets into Nathan Detroit's just in time to keep The Sky from killing old Brandy Bottle.

Baseball Hattie

It comes on springtime, and the little birdies are singing in the trees in Central Park, and the grass is green all around and about, and I am at the Polo Grounds on the opening day of the baseball season, when who do I behold but Baseball Hattie. I am somewhat surprised at this spectacle, as it is years since I see Baseball Hattie, and for all I know she long ago passes to a better and happier world. But there she is, as large as life, and in fact twenty pounds larger, and when I call the attention of Armand Fibleman, the gambler, to her, he gets up and tears right out of the joint as if he sees a ghost, for if there is one thing Armand Fibleman loathes and despises, it is a ghost. I can see that Baseball Hattie is greatly changed, and to tell the truth, I can see that she is getting to be nothing but an old bag. Her hair that is once as black as a yard up a stovepipe is gray, and she is wearing gold-rimmed cheaters, although she seems to be pretty well dressed and looks as if she may be in the money a little bit, at that.

But the greatest change in her is the way she sits there very quiet all afternoon, never once opening her yap, even when many of the customers around her are claiming that Umpire William Klem is Public Enemy No. 1 to 16 inclusive, because they think he calls a close one against the Giants. I am wondering if maybe Baseball Hattie is stricken dumb somewhere back down the years, because I can remember when she is usually making speeches in the grandstand in favor of hanging such characters as Umpire William Klem when they call close ones against the Giants. But Hattie just sits there as if she is in a church while the public clamor goes on about her, and she does not as much as cry out robber, or even you big bum at Umpire William Klem. I see many a baseball bug in my time, male and female, but without doubt the worst bug of them all is Baseball Hattie, and you can say it again. She is most particularly a bug about the Giants, and she never misses a game they play at the Polo Grounds, and in fact she sometimes bobs up watching them play in other cities, which is always very embarrassing to the Giants, as they fear the customers in these cities may get the wrong impression of New York womanhood after listening to Baseball Hattie awhile.

The first time I ever see Baseball Hattie to pay any attention to her is in Philadelphia, a matter of twenty-odd years back, when the Giants are playing a series there, and many citizens of New York, including Armand Fibleman and myself, are present, because the Philadelphia customers are great hands for betting on baseball games in those days, and Armand Fibleman figures he may knock a few of them in the creek. Armand Fibleman is a character who will bet on baseball games from who-laid-the-chunk, and in fact he will bet on anything whatever, because Armand Fibleman is a gambler by trade and has been such since infancy. Personally, I will not bet you four dollars on a baseball game, because in the first place I am not apt to have four dollars, and in the second place I consider horse races a much sounder investment, but I often go around and about with Armand Fibleman, as he is a friend of mine, and sometimes he gives me a little piece of one of his bets for nothing.

Well, what happens in Philadelphia but the umpire forfeits the game in the seventh inning to the Giants by a score of nine to nothing when the Phillies are really leading by five runs, and the reason the umpire takes this action is because he orders several of the Philadelphia players to leave the field for calling him a scoundrel and a rat and a snake in the grass, and also a baboon, and they refuse to take their departure, as they still have more names to call him. Right away the Philadelphia customers become infuriated in a manner you will scarcely believe, for ordinarily a Philadelphia baseball customer is as quiet as a lamb, no matter what you do to him, and in fact in those days a Philadelphia baseball customer is only considered as somebody to do something to.

But these Philadelphia customers are so infuriated that they not only chase the umpire under the stand, but they wait in the street outside the baseball orchard until the Giants change into their street clothes and come out of the clubhouse. Then the Philadelphia customers begin pegging rocks, and one thing and another, at the Giants, and it is a most exciting and disgraceful scene that is spoken of for years afterwards. Well, the Giants march along toward the North Philly station to catch a train for home, dodging the rocks and one thing and another the best they can, and wondering why the Philadelphia gendarmes do not come to the rescue, until somebody notices several gendarmes among the customers doing some of the throwing themselves, so the Giants realize that this is a most inhospitable community, to be sure.

Finally all of them get inside the North Philly station and are safe, except a big, tall, left-handed pitcher by the name of Haystack Duggeler, who just reports to the club the day before and who finds himself surrounded by quite a posse of these infuriated Philadelphia customers, and who is unable to make them understand that he is nothing but a rookie, because he has a Missouri accent, and besides, he is half paralyzed with fear. One of the infuriated Philadelphia customers is armed with a brickbat and is just moving forward to maim Haystack Duggeler with this instrument, when who steps into the situation but Baseball Hattie, who is also on her way to the station to catch a train, and who is greatly horrified by the assault on the Giants.

She seizes the brickbat from the infuriated Philadelphia customer's grasp, and then tags the customer smack-dab between the eyes with his own weapon, knocking him so unconscious that I afterwards hear he does not recover for two weeks, and that he remains practically an imbecile the rest of his days. Then Baseball Hattie cuts loose on the other infuriated Philadelphia customers with language that they never before hear in those parts, causing them to disperse without further ado, and after the last customer is beyond the sound of her voice, she takes Haystack Duggeler by the pitching arm and personally escorts him to the station.

Now out of this incident is born a wonderful romance between Baseball Hattie and Haystack Duggeler, and in fact it is no doubt love at first sight, and about this period Haystack Duggeler begins burning up the league with his pitching, and at the same time giving Manager

Mac plenty of headaches, including the romance with Baseball Hattie, because anybody will tell you that a left-hander is tough enough on a manager without a romance, and especially a romance with Baseball Hattie. It seems that the trouble with Hattie is she is in business up in Harlem, and this business consists of a boarding and rooming house where ladies and gentlemen board and room, and personally I never see anything out of line in the matter, but the rumor somehow gets around, as rumors will do, that in the first place, it is not a boarding and rooming house, and in the second place that the ladies and gentlemen who room and board there are by no means ladies and gentlemen, and especially ladies.

Well, this rumor becomes a terrible knock to Baseball Hattie's social reputation. Furthermore, I hear Manager Mac sends for her and requests her to kindly lay off his ballplayers, and especially off a character who can make a baseball sing high C like Haystack Duggeler. In fact, I hear Manager Mac gives her such a lecture on her civic duty to New York and to the Giants that Baseball Hattie sheds tears, and promises she will never give Haystack another tumble the rest of the season. "You know me, Mac," Baseball Hattie says. "You know I will cut off my nose rather than do anything to hurt your club. I sometimes figure I am in love with this big bloke, but," she says, "maybe it is only gas pushing up around my heart. I will take something for it. To hell with him, Mac!" she says.

So she does not see Haystack Duggeler again, except at a distance, for a long time, and he goes on to win fourteen games in a row, pitching a no-hitter and four two-hitters among them, and hanging up a reputation as a great pitcher, and also as a hundred-per-cent heel.

Haystack Duggeler is maybe twenty-five at this time,

and he comes to the big league with more bad habits than anybody in the history of the world is able to acquire in such a short time. He is especially a great rumpot, and after he gets going good in the league, he is just as apt to appear for a game all mulled up as not. He is fond of all forms of gambling, such as playing cards and shooting craps, but after they catch him with a deck of readers in a poker game and a pair of tops in a crap game, none of the Giants will play with him any more, except of course when there is nobody else to play with. He is ignorant about many little things, such as reading and writing and geography and mathematics, as Haystack Duggeler himself admits he never goes to school any more than he can help, but he is so wise when it comes to larceny that I always figure they must have great tutors back in Haystack's old home town of Booneville, Mo.

And no smarter jobbie ever breathes than Haystack when he is out there pitching. He has so much speed that he just naturally throws the ball past a batter before he can get the old musket off his shoulder, and along with his hard one, Haystack has a curve like the letter Q. With two ounces of brains, Haystack Duggeler will be the greatest pitcher that ever lives. Well, as far as Baseball Hattie is concerned, she keeps her word about not seeing Haystack, although sometimes when he is mulled up he goes around to her boarding and rooming house, and tries to break down the door.

On days when Haystack Duggeler is pitching, she is always in her favorite seat back of third, and while she roots hard for the Giants no matter who is pitching, she puts on extra steam when Haystack is bending them over, and it is quite an experience to hear her crying lay them in there, Haystack, old boy, and strike this big tramp out, Haystack, and other exclamations of a

similar nature, which please Haystack quite some, but
annoy Baseball Hattie's neighbors back of third base,
such as Armand Fibleman, if he happens to be betting
on the other club.

A month before the close of his first season in the
big league, Haystack Duggeler gets so ornery that Manager Mac suspends him, hoping maybe it will cause
Haystack to do a little thinking, but naturally Haystack
is unable to do this, because he has nothing to think
with. About a week later, Manager Mac gets to noticing
how he can use a few ball games, so he starts looking
for Haystack Duggeler, and he finds him tending bar
on Eighth Avenue with his uniform hung up back of
the bar as an advertisement. The baseball writers speak
of Haystack as eccentric, which is a polite way of saying
he is a screwball, but they consider him a most unique
character and are always writing humorous stories about
him, though any one of them will lay you plenty of
nine to five that Haystack winds up an umbay. The
chances are they will raise their price a little, as the
season closes and Haystack is again under suspension
with cold weather coming on and not a dime in his
pants pockets.

It is sometime along in the winter that Baseball Hattie
hauls off and marries Haystack Duggeler, which is a
great surprise to one and all, but not nearly as much
of a surprise as when Hattie closes her boarding and
rooming house and goes to live in a little apartment
with Haystack Duggeler up on Washington Heights.

It seems that she finds Haystack one frosty night sleeping in a hallway, after being around slightly mulled
up for several weeks, and she takes him to her home
and gets him a bath and a shave and a clean shirt and
two boiled eggs and some toast and coffee and a shot
or two of rye whisky, all of which is greatly appreciated

by Haystack, especially the rye whisky. Then Haystack proposes marriage to her and takes a paralyzed oath that if she becomes his wife he will reform, so what with loving Haystack anyway, and with the fix commencing to request more dough off the boarding-and-rooming-house business than the business will stand, Hattie takes him at his word, and there you are. The baseball writers are wondering what Manager Mac will say when he hears these tidings, but all Mac says is that Haystack cannot possibly be any worse married than he is single-o, and then Mac has the club office send the happy couple a little paper money to carry them over the winter. Well, what happens but a great change comes over Haystack Duggeler. He stops bending his elbow and helps Hattie cook and wash the dishes, and holds her hand when they are in the movies, and speaks of his love for her several times a week, and Hattie is as happy as nine dollars' worth of lettuce. Manager Mac is so delighted at the change in Haystack that he has the club office send over more paper money, because Mac knows that with Haystack in shape he is sure of twenty-five games, and maybe the pennant.

In late February, Haystack reports to the training camp down South still as sober as some judges, and the other ballplayers are so impressed by the change in him that they admit him to their poker game again. But of course it is too much to expect a man to alter his entire course of living all at once, and it is not long before Haystack discovers four nines in his hand on his own deal and breaks up the game.

He brings Baseball Hattie with him to the camp, and this is undoubtedly a slight mistake, as it seems the old rumor about her boarding-and-rooming-house business gets around among the ever-loving wives of the other players, and they put on a large chill for her. In fact,

you will think Hattie has the smallpox. Naturally, Baseball Hattie feels the frost, but she never lets on, as it
seems she runs into many bigger and better frosts than
this in her time. Then Haystack Duggeler notices it,
and it seems that it makes him a little peevish toward
Baseball Hattie, and in fact it is said that he gives her
a slight pasting one night in their room, partly because
she has no better social standing and partly because he
is commencing to cop a few sneaks on the local corn
now and then, and Hattie chides him for same.

Well, about this time it appears that Baseball Hattie
discovers that she is going to have a baby, and as soon
as she recovers from her astonishment, she decides that
it is to be a boy who will be a great baseball player,
maybe a pitcher, although Hattie admits she is willing
to compromise on a good second baseman. She also decides that his name is to be Derrill Duggeler, after his
paw, as it seems Derrill is Haystack's real name, and
he is only called Haystack because he claims he once
makes a living stacking hay, although the general opinion is that all he ever stacks is cards. It is really quite
remarkable what a belt Hattie gets out of the idea of
having this baby, though Haystack is not excited about
the matter. He is not paying much attention to Baseball
Hattie by now, except to give her a slight pasting now
and then, but Hattie is so happy about the baby that
she does not mind these pastings.

Haystack Duggeler meets up with Armand Fibleman
along in midsummer. By this time, Haystack discovers
horse racing and is always making bets on the horses,
and naturally he is generally broke, and then I commence running into him in different spots with Armand
Fibleman, who is now betting higher than a cat's back
on baseball games.

It is late August, and the Giants are fighting for the

front end of the league, and an important series with Brooklyn is coming up, and everybody knows that Haystack Duggeler will work in anyway two games of the series, as Haystack can generally beat Brooklyn just by throwing his glove on the mound. There is no doubt but what he has the old Indian sign on Brooklyn, and the night before the first game, which he is sure to work, the gamblers along Broadway are making the Giants two-to-one favorites to win the game.

This same night before the game, Baseball Hattie is home in her little apartment on Washington Heights waiting for Haystack to come in and eat a delicious dinner of pigs' knuckles and sauerkraut, which she personally prepares for him. In fact, she hurries home right after the ball game to get this delicacy ready, because Haystack tells her he will surely come home this particular night, although Hattie knows he is never better than even money to keep his word about anything. But sure enough, in he comes while the pigs' knuckles and sauerkraut are still piping hot, and Baseball Hattie is surprised to see Armand Fibleman with him, as she knows Armand backwards and forwards and does not care much for him, at that. However, she can say the same thing about four million other characters in this town, so she makes Armand welcome, and they sit down and put on the pigs' knuckles and sauerkraut together, and a pleasant time is enjoyed by one and all. In fact, Baseball Hattie puts herself out to entertain Armand Fibleman, because he is the first guest Haystack ever brings home.

Well, Armand Fibleman can be very pleasant when he wishes, and he speaks very nicely to Hattie. Naturally, he sees that Hattie is expecting, and in fact he will have to be blind not to see it, and he seems greatly interested in this matter and asks Hattie many questions, and Hattie is delighted to find somebody to

talk to about what is coming off with her, as Haystack
will never listen to any of her remarks on the subject.
So Armand Fibleman gets to hear all about Baseball
Hattie's son, and how he is to be a great baseball player,
and Armand says is that so, and how nice, and all
this and that, until Haystack Duggeler speaks up as
follows, and to wit:

"Oh, dag-gone her son!" Haystack says. "It is going
to be a girl, anyway, so let us dismiss this topic and
get down to business. Hat," he says, "you fan yourself
into the kitchen and wash the dishes, while Armand
and me talk."

So Hattie goes into the kitchen, leaving Haystack and
Armand sitting there talking, and what are they talking
about but a proposition for Haystack to let the Brooklyn
club beat him the next day so Armand Fibleman can
take the odds and clean up a nice little gob of money,
which he is to split with Haystack. Hattie can hear every
word they say, as the kitchen is next door to the dining
room where they are sitting, and at first she thinks they
are joking, because at this time nobody ever even as
much as thinks of skulduggery in baseball, or anyway,
not much. It seems that at first Haystack is not in favor
of the idea, but Armand Fibleman keeps mentioning
money that Haystack owes him for bets on the horse
races, and he asks Haystack how he expects to continue
betting on the races without fresh money, and Armand
also speaks of the great injustice that is being done Haystack by the Giants in not paying him twice the salary
he is getting, and how the loss of one or two games is
by no means such a great calamity.

Well, finally Baseball Hattie hears Haystack say all
right, but he wishes a thousand dollars then and there
as a guarantee, and Armand Fibleman says this is fine,
and they will go downtown and he will get the money

at once, and now Hattie realizes that maybe they are in earnest, and she pops out of the kitchen and speaks as follows:

"Gentlemen," Hattie says, "you seem to be sober, but I guess you are drunk. If you are not drunk, you must both be daffy to think of such a thing as phenagling around with a baseball game."

"Hattie," Haystack says, "kindly close your trap and go back in the kitchen, or I will give you a bust in the nose."

And with this he gets up and reaches for his hat, and Armand Fibleman gets up, too, and Hattie says like this:

"Why, Haystack," she says, "you are not really serious in this matter, are you?"

"Of course I am serious," Haystack says. "I am sick and tired of pitching for starvation wages, and besides, I will win a lot of games later on to make up for the one I lose tomorrow. Say," he says, "these Brooklyn bums may get lucky tomorrow and knock me loose from my pants, anyway, no matter what I do, so what difference does it make?"

"Haystack," Baseball Hattie says, "I know you are a liar and a drunkard and a cheat and no account generally, but nobody can tell me you will sink so low as to purposely toss off a ball game. Why, Haystack, baseball is always on the level. It is the most honest game in all this world. I guess you are just ribbing me, because you know how much I love it."

"Dry up!" Haystack says to Hattie. "Furthermore, do not expect me home again tonight. But anyway, dry up."

"Look, Haystack," Hattie says, "I am going to have a son. He is your son and my son, and he is going to be a great ballplayer when he grows up, maybe a greater pitcher than you are, though I hope and trust he is not left-handed. He will have your name. If they find out you toss off a game for money, they will throw you out of baseball and you will be disgraced. My son will be known as the son of a crook, and what chance will he have in baseball? Do you think I am going to allow you to do this to him, and to the game that keeps me from going nutty for marrying you?"

Naturally, Haystack Duggeler is greatly offended by Hattie's crack about her son being maybe a greater pitcher than he is, and he is about to take steps, when Armand Fibleman stops him. Armand Fibleman is commencing to be somewhat alarmed at Baseball Hattie's attitude, and he gets to thinking that he hears that people in her delicate condition are often irresponsible, and he fears that she may blow a whistle on this enterprise without realizing what she is doing. So he undertakes a few soothing remarks to her. "Why, Hattie," Armand Fibleman says, "nobody can possibly find out about this little matter, and Haystack will have enough money to send your son to college, if his markers at the race track do not take it all. Maybe you better lie down and rest awhile," Armand says.

But Baseball Hattie does not as much as look at Armand, though she goes on talking to Haystack. "They always find out thievery, Haystack," she says, "especially when you are dealing with a fink like Fibleman. If you deal with him once, you will have to deal with him again and again, and he will be the first to holler copper on you, because he is a stool pigeon in his heart."

"Haystack," Armand Fibleman says, "I think we better be going."

"Haystack," Hattie says, "you can go out of here and stick up somebody or commit a robbery or a murder, and I will still welcome you back and stand by you.

But if you are going out to steal my son's future, I advise you not to go."

"Dry up!" Haystack says. "I am going."

"All right, Haystack," Hattie says, very calm. "But just step into the kitchen with me and let me say one little word to you by yourself, and then I will say no more." Well, Haystack Duggeler does not care for even just one little word more, but Armand Fibleman wishes to get this disagreeable scene over with, so he tells Haystack to let her have her word, and Haystack goes into the kitchen with Hattie, and Armand cannot hear what is said, as she speaks very low, but he hears Haystack laugh heartily and then Haystack comes out of the kitchen, still laughing, and tells Armand he is ready to go.

As they start for the door, Baseball Hattie outs with a long-nosed .38-caliber Colt's revolver, and goes root-a-toot-toot with it, and the next thing anybody knows, Haystack is on the floor yelling bloody murder, and Armand Fibleman is leaving the premises without bothering to open the door. In fact, the landlord afterwards talks some of suing Haystack Duggeler because of the damage Armand Fibleman does to the door. Armand himself afterwards admits that when he slows down for a breather a couple of miles down Broadway he finds splinters stuck all over him.

Well, the doctors come, and the gendarmes come, and there is great confusion, especially as Baseball Hattie is sobbing so she can scarcely make a statement, and Haystack Duggeler is so sure he is going to die that he cannot think of anything to say except oh-oh-oh, but finally the landlord remembers seeing Armand leave with his door, and everybody starts questioning Hattie about this until she confesses that Armand is there all right, and that he tries to bribe Haystack to toss off a ball game, and that she then suddenly finds herself with a revolver in her hand, and everything goes black before her eyes, and she can remember no more until somebody is sticking a bottle of smelling salts under her nose. Naturally, the newspaper reporters put two and two together, and what they make of it is that Hattie tries to plug Armand Fibleman for his rascally offer, and that she misses Armand and gets Haystack, and right away Baseball Hattie is a great heroine, and Haystack is a great hero, though nobody thinks to ask Haystack how he stands on the bribe proposition, and he never brings it up himself.

And nobody will ever offer Haystack any more bribes, for after the doctors get through with him he is shy a left arm from the shoulder down, and he will never pitch a baseball again, unless he learns to pitch right-handed. The newspapers make quite a lot of Baseball Hattie protecting the fair name of baseball. The National League plays a benefit game for Haystack Duggeler and presents him with a watch and a purse of twenty-five thousand dollars, which Baseball Hattie grabs away from him, saying it is for her son, while Armand Fibleman is in bad with one and all.

Baseball Hattie and Haystack Duggeler move to the Pacific Coast, and this is all there is to the story, except that one day some years ago, and not long before he passes away in Los Angeles, a respectable grocer, I run into Haystack when he is in New York on a business trip, and I say to him like this:

"Haystack," I say, "it is certainly a sin and a shame that Hattie misses Armand Fibleman that night and puts you on the shelf. The chances are that but for this little accident you will hang up one of the greatest pitching records in the history of baseball. Personally," I say, "I never see a better left-handed pitcher."

"Look," Haystack says. "Hattie does not miss Fibleman. It is a great newspaper story and saves my name, but the truth is she hits just where she aims. When she calls me into the kitchen before I start out with Fibleman, she shows me a revolver I never before know she has, and says to me, 'Haystack,' she says, 'if you leave with this weasel on the errand you mention, I am going to fix you so you will never make another wrong move with your pitching arm. I am going to shoot it off for you.'

"I laugh heartily," Haystack says. "I think she is kidding me, but I find out different. By the way," Haystack says, "I afterwards learn that long before I meet her, Hattie works for three years in a shooting gallery at Coney Island. She is really a remarkable broad," Haystack says.

I guess I forget to state that the day Baseball Hattie is at the Polo Grounds she is watching the new kid sensation of the big leagues, Derrill Duggeler, shut out Brooklyn with three hits.

He is a wonderful young left-hander.

All Horse Players Die Broke

IT IS DURING the last race meeting at Saratoga, and one evening I am standing out under the elms in front of the Grand Union Hotel thinking what a beautiful world it is, to be sure, for what do I do in the afternoon at the track but grab myself a piece of a ten-to-one shot. I am thinking what a beautiful moon it is, indeed, that is shining down over the park where Mr. Dick Canfield once deals them higher than a cat's back, and how pure and balmy the air is, and also what nice-looking Judys are wandering around and about, although it is only the night before that I am standing in the same spot wondering where I can borrow a Betsy with which to shoot myself smack-dab through the pimple.

In fact, I go around to see a character I know by the name of Solly something, who owns a Betsy, but it seems he has only one cartridge to his name for this Betsy and he is thinking some of either using the cartridge to shoot his own self smack-dab through the pimple, or of going out to the race course and shooting an old catfish by the name of Pair of Jacks that plays him false in the fifth race, and therefore Solly is not in a mood to lend his Betsy to anybody else. So we try to figure out a way we can make one cartridge do for two pimples, and in the meantime Solly outs with a bottle of applejack, and after a couple of belts at this bottle we decide that the sensible thing to do is to take the Betsy out and peddle it for whatever we can, and maybe get a taw for the next day.

Well, it happens that we run into an Italian party from Passaic, N.J., by the name of Guiseppe Palladino, who is called Joe for short, and this Joe is in the money very good at the moment, and he is glad to lend us a pound note on the Betsy, because Joe is such a character as never knows when he may need an extra Betsy, and anyway it is the first time in his experience around the race tracks that anybody ever offers him collateral for a loan. So there Solly and I are with a deuce apiece after we spend the odd dollar for breakfast the next day, and I run my deuce up to a total of twenty-two slugs on the ten-to-one shot in the last heat of the day, and everything is certainly all right with me in every respect.

Well, while I am standing there under the elms, who comes along but a raggedy old Dutchman by the name of Unser Fritz, who is maybe seventy-five years old, come next grass, and who is following the giddyaps since the battle of Gettysburg, as near as anybody can figure out. In fact, Unser Fritz is quite an institution around the race tracks, and is often written up by the newspaper scribes as a terrible example of what a horse player comes to, although personally I always say that what Unser Fritz comes to is not so tough when you figure that he does not do a tap of work in all these years.

In his day, Unser Fritz is a most successful handicapper, a handicapper being a character who can dope out from the form what horses ought to win the races, and as long as his figures turn out all right, a handicapper is spoken of most respectfully by one and all, although of course when he begins missing out for any length of time as handicappers are bound to do, he is no longer spoken of respectfully, or even as a handicapper. He is spoken of as a bum.

It is a strange thing how a handicapper can go along for years doing everything right, and then all of a sudden he finds himself doing everything wrong, and this is the way it is with Unser Fritz. For a long time his figures on the horse races are considered most remarkable, indeed, and as he will bet till the cows come home on his own figures, he generally has plenty of money, and a fiancée by the name of Emerald Em. She is called Emerald Em because she has a habit of wearing a raft of emeralds in rings, and pins, and bracelets, and one thing and another, which are purchased for her by Unser Fritz to express his love, an emerald being a green stone that is considered most expressive of love, if it is big enough. It seems that Emerald Em is very fond of emeralds, especially when they are surrounded by large, coarse diamonds. I hear the old-timers around the race tracks say that when Emerald Em is young, she is a tall, good-looking Judy with yellow hair that is by no means a phony yellow, at that, and with a shape that does not require a bustle such as most Judys always wear in those days.

But then nobody ever hears an old-timer mention any Judy that he remembers from back down the years who is not good-looking, and in fact beautiful. To hear the old-timers tell it, every pancake they ever see when they are young is a double Myrna Loy, though the chances

are, figuring in the law of averages, that some of them
are bound to be rutabagas, the same as now. Anyway,
for years this Emerald Em is known on every race track
from coast to coast as Unser Fritz's fiancée, and is considered quite a remarkable scene, what with her emeralds,
and not requiring any bustle, and everything else.

Then one day Unser Fritz's figures run plumb out
on him, and so does his dough, and so does Emerald
Em, and now Unser Fritz is an old pappy guy, and it
is years since he is regarded as anything but a crumbo
around the race tracks, and nobody remembers much
of his story, or cares a cuss about it, for if there is anything that is a drug on the market around the tracks
it is the story of a broker. How he gets from place to
place, and how he lives after he gets there, is a very
great mystery to one and all, although I hear he often
rides in the horsecars with the horses, when some owner
or trainer happens to be feeling tenderhearted, or he
hitchhikes in automobiles, and sometimes he even walks,
for Unser Fritz is still fairly nimble, no matter how
old he is.

He always has under his arm a bundle of newspapers
that somebody throws away, and every night he sits
down and handicaps the horses running the next day
according to his own system, but he seldom picks any
winners and even if he does pick any winners, he seldom
has anything to bet on them. Sometimes he promotes
a stranger, who does not know he is bad luck to a good
hunting dog, to put down a few dibs on one of his picks,
and once in a while the pick wins, and Unser Fritz
gets a small stake, and sometimes an old-timer who feels
sorry for him will slip him something. But whatever
Unser Fritz gets hold of, he bets off right away on the
next race that comes up, so naturally he never is holding
anything very long.

Well, Unser Fritz stands under the elms with me a
while, speaking of this and that, and especially of the
races, and I am wondering to myself if I will become
as disheveled as Unser Fritz if I keep on following the
races, when he gazes at the Grand Union Hotel, and
says to me like this:

"It looks nice," he says. "It looks cheery-like, with
the lights, and all this and that. It brings back memories
to me. Emma always lives in this hotel whenever we
make Saratoga for the races back in the days when I
am in the money. She always has a suite of two or three
rooms on this side of the hotel. Once she has four. I
often stand here under these trees," Unser Fritz says,
"watching her windows to see what time she puts out
her lights, because, while I trust Emma implicitly, I
know she has a restless nature, and sometimes she cannot
resist returning to scenes of gaiety after I bid her good
night, especially," he says, "with a party by the name
of Pete Shovelin, who runs the restaurant where she
once deals them off the arm."

"You mean she is a biscuit shooter?" I say.

"A waitress," Unser Fritz says. "A good waitress. She
comes of a family of farm folks in this very section,
although I never know much about them," he says.
"Shovelin's is a little hole-in-the-wall up the street here
somewhere which long since disappears. I go there for
my morning java in the old days. I will say one thing
for Shovelin," Unser Fritz says, "he always has good
java. Three days after I first clap eyes on Emma, she
is wearing her first emerald, and is my fiancée. Then
she moves into a suite in the Grand Union. I only wish
you can know Emma in those days," he says. "She is
beautiful. She is a fine character. She is always on the
level, and I love her dearly."

"What do you mean—always on the level?" I say.

"What about this Shovelin party you just mention?"

"Ah," Unser Fritz says, "I suppose I am dull company for a squab, what with having to stay in at night to work on my figures, and Emma likes to go around and about. She is a highly nervous type, and extremely restless, and she cannot bear to hold still very long at a time. But," he says, "in those days it is not considered proper for a young Judy to go around and about without a chaperon, so she goes with Shovelin for her chaperon. Emma never goes anywhere without a chaperon," he says.

Well, it seems that early in their courtship, Unser Fritz learns that he can generally quiet her restlessness with emeralds, if they have diamonds on the side. It seems that these stones have a very soothing effect on her, and this is why he purchases them for her by the bucket. "Yes," Unser Fritz says, "I always think of Emma whenever I am in New York City, and look down Broadway at night with the go lights on."

But it seems from what Unser Fritz tells me that even with the emeralds her restless spells come on her very bad, and especially when he finds himself running short of ready, and is unable to purchase more emeralds for her at the moment, although Unser Fritz claims this is nothing unusual. In fact, he says anybody with any experience with nervous female characters knows that it becomes very monotonous for them to be around people who are short of ready. "But," he says, "not all of them require soothing with emeralds. Some require pearls," he says.

Well, it seems that Emma generally takes a trip without Unser Fritz to break the monotony of his running short of ready, but she never takes one of these trips without a chaperon, because she is very careful about her good name, and Unser Fritz's, too. It seems that in those days Judys have to be more careful about such matters than they do now.

He remembers that once when they are in San Francisco she takes a trip through the Yellowstone with Jockey Gus Kloobus as her chaperon, and is gone three weeks and returns much refreshed, especially as she gets back just as Unser Fritz makes a nice score and has a seidel of emeralds waiting for her. He remembers another time she goes to England with a trainer by the name of Blootz as her chaperon and comes home with an English accent that sounds right cute, to find Unser Fritz going like a house afire at Belmont. "She takes a lot of other trips without me during the time we are engaged," Unser Fritz says, "but," he says, "I always know Emma will return to me as soon as she hears I am back in the money and can purchase more emeralds for her. In fact," he says, "this knowledge is all that keeps me struggling now."

"Look, Fritz," I say, "what do you mean, keeps you going? Do you mean you think Emma may return to you again?"

"Why, sure," Unser Fritz says. "Why, certainly, if I get my rushes again. Why not?" he says. "She knows there will be a pail of emeralds waiting for her. She knows I love her and always will," he says.

Well, I ask him when he sees Emerald Em last, and he says it is 1908 in the old Waldorf-Astoria the night he blows a hundred and sixty thousand betting on a hide called Sir Martin to win the Futurity, and it is all the dough Unser Fritz has at the moment. In fact, he is cleaner than a jay bird, and he is feeling somewhat discouraged. It seems he is waiting on his floor for the elevator, and when it comes down Emerald Em is one of the several passengers, and when the door opens, and Unser Fritz starts to get in, she raises her foot and plants

it in his stomach, and gives him a big push back out
the door and the elevator goes on down without him.

"But, of course," Unser Fritz says, "Emma never likes
to ride in the same elevator with me, because I am not
always tidy enough to suit her in those days, what with
having so much work to do on my figures, and she claims
it is a knock to her socially. Anyway," he says, "this
is the last I see of Emma."

"Why, Fritz," I say, "nineteen-eight is nearly thirty
years back, and if she ever thinks of returning to you,
she will return long before this."

"No," Unser Fritz says. "You see, I never make a
scratch since then. I am never since in the money, so
there is no reason for Emma to return to me. But,"
he says, "wait until I get going good again and you
will see."

Well, I always figure Unser Fritz must be more or
less of an old screwball for going on thinking there is
still a chance for him around the tracks, and now I am
sure of it, and I am about to bid him good evening,
when he mentions that he can use about two dollars
if I happen to have a deuce on me that is not working,
and I will say one thing for Unser Fritz, he seldom
comes right out and asks anybody for anything unless
things are very desperate with him, indeed. "I need it
to pay something on account of my landlady," he says.
"I room with old Mrs. Crob around the corner for over
twenty years, and," he says, "she only charges me a
finnif a week, so I try to keep from getting too far to
the rear with her. I will return it to you the first score
I make."

Well, of course I know this means practically never,
but I am feeling so good about my success at the track
that I slip him a deucer, and it is half an hour later

before I fully realize what I do, and go looking for Fritz to get anyway half of it back. But by this time he disappears, and I think no more of the matter until the next day out at the course when I hear Unser Fritz bets two dollars on a thing by the name of Speed Cart, and it bows down at fifty to one, so I know Mrs. Crob is still waiting for hers.

Now there is Unser Fritz with one hundred slugs, and this is undoubtedly more money than he enjoys since Hickory Slim is a two-year-old. And from here on the story becomes very interesting, and in fact remarkable, because up to the moment Speed Cart hits the wire, Unser Fritz is still nothing but a crumbo, and you can say it again, while from now on he is somebody to point out and say can you imagine such a thing happening? He bets a hundred on a centipede called Marchesa, and down pops Marchesa like a trained pig at twenty to one. Then old Unser Fritz bets two hundred on a caterpillar by the name of Merry Soul, at four to one, and Merry Soul just laughs his way home. Unser Fritz winds up the day betting two thousand more on something called Sharp Practice, and when Sharp Practice wins by so far it looks as if he is a shoo-in, Fritz finds himself with over twelve thousand slugs, and the way the bookmakers in the betting ring are sobbing is really most distressing to hear.

Well, in a week Unser Fritz is a hundred thousand dollars in front, because the way he sends it in is quite astonishing to behold, although the old-timers tell me it is just the way he sends it when he is younger. He is betting only on horses that he personally figures out, and what happens is that Unser Fritz's figures suddenly come to life again, and he cannot do anything wrong. He wins so much dough that he even pays off a few old touches, including my two, and he goes so far as to lend Joe Palladino three dollars on the Betsy that Solly and I hock with Joe for the pound note, as it seems that by this time Joe himself is practically on his way to the poorhouse, and while Unser Fritz has no use whatsoever for a Betsy he cannot bear to see a character such as Joe go to the poorhouse.

But with all the dough Unser Fritz carries in his pockets, and plants in a safe-deposit box in the jug downtown, he looks just the same as ever, because he claims he cannot find time from working on his figures to buy new clothes and dust himself off, and if you tell anybody who does not know who he is that this old crutch is stone rich, the chances are they will call you a liar.

In fact, on a Monday around noon, the clerk in the branch office that a big Fifth Avenue jewelry firm keeps in the lobby of the States Hotel is all ready to yell for the constables when Unser Fritz leans up against the counter and asks to see some jewelry on display in a showcase, as Unser Fritz is by no means the clerk's idea of a customer for jewelry. I am standing in the lobby of the hotel on the off chance that some fresh money may arrive in the city on the late trains that I may be able to connect up with before the races, when I notice Unser Fritz and observe the agitation of the clerk, and presently I see Unser Fritz waving a fistful of bank notes under the clerk's beak, and the clerk starts setting out the jewelry with surprising speed.

I go over to see what is coming off, and I can see that the jewelry Unser Fritz is looking at consists of a necklace of emeralds and diamonds, with a centerpiece the size of the home plate, and some eardrops, and bracelets, and clips of same, and as I approach the scene I hear Unser Fritz ask how much for the lot as if he is dickering for a basket of fish.

"One hundred and one thousand dollars, sir," the

clerk says. "You see, sir, it is a set, and one of the finest things of the kind in the country. We just got it in from our New York store to show a party here, and," he says, "she is absolutely crazy about it, but she states she cannot give us a final decision until five o'clock this afternoon. Confidentially, sir," the clerk says, "I think the real trouble is financial, and doubt that we will hear from her again. In fact," he says, "I am so strongly of this opinion that I am prepared to sell the goods without waiting on her. It is really a bargain at the price," he says.

"Dear me," Unser Fritz says to me, "this is most unfortunate as the sum mentioned is just one thousand dollars more than I possess in all this world. I have twenty thousand on my person, and eighty thousand over in the box in the jug, and not another dime. But," he says, "I will be back before five o'clock and take the lot. In fact," he says, "I will run in right after the third race, and pick it up." Well, at this, the clerk starts putting the jewelry back in the case, and anybody can see that he figures he is on a lob and that he is sorry he wastes so much time, but Unser Fritz says to me like this: "Emma is returning to me," he says.

"Emma who?" I say.

"Why," Unser Fritz says, "my Emma. The one I tell you about not long ago. She must hear I am in the money again, and she is returning just as I always say she will."

"How do you know?" I say. "Do you hear from her, or what?"

"No," Unser Fritz says, "I do not hear from her direct, but Mrs. Crob knows some female relative of Emma's that lives at Ballston Spa a few miles from here, and this relative is in Saratoga this morning to do some shopping, and she tells Mrs. Crob and Mrs. Crob tells me. Emma will be here tonight. I will have these emeralds waiting for her." Well, what I always say is that every guy knows his own business best, and if Unser Fritz wishes to toss his dough off on jewelry, it is none of my put-in, so all I remark is that I have no doubt Emma will be very much surprised, indeed. "No," Unser Fritz says. "She will be expecting them. She always expects emeralds when she returns to me. I love her," he says. "You have no idea how I love her. But let us hasten to the course," he says. "Cara Mia is a right good thing in the third, and I will make just one bet today to win the thousand I need to buy these emeralds."

"But, Fritz," I say, "you will have nothing left for operating expenses after you invest in the emeralds."

"I am not worrying about operating expenses now," Unser Fritz says. "The way my figures are standing up, I can run a spool of thread into a pair of pants in no time. But I can scarcely wait to see the expression on Emma's face when she sees her emeralds. I will have to make a fast trip into town after the third to get my dough out of the box in the jug and pick them up," he says. "Who knows but what this other party that is interested in the emeralds may make her mind up before five o'clock and pop in there and nail them?"

Well, after we get to the race track, all Unser Fritz does is stand around waiting for the third race. He has his figures on the first two races, and ordinarily he will be betting himself a gob on them, but he says he does not wish to take the slightest chance on cutting down his capital at this time, and winding up short of enough dough to buy the emeralds. It turns out that both of the horses Unser Fritz's figures make on top in the first and second races bow down, and Unser Fritz will have his thousand if he only bets a couple of hundred on either of them, but Unser Fritz says he is not sorry he does not bet. He says the finishes in both races are very close, and prove that there is an element of risk in these races. And Unser Fritz says he cannot afford to tamper with the element of risk at this time.

He states that there is no element of risk whatever in the third race, and what he states is very true, as everybody realizes that this mare Cara Mia is a stick-out. In fact, she is such a stick-out that it scarcely figures to be a contest. There are three other horses in the race, but it is the opinion of one and all that if the owners of these horses have any sense they will leave them in the barn and save them a lot of unnecessary lather.

The opening price offered by the bookmakers on Cara Mia is two to five, which means that if you wish to wager on Cara Mia to win you will have to put up five dollars to a bookmaker's two dollars, and everybody agrees that this is a reasonable thing to do in this case unless you wish to rob the poor bookmaker. In fact, this is considered so reasonable that everybody starts running at the bookmakers all at once, and the bookmakers can see if this keeps up they may get knocked off their stools in the betting ring and maybe seriously injured, so they make Cara Mia one to six, and out, as quickly as possible to halt the rush and give them a chance to breathe.

This one to six means that if you wish to wager on Cara Mia to win, you must wager six of your own dollars to one of the bookmaker's dollars, and means that the bookies are not offering any prices whatsoever on Cara Mia running second, or third. You can get almost any price you can think of right quick against any of the other horses winning the race, and place and show prices, too, but asking the bookmakers to lay against Cara Mia running second or third will be something like asking them to bet that Mr. Roosevelt is not President of the United States. Well, I am expecting Unser

Fritz to step in and partake of the two to five on Cara Mia for all the dough he has on his person the moment it is offered, because he is very high indeed on this mare, and in fact I never see anybody any higher on any horse, and it is a price Unser Fritz will not back off from when he is high on anything.

Moreover, I am pleased to think he will make such a wager, because it will give him plenty over and above the price of the emeralds, and as long as he is bound to purchase the emeralds, I wish to see him have a little surplus, because when anybody has a surplus there is always a chance for me. It is when everybody runs out of surpluses that I am handicapped no little. But instead of stepping in and partaking, Unser Fritz keeps hesitating until the opening price gets away from him, and finally he says to me like this:

"Of course," he says, "my figures show Cara Mia cannot possibly lose this race, but," he says, "to guard against any possibility whatever of her losing, I will make an absolute cinch of it. I will bet her third."

"Why, Fritz," I say, "I do not think there is anybody in this world outside of an insane asylum who will give you a price on the peek. Furthermore," I say, "I am greatly surprised at this sign of weakening on your part on your figures."

"Well," Unser Fritz says, "I cannot afford to take a chance on not having the emeralds for Emma when she arrives. Let us go through the betting ring, and see what we can see," he says. So we walk through the betting ring, and by this time it seems that many of the books are so loaded with wagers on Cara Mia to win that they will not accept any more under any circumstances, and I figure that Unser Fritz blows the biggest opportunity of his life in not grabbing the opening. The bookmakers who are loaded are now looking even sadder than somewhat, and this makes them a pitiful spectacle, indeed.

Well, one of the saddest-looking is a character by the name of Slow McCool, but he is a character who will usually give you a gamble and he is still taking Cara Mia at one to six, and Unser Fritz walks up to him and whispers in his ear, and what he whispers is he wishes to know if Slow McCool cares to lay him a price on Cara Mia third. But all that happens is that Slow McCool stops looking sad a minute and looks slightly perplexed, and then he shakes his head and goes on looking sad again. Now Unser Fritz steps up to another sad-looking bookmaker by the name of Pete Phozzler and whispers in his ear, and Pete also shakes his head and after we leave him I look back and see that Pete is standing up on his stool watching Unser Fritz, and still shaking his head. Well, Unser Fritz approaches maybe a dozen other sad-looking bookmakers, and whispers to them, and all he gets is the old head shake, but none of them seem to become angry with Unser Fritz, and I always say that this proves that bookmakers are better than some people think, because, personally, I claim they have a right to get angry with Unser Fritz for insulting their intelligence, and trying to defraud them, too, by asking a price on Cara Mia third.

Finally we come to a character by the name of Willie the Worrier, who is called by this name because he is always worrying about something, and what he is generally worrying about is a short bank roll, or his everloving wife, and sometimes both, though mostly it is his wife. Personally, I always figure she is something to worry about, at that, though I do not consider details necessary. She is a red-headed Judy about half as old as Willie the Worrier, and this alone is enough to start any guy worrying, and what is more she is easily vexed, espe-

cially by Willie. In fact, I remember Solly telling me
that she is vexed with Willie no longer ago than about
II A.M. this very day, and gives him a public reprimand-
ing about something or other in the telegraph office
downtown when Solly happens to be in there hoping
maybe he will receive an answer from a mark in Pitts-
field, Mass., that he sends a tip on a horse. Solly says
the last he hears Willie the Worrier's wife say is that
she will leave him for good this time, but I just see
her over on the clubhouse lawn wearing some right
classy-looking garments, so I judge she does not leave
him as yet, as the clubhouse lawn is not a place to be
waiting for a train.

Well, when Unser Fritz sees that he is in front of
Willie's stand, he starts to move on, and I nudge him
and motion at Willie, and ask him if he does not notice
that Willie is another bookmaker, and Unser Fritz says
he notices him all right, but that he does not care to
offer him any business, because Willie insults him ten
years ago. He says Willie calls him a dirty old Dutch
bum, and while I am thinking what a wonderful memory
Unser Fritz has to remember insults from bookmakers
for ten years, Willie the Worrier, sitting there on his
stool looking out over the crowd, spots Unser Fritz and
yells at him as follows:

"Hellow, Dirty Dutch," he says. "How is the soap
market? What are you looking for around here, Dirty
Dutch? Santa Claus?"

Well, at this, Unser Fritz pushes his way through
the crowd around Willie the Worrier's stand, and gets
close to Willie, and says:

"Yes," he says, "I am looking for Santa Claus. I am
looking for a show price on number two horse, but,"
he says, "I do not expect to get it from the shoemakers
who are booking nowadays."

Now the chances are Willie the Worrier figures Unser Fritz is just trying to get sarcastic with him for the benefit of the crowd around his stand in asking for such a thing as a price on Cara Mia third, and in fact the idea of anybody asking a price third on a horse that some bookmakers will not accept any more wagers on first, or even second, is so humorous that many characters laugh right out loud. "All right," Willie the Worrier says. "No one can ever say he comes to my store looking for a market on anything and is turned down. I will quote you a show price, Dirty Dutch," he says. "You can have one to one hundred." This means that Willie the Worrier is asking Unser Fritz for one hundred dollars to the book's one dollar, if Unser Fritz wishes to bet on Cara Mia dropping in there no worse than third, and of course Willie has no idea Unser Fritz or anybody else will ever take such a price, and the chances are if Willie is not sizzling a little at Unser Fritz, he will not offer such a price, because it sounds foolish.

Furthermore, the chances are if Unser Fritz offers Willie a comparatively small bet at this price, such as may enable him to chisel just a couple of hundred out of Willie's book, Willie will find some excuse to wiggle off, but Unser Fritz leans over and says in a low voice to Willie the Worrier: "A hundred thousand."

Willie nods his head and turns to a clerk alongside him, and his voice is as low as Unser Fritz's as he says to the clerk: "A thousand to a hundred thousand, Cara Mia third."

The clerk's eyes pop open and so does his mouth, but he does not say a word. He just writes something on a pad of paper in his hand, and Unser Fritz offers Willie the Worrier a package of thousand-dollar bills, and says:

"Here is twenty," he says. "The rest is in the jug."

"All right, Dutch," Willie says. "I know you have it, although," he says, "this is the first crack you give me at it. You are on, Dutch," he says. "P. S.," Willie says, "the Dirty does not go any more."

Well, you understand Unser Fritz is betting one hundred thousand dollars against a thousand dollars that Cara Mia will run in the money, and personally I consider this wager a very sound business proposition, indeed, and so does everybody else, for all it amounts to is finding a thousand dollars in the street. There is really nothing that can make Cara Mia run out of the money, the way I look at it, except what happens to her, and what happens is she steps in a hole fifty yards from the finish when she is on top by ten, and breezing, and down she goes all spread out, and of course the other three horses run on past her to the wire, and all this is quite a disaster to many members of the public, including Unser Fritz.

I am standing with him on the rise of the grandstand lawn watching the race, and it is plain to be seen that he is slightly surprised at what happens, and personally, I am practically dumfounded because, to tell the truth, I take a nibble at the opening price of two to five on Cara Mia with a total of thirty slugs, which represents all my capital, and I am thinking what a great injustice it is for them to leave holes in the track for horses to step in, when Unser Fritz says like this:

"Well," he says, "it is horse racing."

And this is all he ever says about the matter, and then he walks down to Willie the Worrier, and tells Willie if he will send a clerk with him, he will go to the jug and get the balance of the money that is now due Willie. "Dutch," Willie says, "it will be a pleasure to accompany you to the jug in person." As Willie is getting down off his stool, somebody in the crowd who hears of the wager gazes at Unser Fritz, and remarks that he is really a game guy, and Willie says:

"Yes," he says, "he is a game guy at that. But," he says, "what about me?" And he takes Unser Fritz by the arm, and they walk away together, and anybody can see that Unser Fritz picks up anyway twenty years or more, and a slight stringhalt, in the last few minutes.

Then it comes on night again in Saratoga, and I am standing out under the elms in front of the Grand Union, thinking that this world is by no means as beautiful as formerly, when I notice a big, fat old Judy with snow-white hair and spectacles standing near me, looking up and down the street. She will weigh a good two hundred pounds, and much of it is around her ankles, but she has a pleasant face, at that, and when she observes me looking at her, she comes over to me, and says:

"I am trying to fix the location of a restaurant where I work many years ago," she says. "It is a place called Shovelin's. The last thing my husband tells me is to see if the old building is still here, but," she says, "it is so long since I am in Saratoga I cannot get my bearings."

"Ma'am," I say, "is your name Emma by any chance, and do they ever call you Emerald Em?"

Well, at this the old Judy laughs, and says:

"Why, yes," she says. "That is what they call me when I am young and foolish. But how do you know?" she says. "I do not remember ever seeing you before in my life."

"Well," I say, "I know a party who once knows you. A party by the name of Unser Fritz."

"Unser Fritz?" she says. "Unser Fritz? Oh," she says, "I wonder if you mean a crazy Dutchman I run around with many years ago? My gracious," she says, "I just barely remember him. He is a great hand for giving me little presents, such as emeralds. When I am young, I think emeralds are right pretty, but," she says, "otherwise I cannot stand him."

"Then you do not come here to see him?" I say.

"Are you crazy, too?" she says. "I am on my way to Ballston Spa to see my grandchildren. I live in Macon, Georgia. If ever you are in Macon, Georgia, drop in at Shovelin's restaurant and get some real Southern fried chicken. I am Mrs. Joe Shovelin," she says. "By the way," she says, "I remember more about that crazy Dutchman. He is a horse player. I always figure he must die long ago and that the chances are he dies broke, too. I remember I hear people say all horse players die broke."

"Yes," I say, "he dies all right, and he dies as you suggest, too," for it is only an hour before that they find old Unser Fritz in a vacant lot over near the railroad station with the Betsy he gets off Joe Palladino in his hand and a bullet hole smack-dab through his pimple.

Nobody blames him much for taking this out, and in fact I am standing there thinking long after Emerald Em goes on about her business that it will be a good idea if I follow his example, only I cannot think where I can find another Betsy, when Solly comes along and stands there with me. I ask Solly if he knows anything new. "No," Solly says, "I do not know anything new, except," he says, "I hear Willie the Worrier and his ever-loving make up again, and she is not going to leave him after all. I hear Willie takes home a squarer in the shape of a batch of emeralds and diamonds that she orders sent up here when Willie is not looking, and that they are fighting about all day. Well," Solly says, "maybe this is love."

That Ever-Loving Wife of Hymie's

IF ANYBODY EVER tells me I will wake up some morning
to find myself sleeping with a horse, I will consider
them very daffy indeed, especially if they tell me it will
be with such a horse as old Mahogany, for Mahogany
is really not much horse. In fact, Mahogany is nothing
but an old bum, and you can say it again, and many
horse players wish he is dead ten thousand times over.

But I will think anybody is daffier still if they tell
me I will wake up some morning to find myself sleeping
with Hymie Banjo Eyes, because as between Mahogany and Hymie Banjo Eyes to sleep with, I will take Mahogany every time, even though Mahogany snores
more than somewhat when he is sleeping. But Mahogany is by no means as offensive to sleep with as Hymie
Banjo Eyes, as Hymie not only snores when he is
sleeping, but he hollers and kicks around and takes on
generally.

He is a short, pudgy little guy who is called Hymie

Banjo Eyes because his eyes bulge out as big and round as banjos, although his right name is Weinstein, or some such, and he is somewhat untidy-looking in spots, for Hymie Banjo Eyes is a guy who does not care if his breakfast gets on his vest, or what. Furthermore, he gabs a lot and thinks he is very smart, and many citizens consider him a pest, in spades. But personally I figure Hymie Banjo Eyes as very harmless, although he is not such a guy as I will ordinarily care to have much truck with.

But there I am one morning waking up to find myself sleeping with both Mahogany and Hymie, and what are we sleeping in but a horse car bound for Miami, and we are passing through North Carolina in a small-time blizzard when I wake up, and Mahogany is snoring and shivering, because it seems Hymie cops the poor horse's blanket to wrap around himself, and I am half frozen and wishing I am back in Mindy's restaurant on Broadway, where all is bright and warm, and that I never see either Mahogany or Hymie in my life.

Of course it is not Mahogany's fault that I am sleeping with him and Hymie, and in fact, for all I know, Mahogany may not consider me any bargain whatever to sleep with. It is Hymie's fault for digging me up in Mindy's one night and explaining to me how wonderful the weather is in Miami in the wintertime, and how we can go there for the races with his stable and make plenty of potatoes for ourselves, although of course I know when Hymie is speaking of his stable he means Mahogany, for Hymie never has more than one horse at any one time in his stable.

Generally it is some broken-down lizard that he buys for about the price of an old wool hat and patches up the best he can, as Hymie Banjo Eyes is a horse trainer by trade, and considering the kind of horses he trains he is not a bad trainer, at that. He is very good indeed

at patching up cripples and sometimes winning races
with them until somebody claims them on him or they
fall down dead, and then he goes and gets himself another cripple and starts all over again.

I hear he buys Mahogany off a guy by the name of
O'Shea for a hundred bucks, although the chances are
if Hymie waits awhile the guy will pay him at least
two hundred to take Mahogany away and hide him,
for Mahogany has bad legs and bum feet, and is maybe
nine years old, and does not win a race since the summer
of 1924, and then it is an accident. But anyway, Mahogany is the stable Hymie Banjo Eyes is speaking of taking
to Miami when he digs me up in Mindy's.

"And just think," Hymie says, "all we need to get
there is the price of a drawing room on the Florida
Special."

Well, I am much surprised by this statement, because
it is the first time I ever hear of a horse needing a drawing room, especially such a horse as Mahogany, but it
seems the drawing room is not to be for Mahogany,
or even for Hymie or me. It seems it is to be for Hymie's
ever-loving wife, a blond doll by the name of 'Lasses,
which he marries out of some night club where she is
what is called an adagio dancer.

It seems that when 'Lasses is very young somebody
once says she is just as sweet as Molasses, and this is
how she comes to get the name of 'Lasses, although
her right name is Maggie Something, and I figure she
must change quite a lot since they begin calling her
'Lasses because at the time I meet her she is sweet just
the same as green grapefruit.

She has a partner in the adagio business by the name
of Donaldo, who picks her up and heaves her around
the night club as if she is nothing but a baseball, and
it is very thrilling indeed to see Donaldo giving 'Lasses
a sling as if he is going to throw her plumb away, which

many citizens say may not be a bad idea, at that, and then catching her by the foot in midair and hauling her back to him.

But one night it seems that Donaldo takes a few slugs of gin before going into this adagio business, and he muffs 'Lasses' foot, although nobody can see how this is possible, because 'Lasses' foot is no more invisible than a boxcar, and 'Lasses keeps on sailing through the air. She finally sails into Hymie Banjo Eyes' stomach as he is sitting at a table pretty well back, and this is the way Hymie and 'Lasses meet, and a romance starts, although it is nearly a week before Hymie recovers enough from the body beating he takes off 'Lasses to go around and see her.

The upshot of the romance is 'Lasses and Hymie get married, although up to the time Donaldo slings her into Hymie's stomach, 'Lasses is going around with Brick McCloskey, the bookmaker, and is very loving with him indeed, but they have a row about something and are carrying the old torch for each other when Hymie happens along.

Some citizens say the reason 'Lasses marries Hymie is because she is all sored up on Brick and that she acts without thinking, as dolls often do, especially blond dolls, although personally I figure Hymie takes all the worst of the situation, as 'Lasses is not such a doll as any guy shall marry without talking it over with his lawyer. 'Lasses is one of these little blondes who is full of short answers, and personally I will just as soon marry a porcupine. But Hymie loves her more than somewhat, and there is no doubt Brick McCloskey is all busted up because 'Lasses takes this runout powder on him, so maybe after all 'Lasses has some kind of appeal which I cannot notice offhand.

"But," Hymie explains to me when he is speaking to me about this trip to Miami, " 'Lasses is not well, what with nerves and one thing and another, and she will have to travel to Miami along with her Pekingese dog, Sooey-pow, because," Hymie says, "it will make her more nervous than somewhat if she has to travel with anybody else. And of course," Hymie says, "no one can expect 'Lasses to travel in anything but a drawing room on account of her health."

Well, the last time I see 'Lasses she is making a sucker of a big sirloin in Bobby's restaurant, and she strikes me as a pretty healthy doll, but of course I never examine her close, and anyway, her health is none of my business.

"Now," Hymie says, "I get washed out at Empire, and I am pretty much in hock here and there and have no dough to ship my stable to Miami, but," he says, "a friend of mine is shipping several horses there and he has a whole car, and he will kindly let me have room in one end of the car for my stable, and you and I can ride in there, too.

"That is," Hymie says, "we can ride in there if you will dig up the price of a drawing room and the two tickets that go with it so 'Lasses' nerves will not be disturbed. You see," Hymie says, "I happen to know you have two hundred and fifty bucks in the jug over here on the corner, because one of the tellers in the jug is a friend of mine, and he tips me off you have this sugar, even though," Hymie says, "you have it in there under another name."

Well, a guy goes up against many daffy propositions as he goes along through life, and the first thing I know I am waking up, like I tell you, to find myself sleeping with Mahogany and Hymie, and as I lay there in the horse car slowly freezing to death, I get to thinking of 'Lasses in a drawing room on the Florida Special, and I hope and trust that she and the Peke are sleeping nice and warm.

The train finally runs out of the blizzard and the

weather heats up somewhat, so it is not so bad riding in the horse car, and Hymie and I pass the time away playing two-handed pinochle. Furthermore, I get pretty well acquainted with Mahogany, and I find he is personally not such a bad old pelter as many thousands of citizens think.

Finally we get to Miami, and at first it looks as if Hymie is going to have a tough time finding a place to keep Mahogany, as all the stable room at the Hialeah track is taken by cash customers, and Hymie certainly is not a cash customer and neither is Mahogany. Personally, I am not worried so much about stable room for Mahogany as I am about stable room for myself, because I am now down to a very few bobs and will need same to eat on.

Naturally, I figure Hymie Banjo Eyes will be joining his ever-loving wife 'Lasses, as I always suppose a husband and wife are an entry, but Hymie tells me 'Lasses is parked in the Roney Plaza over on Miami Beach, and that he is going to stay with Mahogany, because it will make her very nervous to have people around her, especially people who are training horses every day, and who may not smell so good.

Well, it looks as if we will wind up camping out with Mahogany under a palm tree, although many of the palm trees are already taken by other guys camping out with horses, but finally Hymie finds a guy who has a garage back of his house right near the race track, and having no use for this garage since his car blows away in the hurricane of 1926, the guy is willing to let Hymie keep Mahogany in the garage. Furthermore, he is willing to let Hymie sleep in the garage with Mahogany, and pay him now and then.

So Hymie borrows a little hay and grain, such as horses love to eat, off a friend who has a big string at the track, and moves into the garage with Mahogany, and about the same time I run into a guy by the name of Pottsville Legs, out of Pottsville, Pa., and he has a room in a joint downtown, and I move in with him, and it is no worse than sleeping with Hymie Banjo Eyes and Mahogany, at that.

I do not see Hymie for some time after this, but I hear of him getting Mahogany ready for a race. He has the old guy out galloping on the track every morning, and who is galloping him but Hymie himself, because he cannot get any stable boys to do the galloping for him, as they do not wish to waste their time. However, Hymie rides himself when he is a young squirt, so galloping Mahogany is not such a tough job for him, except that it gives him a terrible appetite, and it is very hard for him to find anything to satisfy this appetite with, and there are rumors around that Hymie is eating most of Mahogany's hay and grain.

In the meantime, I am going here and there doing the best I can, and this is not so very good, at that, because never is there such a terrible winter in Miami or so much suffering among the horse players. In the afternoon I go out to the race track, and in the evening I go to the dog tracks, and later to the gambling joints trying to pick up a few honest bobs, and wherever I go I seem to see Hymie's ever-loving wife 'Lasses, and she is always dressed up more than somewhat, and generally she is with Brick McCloskey, for Brick shows up in Miami figuring to do a little business in bookmaking at the track.

When they turn off the books there and put in the mutuels, Brick still does a little booking to big betters who do not wish to put their dough in the mutuels for fear of ruining a price, for Brick is a very large operator at all times. He is not only a large operator, but he is a big, good-looking guy, and how 'Lasses can ever give him the heave-o for such a looking guy as Hymie Banjo Eyes is always a great mystery to me. But then this is the way blondes are.

Of course Hymie probably does not know 'Lasses is running around with Brick McCloskey, because Hymie is too busy getting Mahogany ready for a race to make such spots as 'Lasses and Brick are apt to be, and nobody is going to bother to tell him, because so many ever-loving wives are running around with guys who are not their ever-loving husbands in Miami this winter that nobody considers it any news.

Personally, I figure 'Lasses' running around with Brick is a pretty fair break for Hymie, at that, as it takes plenty of weight off him in the way of dinners, and maybe breakfasts, for all I know, although it seems to me 'Lasses cannot love Hymie as much as Hymie thinks to be running around with another guy. In fact, I am commencing to figure 'Lasses does not care for Hymie Banjo Eyes whatever.

Well, one day I am looking over the entries, and I see where Hymie has old Mahogany in a claiming race at a mile and an eighth, and while it is a cheap race, there are some pretty fair hides in it. In fact, I can figure at least eight out of the nine that are entered to beat Mahogany by fourteen lengths.

Well, I go out to Hialeah very early, and I step around to the garage where Mahogany and Hymie are living, and Hymie is sitting out in front of the garage on a bucket looking very sad, and Mahogany has his beezer stuck out through the door of the garage, and he is looking even sadder than Hymie.

"Well," I say to Hymie Banjo Eyes, "I see the big horse goes today."

"Yes," Hymie says, "the big horse goes today if I can

get ten bucks for the jockey fee, and if I can get a jock after I get the fee. It is a terrible situation," Hymie says. "Here I get Mahogany all readied up for the race of his life in a spot where he can win by as far as from here to Palm Beach and grab a purse worth six hundred fish, and me without as much as a sawbuck to hire one of these hoptoads that are putting themselves away as jocks around here."

"Well," I say, "why do you not speak to 'Lasses, your ever-loving wife, about this situation? I see 'Lasses playing the wheel out at Hollywood last night," I say, "and she has a stack of checks in front of her a greyhound cannot hurdle, and," I say, "it is not like 'Lasses to go away from there without a few bobs off such a start."

"Now there you go again," Hymie says, very impatient, indeed. "You are always making cracks about 'Lasses, and you know very well it will make the poor little doll very nervous if I speak to her about such matters as a sawbuck, because 'Lasses needs all the sawbucks she can get hold of to keep herself and Sooey-pow at the Roney Plaza. By the way," Hymie says, "how much scratch do you have on your body at this time?"

Well, I am never any hand for telling lies, especially to an old friend such as Hymie Banjo Eyes, so I admit I have a ten-dollar note, although naturally I do not mention another tenner which I also have in my pocket, as I know Hymie will wish both of them. He will wish one of my tenners to pay the jockey fee, and he will wish the other to bet on Mahogany, and I am certainly not going to let Hymie throw my dough away betting it on such an old crocodile as Mahogany, especially in a race which a horse by the name of Side Burns is a sure thing to win.

In fact, I am waiting patiently for several days for a chance to bet on Side Burns. So I hold out one sawbuck

on Hymie, and then I go over to the track and forget
all about him and Mahogany until the sixth race is coming up, and I see by the jockey board that Hymie has
a jock by the name of Scroon riding Mahogany, and
while Mahogany is carrying only one hundred pounds,
which is the light weight of the race, I will personally
just as soon have Paul Whiteman up as Scroon.
Personally I do not think Scroon can spell "horse,"
for he is nothing but a dizzy little guy who gets a mount
about once every Pancake Tuesday. But of course Hymie
is not a guy who can pick and choose his jocks, and
the chances are he is pretty lucky to get anybody to
ride Mahogany.

I see by the board where it tells you the approximate
odds that Mahogany is forty to one, and naturally nobody is paying any attention to such a horse, because
it will not be good sense to pay any attention to Mahogany in this race, what with it being his first start in
months, and Mahogany not figuring with these horses,
or with any horses, as far as this is concerned. In fact,
many citizens think Hymie Banjo Eyes is either crazy,
or is running Mahogany in this race for exercise, although nobody who knows Hymie will figure him to
be spending dough on a horse just to exercise him.

The favorite in the race is this horse named Side
Burns, and from the way they are playing him right
from taw you will think he is Twenty Grand. He is
even money on the board, and I hope and trust that
he will finally pay as much as this, because at even money
I consider him a very sound investment, indeed. In fact,
I am willing to take four to five for my dough, and
will consider it money well found, because I figure this
will give me about eighteen bobs to bet on Tony Joe
in the last race, and anybody will tell you that you can
go to sleep on Tony Joe winning, unless something
happens.

There is a little action on several other horses in the race, but of course there is none whatever for Mahogany and the last time I look he is up to fifty. So I buy my ticket on Side Burns, and go out to the paddock to take a peek at the horses, and I see Hymie Banjo Eyes in there saddling Mahogany with his jockey, this dizzy Scroon, standing alongside him in Hymie's colors of red, pink and yellow, and making wisecracks to the guys in the next stall about Mahogany.

Hymie Banjo Eyes sees me and motions me to come into the paddock, so I go in and give Mahogany a pat on the snoot, and the old guy seems to remember me right away, because he rubs his beezer up and down my arm and lets out a little snicker. But it seems to me the old plug looks a bit peaked, and I can see his ribs very plain indeed, so I figure maybe there is some truth in the rumor about Hymie sharing Mahogany's hay and grain, after all.

Well, as I am standing there, Hymie gives this dizzy Scroon his riding instructions, and they are very short, for all Hymie says is as follows:

"Listen," Hymie says, "get off with this horse and hurry right home."

And Scroon looks a little dizzier than somewhat and nods his head, and then turns and tips a wink to Kurtsinger, who is riding the horse in the next stall.

Well, finally the post bugle goes, and Hymie walks back with me to the lawn as the horses are coming out on the track, and Hymie is speaking about nothing but Mahogany.

"It is just my luck," Hymie says, "not to have a bob or two to bet on him. He will win this race as far as you can shoot a rifle, and the reason he will win this far," Hymie says, "is because the track is just soft enough to feel nice and soothing to his sore feet. Furthermore," Hymie says, "after lugging my one hundred and forty pounds around every morning for two weeks, Mahogany will think it is Christmas when he finds nothing but this Scroon's one hundred pounds on his back.

"In fact," Hymie says, "if I do not need the purse money, I will not let him run today, but will hide him for a bet. But," he says, " 'Lasses must have five yards at once, and you know how nervous she will be if she does not get the five yards. So I am letting Mahogany run," Hymie says, "and it is a pity."

"Well," I says, "why do you not promote somebody to bet on him for you?"

"Why," Hymie says, "if I ask one guy I ask fifty. But they all think I am out of my mind to think Mahogany can beat such horses as Side Burns and the rest. Well," he says, "they will be sorry. By the way," he says, "do you have a bet down of any kind?"

Well, now, I do not wish to hurt Hymie's feelings by letting him know I bet on something else in the race, so I tell him I do not play this race at all, and he probably figures it is because I have nothing to bet with after giving him the sawbuck. But he keeps on talking as we walk over in front of the grandstand, and all he is talking about is what a tough break it is for him not to have any dough to bet on Mahogany. By this time the horses are at the post a little way up the track, and as we are standing there watching them, Hymie Banjo Eyes goes on talking, half to me and half to himself, but out loud.

"Yes," he says, "I am the unluckiest guy in all the world. Here I am," he says, "with a race that is a kick in the pants for my horse at fifty to one, and me without a quarter to bet. It is certainly a terrible thing to be poor," Hymie says. "Why," he says, "I will bet my life on my horse in this race, I am so sure of winning. I will bet my clothes. I will bet all I ever hope to

have. In fact," he says, "I will even bet my ever-loving
wife, this is how sure I am."

Now of course this is only the way horse players rave
when they are good and heated up about the chances
of a horse, and I hear such conversations as this maybe
a million times, and never pay any attention to it whatever, but as Hymie makes this crack about betting his
ever-loving wife, a voice behind us says as follows:
"Against how much?"

Naturally, Hymie and I look around at once, and who
does the voice belong to but Brick McCloskey. Of course
I figure Brick is kidding Hymie Banjo Eyes, but Brick's
voice is as cold as ice as he says to Hymie like this:

"Against how much will you bet your wife your horse
wins this race?" he says. "I hear you saying you are
sure this old buzzard meat you are running will win,"
Brick says, "so let me see how sure you are. Personally,"
Brick says, "I think they ought to prosecute you for
running a broken-down hound like Mahogany on the
ground of cruelty to animals, and furthermore," Brick
says, "I think they ought to put you in an insane asylum
if you really believe your old dog has a chance. But I
will give you a bet," he says. "How much do you wish
me to lay against your wife?"

Well, this is very harsh language indeed, and I can
see that Brick is getting something off his chest he is
packing there for some time. The chances are he is putting the blast on poor Hymie Banjo Eyes on account
of Hymie grabbing 'Lasses from him, and of course
Brick McCloskey never figures for a minute that Hymie
will take his question seriously. But Hymie answers
like this:

"You are a price maker," he says. "What do you lay?"

Now this is a most astonishing reply, indeed, when
you figure that Hymie is asking what Brick will bet

against Hymie's ever-loving wife 'Lasses, and I am very sorry to hear Hymie ask, especially as I happen to turn around and find that nobody but 'Lasses herself is listening in on the conversation, and the chances are her face will be very white, if it is not for her make-up, 'Lasses being a doll who goes in for make-up more than somewhat.

"Yes," Brick McCloskey says, "I am a price maker, all right, and I will lay you a price. I will lay you five C's against your wife that your plug does not win," he says.

Brick looks at 'Lasses as he says this, and 'Lasses looks at Brick, and personally I will probably take a pop at a guy who looks at my ever-loving wife in such a way, if I happen to have any ever-loving wife, and maybe I will take a pop at my ever-loving wife, too, if she looks back at a guy in such a way, but of course Hymie is not noticing such things as looks at this time, and in fact he does not see 'Lasses as yet. But he does not hesitate in answering Brick.

"You are a bet," says Hymie. "Five hundred bucks against my ever-loving wife 'Lasses. It is a chiseler's price such as you always lay," he says, "and the chances are I can do better if I have time to go shopping around, but as it is," he says, "it is like finding money and I will not let you get away. But be ready to pay cash right after the race, because I will not accept your paper."

Well, I hear of many a strange bet on horse races, but never before do I hear of a guy betting his ever-loving wife, although to tell you the truth I never before hear of a guy getting the opportunity to bet his wife on a race. For all I know, if bookmakers take wives as a steady thing there will be much action in such matters at every track.

But I can see that both Brick McCloskey and Hymie Banjo Eyes are in dead earnest, and about this time 'Lasses tries to cop a quiet sneak, and Hymie sees her and speaks to her as follows:

"Hello, Baby," Hymie says. "I will have your five yards for you in a few minutes and five more to go with it, as I am just about to clip a sucker. Wait here with me, Baby," Hymie says.

"No," 'Lasses says; "I am too nervous to wait here. I am going down by the fence to root your horse in," she says, but as she goes away I see another look pass between her and Brick McCloskey.

Well, all of a sudden Cassidy gets the horses in a nice line and lets them go, and as they come busting down past the stand the first time who is right there on top but old Mahogany, with this dizzy Scroon kicking at his skinny sides and yelling in his ears. As they make the first turn, Scroon has Mahogany a length in front, and he moves him out another length as they hit the back side.

Now I always like to watch the races from a spot away up the lawn, as I do not care to have anybody much around me when the tough finishes come along in case I wish to bust out crying, so I leave Hymie Banjo Eyes and Brick McCloskey still glaring at each other and go to my usual place, and who is standing there, too, all by herself but 'Lasses. And about this time the horses are making the turn into the stretch and Mahogany is still on top, but something is coming very fast on the outside. It looks as if Mahogany is in a tough spot, because halfway down the stretch the outside horse nails him and looks him right in the eye, and who is it but the favorite, Side Burns.

They come on like a team, and I am personally giving Side Burns a great ride from where I am standing, when

I hear a doll yelling out loud, and who is the doll but 'Lasses, and what is she yelling but the following: "Come on with him, jock!"

Furthermore, as she yells, 'Lasses snaps her fingers like a crap shooter and runs a couple of yards one way and then turns and runs a couple of yards back the other way, so I can see that 'Lasses is indeed of a nervous temperament, just as Hymie Banjo Eyes is always telling me, although up to this time I figure her nerves are the old alzo.

"Come on!" 'Lasses yells again. "Let him roll!" she yells. "Ride him, boy!" she yells. "Come on with him, Frankie!"

Well, I wish to say that 'Lasses' voice may be all right if she is selling tomatoes from door to door, but I will not care to have her using it around me every day for any purpose whatever, because she yells so loud I have to move off a piece to keep my eardrums from being busted wide open. She is still yelling when the horses go past the finish line, the snozzles of old Mahogany and Side Burns so close together that nobody can hardly tell which is which.

In fact, there is quite a wait before the numbers go up, and I can see 'Lasses standing there with her program all wadded up in her fist as she watches the board, and I can see she is under a very terrible nervous strain indeed, and I am very sorry I go around thinking her nerves are the old alzo. Pretty soon the guy hangs out No. 9, and No. 9 is nobody but old Mahogany, and at this I hear 'Lasses screech, and all of a sudden she flops over in a faint, and somebody carries her under the grand stand to revive her, and I figure her nerves bog down entirely, and I am sorrier than ever for thinking bad thoughts of her.

I am also very, very sorry I do not bet my sawbuck

on Mahogany, especially when the board shows he pays
$102, and I can see where Hymie Banjo Eyes is right
about the weight and all, but I am glad Hymie wins
the purse and also the five C's off of Brick McCloskey
and that he saves his ever-loving wife, because I figure
Hymie may now pay me back a few bobs.

I do not see Hymie or Brick or 'Lasses again until
the races are over, and then I hear of a big row going
on under the stand, and go to see what is doing, and
who is having the row but Hymie Banjo Eyes and Brick
McCloskey. It seems that Hymie hits Brick a clout on
the beezer that stretches Brick out, and it seems that
Hymie hits Brick this blow because as Brick is paying
Hymie the five C's he makes the following crack:

"I do not mind losing the dough to you, Banjo Eyes,"
Brick says, "but I am sore at myself for overlaying the
price. It is the first time in all the years I am booking
that I make such an overlay. The right price against
your wife," Brick says, "is maybe two dollars and a
half."

Well, as Brick goes down with a busted beezer from
Hymie's punch, and everybody is much excited, who
steps out of the crowd around them and throws her
arms around Hymie Banjo Eyes, but his ever-loving wife
'Lasses, and as she kisses Hymie smack dab in the mush,
'Lasses says as follows:

"My darling Hymie," she says, "I hear what this big
flannelmouth says about the price on me, and," she says,
"I am only sorry you do not cripple him for life. I know
now I love you, and only you, Hymie," she says, "and
I will never love anybody else. In fact," 'Lasses says,
"I just prove my love for you by almost wrecking my
nerves in rooting Mahogany home. I am still weak,"
she says, "but I have strength enough left to go with
you to the Sunset Inn for a nice dinner, and you can

give me my money then. Furthermore," 'Lasses says, "now that we have a few bobs, I think you better find another place for Mahogany to stay, as it does not look nice for my husband to be living with a horse."

Well, I am going by the jockey house on my way home, thinking how nice it is that Hymie Banjo Eyes will no longer have to live with Mahogany, and what a fine thing it is to have a loyal, ever-loving wife such as 'Lasses, who risks her nerves rooting for her husband's horse, when I run into this dizzy Scroon in his street clothes, and wishing to be friendly, I say to him like this:

"Hello, Frankie," I say. "You put up a nice ride today."

"Where do you get this 'Frankie'?" Scroon says. "My name is Gus."

"Why," I say, commencing to think of this and that, "so it is, but is there a jock called Frankie in the sixth race with you this afternoon?"

"Sure," Scroon says. "Frankie Madeley. He rides Side Burns, the favorite; and I make a sucker of him in the stretch run."

But of course I never mention to Hymie Banjo Eyes that I figure his ever-loving wife roots herself into a dead faint for the horse that will give her to Brick McCloskey, because for all I know she may think Scroon's name is Frankie, at that.

Hold 'Em, Yale!

WHAT I AM DOING in New Haven on the day of a very
large football game between the Harvards and the Yales
is something which calls for quite a little explanation,
because I am not such a guy as you will expect to find
in New Haven at any time, and especially on the day
of a large football game.

But there I am, and the reason I am there goes back
to a Friday night when I am sitting in Mindy's restaurant on Broadway thinking of very little except how I
can get hold of a few potatoes to take care of the old
overhead. And while I am sitting there, who comes in
but Sam the Gonoph, who is a ticket speculator by trade,
and who seems to be looking all around and about.

Well, Sam the Gonoph gets to talking to me, and it
turns out that he is looking for a guy by the name of
Gigolo Georgie, who is called Gigolo Georgie because
he is always hanging around night clubs wearing a little
mustache and white spats, and dancing with old dolls.

In fact, Gigolo Georgie is nothing but a gentleman bum, and I am surprised that Sam the Gonoph is looking for him.

But it seems that the reason Sam the Gonoph wishes to find Gigolo Georgie is to give him a good punch in the snoot, because it seems that Gigolo Georgie promotes Sam for several duckets to the large football game between the Harvards and the Yales to sell on commission, and never kicks back anything whatever to Sam. Naturally Sam considers Gigolo Georgie nothing but a rascal for doing such a thing to him, and Sam says he will find Gigolo Georgie and give him a going-over if it is the last act of his life.

Well, then, Sam explains to me that he has quite a few nice duckets for the large football game between the Harvards and the Yales and that he is taking a crew of guys with him to New Haven the next day to hustle these duckets, and what about me going along and helping to hustle these duckets and making a few bobs for myself, which is an invitation that sounds very pleasant to me, indeed.

Now of course it is very difficult for anybody to get nice duckets to a large football game between the Harvards and the Yales unless they are personally college guys, and Sam the Gonoph is by no means a college guy. In fact, the nearest Sam ever comes to a college is once when he is passing through the yard belonging to the Princetons, but Sam is on the fly at the time as a gendarme is after him, so he does not really see much of the college.

But every college guy is entitled to duckets to a large football game with which his college is connected, and it is really surprising how many college guys do not care to see large football games even after they get their duckets, especially if a ticket spec such as Sam the

Gonoph comes along offering them a few bobs more than
the duckets are worth. I suppose this is because a college
guy figures he can see a large football game when he
is old, while many things are taking place around and
about that it is necessary for him to see while he is
young enough to really enjoy them, such as the Follies.

Anyway, many college guys are always willing to listen to reason when Sam the Gonoph comes around offering to buy their duckets, and then Sam takes these
duckets and sells them to customers for maybe ten times
the price the duckets call for, and in this way Sam does
very good for himself.

I know Sam the Gonoph for maybe twenty years,
and always he is speculating in duckets of one kind and
another. Sometimes it is duckets for the world's series,
and sometimes for big fights, and sometimes it is duckets
for nothing but lawn-tennis games, although why anybody wishes to see such a thing as lawn tennis is always
a very great mystery to Sam the Gonoph and everybody
else.

But in all those years I see Sam dodging around under
the feet of the crowds of these large events, or running
through the special trains offering to buy or sell duckets,
I never hear of Sam personally attending any of these
events except maybe a baseball game, or a fight, for
Sam has practically no interest in anything but a little
profit on his duckets.

He is a short, chunky, black-looking guy with a big
beezer, and he is always sweating even on a cold day,
and he comes from down around Essex Street, on the
lower East Side. Moreover, Sam the Gonoph's crew generally comes from the lower East Side, too, for as Sam
goes along he makes plenty of potatoes for himself and
branches out quite some, and has a lot of assistants hustling duckets around these different events.

When Sam is younger the cops consider him hard
to get along with, and in fact his monicker, the Gonoph,
comes from his young days down on the lower East
Side, and I hear it is Yiddish for thief, but of course
as Sam gets older and starts gathering plenty of potatoes,
he will not think of stealing anything. At least not much,
and especially if it is anything that is nailed down.

Well, anyway, I meet Sam the Gonoph and his crew
at the information desk in Grand Central the next morning, and this is how I come to be in New Haven on
the day of the large football game between the Harvards
and the Yales.

For such a game as this, Sam has all his best hustlers,
including such as Jew Louie, Nubbsy Taylor, Benny
South Street and old Liverlips, and to look at these parties you will never suspect that they are topnotch ducket
hustlers. The best you will figure them is a lot of guys
who are not to be met up with in a dark alley, but
then ducket-hustling is a rough-and-tumble dodge and
it will scarcely be good policy to hire female impersona-
tors.

Now while we are hustling these duckets out around
the main gates of the Yale Bowl I notice a very beautiful
little doll of maybe sixteen or seventeen standing around
watching the crowd, and I can see she is waiting for
somebody, as many dolls often do at football games.
But I can also see that this little doll is very much worried as the crowd keeps going in, and it is getting on
toward game time. In fact, by and by I can see this
little doll has tears in her eyes and if there is anything
I hate to see it is tears in a doll's eyes.

So finally I go over to her, and I say as follows: "What
is eating you, little miss?"

"Oh," she says, "I am waiting for Elliot. He is to
come up from New York and meet me here to take
me to the game, but he is not here yet, and I am afraid

something happens to him. Furthermore," she says, the tears in her eyes getting very large, indeed, "I am afraid I will miss the game because he has my ticket."

"Why," I say, "this is a very simple proposition. I will sell you a choice ducket for only a sawbuck, which is ten dollars in your language, and you are getting such a bargain only because the game is about to begin, and the market is going down."

"But," she says, "I do not have ten dollars. In fact, I have only fifty cents left in my purse, and this is worrying me very much, for what will I do if Elliot does not meet me? You see," she says, "I come from Miss Peevy's school at Worcester, and I only have enough money to pay my railroad fare here, and of course I cannot ask Miss Peevy for any money as I do not wish her to know I am going away."

Well, naturally all this is commencing to sound to me like a hard-luck story such as any doll is apt to tell, so I go on about my business because I figure she will next be trying to put the lug on me for a ducket, or maybe for her railroad fare back to Worcester, although generally dolls with hard-luck stories live in San Francisco.

She keeps on standing there, and I notice she is now crying more than somewhat, and I get to thinking to myself that she is about as cute a little doll as ever I see, although too young for anybody to be bothering much about. Furthermore, I get to thinking that maybe she is on the level, at that, with her story.

Well, by this time the crowd is nearly all in the Bowl, and only a few parties such as coppers and hustlers of one kind and another are left standing outside, and there is much cheering going on inside, when Sam the Gonoph comes up looking very much disgusted, and speaks as follows:

"What do you think?" Sam says. "I am left with seven

duckets on my hands, and these guys around here will not pay as much as face value for them, and they stand me better than three bucks over that. Well," Sam says, "I am certainly not going to let them go for less than they call for if I have to eat them. What do you guys say we use these duckets ourselves and go in and see the game? Personally," Sam says, "I often wish to see one of these large football games just to find out what makes suckers willing to pay so much for duckets."

Well, this seems to strike one and all, including myself, as a great idea, because none of the rest of us ever see a large football game either, so we start for the gate, and as we pass the little doll who is still crying, I say to Sam the Gonoph like this:

"Listen, Sam," I say, "you have seven duckets, and we are only six, and here is a little doll who is stood up by her guy, and has no ducket, and no potatoes to buy one with, so what about taking her with us?"

Well, this is all right with Sam the Gonoph, and none of the others object, so I step up to the little doll and invite her to go with us, and right away she stops crying and begins smiling, and saying we are very kind indeed. She gives Sam the Gonoph an extra big smile, and right away Sam is saying she is very cute, indeed, and then she gives old Liverlips an even bigger smile, and what is more she takes old Liverlips by the arm and walks with him, and old Liverlips is not only very much astonished, but very much pleased. In fact, old Liverlips begins stepping out very spry, and Liverlips is not such a guy as cares to have any part of dolls, young or old.

But while walking with old Liverlips, the little doll talks very friendly to Jew Louie and to Nubbsy Taylor and Benny South Street, and even to me, and by and by you will think to see us that we are all her uncles, although of course if this little doll really knows who she is with, the chances are she will start chucking faints one after the other.

Anybody can see that she has very little experience in this wicked old world, and in fact is somewhat rattle-headed, because she gabs away very freely about her personal business. In fact, before we are in the Bowl she lets it out that she runs away from Miss Peevy's school to elope with this Elliot, and she says the idea is they are to be married in Hartford after the game. In fact, she says Elliot wishes to go to Hartford and be married before the game.

"But," she says, "my brother John is playing substitute with the Yales today, and I cannot think of getting married to anybody before I see him play, although I am much in love with Elliot. He is a wonderful dancer," she says, "and very romantic. I meet him in Atlantic City last summer. Now we are eloping," she says, "because my father does not care for Elliot whatever. In fact, my father hates Elliot, although he only sees him once, and it is because he hates Elliot so that my father sends me to Miss Peevy's school in Worcester. She is an old pill. Do you not think my father is unreasonable?" she says.

Well, of course none of us have any ideas on such propositions as this, although old Liverlips tells the little doll he is with her right or wrong, and pretty soon we are inside the Bowl and sitting in seats as good as any in the joint. It seems we are on the Harvards' side of the field, although of course I will never know this if the little doll does not mention it.

She seems to know everything about this football business, and as soon as we sit down she tries to point out her brother playing substitute for the Yales, saying he is the fifth guy from the end among a bunch of guys sitting on a bench on the other side of the field all wrapped in blankets. But we cannot make much of him from where we sit, and anyway it does not look to me as if he has much of a job.

It seems we are right in the middle of all the Harvards and they are making an awful racket, what with yelling, and singing, and one thing and another, because it seems the game is going on when we get in, and that the Harvards are shoving the Yales around more than somewhat. So our little doll lets everybody know she is in favor of the Yales by yelling, "Hold 'em, Yale!"

Personally, I cannot tell which are the Harvards and which are the Yales at first, and Sam the Gonoph and the others are as dumb as I am, but she explains the Harvards are wearing the red shirts and the Yales the blue shirts, and by and by we are yelling for the Yales to hold 'em, too, although of course it is only on account of our little doll wishing the Yales to hold 'em, and not because any of us care one way or the other.

Well, it seems that the idea of a lot of guys and a little doll getting right among them and yelling for the Yales to hold 'em is very repulsive to the Harvards around us, although any of them must admit it is very good advice to the Yales, at that, and some of them start making cracks of one kind and another, especially at our little doll. The chances are they are very jealous because she is outyelling them, because I will say one thing for our little doll, she can yell about as loud as anybody I ever hear, male or female.

A couple of Harvards sitting in front of old Liverlips are imitating our little doll's voice, and making guys around them laugh very heartily, but all of a sudden these parties leave their seats and go away in great haste, their faces very pale, indeed, and I figure maybe they are both taken sick the same moment, but afterwards I learn that Liverlips takes a big shiv out of his pocket

and opens it and tells them very confidentially that he
is going to carve their ears off.

Naturally, I do not blame the Harvards for going away
in great haste, for Liverlips is such a looking guy as
you will figure to take great delight in carving off ears.
Furthermore, Nubbsy Taylor and Benny South Street
and Jew Louie and even Sam the Gonoph commence
exchanging such glances with other Harvards around
us who are making cracks at our little doll that presently
there is almost a dead silence in our neighborhood, except for our little doll yelling, "Hold 'em, Yale!" You
see by this time we are all very fond of our little doll
because she is so cute-looking and has so much zing
in her, and we do not wish anybody making cracks at
her or at us either, and especially at us.

In fact, we are so fond of her that when she happens
to mention that she is a little chilly, Jew Louie and
Nubbsy Taylor slip around among the Harvards and
come back with four steamer rugs, six mufflers, two
pairs of gloves, and a thermos bottle full of hot coffee
for her, and Jew Louie says if she wishes a mink coat
to just say the word. But she already has a mink coat.
Furthermore, Jew Louie brings her a big bunch of red
flowers that he finds on a doll with one of the Harvards,
and he is much disappointed when she says it is the
wrong color for her.

Well, finally the game is over, and I do not remember
much about it, although afterwards I hear that our little
doll's brother John plays substitute for the Yales very
good. But it seems that the Harvards win, and our little
doll is very sad indeed about this, and is sitting there
looking out over the field, which is now covered with
guys dancing around as if they all suddenly go daffy,
and it seems they are all Harvards, because there is really
no reason for the Yales to do any dancing.

All of a sudden our little doll looks toward one end
of the field, and says as follows: "Oh, they are going
to take our goal posts!"

Sure enough, a lot of the Harvards are gathering
around the posts at this end of the field, and are pulling
and hauling at the posts, which seem to be very stout
posts, indeed. Personally, I will not give you eight cents
for these posts, but afterwards one of the Yales tells
me that when a football team wins a game it is considered the proper caper for this team's boosters to grab
the other guy's goal posts. But he is not able to tell
me what good the posts are after they get them, and
this is one thing that will always be a mystery to me.

Anyway, while we are watching the goings-on around
the goal posts, our little doll says come on and jumps
up and runs down an aisle and out on to the field, and
into the crowd around the goal posts, so naturally we
follow her. Somehow she manages to wiggle through
the crowd of Harvards around the posts, and the next
thing anybody knows she shins up one of the posts faster
than you can say scat, and pretty soon is roosting out
on the cross-bar between the posts like a chipmunk.

Afterwards she explains that her idea is the Harvards
will not be ungentlemanly enough to pull down the
goal posts with a lady roosting on them, but it seems
these Harvards are no gentlemen, and keep on pulling,
and the posts commence to teeter, and our little doll
is teetering with them, although of course she is in no
danger if she falls because she is sure to fall on the
Harvards' noggins, and the way I look at it, the noggin
of anybody who will be found giving any time to pulling
down goal posts is apt to be soft enough to break a
very long fall.

Now Sam the Gonoph and old Liverlips and Nubbsy
Taylor and Benny South Street and Jew Louie and I

reach the crowd around the goal posts at about the same time, and our little doll sees us from her roost and yells to us as follows: "Do not let them take our posts!"

Well, about this time one of the Harvards who seems to be about nine feet high reaches over six other guys and hits me on the chin and knocks me so far that when I pick myself up I am pretty well out of the way of everybody and have a chance to see what is going on.

Afterwards somebody tells me that the guy probably thinks I am one of the Yales coming to the rescue of the goal posts, but I wish to say I will always have a very low opinion of college guys, because I remember two other guys punch me as I am going through the air, unable to defend myself.

Now Sam the Gonoph and Nubbsy Taylor and Jew Louie and Benny South Street and old Liverlips somehow manage to ease their way through the crowd until they are under the goal posts, and our little doll is much pleased to see them, because the Harvards are now making the posts teeter more than somewhat with their pulling, and it looks as if the posts will go any minute.

Of course Sam the Gonoph does not wish any trouble with these parties, and he tries to speak nicely to the guys who are pulling at the posts, saying as follows:

"Listen," Sam says, "the little doll up there does not wish you to take these posts."

Well, maybe they do not hear Sam's words in the confusion, or if they do hear them they do not wish to pay any attention to them, for one of the Harvards mashes Sam's derby hat down over his eyes, and another smacks old Liverlips on the left ear, while Jew Louie and Nubbsy Taylor and Benny South Street are shoved around quite some.

"All right," Sam the Gonoph says, as soon as he can pull his hat off his eyes, "all right, gentlemen, if you wish to play this way. Now, boys, let them have it!"

So Sam the Gonoph and Nubbsy Taylor and Jew Louie and Benny South Street and old Liverlips begin letting them have it, and what they let them have it with is not only their dukes, but with the good old difference in their dukes, because these guys are by no means suckers when it comes to a battle, and they all carry something in their pockets to put in their dukes in case of a fight, such as a dollar's worth of nickels rolled up tight.

Furthermore, they are using the old leather, kicking guys in the stomach when they are not able to hit them on the chin, and Liverlips is also using his noodle to good advantage, grabbing guys by their coat lapels and yanking them into him so he can butt them between the eyes with his noggin, and I wish to say that old Liverlips' noggin is a very dangerous weapon at all times.

Well, the ground around them is soon covered with Harvards, and it seems that some Yales are also mixed up with them, being Yales who think Sam the Gonoph and his guys are other Yales defending the goal posts, and wishing to help out. But of course Sam the Gonoph and his guys cannot tell the Yales from the Harvards, and do not have time to ask which is which, so they are just letting everybody have it who comes along. And while all this is going on our little doll is sitting up on the cross-bar and yelling plenty of encouragement to Sam and his guys.

Now it turns out that these Harvards are by no means soft touches in a scrabble such as this, and as fast as they are flattened they get up and keep belting away, and while the old experience is running for Sam the Gonoph and Jew Louie and Nubbsy Taylor and Benny South Street and old Liverlips early in the fight, the Harvards have youth in their favor.

Pretty soon the Harvards are knocking down Sam the Gonoph, then they start knocking down Nubbsy Taylor, and by and by they are knocking down Benny South Street and Jew Louie and Liverlips, and it is so much fun that the Harvards forget all about the goal posts. Of course as fast as Sam the Gonoph and his guys are knocked down they also get up, but the Harvards are too many for them, and they are getting an awful shellacking when the nine-foot guy who flattens me, and who is knocking down Sam the Gonoph so often he is becoming a great nuisance to Sam, sings out:

"Listen," he says, "these are game guys, even if they do go to Yale. Let us cease knocking them down," he says, "and give them a cheer."

So the Harvards knock down Sam the Gonoph and Nubbsy Taylor and Jew Louie and Benny South Street and old Liverlips just once more and then all the Harvards put their heads together and say rah-rah-rah, very loud, and go away, leaving the goal posts still standing, with our little doll still roosting on the cross-bar, although afterwards I hear some Harvards who are not in the fight get the posts at the other end of the field and sneak away with them. But I always claim these posts do not count.

Well, sitting there on the ground because he is too tired to get up from the last knockdown, and holding one hand to his right eye, which is closed tight, Sam the Gonoph is by no means a well guy, and all around and about him is much suffering among his crew. But our little doll is hopping up and down chattering like a jaybird and running between old Liverlips, who is stretched out against one goal post, and Nubbsy Taylor, who is leaning up against the other, and she is trying to mop the blood off their kissers with a handkerchief the size of a postage stamp.

Benny South Street is laying across Jew Louie and both are still snoring from the last knockdown, and the Bowl is now pretty much deserted except for the newspaper scribes away up in the press box, who do not seem to realize that the Battle of the Century just comes off in front of them. It is coming on dark, when all of a sudden a guy pops up out of the dusk wearing white spats and an overcoat with a fur collar, and he rushes up to our little doll.

"Clarice," he says, "I am looking for you high and low. My train is stalled for hours behind a wreck the other side of Bridgeport, and I get here just after the game is over. But," he says, "I figure you will be waiting somewhere for me. Let us hurry on to Hartford, darling," he says.

Well, when he hears this voice, Sam the Gonoph opens his good eye wide and takes a peek at the guy. Then all of a sudden Sam jumps up and wobbles over to the guy and hits him a smack between the eyes. Sam is wobbling because his legs are not so good from the shellacking he takes off the Harvards, and furthermore he is away off in his punching as the guy only goes to his knees and comes right up standing again as our little doll lets out a screech and speaks as follows:

"Oo-oo!" she says. "Do not hit Elliot! He is not after our goal posts!"

"Elliot?" Sam the Gonoph says. "This is no Elliot. This is nobody but Gigolo Georgie. I can tell him by his white spats," Sam says, "and I am now going to get even for the pasting I take from the Harvards."

Then he nails the guy again and this time he seems to have a little more on his punch, for the guy goes down and Sam the Gonoph gives him the leather very good, although our little doll is still screeching, and begging Sam not to hurt Elliot. But of course the rest of us know it is not Elliot, no matter what he may tell her, but only Gigolo Georgie.

Well, the rest of us figure we may as well take a little something out of Georgie's hide, too, but as we start for him he gives a quick wiggle and hops to his feet and tears across the field, and the last we see of him is his white spats flying through one of the portals.

Now a couple of other guys come up out of the dusk, and one of them is a tall, fine-looking guy with a white mustache and anybody can see that he is somebody, and what happens but our little doll runs right into his arms and kisses him on the white mustache and calls him daddy and starts to cry more than somewhat, so I can see we lose our little doll then and there. And now the guy with the white mustache walks up to Sam the Gonoph and sticks out his duke and says as follows:

"Sir," he says, "permit me the honor of shaking the hand which does me the very signal service of chastising the scoundrel who just escapes from the field. And," he says, "permit me to introduce myself to you. I am J. Hildreth Van Cleve, president of the Van Cleve Trust. I am notified early today by Miss Peevy of my daughter's sudden departure from school, and we learn she purchases a ticket for New Haven. I at once suspect this fellow has something to do with it. Fortunately," he says, "I have these private detectives here keeping tab on him for some time, knowing my child's schoolgirl infatuation for him, so we easily trail him here. We are on the train with him, and arrive in time for your last little scene with him. Sir," he says, "again I thank you."

"I know who you are, Mr. Van Cleve," Sam the Gonoph says. "You are the Van Cleve who is down to his last forty million. But," he says, "do not thank me for putting the slug on Gigolo Georgie. He is a bum in spades, and I am only sorry he fools your nice little kid even for a minute, although," Sam says, "I figure she must be dumber than she looks to be fooled by such a guy as Gigolo Georgie."

"I hate him," the little doll says. "I hate him because he is a coward. He does not stand up and fight when he is hit like you and Liverlips and the others. I never wish to see him again."

"Do not worry," Sam the Gonoph says. "I will be too close to Gigolo Georgie as soon as I recover from my wounds for him to stay in this part of the country."

Well, I do not see Sam the Gonoph or Nubbsy Taylor or Benny South Street or Jew Louie or Liverlips for nearly a year after this, and then it comes on fall again and one day I get to thinking that here it is Friday and the next day the Harvards are playing the Yales a large football game in Boston.

I figure it is a great chance for me to join up with Sam the Gonoph again to hustle duckets for him for this game, and I know Sam will be leaving along about midnight with his crew. So I go over to the Grand Central station at such a time, and sure enough he comes along by and by, busting through the crowd in the station with Nubbsy Taylor and Benny South Street and Jew Louie and old Liverlips at his heels, and they seem very much excited.

"Well, Sam," I say, as I hurry along with them, "here I am ready to hustle duckets for you again, and I hope and trust we do a nice business."

"Duckets!" Sam the Gonoph says. "We are not hustling duckets for this game, although you can go with us, and welcome. We are going to Boston," he says, "to root for the Yales to kick hell out of the Harvards and we are going as the personal guests of Miss Clarice Van Cleve and her old man."

"Hold 'em, Yale!" old Liverlips says, as he pushes me to one side and the whole bunch goes trotting through the gate to catch their train, and I then notice they are all wearing blue feathers in their hats with a little white Y on these feathers such as college guys always wear at football games, and that moreover Sam the Gonoph is carrying a Yale pennant.

A Story Goes with It

ONE NIGHT I am in a gambling joint in Miami watching the crap game and thinking what a nice thing it is, indeed, to be able to shoot craps without having to worry about losing your potatoes.

Many of the high shots from New York and Detroit and St. Louis and other cities are around the table, and there is quite some action in spite of the hard times. In fact, there is so much action that a guy with only a few bobs on him, such as me, will be considered very impolite to be pushing into this game, because they are packed in very tight around the table.

I am maybe three guys back from the table, and I am watching the game by standing on tiptoe peeking over their shoulders, and all I can hear is Goldie, the stick man, hollering money-money-money every time some guy makes a number, so I can see the dice are very warm indeed, and that the right betters are doing first-rate.

By and by a guy by the name of Guinea Joe, out of
Trenton, picks up the dice and starts making numbers
right and left, and I know enough about this Guinea
Joe to know that when he starts making numbers anybody will be very foolish indeed not to follow his hand,
although personally I am generally a wrong better
against the dice, if I bet at all.

Now all I have in my pocket is a sawbuck, and the
hotel stakes are coming up on me the next day, and I
need this saw, but with Guinea Joe hotter than a forty-
five it will be overlooking a big opportunity not to go
along with him, so when he comes out on an eight,
which is a very easy number for Joe to make when he
is hot, I dig up my sawbuck, and slide it past the three
guys in front of me to the table, and I say to Lefty
Park, who is laying against the dice, as follows: "I will
take the odds, Lefty."

Well, Lefty looks at my sawbuck and nods his head,
for Lefty is not such a guy as will refuse any bet, even
though it is as modest as mine, and right away Goldie
yells money-money-money, so there I am with twenty-
two dollars.

Next Guinea Joe comes out on a nine, and naturally
I take thirty to twenty for my sugar, because nine is
nothing for Joe to make when he is hot. He makes the
nine just as I figure, and I take two to one for my half
a yard when he starts looking for a ten, and when he
makes the ten I am right up against the table, because
I am now a guy with means.

Well, the upshot of the whole business is that I finally
find myself with three hundred bucks, and when it looks
as if the dice are cooling off, I take out and back off
from the table, and while I am backing off I am trying
to look like a guy who loses all his potatoes, because
there are always many wolves waiting around crap

games and one thing and another in Miami this season, and what they are waiting for is to put the bite on anybody who happens to make a little scratch.

In fact, nobody can remember when the bite is as painful as it is in Miami this season, what with the unemployment situation among many citizens who come to Miami expecting to find work in the gambling joints, or around the race track. But almost as soon as these citizens arrive, the gambling joints are all turned off, except in spots, and the bookmakers are chased off the track and the mutuels put in, and the consequences are the suffering is most intense. It is not only intense among the visiting citizens, but it is quite intense among the Miami landlords, because naturally if a citizen is not working, nobody can expect him to pay any room rent, but the Miami landlords do not seem to understand this situation, and are very unreasonable about their room rent.

Anyway, I back through quite a crowd without anybody biting me, and I am commencing to figure I may escape altogether and get to my hotel and hide my dough before the news gets around that I win about five G's, which is what my winning is sure to amount to by the time the rumor reaches all quarters of the city.

Then, just as I am thinking I am safe, I find I am looking a guy by the name of Hot Horse Herbie in the face, and I can tell from Hot Horse Herbie's expression that he is standing there watching me for some time, so there is no use in telling him I am washed out in the game. In fact, I cannot think of much of anything to tell Hot Horse Herbie that may keep him from putting the bite on me for at least a few bobs, and I am greatly astonished when he does not offer to bite me at all, but says to me like this:

"Well," he says, "I am certainly glad to see you make

such a nice score. I will be looking for you tomorrow at the track, and will have some big news for you."

Then he walks away from me and I stand there with my mouth open looking at him, as it is certainly a most unusual way for Herbie to act. It is the first time I ever knew Herbie to walk away from a chance to bite somebody, and I can scarcely understand such actions, for Herbie is such a guy as will not miss a bite, even if he does not need it.

He is a tall, thin guy, with a sad face and a long chin, and he is called Hot Horse Herbie because he nearly always has a very hot horse to tell you about. He nearly always has a horse that is so hot it is fairly smoking, a hot horse being a horse that cannot possibly lose a race unless it falls down dead, and while Herbie's hot horses often lose without falling down dead, this does not keep Herbie from coming up with others just as hot.

In fact, Hot Horse Herbie is what is called a hustler around the race tracks, and his business is to learn about these hot horses, or even just suspect about them, and then get somebody to bet on them, which is a very legitimate business indeed, as Herbie only collects a commission if the hot horses win, and if they do not win Herbie just keeps out of sight awhile from whoever he gets to bet on the hot horses. There are very few guys in this world who can keep out of sight better than Hot Horse Herbie, and especially from old Cap Duhaine, of the Pinkertons, who is always around pouring cold water on hot horses.

In fact, Cap Duhaine, of the Pinkertons, claims that guys such as Hot Horse Herbie are nothing but touts, and sometimes he heaves them off the race track altogether, but of course Cap Duhaine is a very unsentimental old guy and cannot see how such characters as Hot

Horse Herbie add to the romance of the turf.

Anyway, I escape from the gambling joint with all my scratch on me, and hurry to my room and lock myself in for the night, and I do not show up in public until along about noon the next day, when it is time to go over to the coffee shop for my java. And of course by this time the news of my score is all over town, and many guys are taking dead aim at me.

But naturally I am now able to explain to them that I have to wire most of the three yards I win to Nebraska to save my father's farm from being seized by the sheriff, and while everybody knows I do not have a father, and that if I do have a father I will not be sending him money for such a thing as saving his farm, with times what they are in Miami, nobody is impolite enough to doubt my word except a guy by the name of Pottsville Legs, who wishes to see my receipts from the telegraph office when I explain to him why I cannot stake him to a double sawbuck.

I do not see Hot Horse Herbie until I get to the track, and he is waiting for me right inside the grandstand gate, and as soon as I show up he motions me off to one side and says to me like this:

"Now," Herbie says, "I am very smart indeed about a certain race today. In fact," he says, "if any guy knowing what I know does not bet all he can rake and scrape together on a certain horse, such a guy ought to cut his own throat and get himself out of the way forever. What I know," Herbie says, "is enough to shake the foundations of this country if it gets out. Do not ask any questions," he says, "but get ready to bet all the sugar you win last night on this horse I am going to mention to you, and all I ask you in return is to bet fifty on me. And," Herbie says, "kindly do not tell me you leave your money in your other pants, because I know you do not have any other pants."

"Now, Herbie," I say, "I do not doubt your information, because I know you will not give out information unless it is well founded. But," I say, "I seldom stand for a tip, and as for betting fifty for you, you know I will not bet fifty even for myself if somebody guarantees me a winner. So I thank you, Herbie, just the same," I say, "but I must do without your tip," and with this I start walking away.

"Now," Herbie says, "wait a minute. A story goes with it," he says.

Well, of course this is a different matter entirely. I am such a guy as will always listen to a tip on a horse if a story goes with the tip. In fact, I will not give you a nickel for a tip without a story, but it must be a first-class story, and most horse players are the same way. In fact, there are very few horse players who will not listen to a tip if a story goes with it, for this is the way human nature is. So I turn and walk back to Hot Horse Herbie, and say to him like this:

"Well," I say, "let me hear the story, Herbie."

"Now," Herbie says, dropping his voice away down low, in case old Cap Duhaine may be around somewhere listening, "it is the third race, and the horse is a horse by the name of Never Despair. It is a boat race," Herbie says. "They are going to shoo in Never Despair. Everything else in the race is a cooler," he says.

"Well," I say, "this is just an idea, Herbie, and not a story."

"Wait a minute," Herbie says. "The story that goes with it is a very strange story indeed. In fact," he says, "it is such a story as I can scarcely believe myself, and I will generally believe almost any story, including," he says, "the ones I make up out of my own head. Anyway, the story is as follows:

"Never Despair is owned by an old guy by the name of Seed Mercer," Herbie says. "Maybe you remember seeing him around. He always wears a black slouch hat and gray whiskers," Herbie says, "and he is maybe a hundred years old, and his horses are very terrible horses indeed. In fact," Herbie says, "I do not remember seeing any more terrible horses in all the years I am around the track, and," Herbie says, "I wish to say I see some very terrible horses indeed.

"Now," Herbie says, "old Mercer has a granddaughter who is maybe sixteen years old, come next grass, by the name of Lame Louise, and she is called Lame Louise because she is all crippled up from childhood by infantile what-is-this, and can scarcely navigate, and," Herbie says, "her being crippled up in such a way makes old Mercer feel very sad, for she is all he has in the world, except these terrible horses."

"It is a very long story, Herbie," I say, "and I wish to see Moe Shapoff about a very good thing in the first race."

"Never mind Moe Shapoff," Herbie says. "He will only tell you about a bum by the name of Zachary in the first race, and Zachary has no chance whatever. I make Your John a standout in the first," he says.

"Well," I say, "let us forget the first and go on with your story, although it is commencing to sound all mixed up to me."

"Now," Herbie says, "it not only makes old man Mercer very sad because Lame Louise is all crippled up, but," he says, "it makes many of the jockeys and other guys around the race track very sad, because," he says, "they know Lame Louise since she is so high and she always has a smile for them, and especially for Jockey Scroon. In fact," Herbie says, "Jockey Scroon is even more sad about Lame Louise than old man Mercer, because Jockey Scroon loves Lame Louise."

"Why," I say, very indignant, "Jockey Scroon is noth-

ing but a little burglar. Why," I say, "I see Jockey Scroon
do things to horses I bet on that he will have to answer
for on the Judgment Day, if there is any justice at such
a time. Why," I say, "Jockey Scroon is nothing but a
Gerald Chapman in his heart, and so are all other
jockeys."

"Yes," Hot Horse Herbie says, "what you say is very,
very true, and I am personally in favor of the electric
chair for all jockeys, but," he says, "Jockey Scroon loves
Lame Louise just the same, and is figuring on making
her his ever-loving wife when he gets a few bobs together, which," Herbie says, "makes Louise eight to five
in my line to be an old maid. Jockey Scroon rooms with
me downtown," Herbie says, "and he speaks freely to
me about his love for Louise. Furthermore," Herbie
says, "Jockey Scroon is personally not a bad little guy,
at that, although of course being a jockey he is sometimes
greatly misunderstood by the public.

"Anyway," Hot Horse Herbie says, "I happen to go
home early last night before I see you at the gambling
joint, and I hear voices coming out of my room, and
naturally I pause outside the door to listen, because for
all I know it may be the landlord speaking about the
room rent, although," Herbie says, "I do not figure my
landlord to be much worried at this time because I see
him sneak into my room a few days before and take a
lift at my trunk to make sure I have belongings in the
same, and it happens I nail the trunk to the floor before-
hand, so not being able to lift it, the landlord is bound
to figure me a guy with property.

"These voices," Herbie says, "are mainly soprano
voices, and at first I think Jockey Scroon is in there
with some dolls, which is by no means permissible in
my hotel, but, after listening awhile, I discover they
are the voices of young boys, and I make out that these

boys are nothing but jockeys, and they are the six jockeys who are riding in the third race, and they are fixing up this race to be a boat race, and to shoo in Never Despair, which Jockey Scroon is riding.

"And," Hot Horse Herbie says, "the reason they are fixing up this boat race is the strangest part of the story. It seems," he says, "that Jockey Scroon hears old man Mercer talking about a great surgeon from Europe who is a shark on patching up cripples such as Lame Louise, and who just arrives at Palm Beach to spend the winter, and old man Mercer is saying how he wishes he has dough enough to take Lame Louise to this guy so he can operate on her, and maybe make her walk good again.

"But of course," Herbie says, "it is well known to one and all that old man Mercer does not have a quarter, and that he has no way of getting a quarter unless one of his terrible horses accidentally wins a purse. So," Herbie says, "it seems these jockeys get to talking it over among themselves, and they figure it will be a nice thing to let old man Mercer win a purse such as the thousand bucks that goes with the third race today, so he can take Lame Louise to Palm Beach, and now you have a rough idea of what is coming off.

"Furthermore," Herbie says, "these jockeys wind up their meeting by taking a big oath among themselves that they will not tell a living soul what is doing so nobody will bet on Never Despair, because," he says, "these little guys are smart enough to see if there is any betting on such a horse there may be a very large squawk afterwards. And," he says, "I judge they keep their oath because Never Despair is twenty to one in the morning line, and I do not hear a whisper about him, and you have the tip all to yourself."

"Well," I say, "so what?" For this story is now com-

mencing to make me a little tired, especially as I hear
the bell for the first race, and I must see Moe Shapoff.

"Why," Hot Horse Herbie says, "so you bet every
nickel you can rake and scrape together on Never Despair, including the twenty you are to bet for me for
giving you this tip and the story that goes with it."

"Herbie," I say, "it is a very interesting story indeed,
and also very sad, but," I say, "I am sorry it is about
a horse Jockey Scroon is to ride, because I do not think
I will ever bet on anything Jockey Scroon rides if they
pay off in advance. And," I say, "I am certainly not
going to bet twenty for you or anybody else."

"Well," Hot Horse Herbie says, "I will compromise
with you for a pound note, because I must have something going for me on this boat race."

So I give Herbie a fiver, and the chances are this is
about as strong as he figures from the start, and I forget
all about his tip and the story that goes with it, because
while I enjoy a story with a tip, I feel that Herbie over-
does this one.

Anyway, no handicapper alive can make Never Despair win the third race off the form, because this race
is at six furlongs, and there is a barrel of speed in it,
and anybody can see that old man Mercer's horse is
away over his head. In fact, The Dancer tells me that
any one of the other five horses in this race can beat
Never Despair doing anything from playing hockey to
putting the shot, and everybody else must think the
same thing because Never Despair goes to forty to one.

Personally, I like a horse by the name of Loose Living,
which is a horse owned by a guy by the name of Bill
Howard, and I hear Bill Howard is betting plenty away
on his horse, and any time Bill Howard is betting away
on his horse a guy will be out of his mind not to bet on
this horse, too, as Bill Howard is very smart indeed.

Loose Living is two to one in the first line, but by and by I judge the money Bill Howard bets away commences to come back to the track, and Loose Living winds up seven to ten, and while I am generally not a seven-to-ten guy, I can see that here is a proposition I cannot overlook.

So, naturally, I step up to the mutuel window and invest in Loose Living. In fact, I invest everything I have on me in the way of scratch, amounting to a hundred and ten bucks, which is all I have left after taking myself out of the hotel stakes and giving Hot Horse Herbie the finnif, and listening to what Moe Shapoff has to say about the first race, and also getting beat a snoot in the second.

When I first step up to the window, I have no idea of betting all my scratch on Loose Living, but while waiting in line there I get to thinking what a cinch Loose Living is, and how seldom such an opportunity comes into a guy's life, so I just naturally set it all in.

Well, this is a race which will be remembered by one and all to their dying day, as Loose Living beats the barrier a step, and is two lengths in front before you can say Jack Robinson, with a thing by the name of Callipers second by maybe half a length, and with the others bunched except Never Despair, and where is Never Despair but last, where he figures.

Now any time Loose Living busts on top there is no need worrying any more about him, and I am thinking I better get in line at the pay-off window right away, so I will not have to wait long to collect my sugar. But I figure I may as well stay and watch the race, although personally I am never much interested in watching races. I am interested only in how a race comes out.

As the horses hit the turn into the stretch, Loose Living is just breezing, and anybody can see that he is going to laugh his way home from there. Callipers is still second, and a thing called Goose Pimples is third, and I am surprised to see that Never Despair now struggles up to fourth with Jockey Scroon belting away at him with his bat quite earnestly. Furthermore, Never Despair seems to be running very fast, though afterwards I figure this may be because the others are commencing to run very slow.

Anyway, a very strange spectacle now takes place in the stretch, as all of a sudden Loose Living seems to be stopping, as if he is waiting for a street car, and what is all the more remarkable Callipers and Goose Pimples also seem to be hanging back, and the next thing anybody knows, here comes Jockey Scroon on Never Despair sneaking through on the rail, and personally it looks to me as if the jock on Callipers moves over to give Jockey Scroon plenty of elbow room, but of course the jock on Callipers may figure Jockey Scroon has diphtheria, and does not wish to catch it.

Loose Living is out in the middle of the track, anyway, so he does not have to move over. All Loose Living has to do is to keep on running backwards as he seems to be doing from the top of the stretch, to let Jockey Scroon go past on Never Despair to win the heat by a length.

Well, the race is practically supernatural in many respects, and the judges are all upset over it, and they haul all the jocks up in the stand and ask them many questions, and not being altogether satisfied with the answers, they ask these questions over several times. But all the jocks will say is that Never Despair sneaks past them very unexpectedly indeed, while Jockey Scroon, who is a pretty fresh duck at that, wishes to know if he is supposed to blow a horn when he is slipping through a lot of guys sound asleep.

But the judges are still not satisfied, so they go prowling around investigating the betting, because naturally when a boat race comes up there is apt to be some reason for it, such as the betting, but it seems that all the judges find is that one five-dollar win ticket is sold on Never Despair in the mutuels, and they cannot learn of a dime being bet away on the horse. So there is nothing much the judges can do about the proposition, except give the jocks many hard looks, and the jocks are accustomed to hard looks from the judges, anyway.

Personally, I am greatly upset by this business, especially when I see that Never Despair pays $86.34, and for two cents I will go right up in the stand and start hollering copper on these little Jesse Jameses for putting on such a boat race and taking all my hard-earned potatoes away from me, but before I have time to do this, I run into The Dancer, and he tells me that Dedicate in the next race is the surest thing that ever goes to the post, and at five to one, at that. So I have to forget everything while I bustle about to dig up a few bobs to bet on Dedicate, and when Dedicate is beat a whisker, I have to do some more bustling to dig up a few bobs to bet on Vesta in the fifth, and by this time the third race is such ancient history that nobody cares what happens in it.

It is nearly a week before I see Hot Horse Herbie again, and I figure he is hiding out on everybody because he has this dough he wins off the fiver I give him, and personally I consider him a guy with no manners not to be kicking back the fin, at least. But before I can mention the fin, Herbie gives me a big hello, and says to me like this:

"Well," he says, "I just see Jockey Scroon, and Jockey Scroon just comes back from Palm Beach, and the operation is a big success, and Lame Louise will walk as good as anybody again, and old Mercer is tickled silly. But,"

Herbie says, "do not say anything out loud, because the judges may still be trying to find out what comes off in the race."

"Herbie," I say, very serious, "do you mean to say the story you tell me about Lame Louise, and all this and that, the other day is on the level?"

"Why," Herbie says, "certainly it is on the level, and I am sorry to hear you do not take advantage of my information. But," he says, "I do not blame you for not believing my story, because it is a very long story for anybody to believe. It is not such a story," Herbie says, "as I will tell to any one if I expect them to believe it. In fact," he says, "it is so long a story that I do not have the heart to tell it to anybody else but you, or maybe I will have something running for me on the race.

"But," Herbie says, "never mind all this. I will be plenty smart about a race tomorrow. Yes," Herbie says, "I will be wiser than a treeful of owls, so be sure and see me if you happen to have any coconuts."

"There is no danger of me seeing you," I say, very sad, because I am all sorrowed up to think that the story he tells me is really true. "Things are very terrible with me at this time," I say, "and I am thinking maybe you can hand me back my finnif, because you must do all right for yourself with the fiver you have on Never Despair at such a price."

Now a very strange look comes over Hot Horse Herbie's face, and he raises his right hand, and says to me like this:

"I hope and trust I drop down dead right here in front of you," Herbie says, "if I bet a quarter on the horse. It is true," he says, "I am up at the window to buy a ticket on Never Despair, but the guy who is selling the tickets is a friend of mine by the name of Heeby

Rosenbloom, and Heeby whispers to me that Big Joe
Gompers, the guy who owns Callipers, just bets half a
hundred on his horse, and," Herbie says, "I know Joe
Gompers is such a guy as will not bet half a hundred
on anything he does not get a Federal Reserve guarantee
with it.

"Anyway," Herbie says, "I get to thinking about what
a bad jockey this Jockey Scroon is, which is very bad
indeed, and," he says, "I figure that even if it is a boat
race it is no even-money race they can shoo him in, so
I buy a ticket on Callipers."

"Well," I say, "somebody buys one five-dollar ticket
on Never Despair, and I figure it can be nobody but
you."

"Why," Hot Horse Herbie says, "do you not hear
about this? Why," he says, "Cap Duhaine, of the Pinkertons, traces this ticket and finds it is bought by a guy
by the name of Steve Harter, and the way this guy Harter comes to buy it is very astonishing. It seems," Herbie
says, "that this Harter is a tourist out of Indiana who
comes to Miami for the sunshine, and who loses all his
dough but six bucks against the faro bank at Hollywood.

"At the same time," Herbie says, "the poor guy gets
a telegram from his ever-loving doll back in Indiana
saying she no longer wishes any part of him.

"Well," Herbie says, "between losing his dough and
his doll, the poor guy is practically out of his mind,
and he figures there is nothing left for him to do but
knock himself off.

"So," Herbie says, "this Harter spends one of his six
bucks to get to the track, figuring to throw himself under
the feet of the horses in the first race and let them kick
him to a jelly. But he does not get there until just as
the third race is coming up and," Herbie says, "he sees
this name 'Never Despair,' and he figures it may be a

hunch, so he buys himself a ticket with his last fiver.
Well, naturally," Herbie says, "when Never Despair
pops down, the guy forgets about letting the horses kick
him to a jelly, and he keeps sending his dough along
until he runs nothing but a nubbin into six G's on
the day.

"Then," Herbie says, "Cap Duhaine finds out that
the guy, still thinking of Never Despair, calls his ever-
loving doll on the phone, and finds she is very sorry
she sends him the wire and that she really loves him
more than somewhat, especially," Herbie says, "when
she finds out about the six G's. And the last anybody
hears of the matter, this Harter is on his way home to
get married, so Never Despair does quite some good
in this wicked old world, after all.

"But," Herbie says, "let us forget all this, because
tomorrow is another day. Tomorrow," he says, "I will
tell you about a thing that goes in the fourth which is
just the same as wheat in the bin. In fact," Hot Horse
Herbie says, "if it does not win, you can never speak
to me again."

"Well," I say, as I start to walk away, "I am not interested in any tip at this time."

"Now," Herbie says, "wait a minute. A story goes
with it."

"Well," I say, coming back to him, "let me hear the
story."

Johnny One-Eye

THIS CAT I am going to tell you about is a very small cat, and in fact it is only a few weeks old, consequently it is really nothing but an infant cat. To tell the truth, it is just a kitten.

It is gray and white and very dirty and its fur is all frowzled up, so it is a very miserable-looking little kitten to be sure the day it crawls through a broken basement window into an old house in East Fifty-third Street over near Third Avenue in the city of New York and goes from room to room saying mer-ow, mer-ow in a low, weak voice until it comes to a room at the head of the stairs on the second story where a guy by the name of Rudolph is sitting on the floor thinking of not much.

One reason Rudolph is sitting on the floor is because there is nothing else to sit on as this is an empty house that is all boarded up for years and there is no furniture whatever in it, and another reason is that Rudolph has a .38 slug in his side and really does not feel like doing much of anything but sitting. He is wearing a derby hat and his overcoat as it is in the wintertime and very cold and he has an automatic Betsy on the floor beside him and naturally he is surprised quite some when the little kitten comes mer-owing into the room and he picks up the Betsy and points it at the door in case anyone he does not wish to see is with the kitten. But when he observes that it is all alone, Rudolph puts the Betsy down again and speaks to the kitten as follows:

"Hello, cat," he says.

Of course the kitten does not say anything in reply except mer-ow but it walks right up to Rudolph and climbs on his lap, although the chances are if it knows who Rudolph is, it will hightail it out of there quicker than anybody can say scat. There is enough daylight coming through the chinks in the boards over the windows for Rudolph to see that the kitten's right eye is in bad shape, and in fact it is bulged half out of its head in a most distressing manner and it is plain to be seen that the sight is gone from this eye. It is also plain to be seen that the injury happens recently and Rudolph gazes at the kitten a while and starts to laugh and says like this:

"Well, cat," he says, "you seem to be scuffed up almost as much as I am. We make a fine pair of invalids here together. What is your name, cat?"

Naturally the kitten does not state its name but only goes mer-ow and Rudolph says, "All right, I will call you Johnny. Yes," he says, "your tag is now Johnny One-Eye."

Then he puts the kitten in under his overcoat and pretty soon it gets warm and starts to purr and Rudolph says:

"Johnny," he says, "I will say one thing for you and that is you are plenty game to be able to sing when you are hurt as bad as you are. It is more than I can do."

But Johnny only goes mer-ow again and keeps on purring and by and by it falls sound asleep under Rudolph's coat, and Rudolph is wishing the pain in his side will let up long enough for him to do the same.

Well, I suppose you are saying to yourself, what is this Rudolph doing in an old empty house with a slug in his side, so I will explain that the district attorney is responsible for this situation. It seems that the D.A. appears before the grand jury and tells it that Rudolph is an extortion guy and a killer and I do not know what all else, though some of these statements are without doubt a great injustice to Rudolph as, up to the time the D.A. makes them, Rudolph does not kill anybody of any consequence in years.

It is true that at one period of his life he is considered a little wild but this is in the 1920's when everybody else is, too, and for seven or eight years he is all settled down and is engaged in business organization work, which is very respectable work, indeed. He organizes quite a number of businesses on a large scale and is doing very good for himself. He is living quietly in a big hotel all alone, as Rudolph is by no means a family guy, and he is highly spoken of by one and all when the D.A. starts poking his nose into his affairs, claiming that Rudolph has no right to be making money out of the businesses, even though Rudolph gives these businesses plenty of first-class protection.

In fact, the D.A. claims that Rudolph is nothing but a racket guy and a great knock to the community, and all this upsets Rudolph no little when it comes to his ears in a roundabout way. So he calls up his lawbooks and requests legal advice on the subject, and lawbooks says the best thing he can think of for Rudolph to do is to become as inconspicuous as possible right away but to please not mention to anyone that he gives this advice.

Lawbooks says he understands the D.A. is requesting indictments and is likely to get them and furthermore that he is rounding up certain parties that Rudolph is once associated with and trying to get them to remember incidents in Rudolph's early career that may not be entirely to his credit. Lawbooks says he hears that one of these parties is a guy by the name of Cute Freddy and that Freddy makes a deal with the D.A. to lay off of him if he tells everything he knows about Rudolph, so under the circumstances a long journey by Rudolph will be in the interest of everybody concerned.

So Rudolph decides to go on a journey but then he gets to thinking that maybe Freddy will remember a little matter that Rudolph long since dismisses from his mind and does not wish to have recalled again, which is the time he and Freddy do a job on a guy by the name of The Icelander in Troy years ago and he drops around to Freddy's house to remind him to be sure not to remember this.

But it seems that Freddy, who is an important guy in business organization work himself, though in a different part of the city than Rudolph, mistakes the purpose of Rudolph's visit and starts to out with his rooty-toot-toot, and in order to protect himself it is necessary for Rudolph to take his Betsy and give Freddy a little tattooing. In fact, Rudolph practically crochets his monogram on Freddy's chest and leaves him exceptionally deceased.

But as Rudolph is departing from the neighborhood, who bobs up but a young guy by the name of Buttsy Fagan, who works for Freddy as a chauffeur and one thing and another, and who is also said to be able to put a slug through a keyhole at forty paces without touching the sides, though I suppose it will have to be a pretty good-sized keyhole. Anyway, he takes a long-distance crack at Rudolph as Rudolph is rounding a corner but all Buttsy can see of Rudolph at the moment is a little piece of his left side and this is what Buttsy hits, although no one knows it at the time, except of course Rudolph, who just keeps on departing.

Now this incident causes quite a stir in police circles, and the D.A. is very indignant over losing a valuable witness, and when they are unable to locate Rudolph at once, a reward of five thousand dollars is offered for information leading to his capture alive or dead and some think they really mean dead. Indeed, it is publicly stated that it is not a good idea for anyone to take any chances with Rudolph as he is known to be armed and is such a character as will be sure to resent being captured, but they do not explain that this is only because Rudolph knows the D.A. wishes to place him in the old rocking chair at Sing Sing and that Rudolph is quite allergic to the idea.

Anyway, the cops go looking for Rudolph in Hot Springs and Miami and every other place except where he is, which is right in New York wandering around town with the slug in his side, knocking at the doors of old friends requesting assistance. But all the old friends do for him is to slam the doors in his face and forget they ever see him, as the D.A. is very tough on parties who assist guys he is looking for, claiming that this is something most illegal called harboring fugitives. Besides Rudolph is never any too popular at best with his old friends as he always plays pretty much of a lone duke and takes the big end of everything for his.

He cannot even consult a doctor about the slug in his side as he knows that nowadays the first thing a doctor will do about a guy with a gunshot wound is to report him to the cops, although Rudolph can remember when there is always a sure-footed doctor around who will consider it a privilege and a pleasure to treat him and keep his trap closed about it. But of course this is in the good old days and Rudolph can see they are gone forever. So he just does the best he can about the slug and goes on wandering here and there and around and about and the blats keep printing his picture and saying, Where is Rudolph?

Where he is some of the time is in Central Park trying to get some sleep, but of course even the blats will consider it foolish to go looking for Rudolph there in such cold weather, as he is known as a guy who enjoys his comfort at all times. In fact, it is comfort that Rudolph misses more than anything as the slug is commencing to cause him great pain and naturally the pain turns Rudolph's thoughts to the author of same and he remembers that he once hears somebody say that Buttsy lives over in East Fifty-third Street.

So one night Rudolph decides to look Buttsy up and cause him a little pain in return, and he is moseying through Fifty-third when he gets so weak he falls down on the sidewalk in front of the old house and rolls down a short flight of steps that lead from the street level to a little railed-in areaway and ground floor or basement door, and before he stops rolling he brings up against the door itself and it creaks open inward as he bumps it. After he lays there a while Rudolph can see that the house is empty and he crawls on inside.

Then, when he feels stronger, Rudolph makes his way upstairs because the basement is damp and mice keep trotting back and forth over him and eventually he winds up in the room where Johnny One-Eye finds him the following afternoon, and the reason Rudolph settles down in this room is because it commands the stairs. Naturally, this is important to a guy in Rudolph's situation, though after he is sitting there for about fourteen hours before Johnny comes along he can see that he is not going to be much disturbed by traffic. But he considers it a very fine place, indeed, to remain planted until he is able to resume his search for Buttsy.

Well, after a while Johnny One-Eye wakes up and comes from under the coat and looks at Rudolph out of his good eye and Rudolph waggles his fingers and Johnny plays with them, catching one finger in his front paws and biting it gently and this pleases Rudolph no little as he never before has any personal experience with a kitten. However, he remembers observing one when he is a boy down in Houston Street, so he takes a piece of paper out of his pocket and makes a little ball of it and rolls it along the floor and Johnny bounces after it very lively indeed. But Rudolph can see that the bad eye is getting worse and finally he says to Johnny like this:

"Johnny," he says, "I guess you must be suffering more than I am. I remember there are some pet shops over on Lexington Avenue not far from here and when it gets good and dark I am going to take you out and see if we can find a cat croaker to do something about your eye. Yes, Johnny," Rudolph says, "I will also get you something to eat. You must be starved."

Johnny One-Eye says mer-ow to this and keeps on playing with the paper ball but soon it comes on dark outside and inside, too, and, in fact, it is so dark inside that Rudolph cannot see his hand before him. Then he puts his Betsy in a side pocket of his overcoat and picks up Johnny and goes downstairs, feeling his way in the dark and easing along a step at a time until he gets to the basement door. Naturally, Rudolph does not wish to strike any matches because he is afraid someone outside may see the light and get nosey.

By moving very slowly, Rudolph finally gets to Lexington Avenue and while he is going along he remembers the time he walks from 125th Street in Harlem down to 110th with six slugs in him and never feels as bad as he does now. He gets to thinking that maybe he is not the guy he used to be, which of course is very true, as Rudolph is now forty-odd years of age and is fat around the middle and getting bald, and he also does some thinking about what a pleasure it will be to him to find this Buttsy and cause him the pain he is personally suffering.

There are not many people in the streets and those that are go hurrying along because it is so cold and none of them pay any attention to Rudolph or Johnny One-Eye either, even though Rudolph staggers a little now and then like a guy who is rummed up, although of course it is only weakness. The chances are he is also getting a little feverish and light-headed because finally he stops a cop who is going along swinging his arms to keep warm and asks him if he knows where there is a pet shop, and it is really most indiscreet of such a guy as Rudolph to be interviewing cops. But the cop just points up the street and goes on without looking twice at Rudolph and Rudolph laughs and pokes Johnny with a finger and says:

"No, Johnny One-Eye," he says, "the cop is not a dope for not recognizing Rudolph. Who can figure the hottest guy in forty-eight states to be going along a street with a little cat in his arms? Can you, Johnny?"

Johnny says mer-ow and pretty soon Rudolph comes to the pet shop the cop points out. Rudolph goes inside and says to the guy like this:

"Are you a cat croaker?" Rudolph says. "Do you know what to do about a little cat that has a hurt eye?"

"I am a kind of a vet," the guy says.

"Then take a glaum at Johnny One-Eye here and see what you can do for him," Rudolph says.

Then he hands Johnny over to the guy and the guy looks at Johnny a while and says:

"Mister," he says, "the best thing I can do for this cat is to put it out of its misery. You better let me give it something right now. It will just go to sleep and never know what happens."

Well, at this, Rudolph grabs Johnny One-Eye out of the guy's hands and puts him under his coat and drops a duke on the Betsy in his pocket as if he is afraid the guy will take Johnny away from him again and he says to the guy like this:

"No, no, no," Rudolph says. "I cannot bear to think of such a thing. What about some kind of an operation? I remember they take a bum lamp out of Joe the Goat at Bellevue one time and he is okay now."

"Nothing will do your cat any good," the guy says. "It is a goner. It will start having fits pretty soon and die sure. What is the idea of trying to save such a cat as this? It is no kind of a cat to begin with. It is just a cat. You can get a million like it for a nickel."

"No," Rudolph says, "this is not just a cat. This is Johnny One-Eye. He is my only friend in the world. He is the only living thing that ever comes pushing up against me warm and friendly and trusts me in my whole life. I feel sorry for him."

"I feel sorry for him, too," the guy says. "I always feel sorry for animals that get hurt and for people."

"I do not feel sorry for people," Rudolph says. "I only feel sorry for Johnny One-Eye. Give me some kind of stuff that Johnny will eat."

"Your cat wants milk," the guy says. "You can get some at the delicatessen store down at the corner. Mister," he says, "you look sick yourself. Can I do anything for you?"

But Rudolph only shakes his head and goes on out and down to the delicatessen joint where he buys a bottle of milk and this transaction reminds him that he is very short in the moo department. In fact, he can find only a five-dollar note in his pockets and he remembers that he has no way of getting any more when this runs out, which is a very sad predicament indeed for a guy who is accustomed to plenty of moo at all times.

Then Rudolph returns to the old house and sits down on the floor again and gives Johnny One-Eye some of the milk in his derby hat as he neglects buying something for Johnny to drink out of. But Johnny offers no complaint. He laps up the milk and curls himself into a wad in Rudolph's lap and purrs.

Rudolph takes a swig of the milk himself but it makes him sick, for by this time Rudolph is really far from being in the pink of condition. He not only has the pain in his side but he has a heavy cold which he probably catches from lying on the basement floor or maybe sleeping in the park and he is wheezing no little. He commences to worry that he may get too ill to continue looking for Buttsy, as he can see that if it is not for Buttsy he will not be in this situation, suffering the way he is, but on a long journey to some place.

He takes to going off into long stretches of a kind of stupor and every time he comes out of one of these stupors the first thing he does is to look around for Johnny One-Eye and Johnny is always right there either playing with the paper ball or purring in Rudolph's lap. He is a great comfort to Rudolph but after a while Rudolph notices that Johnny seems to be running out of zip and he also notices that he is running out of zip himself especially when he discovers that he is no longer able to get to his feet.

It is along in the late afternoon of the day following the night Rudolph goes out of the house that he hears someone coming up the stairs and naturally he picks up his Betsy and gets ready for action when he also hears a very small voice calling kitty, kitty, kitty, and he realizes that the party that is coming can be nobody but a child. In fact, a minute later a little pretty of maybe six years of age comes into the room all out of breath and says to Rudolph like this:

"How do you do?" she says. "Have you seen my kitty?"

Then she spots Johnny One-Eye in Rudolph's lap and runs over and sits down beside Rudolph and takes Johnny in her arms, and at first Rudolph is inclined to resent this and has a notion to give her a good boffing but he is too weak to exert himself in such a manner.

"Who are you?" Rudolph says to the little pretty, "and," he says, "where do you live and how do you get in this house?"

"Why," she says, "I am Elsie, and I live down the street and I am looking everywhere for my kitty for three days and the door is open downstairs and I know kitty likes to go in doors that are open so I came to find her and here she is."

"I guess I forgot to close it last night," Rudolph says. "I seem to be very forgetful lately."

"What is your name?" Elsie asks, "and why are you sitting on the floor in the cold and where are all your chairs? Do you have any little girls like me and do you love them dearly?"

"No," Rudolph says. "By no means and not at all."

"Well," Elsie says, "I think you are a nice man for taking care of my kitty. Do you love kitty?"

"Look," Rudolph says, "his name is not kitty. His name is Johnny One-Eye, because he has only one eye."

"I call her kitty," Elsie says. "But," she says, "Johnny One-Eye is a nice name too and if you like it best I will call her Johnny and I will leave her here with you to take care of always and I will come to see her every day. You see," she says, "if I take Johnny home Buttsy will only kick her again."

"Buttsy?" Rudolph says. "Do I hear you say Buttsy? Is his other name Fagan?"

"Why, yes," Elsie says. "Do you know him?"

"No," Rudolph says, "but I hear of him. What is he to you?"

"He is my new daddy," Elsie says. "My other one and my best one is dead and so my mamma makes Buttsy my new one. My mamma says Buttsy is her mistake. He is very mean. He kicks Johnny and hurts her eye and makes her run away. He kicks my mamma too. Buttsy kicks everybody and everything when he is mad and he is always mad."

"He is a louse to kick a little cat," Rudolph says.

"Yes," Elsie says, "that is what Mr. O'Toole says he is for kicking my mamma but my mamma says it is not a nice word and I am never to say it out loud."

"Who is Mr. O'Toole?" Rudolph says.

"He is the policeman," Elsie says. "He lives across the street from us and he is very nice to me. He says Buttsy is the word you say just now, not only for kicking my mamma but for taking her money when she brings it home from work and spending it so she cannot buy me nice things to wear. But do you know what?" Elsie says. "My mamma says some day Buttsy is going far away and then she will buy me lots of things and send me to school and make me a lady."

Then Elsie begins skipping around the room with Johnny One-Eye in her arms and singing I am going

to be a lady, I am going to be a lady, until Rudolph
has to tell her to pipe down because he is afraid somebody may hear her. And all the time Rudolph is thinking
of Buttsy and regretting that he is unable to get on
his pins and go out of the house.

"Now I must go home," Elsie says, "because this is
a night Buttsy comes in for his supper and I have to
be in bed before he gets there so I will not bother him.
Buttsy does not like little girls. Buttsy does not like
little kittens. Buttsy does not like little anythings. My
mamma is afraid of Buttsy and so am I. But," she says,
"I will leave Johnny here with you and come back tomorrow to see her."

"Listen, Elsie," Rudolph says, "does Mr. O'Toole
come home tonight to his house for his supper, too?"

"Oh, yes," Elsie says. "He comes home every night.
Sometimes when there is a night Buttsy is not coming
in for his supper my mamma lets me go over to Mr.
O'Toole's and I play with his dog Charley but you must
never tell Buttsy this because he does not like O'Toole
either. But this is a night Buttsy is coming and that is
why my mamma tells me to get in early."

Now Rudolph takes an old letter out of his inside
pocket and a pencil out of another pocket and he scrib-
bles a few lines on the envelope and stretches himself
out on the floor and begins groaning oh, oh, oh, and
then he says to Elsie like this:

"Look, Elsie," he says, "you are a smart little kid and
you pay strict attention to what I am going to say to
you. Do not go to bed tonight until Buttsy gets in.
Then," Rudolph says, "you tell him you come in this
old house looking for your cat and that you hear somebody groaning like I do just now in the room at the
head of the stairs and that you find a guy who says
his name is Rudolph lying on the floor so sick he cannot

move. Tell him the front door of the basement is open. But," Rudolph says, "you must not tell him that Rudolph tells you to say these things. Do you understand?"

"Oh," Elsie says, "do you want him to come here? He will kick Johnny again if he does."

"He will come here, but he will not kick Johnny," Rudolph says. "He will come here, or I am the worst guesser in the world. Tell him what I look like, Elsie. Maybe he will ask you if you see a gun. Tell him you do not see one. You do not see a gun, do you, Elsie?"

"No," Elsie says, "only the one in your hand when I come in but you put it under your coat. Buttsy has a gun and Mr. O'Toole has a gun but Buttsy says I am never, never to tell anybody about this or he will kick me the way he does my mamma."

"Well," Rudolph says, "you must not remember seeing mine, either. It is a secret between you and me and Johnny One-Eye. Now," he says, "if Buttsy leaves the house to come and see me, as I am pretty sure he will, you run over to Mr. O'Toole's house and give him this note, but do not tell Buttsy or your mamma either about the note. If Buttsy does not leave, it is my hard luck but you give the note to Mr. O'Toole anyway. Now tell me what you are to do, Elsie," Rudolph says, "so I can see if you have got everything correct."

"I am to go on home and wait for Buttsy," she says, "and I am to tell him Rudolph is lying on the floor of this dirty old house with a fat stomach and a big nose making noises and that he is very sick and the basement door is open and there is no gun if he asks me, and when Buttsy comes to see you I am to take this note to Mr. O'Toole but Buttsy and my mamma are not to know I have the note and if Buttsy does not leave I am to give it to Mr. O'Toole anyway and you are to stay here and take care of Johnny my kitten."

"That is swell," Rudolph says. "Now you run along."

So Elsie leaves and Rudolph sits up again against the wall because his side feels easier this way and Johnny One-Eye is in his lap purring very low and the dark comes on until it is blacker inside the room than in the middle of a tunnel and Rudolph feels that he is going into another stupor and he has a tough time fighting it off.

Afterward some of the neighbors claim they remember hearing a shot inside the house and then two more in quick succession and then all is quiet until a little later when Officer O'Toole and half a dozen other cops and an ambulance with a doctor come busting into the street and swarm into the joint with their guns out and their flashlights going. The first thing they find is Buttsy at the foot of the stairs with two bullet wounds close together in his throat, and naturally he is real dead.

Rudolph is still sitting against the wall with what seems to be a small bundle of bloody fur in his lap but which turns out to be what is left of this little cat I am telling you about, although nobody pays any attention to it at first. They are more interested in getting the come-alongs on Rudolph's wrists, but before they move him he pulls his clothes aside and shows the doctor where the slug is in his side and the doctor takes one glaum and shakes his head and says:

"Gangrene," he says. "I think you have pneumonia, too, from the way you are blowing."

"I know," Rudolph says. "I know this morning. Not much chance, hey, croaker?"

"Not much," the doctor says.

"Well, cops," Rudolph says, "load me in. I do not suppose you want Johnny, seeing that he is dead."

"Johnny who?" one of the cops says.

"Johnny One-Eye," Rudolph says. "This little cat here in my lap. Buttsy shoots Johnny's only good eye out and takes most of his noodle with it. I never see a more wonderful shot. Well, Johnny is better off but I feel sorry about him as he is my best friend down to the last."

Then he begins to laugh and the cop asks him what tickles him so much and Rudolph says:

"Oh," he says, "I am thinking of the joke on Buttsy. I am positive he will come looking for me, all right, not only because of the little altercation between Cute Freddy and me but because the chances are Buttsy is greatly embarrassed by not tilting me over the first time, as of course he never knows he wings me. Furthermore," Rudolph says, "and this is the best reason of all, Buttsy will realize that if I am in his neighborhood it is by no means a good sign for him, even if he hears I am sick.

"Well," Rudolph says, "I figure that with any kind of a square rattle I will have a better chance of nailing him than he has of nailing me, but that even if he happens to nail me, O'Toole will get my note in time to arrive here and nab Buttsy on the spot with his gun on him. And," Rudolph says, "I know it will be a great pleasure to the D.A. to settle Buttsy for having a gun on him.

"But," Rudolph says, "as soon as I hear Buttsy coming on the sneaksby up the stairs, I can see I am taking all the worst of it because I am now wheezing like a busted valve and you can hear me a block away except when I hold my breath, which is very difficult indeed, considering the way I am already greatly tuckered out. No," Rudolph says, "it does not look any too good for me as Buttsy keeps coming up the stairs, as I can tell he is doing by a little faint creak in the boards now and then. I am in no shape to maneuver around the room and pretty soon he will be on the landing and then all he will have to do is to wait there until he hears me which he is bound to do unless I stop breathing altogether. Naturally," Rudolph says, "I do not care to risk a blast in the dark without knowing where he is, as something tells me Buttsy is not a guy you can miss in safety.

"Well," Rudolph says, "I notice several times before this that in the dark Johnny One-Eye's good glim shines like a big spark, so when I feel Buttsy is about to hit the landing, although of course I cannot see him, I flip Johnny's ball of paper across the room to the wall just opposite the door, and tough as he must be feeling Johnny chases after it when he hears it light. I figure Buttsy will hear Johnny playing with the paper and see his eye shining and think it is me and take a pop at it and that his gun flash will give me a crack at him.

"It all works out just like I dope it," Rudolph says, "but," he says, "I never give Buttsy credit for being such a marksman as to be able to hit a cat's eye in the dark. If I know this, maybe I will never stick Johnny out in front the way I do. It is a good thing I never give Buttsy a second shot. He is a lily. Yes," Rudolph says, "I can remember when I can use a guy like him."

"Buttsy is no account," the cop says. "He is a good riddance. He is the makings of a worse guy than you."

"Well," Rudolph says, "it is a good lesson to him for kicking a little cat."

Then they take Rudolph to a hospital and this is where I see him and piece out this story of Johnny One-Eye, and Officer O'Toole is at Rudolph's bedside keeping guard over him, and I remember that not long before Rudolph chalks out he looks at O'Toole and says to him like this:

"Copper," he says, "there is no chance of them outjuggling the kid on the reward moo, is there?"

"No," O'Toole says, "no chance. I keep the note you send me by Elsie saying she will tell me where you are. It is information leading to your capture just as the reward offer states. Rudolph," he says, "it is a nice thing you do for Elsie and her mother, although," he says, "it is not nearly as nice as icing Buttsy for them."

"By the way, copper," Rudolph says, "there is the remainders of a pound note in my pants pocket when I am brought here. I want you to do me a favor. Get it from the desk and buy Elsie another cat and name it Johnny, will you?"

"Sure," O'Toole says. "Anything else?"

"Yes," Rudolph says, "be sure it has two good eyes."

The Melancholy Dane

IT IS A MATTER of maybe two years back that I run into
Ambrose Hammer, the newspaper scribe, one evening
on Broadway and he requests me to attend the theater
with him, as Ambrose is what is called a dramatic critic
and his racket is to witness all the new plays and write
what he thinks about them in a morning blat.

I often hear the actors and the guys who write the
plays talking about Ambrose in Mindy's restaurant
when they get the last edition and read what he has
to say, and as near as I can make out, they feel that
he is nothing but a low criminal type because it seems
that Ambrose practically murders one and all connected
with any new play. So I say to him like this:

"No, Ambrose," I say, "I may happen to know the
guy who writes the play you are going to see, or one
of the actors, and as I understand it is always about
nine to five that you will put the blister on a new play,
I will be running the risk of hurting myself socially

along Broadway. Furthermore," I say, "where is Miss
Channelle Cooper who accompanies you to the new
plays for the past six months hand-running?"

"Oh," Ambrose says, "you need not worry about the
guy who writes this play, as his name is Shakespeare
and he is dead quite a spell. You need not worry about
any of the actors, either, as they are just a bunch of
plumbers that no one ever hears of before, except maybe
the leading one who has some slight notoriety. And,
as for Miss Channelle Cooper, I do not know where
she is at this particular moment and, not to give you
a short answer, I do not give a D and an A and an M
and an N."

"Why, Ambrose," I say, "the last time we meet, you
tell me that you are on fire with love for Miss Channelle
Cooper, although, of course," I say, "you are on fire
with love for so many different broads since I know
you that I am surprised you are not reduced to ashes
long ago."

"Look," Ambrose says, "let us not discuss such a tender subject as Miss Cooper at this time or I am apt to
break into tears and be in no mood to impartially per-
form my stern duty toward this play. All I know is
she sends me a letter by messenger this morning, stating
that she cannot see me tonight because her grandmother's diabetes is worse and she has to go to Yonkers to
see her.

"And," Ambrose goes on, "I happen to know that
in the first place her grandmother does not have diabetes
but only a tumor, and in the second place she does not
live in Yonkers but in Greenwich Village, and in the
third place Miss Cooper is seen late this afternoon having tea at the Plaza with an eighteen-carat hambola by
the name of Mansfield Sothern. I wonder," Ambrose
says, "if the bim is ever born who can tell the truth?"

"No, Ambrose," I say, "or anyway not yet. But," I say, "I am surprised to hear Miss Cooper turns out unstable, as she always strikes me as the reliable sort and very true to you, or at least as true as you can expect these days. In fact," I say, "I have it on good authority that she turns down Lefty Lyons, the slot-machine king, who offers to take charge of her career and buy a night club for her. But of course Mansfield Sothern is something else again. I often enjoy his comedy on the stage."

"He is a hunk of Smithfield who steals the names of two great actors to make one for himself," Ambrose says. "I will admit that he is sometimes endurable in musical comedy, if you close your eyes when he is on the boards and make believe he is somebody else, but, like all actors, he is egotistical enough to think he can play Hamlet. In fact," Ambrose says, "he is going to do it tonight and I can scarcely wait."

Well, I finally go to the theater with Ambrose and it is quite a high-toned occasion with nearly everybody in the old thirteen-and-odd because Mansfield Sothern has a big following in musical comedy and it seems that his determination to play Hamlet produces quite a sensation, though Ambrose claims that most of those present are members of Mansfield's personal claque from café society and he also claims that it is all nothing but a plot to make Mansfield seem important.

Personally, I am not a Shakespeare man, although I see several of his plays before and, to tell you the truth, I am never able to savvy them, though naturally I do not admit this in public as I do not wish to appear unintelligent. But I stick with Ambrose through the first act of this one and I observe that Mansfield Sothern is at least a right large Hamlet and has a voice that makes him sound as if he is talking from down in a coal mine, though what he is talking about is not clear to me and consequently does not arouse my interest.

So as Ambrose seems very thoughtful and paying no attention to me, I quietly take my departure and go to Mindy's where some hours later along in the early morning, I notice Miss Channelle Cooper and this gee Mansfield Sothern reading Ambrose's column, and Mansfield is shedding tears on the paper until the printer's ink runs down into his bacon and eggs. Naturally, I go out and buy a paper at once to see what causes his distress and I find that Ambrose writes about the play as follows:

"After Mansfield Sothern's performance of Hamlet at the Todd Theater last night, there need no longer be controversy as to the authorship of the immortal drama. All we need do is examine the graves of Shakespeare and Bacon, and the one that has turned over is it."

Now I do not clap eyes on Ambrose Hammer again until the other evening when he enters Mindy's at dinnertime, walking with a cane and gimping slightly. Furthermore, he is no longer roly-poly, but quite thin and he gives me a huge hello and sits down at my table and speaks to me as follows:

"Well, well," Ambrose says, "this is indeed a coincidence. The last time we meet I take you to a theater and now I am going to take you again on my first night back in harness. How is the *gedemte brust* and the *latkas* you are devouring?"

"The *latkas* are all right, Ambrose," I say, "but the *brust* is strictly second run. The war conditions are such that we must now take what we can get, even when it comes to *brust*. I do not see you for a spell, Ambrose. Are you absent from the city and why are you packing the stick?"

"Why," Ambrose says, "I am overseas and I am wounded in North Africa. Do you mean to tell me I am not missed in these parts?"

"Well, Ambrose," I say, "now that you mention it,

I do remember hearing you are mixed up in the war business, but we are so busy missing other personalities that we do not get around to missing you as yet. And as for going to the theater with you, I must pass, because the last time you steer me up against a most unenjoyable evening. By the way, Ambrose," I say, "I wonder what ever becomes of that bloke Mansfield Sothern and Miss Channelle Cooper. And what are you doing in North Africa, anyway?"

I am in North Africa (Ambrose says) risking my life for my paper as a war correspondent because one day my editor calls me into his office and speaks to me as follows:

"Hammer," he says, "kindly go to the front and send us back human-interest stories about our soldiers. Our soldiers are what our readers are interested in. Please eat with them and sleep with them and tell us how they live and what they think about and how they talk and so forth and so on."

So I go to London, and from London, I go to North Africa on a transport, and on this voyage I endeavor to start following my instructions at once, but I find that eating with the soldiers has its disadvantages as they can eat much faster than I can because of their greater experience and I am always getting shut out on the choicer tidbits.

And when I ask one of them if I can sleep with him, he gives me a strange look, and afterward I have a feeling that I am the subject of gossip among these gees. Furthermore, when I try to listen in on their conversation to learn how they talk, some of them figure I am a stool pigeon for the officers and wish to dunk me in the ocean. It is by no means a soft touch to be a war correspondent who is supposed to find out how the soldiers live and how they talk and what they think about, and when I mention my difficulties to one of the officers, he says I may get closer to the boys if I enlist, but naturally I figure this will be carrying war correspondenting too far.

But I write these human-interest stories just the same and I think they are pretty good even if I do hear a guy in the censor's office call me the poor man's Quentin Reynolds, and I always mingle with the soldiers as much as possible to get their atmosphere and finally when they learn I am kindly disposed toward them and generally have plenty of cigarettes, they become quite friendly.

I am sorry I do not have time to tell you a great deal about my terrible personal experiences at the front, but I am putting them all in the book I am writing, and you can buy a copy of it later. In fact, I have enough terrible experiences for three books, only my publisher states that he thinks one book per war correspondent is sufficient for the North African campaign. He says that the way correspondents are writing books on North Africa with Sicily and Italy coming up, he does not figure his paper supply to last the war out.

I first arrive at a place called Algiers in North Africa and I find it is largely infested by Arabs and naturally I feel at home at once, as in my younger days in show business, when I am working for a booking office, I personally book a wonderful Arab acrobatic troop consisting of a real Arab by the name of Punchy, two guys by the name of O'Shea, and a waffle who is known as Little Oran, though her square monicker is really Magnolia Shapiro.

Consequently, I have great sentiment for Arabs, and the sights and scenes and smells of Algiers keep me thinking constantly of the good old days, especially the smells. But I will not tax your patience with the details of my stay in Algiers because, by the time I reach there, the war moves away off to a place called Tunisia and I am willing to let it stay there without my presence. Then, after a week, my editor sends me a sharp message asking why I am not at the front getting human-interest stories instead of loitering in Algiers wasting my time on some tamale, although, as a matter of fact, I am not wasting my time. And how he learns about the tamale I have no idea, as she does not speak a word of English.

However, one way and another I proceed to a place called Bone and then I continue on from there one way and another, but mostly in a little consumptive car, in the general direction of Tunis, and as I go, I keep asking passing British and American soldiers where is the front. And they say the front is up front, and I keep going and in my travels I get very sick and tired of the war because the enemy is always dropping hot apples all over the landscape out of planes, and sprinkling the roads with bullets or throwing big shells that make the most uncouth noises around very carelessly indeed.

Naturally, this impedes and delays my progress quite some because, from time to time, I am compelled to pause and dismount from my little bucket and seek refuge from these missiles in holes in the earth, and, when I cannot find a hole, I seek the refuge by falling on my face on the ground. In fact, I fall so often on my face that I am commencing to fear I will wind up with a pug nose.

Part of the time I am traveling with another newspaper scribe by the name of Herbert something, but he goes to Foldsville on me soon after we leave Bone, with a case of heartburn caused by eating Army rations, which reminds me that I must speak to the F.B.I. about these rations some day as it is my opinion that the books of the guy who invents them should be looked over to see which side he is betting on.

Well, all the time I keep asking where is the front, and all the time the soldiers say the front is up front. But I do not seem to ever find the front and, in fact, I later learn from an old soldier that nobody ever finds the front because by the time they get to where it ought to be, the front is apt to be the rear or the middle, and it is all very confusing to be sure.

Early one morning, I arrive at what seems to be the ruins of a little town, and at the same moment, an enemy battery on a hill a couple of miles away starts throwing big biscuits into the town, although I do not see hide or hair of anyone there, and whether it is because they think some of our troops are in the town or just have a personal grudge against me, I never learn.

Anyway, all of a sudden something nudges my little wagon from under me and knocks it into pieces the size of confetti and at the same moment I feel a distinct sensation of pain in my Francesca. It comes to my mind that I am wounded and I lie there with what I know is blood running down the inside of my pants leg which gives me a most untidy feeling, indeed, and what is more, I am mentally depressed quite some as I am already behind with my copy and I can see where this will delay me further and cause my editor to become most peevish.

But there is nothing I can do about it, only to keep on lying there and to try to stop the blood as best I can and wait for something to happen and also to hope that my mishap does not inconvenience my editor too greatly.

It is coming on noon, and all around and about it is very quiet, and nothing whatever seems to be stirring anywhere when who appears but a big guy in our uniform, and he seems more surprised than somewhat when he observes me, as he speaks to me as follows:

"Goodness me!" he says. "What is this?"

"I am wounded," I say.

"Where?" he says.

"In the vestibule," I say.

Then he drops on one knee beside me and outs with a knife and cuts open my pants and looks at the wound, and as he gets to his feet, he says to me like this:

"Does it hurt?" he says. "Are you suffering greatly?"

"Sure I am," I say. "I am dying."

Now the guy laughs ha-ha-ha-ha, as if he just hears a good joke and he says, "Look at me, Hammer," he says. "Do you not recognize me?"

Naturally I look and I can see that he is nobody but this Mansfield Sothern, the actor, and of course I am greatly pleased at the sight of him.

"Mansfield," I say, "I am never so glad to see an old friend in my life."

"What do you mean by old friend?" Mansfield says. "I am not your old friend. I am not even your new friend. Hammer," he says, "are you really in great pain?"

"Awful," I say. "Please get me to a doctor."

Well, at this, he laughs ha-ha-ha-ha again and says, "Hammer, all my professional life, I am hoping to one day see a dramatic critic suffer, and you have no idea what pleasure you are now giving me, but I think it only fair for you to suffer out loud with groans and one thing and another. Hammer," Mansfield says, "I am enjoying a privilege that any actor will give a squillion dollars to experience."

"Look, Mansfield," I say, "kindly cease your clowning and take me somewhere. I am in great agony."

"Ha-ha-ha-ha," Mansfield Sothern ha-has. "Hammer, I cannot get you to a doctor because the Jeremiahs seem to be between us and our lines. I fear they nab the rest of my patrol. It is only by good luck that I elude them myself and then, lo and behold, I find you. I do not think there are any of the enemy right around this spot at the moment and I am going to lug you into yonder building, but it is not because I take pity on you. It is only because I wish to keep you near me so I can see you suffer."

Then he picks me up in his arms and carries me inside the walls of what seems to be an old inn, though it has no roof and no windows or doors, and even the walls are a little shaky from much shellfire, and he puts me down on the floor and washes my wound with water from his canteen and puts sulfa powder on my wound and gives me some to swallow, and all the time he is talking a blue streak.

"Hammer," he says, "do you remember the night I give my performance of Hamlet and you knock my brains out? Well, you are in no more agony now than I am then. I die ten thousand deaths when I read your criticism. Furthermore, you alienate the affections of Miss Channelle Cooper from me, because she thinks you are a great dramatic critic, and when you say I am a bad Hamlet, she believes you and cancels our engagement. She says she cannot bear the idea of being married to a bad Hamlet. Hammer," he says, "am I a bad Hamlet?"

"Mansfield," I say, "I now regret I cause you anguish."

"Mr. Sothern to you," Mansfield says. "Hammer," he says, "I hear you only see two acts of my Hamlet."

"That is true," I say. "I have to hasten back to my office to write my review."

"Why," he says, "how dare you pass on the merits of an artist on such brief observation? Does your mad jealousy of me over Miss Channelle Cooper cause you to forget you are a human being and make a hyena of you? Or are all dramatic critics just naturally hyenas, as I suspect?"

"Mansfield," I say, "while I admit to much admiration and, in fact, love for Miss Channelle Cooper, I never permit my emotions to bias my professional efforts. When I state you are a bad Hamlet, I state my honest conviction and, while I now suffer the tortures of the damned, I still state it."

"Hammer," Mansfield Sothern says, "listen to me and observe me closely because I am now going to run through the gravediggers' scene for you which you do not see me do, and you can tell me afterward if Barrymore or Leslie Howard or Maurice Evans ever gives a finer performance."

And with this, what does he do but pick up a big stone from the floor and strike a pose and speak as follows:

" 'Alas, poor Yorick! I knew him, Horatio; a fellow of infinite jest, of most excellent fancy; he hath borne me on his back a thousand times; and now, how abhorred in my imagination it is! my gorge rises at it. Here hung those lips that I have kissed I know not how oft. Where be your gibes now? your gambols? your songs? your flashes of merriment, that were wont to set the tables on a roar? Not one, now, to mock your own grinning? quite chapfallen? Now get you to my lady's chamber, and tell her, let her paint an inch thick, to this favour she must come; make her laugh at that. Pr'ythee, Horatio, tell me one thing.' "

Now Mansfield stops and looks at me and says: "Come, come, Hammer, you are Horatio. Throw me the line."

So I try to remember what Horatio remarks at this point in Hamlet and finally I say, " 'How is that, my lord?' "

"No, no," Mansfield says. "Not 'How is that?' but 'What's that?' And you presume to criticize me!"

"All right, Mansfield," I say. " 'What's that, my lord?' "

And Mansfield says, " 'Dost thou think Alexander looked o' this fashion i' the earth?' "

I say, " 'E'en so.' "

" 'And smelt so? pah!" Mansfield says, and with this, he throws the stone to the floor, and at the same moment I hear another noise and, on looking around, what do I see in the doorway but two German officers covered with dust, and one of them says in English like this:

"What is going on here?"

Naturally, I am somewhat nonplused at the sight of these guys, but Mansfield Sothern does not seem to notice them and continues reciting in a loud voice.

"He is an actor in civil life," I say to the German. "He is now presenting his version of Hamlet to me."

" 'To what base uses we may return, Horatio!' " Mansfield Sothern says. " 'Why may not imagination trace the noble dust of Alexander—' "

" 'Till he finds it stopping a bunghole?' " the German cuts in, and then Mansfield looks at him and says:

" 'Find,' not 'finds,' " he says.

"Quite right," the German says. "Well, you are now prisoners. I will send some of my soldiers to pick you up immediately. Do not attempt to leave this place or you will be shot, as we have the town surrounded."

Then the two depart and Mansfield stops reciting at once and says, "Let us duffy out of here. It is growing dark outside, and I think we can make it. Are you still suffering first class, Hammer?"

"Yes," I say, "and I cannot walk an inch, either."

So Mansfield laughs ha-ha-ha and picks me up again as easy as if I am nothing but a bag of wind and carries me out through what seems to have been a back door to the joint, but before we go into the open, he throws himself face downward on the ground and tells me to pull myself on his back and hook my arms around his neck and hold on, and I do same. Then he starts crawling along like he is a turtle and I am its shell. Naturally, our progress is very slow, especially as we hear guys everywhere around us in the dark talking in German.

Every few yards, Mansfield has to stop to rest, and I roll off his back until he is ready to start again and, during one of these halts, he whispers, "Hammer, are you still suffering?"

"Yes," I say.

"Good," Mansfield says, and then he goes on crawling.

I do not know how far he crawls with me aboard him because I am getting a little groggy, but I do remember him whispering very softly to himself like this:

> " 'Imperious Caesar, dead and turn'd to clay,
> Might stop a hole to keep the wind away.' "

Well, Mansfield crawls and crawls and crawls until he crawls himself and me right into a bunch of our guys, and the next thing I know is I wake up in a hospital, and who is sitting there beside me but Mansfield Sothern and, when he sees I am awake, he says like this:

" 'O, I die, Horatio.' "

"Mansfield," I say, "kindly cheese it and permit me to thank you for saving my life."

"Hammer," he says, "the pleasure is all mine. I am sustained on my long crawl (which they tell me is a new world record for crawling with a guy on the deck of the crawler) by the thought that I have on my back a dramatic critic who is suffering keenly every inch of the way.

"I suppose," he says, "that you hear I am decorated for rescuing you, but kindly keep it quiet, as the Actors' Guild will never forgive me for rescuing a critic. Also, Hammer, I am being sent home to organize overseas entertainment for my comrades, and naturally it will

be along Shakespearean lines. Tell me, Hammer, do you
observe your nurse as yet?"

And, with this, Mansfield points to a doll in uniform
standing not far away, and I can see that it is nobody
but Miss Channelle Cooper, and I can also see that she
is hoping she is looking like Miss Florence Nightingale.
When she notices I am awake, she starts toward my
cot, but at her approach, Mansfield Sothern gets up and
departs quite hastily without as much as saying boo to
her and as she stands looking at him, tears come to her
eyes and I can see that a coolness must still prevail between them.

Naturally, I am by no means displeased by this situation because the sight of Miss Channelle Cooper even
in a nurse's uniform brings back fond memories to me
and, in fact, I feel all my old love for her coming up
inside me like a lump and, as she reaches my bedside,
I can scarcely speak because of my emotion.

"You must be quiet, Ambrose," she says. "You know
you are delirious for days and days, and in your delirium
you say things about me that cause me much embarrass-
ment. Does Mansfield happen to mention my name?"

"No," I say. "Forget him, Channelle. He is a cad as
well as a bad Hamlet."

But the tears in her eyes increase, and suddenly she
leaves me and I do not see her for some days afterward
and, in fact, I do not even think of her because my
editor is sending me messages wishing to know what
I am doing in a hospital on his time and to get out of
there at once, and what do I mean by putting a horse
in my last expense account, which of course is an error
in bookkeeping due to my haste in making out the account. What I intend putting in is a hearse, as I figure
that my editor will be too confused by such an unexpected item to dispute it.

So here I am back in the good old U.S.A. (Ambrose

says) and now as I previously state I am going to take
you to the theater again with me, and who are you going
to see but our old friend Mansfield Sothern playing
Hamlet once more!

Now this propect by no means thrills me, but I am
unable to think of a good out at once, so I accompany
Ambrose, and when we arrive at the theater, we find
the manager, who is a guy by the name of Thomas Bodkin, walking up and down in front of the joint and
speaking in the most disparaging terms of actors, and
customers are milling around the lobby and on the side-
walks outside.

They are going up to Thomas Bodkin and saying,
"What is the matter, Bodkin?" and "When does the curtain go up?" and "Who do you think you are?" and all
this and that, which only causes him to become very
disrespectful indeed in his expressions about actors and,
in fact, he is practically libelous, and it is several minutes
before Ambrose and I can figure out the nature of his
emotion.

Then we learn that what happens is that Mansfield
Sothern collapses in his dressing room a few minutes
before the curtain is to rise, and, as the gaff is all sold
out, it is naturally a terrible predicament for Thomas
Bodkin, as he may have to refund the money, and thinking of this has Thomas on the verge of a collapse himself.

"Hammer," he says to Ambrose, "you will do me a
favor if you will go backstage and see if you can find
out what is eating this hamdonny. I am afraid to trust
myself to even look at him at the moment."

So Ambrose and I go around to the stage entrance
and up to Mansfield Sothern's dressing room, and there
is Mansfield sprawled in a chair in his Hamlet make-
up, while his dresser, an old stovelid by the name of
Crichton, is swabbing Mansfield's brow with a towel

and speaking soothing words to him in a Southern accent.

"Why, Mansfield," Ambrose says, "what seems to ail you that you keep an eager audience waiting and put Thomas Bodkin in a condition bordering on hysteria?"

"I cannot go on," Mansfield says. "My heart is too heavy. I just learn of your return and, as I am sitting here thinking of how you must make plenty of hay-hay with Miss Channelle Cooper when you are lying there under her loving care in North Africa and telling her what a bad Hamlet I am, I am overcome with grief. Ambrose," he says, "is there any hope of you being crippled for life?"

"No," Ambrose says. "Come, come, Mansfield," he says. "Pull yourself together. Think of your career and of poor Thomas Bodkin and the box-office receipts. Remember the ancient tradition of the theater: The show must go on—although, personally, I do not always see why."

"I cannot," Mansfield says. "Her face will rise before me, and my words will choke me as I think of her in another's arms. Ambrose, I am in bad shape, but I am man enough to congratulate you. I hope and trust you will always be happy with Miss Channelle Cooper, even if you are a dramatic critic. But I cannot go on in my present state of mind. I am too melancholy even for Hamlet."

"Oh," Ambrose says, "do not worry about Miss Channelle Cooper. She loves you dearly. The last time I see her, I request her to be my ever-loving wife when this cruel war is over, but she says it can never be, as she loves only you. I say all right; if she wishes to love a bad Hamlet instead of a good correspondent, to go ahead. And then," Ambrose says, "Miss Channelle Cooper speaks to me as follows:

" 'No, Ambrose,' she says. 'He is not a bad Hamlet. A better judge than you says he is a fine Hamlet. Professor Bierbauer, the great dramatic coach of Heidelberg, now a colonel in the German army, tells me he witnesses a performance by Mansfield in a ruined tavern in a town near the front, that, under the conditions, is the most magnificent effort of the kind he ever views.'

"It seems," Ambrose says, "that the professor is wounded and captured by our guys when they retake the town, and, at the moment Miss Channelle Cooper is addressing me, he is one of her patients in a nearby ward, where I have no doubt he gets quite an earful on your history and her love. Where are you going, Mansfield?"

"Why," Mansfield says, "I am going around the corner to send a cablegram to Miss Channelle Cooper, telling her I reciprocate her love and also requesting her to get Professor Bierbauer's opinion in writing for my scrapbook."

Well, I wait up in Mindy's restaurant with Mansfield to get the last editions containing the reviews of the critics and, naturally, the first review we turn to is Ambrose Hammer's, and at Mansfield's request I read it aloud as follows:

" 'Mansfield Sothern's inspired performance of Hamlet at the Todd Theater last night leads us to the hope that in this sterling young actor we have a new dramatic force of the power in Shakespearean roles of all the mighty figures of another day, perhaps including even the immortal Edwin Booth.'

"Well, Mansfield," I say, when I finish, "I think Ambrose now pays you off in full on your account with him, including saving his life, what with giving you Miss Channelle Cooper and this wonderful boost, which, undoubtedly, establishes your future in the theater."

"Humph!" Mansfield says. "It seems a fair appraisal, at that, and I will send a clipping to Miss Channelle Cooper at once, but," he says, "there is undoubtedly a streak of venom left in Ambrose Hammer. Else, why does he ring in Booth?"

The Hottest Guy in the World

I WISH TO SAY I am very nervous indeed when Big Jule pops into my hotel room one afternoon, because anybody will tell you that Big Jule is the hottest guy in the whole world at the time I am speaking about.

In fact, it is really surprising how hot he is. They wish to see him in Pittsburgh, Pa., about a matter of a mail truck being robbed, and there is gossip about him in Minneapolis, Minn., where somebody takes a fifty G pay roll off a messenger in cash money, and slugs the messenger around somewhat for not holding still.

Furthermore, the Bankers' Association is willing to pay good dough to talk to Big Jule out in Kansas City, Mo., where a jug is knocked off by a stranger, and in the confusion the paying teller, and the cashier, and the second vice president are clouted about, and the day watchman is hurt, and two coppers are badly bruised, and over fifteen G's is removed from the counters, and never returned.

Then there is something about a department store in Canton, O., and a flour mill safe in Toledo, and a grocery in Spokane, Wash., and a branch postoffice in San Francisco, and also something about a shooting match in Chicago, but of course this does not count so much, as only one party is fatally injured. However, you can see that Big Jule is really very hot, what with the coppers all over the country looking for him high and low. In fact, he is practically on fire.

Of course I do not believe Big Jule does all the things the coppers say, because coppers always blame everything no matter where it happens on the most prominent guy they can think of, and Big Jule is quite prominent all over the U.S.A. The chances are he does not do more than half these things, and he probably has a good alibi for the half he does do, at that, but he is certainly hot, and I do not care to have hot guys around me, or even guys who are only just a little bit warm.

But naturally I am not going to say this to Big Jule when he pops in on me, because he may think I am inhospitable, and I do not care to have such a rap going around and about on me, and furthermore Jule may become indignant if he thinks I am inhospitable, and knock me on my potato, because Big Jule is quick to take offense.

So I say hello to Big Jule, very pleasant, and ask him to have a chair by the window where he can see the citizens walking to and fro down in Eighth Avenue and watch the circus wagons moving into Madison Square Garden by way of the Forty-ninth Street side, for the circus always shows in the Garden in the spring before going out on the road. It is a little warm, and Big Jule takes off his coat, and I can see he has one automatic slung under his arm, and another sticking down in the waistband of his pants, and I hope and trust that no

copper steps into the room while Big Jule is there because it is very much against the law for guys to go
around rodded up this way in New York City.

"Well, Jule," I say, "this is indeed a very large surprise
to me, and I am glad to see you, but I am thinking
maybe it is very foolish for you to be popping into New
York just now, what with all the heat around here, and
the coppers looking to arrest people for very little."

"I know," Jule says. "I know. But they do not have
so very much on me around here, no matter what people
say, and a guy gets homesick for his old home town,
especially a guy who is stuck away where I am for the
past few months. I get homesick for the lights and the
crowds on Broadway, and for the old neighborhood.
Furthermore, I wish to see my maw. I hear she is
sick and may not live, and I wish to see her before she
goes."

Well, naturally anybody will wish to see their maw
under such circumstances, but Big Jule's maw lives over
in West Forty-ninth Street near Eleventh Avenue, and
who is living in the very same block but Johnny Brannigan, the strong-arm copper, and it is a hundred to one
if Big Jule goes nosing around his old neighborhood,
Johnny Brannigan will hear of it, and if there is one
guy Johnny Brannigan does not care for, it is Big Jule,
although they are kids together.

But it seems that even when they are kids they have
very little use for each other, and after they grow up
and Johnny gets on the strong-arm squad, he never
misses a chance to push Big Jule around, and sometimes
trying to boff Big Jule with his blackjack, and it is well
known to one and all that before Big Jule leaves town
the last time, he takes a punch at Johnny Brannigan,
and Johnny swears he will never rest until he puts Big
Jule where he belongs, although where Big Jule belongs,
Johnny does not say.

So I speak of Johnny living in the same block with Big Jule's maw to Big Jule, but it only makes him mad. "I am not afraid of Johnny Brannigan," he says. "In fact," he says, "I am thinking for some time lately that maybe I will clip Johnny Brannigan good while I am here. I owe Johnny Brannigan a clipping. But I wish to see my maw first, and then I will go around and see Miss Kitty Clancy. I guess maybe she will be much surprised to see me, and no doubt very glad."

Well, I figure it is a sure thing Miss Kitty Clancy will be surprised to see Big Jule, but I am not so sure about her being glad, because very often when a guy is away from a doll for a year or more, no matter how ever-loving she may be, she may get to thinking of someone else, for this is the way dolls are, whether they live on Eleventh Avenue or over on Park. Still, I remember hearing that this Miss Kitty Clancy once thinks very well of Big Jule, although her old man, Jack Clancy, who runs a speakeasy, always claims it is a big knock to the Clancy family to have such a character as Big Jule hanging around.

"I often think of Miss Kitty Clancy the past year or so," Big Jule says, as he sits there by the window, watching the circus wagons, and the crowds. "I especially think of her the past few months. In fact," he says, "thinking of Miss Kitty Clancy is about all I have to do where I am at, which is in an old warehouse on the Bay of Fundy outside of a town that is called St. Johns, or some such, up in Canada, and thinking of Miss Kitty Clancy all this time, I find out I love her very much indeed.

"I go to this warehouse," Big Jule says, "after somebody takes a jewelry store in the town, and the coppers start in blaming me. This warehouse is not such a place as I will choose myself if I am doing the choosing, because it is an old fur warehouse, and full of strange smells, but in the excitement around the jewelry store, somebody puts a slug in my hip, and Leon Pierre carries me to the old warehouse, and there I am until I get well.

"It is very lonesome," Big Jule says. "In fact, you will be surprised how lonesome it is, and it is very, very cold, and all I have for company is a lot of rats. Personally, I never care for rats under any circumstances because they carry disease germs, and are apt to bite a guy when he is asleep, if they are hungry, which is what these rats try to do to me.

"The warehouse is away off by itself," Jule says, "and nobody ever comes around there except Leon Pierre to bring me grub and dress my hip, and at night it is very still, and all you can hear is the wind howling around outside, and the rats running here and there. Some of them are very, very large rats. In fact, some of them seem about the size of rabbits, and they are pretty fresh, at that. At first I am willing to make friends with these rats, but they seem very hostile, and after they take a few nips at me I can see there is no use trying to be nice to them, so I have Leon Pierre bring me a lot of ammunition for my rods every day and I practice shooting at the rats.

"The warehouse is so far off there is no danger of anybody hearing the shooting," Big Jule says, "and it helps me pass the time away. I get so I can hit a rat sitting, or running, or even flying through the air, because these warehouse rats often leap from place to place like mountain sheep, their idea being generally to take a good nab at me as they fly past.

"Well, sir," Jule says, "I keep score on myself one day, and I hit fifty rats hand running without a miss, which I claim makes me the champion rat shooter of the world with a forty-five automatic, although of course," he says, "if anybody wishes to challenge me to a rat shooting match I am willing to take them on for a side bet. I get so I can call my shots on the rats, and in fact several times I say to myself, I will hit this one in the right eye, and this one in the left eye, and it always turns out just as I say, although sometimes when you hit a rat with a forty-five up close it is not always possible to tell afterwards just where you hit him, because you seem to hit him all over.

"By and by," Jule says, "I seem to discourage the rats somewhat, and they get so they play the chill for me and do not try to nab me even when I am asleep. They find out that no rat dast poke his whiskers out at me or he will get a very close shave. So I have to look around for other amusement, but there is not much doing in such a place, although I finally find a bunch of doctors' books which turn out to be very interesting reading. It seems these books are left there by some croaker who retires there to think things over after experimenting on his ever-loving wife with a knife. In fact, it seems he cuts his ever-loving wife's head off, and she does not continue living, so he takes his books and goes to the warehouse and remains there until the law finds him, and hangs him up very high, indeed.

"Well, the books are a great comfort to me, and I learn many astonishing things about surgery, but after I read all the books there is nothing for me to do but think, and what I think about is Miss Kitty Clancy, and how much pleasure we have together walking around and about and seeing movie shows, and all this and that, until her old man gets so tough with me. Yes, I will be very glad to see Miss Kitty Clancy, and the old neighborhood, and my maw again."

Well, finally nothing will do Big Jule but he must take a stroll over into his old neighborhood, and see if he cannot see Miss Kitty Clancy, and also drop in on his maw, and he asks me to go along with him. I can think of a million things I will rather do than take a stroll with Big Jule, but I do not wish him to think I am snobbish, because as I say, Big Jule is quick to take offense. Furthermore, I figure that at such an hour of the day he is less likely to run into Johnny Brannigan or any other coppers who know him than at any other time, so I say I will go with him, but as we start out, Big Jule puts on his rods.

"Jule," I say, "do not take any rods with you on a stroll, because somebody may happen to see them, such as a copper, and you know they will pick you up for carrying a rod in this town quicker than you can say Jack Robinson, whether they know who you are or not. You know the Sullivan law is very strong against guys carrying rods in this town."

But Big Jule says he is afraid he will catch cold if he goes out without his rods, so we go down into Forty-ninth Street and start west toward Madison Square Garden, and just as we reach Eighth Avenue and are standing there waiting for the traffic to stop, so we can cross the street, I see there is quite some excitement around the Garden on the Forty-ninth Street side, with people running every which way, and yelling no little, and looking up in the air.

So I look up myself, and what do I see sitting up there on the edge of the Garden roof but a big ugly-faced monkey. At first I do not recognize it as a monkey, because it is so big I figure maybe it is just one of the prize fight managers who stand around on this side of the Garden all afternoon waiting to get a match for their fighters, and while I am somewhat astonished to see a prize fight manager in such a position, I figure maybe he is doing it on a bet. But when I take a second

look I see that it is indeed a big monk, and an exceptionally homely monk at that, although personally I never
see any monks I consider so very handsome, anyway.
Well, this big monk is holding something in its arms,
and what it is I am not able to make out at first, but
then Big Jule and I cross the street to the side opposite
the Garden, and now I can see that the monk has a
baby in its arms. Naturally I figure it is some kind of
advertising dodge put on by the Garden to ballyhoo
the circus, or maybe the fight between Sharkey and
Risko which is coming off after the circus, but guys
are still yelling and running up and down, and dolls
are screaming until finally I realize that a most surprising situation prevails.

It seems that the big monk up on the roof is nobody
but Bongo, who is a gorilla belonging to the circus,
and one of the very few gorillas of any account in this
country, or anywhere else, as far as this goes, because
good gorillas are very scarce, indeed. Well, it seems that
while they are shoving Bongo's cage into the Garden,
the door becomes unfastened, and the first thing anybody knows, out pops Bongo, and goes bouncing along
the street where a lot of the neighbors' children are
playing games on the sidewalk, and a lot of mammas
are sitting out in the sun alongside baby buggies containing their young. This is a very common sight in side
streets such as West Forty-ninth on nice days, and by
no means unpleasant, if you like mammas and their
young.

Now what does this Bongo do but reach into a baby
buggy which a mamma is pushing past on the sidewalk
on the Garden side of the street, and snatch out a baby,
though what Bongo wants with this baby nobody knows
to this day. It is a very young baby, and not such a
baby as is fit to give a gorilla the size of Bongo any

kind of struggle, so Bongo has no trouble whatever in handling it. Anyway, I always hear a gorilla will make a sucker out of a grown man in a battle, though I wish to say I never see a battle between a gorilla and a grown man. It ought to be a first class drawing card, at that.

Well, naturally the baby's mamma puts up quite a squawk about Bongo grabbing her baby, because no mamma wishes her baby to keep company with a gorilla, and this mamma starts in screaming very loud, and trying to take the baby away from Bongo, so what does Bongo do but run right up on the roof of the Garden by way of a big electric sign which hangs down on the Forty-ninth Street side. And there old Bongo sits on the edge of the roof with the baby in his arms, and the baby is squalling quite some, and Bongo is making funny noises, and showing his teeth as the folks commence gathering in the street below.

There is a big guy in his shirt sleeves running through the crowd waving his hands, and trying to shush everybody, and saying "Quiet, please" over and over, but nobody pays any attention to him. I figure this guy has something to do with the circus, and maybe with Bongo, too. A traffic copper takes a peek at the situation, and calls for the reserves from the Forty-seventh Street station, and somebody else sends for the fire truck down the street, and pretty soon cops are running from every direction, and the fire engines are coming, and the big guy in his shirt sleeves is more excited than ever.

"Quiet, please," he says. "Everybody keep quiet, because if Bongo becomes disturbed by the noise he will throw the baby down in the street. He throws everything he gets his hands on," the guy says. "He acquires this habit from throwing coconuts back in his old home country. Let us get a life net, and if you all keep quiet we may be able to save the baby before Bongo starts heaving it like a coconut."

Well, Bongo is sitting up there on the edge of the roof about seven stories above the ground peeking down with the baby in his arms, and he is holding this baby just like a mamma would, but anybody can see that Bongo does not care for the row below, and once he lifts the baby high above his head as if to bean somebody with it. I see Big Nig, the crap shooter, in the mob, and afterwards I hear he is around offering to lay seven to five against the baby, but everybody is too excited to bet on such a proposition, although it is not a bad price, at that.

I see one doll in the crowd on the sidewalk on the side of the street opposite the Garden who is standing perfectly still staring up at the monk and the baby with a very strange expression on her face, and the way she is looking makes me take a second gander at her, and who is it but Miss Kitty Clancy. Her lips are moving as she stands there staring up, and something tells me Miss Kitty Clancy is saying prayers to herself, because she is such a doll as will know how to say prayers on an occasion like this.

Big Jule sees her about the same time I do, and Big Jule steps up beside Miss Kitty Clancy, and says hello to her, and though it is over a year since Miss Kitty Clancy sees Big Jule she turns to him and speaks to him as if she is talking to him just a minute before. It is very strange indeed the way Miss Kitty Clancy speaks to Big Jule as if he has never been away at all.

"Do something, Julie," she says. "You are always the one to do something. Oh, please do something, Julie."

Well Big Jule never answers a word, but steps back in the clear of the crowd and reaches for the waistband of his pants, when I grab him by the arm and say to him like this:

"My goodness, Jule," I say, "what are you going to do?"

"Why," Jule says, "I am going to shoot this thieving monk before he takes a notion to heave the baby on somebody down here. For all I know," Jule says, "he may hit me with it, and I do not care to be hit with anybody's baby."

"Jule," I say, very earnestly, "do not pull a rod in front of all these coppers, because if you do they will nail you sure, if only for having the rod, and if you are nailed you are in a very tough spot, indeed, what with being wanted here and there. Jule," I say, "you are hotter than a forty-five all over this country, and I do not wish to see you nailed. Anyway," I say, "you may shoot the baby instead of the monk, because anybody can see it will be very difficult to hit the monk up there without hitting the baby. Furthermore, even if you do hit the monk it will fall into the street, and bring the baby with it."

"You speak great foolishness," Jule says. "I never miss what I shoot at. I will shoot the monk right between the eyes, and this will make him fall backwards, not forwards, and the baby will not be hurt because anybody can see it is no fall at all from the ledge to the roof behind. I make a study of such propositions," Jule says, "and I know if a guy is in such a position as this monk sitting on a ledge looking down from a high spot his defensive reflexes tend backwards, so this is the way he is bound to fall if anything unexpected comes up on him such as a bullet between the eyes. I read all about it in the doctors' books," Jule says.

Then all of a sudden up comes his hand, and in his hand is one of his rods, and I hear a sound like ker-bap. When I come to think about it afterwards, I do not remember Big Jule even taking aim like a guy will generally do if he is shooting at something sitting, but old Bongo seems to lift up a little bit off the ledge at the crack of the gun and then he keels over backwards, the baby still in his arms, and squalling more than somewhat, and Big Jule says to me like this:

"Right between the eyes, and I will bet on it," he says, "although it is not much of a target, at that."

Well, nobody can figure what happens for a minute, and there is much silence except from the guy in his shirt sleeves who is expressing much indignation with Big Jule and saying the circus people will sue him for damages sure if he has hurt Bongo because the monk is worth $100,000, or some such. I see Miss Kitty Clancy kneeling on the sidewalk with her hands clasped, and looking upwards, and Big Jule is sticking his rod back in his waistband again.

By this time some guys are out on the roof getting through from the inside of the building with the idea of heading Bongo off from that direction, and they let out a yell, and pretty soon I see one of them holding the baby up so everyone in the street can see it. A couple of other guys get down near the edge of the roof and pick up Bongo and show him to the crowd, as dead as a mackerel, and one of the guys puts a finger between Bongo's eyes to show where the bullet hits the monk, and Miss Kitty Clancy walks over to Big Jule and tries to say something to him, but only busts out crying very loud.

Well, I figure this is a good time for Big Jule and me to take a walk, because everybody is interested in what is going on up on the roof, and I do not wish the circus people to get a chance to serve a summons in a damage suit on Big Jule for shooting the valuable monk. Furthermore, a couple of coppers in harness are looking Big Jule over very critically, and I figure they are apt to put the old sleeve on Jule any second.

All of a sudden a slim young guy steps up to Big Jule and says to him like this:

"Jule," he says, "I want to see you," and who is it but Johnny Brannigan. Naturally Big Jule starts reaching for a rod, but Johnny starts him walking down the street so fast Big Jule does not have time to get in action just then.

"No use getting it out, Jule," Johnny Brannigan says. "No use, and no need. Come with me, and hurry."

Well, Big Jule is somewhat puzzled because Johnny Brannigan is not acting like a copper making a collar, so he goes along with Johnny, and I follow after them, and halfway down the block Johnny stops a Yellow short, and hustles us into it and tells the driver to keep shoving down Eighth Avenue.

"I am trailing you ever since you get in town, Jule," Johnny Brannigan says. "You never have a chance around here. I was going over to your maw's house to put the arm on you figuring you are sure to go there, when the thing over by the Garden comes off. Now I am getting out of this cab at the next corner, and you go on and see your maw, and then screw out of town as quick as you can, because you are red-hot around here, Jule.

"By the way," Johnny Brannigan says, "do you know it is my kid you save, Jule? Mine and Kitty Clancy's? We are married a year ago today."

Well, Big Jule looks very much surprised for a moment, and then he laughs, and says like this: "Well, I never know it is Kitty Clancy's but I figure it for yours the minute I see it because it looks like you."

"Yes," Johnny Brannigan says, very proud. "Everybody says he does."

"I can see the resemblance even from a distance," Big Jule says. "In fact," he says, "it is remarkable how much you look alike. But," he says, "for a minute, Johnny, I am afraid I will not be able to pick out the right face between the two on the roof because it is very hard to tell the monk and your baby apart."

Dream Street Rose

OF AN EARLY EVENING when there is nothing much doing anywhere else, I go around to Good Time Charley's little speak in West Forty-seventh Street that he calls the Gingham Shoppe, and play a little klob with Charley, because business is quiet in the Gingham Shoppe at such an hour, and Charley gets very lonesome.

He once has a much livelier spot in Forty-eighth Street that he calls the Crystal Room, but one night a bunch of G-guys step into the joint and bust it wide open, besides confiscating all of Charley's stock of merchandise. It seems that these G-guys are members of a squad that comes on from Washington, and being strangers in the city they do not know that Good Time Charley's joint is not supposed to be busted up, so they go ahead and bust it, just the same as if it is any other joint.

Well, this action causes great indignation in many quarters, and a lot of citizens advise Charley to see some-

body about it. But Charley says no. Charley says if this
is the way the government is going to treat him after
the way he walks himself bow-legged over in France
with the Rainbow Division, making the Germans hard
to catch, why, all right. But he is not going to holler
copper about it, although Charley says he has his own
opinion of Mr. Hoover, at that.

Personally, I greatly admire Charley for taking the
disaster so calmly, especially as it catches him with very
few potatoes. Charley is a great hand for playing the
horses with any dough he makes out of the Crystal
Room, and this particular season the guys who play
the horses are being murdered by the bookies all over
the country, and are in terrible distress.

So I know if Charley is not plumb broke that he has
a terrible crack across his belly, and I am not surprised
that I do not see him for a couple of weeks after the
government guys knock off the Crystal Room. I hear
rumors that he is at home reading the newspapers very
carefully every day, especially the obituary notices, for
it seems that Charley figures that some of the G-guys
may be tempted to take a belt or two at the merchandise
they confiscate, and Charley says if they do, he is even
for life.

Finally I hear that Charley is seen buying a bolt of
gingham in Bloomington's one day, so I know he will
be in action again very soon, for all Charley needs to
go into action is a bolt of gingham and a few bottles
of Golden Wedding. In fact, I know Charley to go into
action without the gingham, but as a rule he likes to
drape a place of business with gingham to make it seem
more homelike to his customers, and I wish to say that
when it comes to draping gingham, Charley can make
a sucker of Joseph Urban, or anybody else.

Well, when I arrive at the Gingham Shoppe this night

I am talking about, which is around ten o'clock, I find Charley in a very indignant state of mind, because an old tomato by the name of Dream Street Rose comes in and tracks up his floor, just after Charley gets through mopping it up, for Charley does his mopping in person, not being able as yet to afford any help.

Rose is sitting at a table in a corner, paying no attention to Charley's remarks about wiping her feet on the welcome mat at the door before she comes in, because Rose knows there is no welcome mat at Charley's door, anyway, but I can see where Charley has a right to a few beefs, at that, as she leaves a trail of black hoofprints across the clean floor as if she is walking around in mud somewhere before she comes in, although I do not seem to remember that it is raining when I arrive.

Now this Dream Street Rose is an old doll of maybe fifty-odd, and is a very well-known character around and about, as she is wandering through the Forties for many a year, and especially through West Forty-seventh Street between Sixth and Seventh Avenues, and this block is called Dream Street. And the reason it is called Dream Street is because in this block are many characters of one kind and another who always seem to be dreaming of different matters.

In Dream Street there are many theatrical hotels, and rooming houses, and restaurants, and speaks, including Good Time Charley's Gingham Shoppe, and in the summer time the characters I mention sit on the stoops or lean against the railings along Dream Street, and the gab you hear sometimes sounds very dreamy indeed. In fact, it sometimes sounds very pipe-dreamy.

Many actors, male and female, and especially vaudeville actors, live in the hotels and rooming houses, and vaudeville actors, both male and female, are great hands for sitting around dreaming out loud about how they will practically assassinate the public in the Palace if ever they get a chance.

Furthermore, in Dream Street are always many hand bookies and horse players, who sit on the church steps on the cool side of Dream Street in the summer and dream about big killings on the races, and there are also nearly always many fight managers, and sometimes fighters, hanging out in front of the restaurants, picking their teeth and dreaming about winning championships of the world, although up to this time no champion of the world has yet come out of Dream Street.

In this street you see burlesque dolls, and hoofers, and guys who write songs, and saxophone players, and newsboys, and newspaper scribes, and taxi drivers, and blind guys, and midgets, and blondes with Pomeranian pooches, or maybe French poodles, and guys with whiskers, and night-club entertainers, and I do not know what all else. And all of these characters are interesting to look at, and some of them are very interesting to talk to, although if you listen to several I know long enough, you may get the idea that they are somewhat daffy, especially the horse players.

But personally I consider all horse players more or less daffy anyway. In fact, the way I look at it, if a guy is not daffy he will not be playing the horses.

Now this Dream Street Rose is a short, thick-set, square-looking old doll, with a square pan, and square shoulders, and she has heavy iron-gray hair that she wears in a square bob, and she stands very square on her feet. In fact, Rose is the squarest-looking doll I ever see, and she is as strong and lively as Jim Londos, the wrestler. In fact, Jim Londos will never be any better than six to five in my line over Dream Street Rose, if she is in any kind of shape. Nobody in this town wishes any truck with Rose if she has a few shots of grog in her, and especially Good Time Charley's grog, for she can fight like the dickens when she is grogged up. In fact, Rose holds many a decision in this town, especially over coppers, because if there is one thing she hates and despises more than somewhat it is a copper, as coppers are always heaving her into the old can when they find her jerking citizens around and cutting up other didoes.

For many years Rose works in the different hotels along Dream Street as a chambermaid. She never works in any one hotel very long, because the minute she gets a few bobs together she likes to go out and enjoy a little recreation, such as visiting around the speaks, although she is about as welcome in most speaks as a G-guy with a search warrant. You see, nobody can ever tell when Rose may feel like taking the speak apart, and also the customers.

She never has any trouble getting a job back in any hotel she ever works in, for Rose is a wonderful hand for making up beds, although several times, when she is in a hurry to get off, I hear she makes up beds with guests still in them, which causes a few mild beefs to the management, but does not bother Rose. I speak of this matter only to show you that she is a very quaint character indeed, and full of zest.

Well, I sit down to play klob with Good Time Charley, but about this time several customers come into the Gingham Shoppe, so Charley has to go and take care of them, leaving me alone. And while I am sitting there alone I hear Dream Street Rose mumbling to herself over in the corner, but I pay no attention to her, although I wish to say I am by no means unfriendly with Rose.

In fact, I say hello to her at all times, and am always very courteous to her, as I do not wish to have her bawling me out in public, and maybe circulating rumors about me, as she is apt to do, if she feels I am snubbing her.

Finally I notice her motioning to me to come over to her table, and I go over at once and sit down, because I can see that Rose is well grogged up at this time, and I do not care to have her attracting my attention by chucking a cuspidor at me. She offers me a drink when I sit down, but of course I never drink anything that is sold in Good Time Charley's, as a personal favor to Charley. He says he wishes to retain my friendship.

So I just sit there saying nothing much whatever, and Rose keeps on mumbling to herself, and I am not able to make much of her mumbling, until finally she looks at me and says to me like this:

"I am now going to tell you about my friend," Rose says.

"Well, Rose," I say, "personally I do not care to hear about your friend, although," I say, "I have no doubt that what you wish to tell me about this friend is very interesting. But I am here to play a little klob with Good Time Charley, and I do not have time to hear about your friend."

"Charley is busy selling his poison to the suckers," Rose says. "I am now going to tell you about my friend. It is quite a story," she says. "You will listen."

So I listen.

It is a matter of thirty-five years ago [Dream Street Rose says] and the spot is a town in Colorado by the name of Pueblo, where there are smelters and one thing and another. My friend is at this time maybe sixteen or seventeen years old, and a first-class looker in every respect. Her papa is dead, and her mamma runs a boardinghouse for the guys who work in the smelters, and who are very hearty eaters. My friend deals them off the arm for the guys in her mamma's boardinghouse to save her mamma the expense of a waitress.

Now among the boarders in this boardinghouse are many guys who are always doing a little pitching to my friend, and trying to make dates with her to take her places, but my friend never gives them much of a tumble, because after she gets through dealing them off the arm all day her feet generally pain her too much to go anywhere on them except to the hay.

Finally, however, along comes a tall, skinny young guy from the East by the name of Frank something, who has things to say to my friend that are much more interesting than anything that has ever been said to her by a guy before, including such things as love and marriage, which are always very interesting subjects to any young doll.

This Frank is maybe twenty-five years old, and he comes from the East with the idea of making his fortune in the West, and while it is true that fortunes are being made in the West at this time, there is little chance that Frank is going to make any part of a fortune, as he does not care to work very hard. In fact, he does not care to work at all, being much more partial to playing a little poker, or shooting a few craps, or maybe hustling a sucker around Mike's poolroom on Santa Fe Avenue, for Frank is an excellent pool player, especially when he is playing a sucker.

Now my friend is at this time a very innocent young doll, and a good doll in every respect, and her idea of love includes a nice little home, and children running here and there and around and about, and she never has a wrong thought in her life, and believes that everybody else in the world is like herself. And the chances are if this Frank does not happen along, my friend will marry a young guy in Pueblo by the name of Higginbottom, who is very fond of her indeed, and who is a decent young guy and afterwards makes plenty of potatoes in the grocery dodge.

But my friend goes very daffy over Frank and cannot see anybody but him, and the upshot of it all is she runs away with him one day to Denver, being dumb enough to believe that he means it when he tells her that he loves her and is going to marry her. Why Frank ever bothers with such a doll as my friend in the first place is always a great mystery to one and all, and the only way anybody can explain it is that she is young and fresh, and he is a heel at heart.

"Well, Rose," I say, "I am now commencing to see the finish of this story about your friend, and," I say, "it is such a story as anybody can hear in a speak at any time in this town, except," I say, "maybe your story is longer than somewhat. So I will now thank you, and excuse myself, and play a little klob with Good Time Charley."

"You will listen," Dream Street Rose says, looking me slap-dab in the eye.

So I listen.

Moreover, I notice now that Good Time Charley is standing behind me, bending in an ear, as it seems that his customers take the wind after a couple of slams of Good Time Charley's merchandise, a couple of slams being about all that even a very hardy customer can stand at one session.

Of course [Rose goes on] the chances are Frank never intends marrying my friend at all, and she never knows until long afterward that the reason he leads her to the parson is that the young guy from Pueblo by the name of Higginbottom catches up with them at the old Windsor Hotel where they are stopping and privately pokes a six-pistol against Frank's ribs and promises faithfully to come back and blow a hole in Frank you can throw a watermelon through if Frank tries any phenagling around with my friend.

Well, in practically no time whatever, love's young dream is over as far as my friend is concerned. This Frank turns out to be a most repulsive character indeed, especially if you are figuring him as an ever-loving husband. In fact, he is no good. He mistreats my friend in every way any guy ever thought of mistreating a doll, and besides the old established ways of mistreating a doll, Frank thinks up quite a number of new ways, being really quite ingenious in this respect.

Yes, this Frank is one-hundred-per-cent heel.

It is not so much that he gives her a thumping now and then, because, after all, a thumping wears off, and hurts heal up, even when they are such hurts as a broken nose and fractured ribs, and once an ankle cracked by a kick. It is what he does to her heart, and to her innocence. He is by no means a good husband, and does not know how to treat an ever-loving wife with any respect, especially as he winds up by taking my friend to San Francisco and hiring her out to a very loose character there by the name of Black Emanuel, who has a dance joint on the Barbary Coast, which, at the time I am talking about, is hotter than a stove. In this joint my friend has to dance with the customers, and get them to buy beer for her and one thing and another, and this occupation is most distasteful to my friend, as she never cares for beer.

It is there Frank leaves her for good after giving her an extra big thumping for a keepsake, and when my friend tries to leave Black Emanuel's to go looking for her ever-loving husband, she is somewhat surprised to hear Black Emanuel state that he pays Frank three C's for her to remain there and continue working. Furthermore, Black Emanuel resumes the thumpings where Frank leaves off, and by and by my friend is much bewildered and down-hearted and does not care what happens to her.

Well, there is nothing much of interest in my friend's life for the next thirty-odd years, except that she finally gets so she does not mind the beer so much, and, in fact, takes quite a fondness for it, and also for light wines and Bourbon whisky, and that she comes to realize that Frank does not love her after all, in spite of what he says. Furthermore, in later years, after she drifts around the country quite some, in and out of different joints, she realizes that the chances are she will never have a nice little home, with children running here and there, and she often thinks of what a disagreeable influence Frank has on her life.

In fact, this Frank is always on her mind more than somewhat. In fact, she thinks of him night and day, and says many a prayer that he will do well. She manages to keep track of him, which is not hard to do, at that, as Frank is in New York, and is becoming quite a guy in business, and is often in the newspapers. Maybe his success is due to my friend's prayers, but the chances are it is more because he connects up with some guy who has an invention for doing something very interesting to steel, and by grabbing an interest in this invention Frank gets a shove toward plenty of potatoes. Furthermore, he is married, and is raising up a family.

About ten or twelve years ago my friend comes to New York, and by this time she is getting a little faded around the edges. She is not so old, at that, but the air of the Western and Southern joints is bad on the complexion, and beer is no good for the figure. In fact, my friend is now quite a haybag, and she does not get any better-looking in the years she spends in New York as she is practically all out of the old sex appeal, and has to do a little heavy lifting to keep eating. But she never forgets to keep praying that Frank will continue to do well, and Frank certainly does this, as he is finally spoken of everywhere very respectfully as a millionaire and a high-class guy.

In all the years she is in New York my friend never runs into Frank, as Frank is by no means accustomed to visiting the spots where my friend hangs out, but my friend goes to a lot of bother to get acquainted with a doll who is a maid for some time in Frank's town house in East Seventy-fourth Street, and through this doll my friend keeps a pretty fair line on the way Frank lives. In fact, one day when Frank and his family are absent, my friend goes to Frank's house with her friend, just to see what it looks like, and after an hour there my friend has the joint pretty well cased.

And now my friend knows through her friend that on very hot nights such as tonight Frank's family is bound to be at their country place at Port Washington, but that Frank himself is spending the night at this town house, because he wishes to work on a lot of papers of some kind. My friend knows through her friend that all of Frank's servants are at Port Washington, too, except my friend's friend, who is in charge of the town house, and Frank's valet, a guy by the name of Sloggins.

Furthermore, my friend knows through her friend that both her friend and Sloggins have a date to go to a movie at eight-thirty, to be gone a couple of hours, as it seems Frank is very big-hearted about giving his servants time off for such a purpose when he is at home alone; although one night he squawks no little when my friend is out with her friend drinking a little beer, and my friend's friend loses her door key and has to ring the bell of the servants' entrance, and rousts Frank out of a sound sleep.

Naturally, my friend's friend will be greatly astonished if she ever learns that it is with this key that my
friend steps into Frank's house along about nine o'clock
tonight. An electric light hangs over the servants' entrance, and my friend locates the button that controls
this light just inside the door and turns it off, as my
friend figures that maybe Frank and his family will not
care to have their high-class neighbors, or anyone else,
see an old doll who has no better hat than she is wearing,
entering or leaving their house at such an hour.

It is an old-fashioned sort of house, four or five stories
high, with the library on the third floor in the rear,
looking out through French windows over a nice little
garden, and my friend finds Frank in the library where
she expects to find him, because she is smart enough
to figure that a guy who is working on papers is not
apt to be doing this work in the cellar.

But Frank is not working on anything when my friend
moves in on him. He is dozing in a chair by the window,
and, looking at him after all these years, she finds something of a change, indeed. He is much heavier than he
is thirty-five years back, and his hair is white, but he
looks pretty well to my friend, at that, as she stands
there for maybe five minutes watching him. Then he
seems to realize somebody is in the room, as sleeping
guys will do, for his regular breathing stops with a snort,
and he opens his eyes, and looks into my friend's eyes,
but without hardly stirring. And finally my friend
speaks to Frank as follows:

"Well, Frank," she says, "do you know me?"

"Yes," he says, after a while, "I know you. At first
I think maybe you are a ghost, as I once hear something
about your being dead. But," he says, "I see now the
report is a canard. You are too fat to be a ghost."

Well, of course, this is a most insulting crack, indeed,
but my friend passes it off as she does not wish to get

in any arguments with Frank at this time. She can see that he is upset more than somewhat and he keeps looking around the room as if he hopes he can see somebody else he can cut in on the conversation. In fact, he acts as if my friend is by no means a welcome visitor.

"Well, Frank," my friend says, very pleasant, "there you are, and here I am. I understand you are now a wealthy and prominent citizen of this town. I am glad to know this, Frank," she says. "You will be surprised to hear that for years and years I pray that you will do well for yourself and become a big guy in every respect, with a nice family, and everything else. I judge my prayers are answered," she says. "I see by the papers that you have two sons at Yale, and a daughter in Vassar, and that your ever-loving wife is getting to be very high mucky-mucky in society. Well, Frank," she says, "I am very glad. I pray something like all this will happen to you."

Now, at such a speech, Frank naturally figures that my friend is all right, at that, and the chances are he also figures that she still has a mighty soft spot in her heart for him, just as she has in the days when she deals them off the arm to keep him in gambling and drinking money. In fact, Frank brightens up somewhat, and he says to my friend like this:

"You pray for my success?" he says. "Why, this is very thoughtful of you, indeed. Well," he says, "I am sitting on top of the world, I have everything to live for."

"Yes," my friend says, "and this is exactly where I pray I will find you. On top of the world," she says, "and with everything to live for. It is where I am when you take my life. It is where I am when you kill me as surely as if you strangle me with your hands. I always pray you will not become a bum," my friend says, "because a bum has nothing to live for, anyway. I want to find you liking to live, so you will hate so much to die."

Naturally, this does not sound so good to Frank, and he begins all of a sudden to shake and shiver and to stutter somewhat.

"Why," he says, "what do you mean? Are you going to kill me?"

"Well," my friend says, "that remains to be seen. Personally," she says, "I will be much obliged if you will kill yourself, but it can be arranged one way or the other. However, I will explain the disadvantages of me killing you.

"The chances are," my friend says, "if I kill you I will be caught and a very great scandal will result, because," she says, "I have on my person the certificate of my marriage to you in Denver, and something tells me you never think to get a divorce. So," she says, "you are a bigamist."

"I can pay," Frank says. "I can pay plenty."

"Furthermore," my friend says, paying no attention to his remark, "I have a sworn statement from Black Emanuel about your transaction with him, for Black Emanuel gets religion before he dies from being shivved by Johnny Mizzoo, and he tries to round himself up by confessing all the sins he can think of, which are quite a lot. It is a very interesting statement," my friend says.

"Now then," she says, "if you knock yourself off you will leave an unsullied, respected name. If I kill you, all the years and effort you have devoted to building up your reputation will go for nothing. You are past sixty," my friend says, "and any way you figure it, you do not have so very far to go. If I kill you," she says, "you will go in horrible disgrace, and everybody around you will feel the disgrace, no matter how much dough you leave them. Your children will hang their heads in shame. Your ever-loving wife will not like it," my friend says.

"I wait on you a long time, Frank," my friend says. "A dozen times in the past twenty years I figure I may as well call on you and close up my case with you, but," she says, "then I always persuade myself to wait a little longer so you would rise higher and higher and life will be a bit sweeter to you. And there you are, Frank," she says, "and here I am."

Well, Frank sits there as if he is knocked plumb out, and he does not answer a word; so finally my friend outs with a large John Roscoe which she is packing in the bosom of her dress, and tosses it in his lap, and speaks as follows:

"Frank," she says, "do not think it will do you any good to pot me in the back when I turn around, because," she says, "you will be worse off than ever. I leave plenty of letters scattered around in case anything happens to me. And remember," she says, "if you do not do this job yourself, I will be back. Sooner or later, I will be back."

So [Dream Street Rose says] my friend goes out of the library and down the stairs, leaving Frank sprawled out in his chair, and when she reaches the first floor she hears what may be a shot in the upper part of the house, and then again may be only a door slamming. My friend never knows for sure what it is, because a little later as she nears the servants' entrance she hears quite a commotion outside, and a guy cussing a blue streak, and a doll tee-heeing, and pretty soon my friend's friend, the maid, and Sloggins, the valet, come walking in.

Well, my friend just has time to scroonch herself back

in a dark corner, and they go upstairs, the guy still cussing and the doll still giggling, and my friend cannot make out what it is all about except that they come home earlier than she figures. So my friend goes tippytoe out of the servants' entrance, to grab a taxi not far from the house and get away from this neighborhood, and now you will soon hear of the suicide of a guy who is a millionaire, and it will be all even with my friend.

"Well, Rose," I say, "it is a nice long story, and full of romance and all this and that, and," I say, "of course I will never be ungentlemanly enough to call a lady a liar, but," I say, "if it is not a lie, it will do until a lie comes along."

"All right," Rose says. "Anyway, I tell you about my friend. Now," she says, "I am going where the liquor is better, which can be any other place in town, because," she says, "there is no chance of liquor anywhere being any worse."

So she goes out, making more tracks on Good Time Charley's floor, and Charley speaks most impolitely of her after she goes, and gets out his mop to clean the floor, for one thing about Charley, he is as neat as a pin, and maybe neater.

Well, along toward one o'clock I hear a newsboy in the street outside yelling something I cannot make out, because he is yelling as if he has a mouthful of mush, as newsboys are bound to do. But I am anxious to see what goes in the first race at Belmont, on account of having a first-class tip, so I poke my noggin outside Good Time Charley's and buy a paper, and across the front page, in large letters, it states that the wealthy Mr. Frank Billingsworth McQuiggan knocks himself off by putting a slug through his own noggin.

It says Mr. McQuiggan is found in a chair in his li-

brary as dead as a doornail with the pistol in his lap
with which he knocks himself off, and the paper states
that nobody can figure what causes Mr. McQuiggan to
do such a thing to himself as he is in good health and
has plenty of potatoes and is at the peak of his career.
Then there is a lot about his history.

When Mr. McQuiggan is a young fellow returning
from a visit to the Pacific Coast with about two hundred
dollars in his pocket after paying his railroad fare, he
meets in the train Jonas Calloway, famous inventor of
the Calloway steel process. Calloway also then young,
is desperately in need of funds and he offers Mr.
McQuiggan a third interest in his invention for what
now seems the paltry sum of one hundred dollars. Mr.
McQuiggan accepts the offer and thus paves the way
to his own fortune.

I am telling all this to Good Time Charley while he
is mopping away at the floor, and finally I come on a
paragraph down near the finish which goes like this:
"The body was discovered by Mr. McQuiggan's faithful
valet, Thomas Sloggins, at eleven o'clock. Mr. McQuiggan was then apparently dead a couple of hours. Sloggins
returned home shortly before ten o'clock with another
servant after changing his mind about going to a movie.
Instead of going to see his employer at once, as is his
usual custom, Sloggins went to his own quarters and
changed his clothes.

" 'The light over the servants' entrance was out when
I returned home,' the valet said, 'and in the darkness I
stumbled over some scaffolding and other material left
near this entrance by workmen who are to regravel the
roof of the house tomorrow, upsetting all over the en-
tranceway a large bucket of tar, much of which got on
my apparel when I fell, making a change necessary before going to see Mr. McQuiggan.' "

Well, Good Time Charley keeps on mopping harder than ever, though finally he stops a minute and speaks to me as follows:

"Listen," Charley says, "understand I do not say the guy does not deserve what he gets, and I am by no means hollering copper, but," Charley says, "if he knocks himself off, how does it come the rod is still in his lap where Dream Street Rose says her friend tosses it? Well, never mind," Charley says, "but can you think of something that will remove tar from a wood floor? It positively will not mop off."

For a Pal

A romance of that curious and most exciting
thoroughfare known as Broadway

FOR a matter of maybe fifteen years or more, Little Yid
and Blind Benny are pals, and this is considered a very
good thing for Benny because he is as blind as a bat,
and maybe blinder, while Yid can see as good as anybody
and sometimes better.

So Little Yid does the seeing for Benny, explaining
in his own way to Benny just what he sees, such as a
horse race or a baseball game or a prize fight or a play
or a moving picture or anything else, for Yid and Blind
Benny are great hands for going around and about wherever anything is coming off, no matter what, and up
to the time this doll Mary Marble comes into their lives
they are as happy as two pups in a basket.

How Benny comes to go blind I do not know, and
nobody else along Broadway seems to know either, and

in fact nobody cares, although I once hear Regret, the horse player, say it is probably in sympathy with the judges at the race track, Regret being such a guy as claims all these judges are very blind indeed. But of course Regret is sore at these race-track judges because they always call the wrong horse for him in the close finishes.

Little Yid tells me that Blind Benny is once a stick man in a gambling joint in Denver, and a very good stick man, at that, and one night a fire comes off in a flop house on Larimer Street, and Blind Benny, who is not blind at this time, runs into the fire to haul out an old guy who has more smoke in him than somewhat, and a rush of flames burns Benny's eyes so bad he loses his sight.

Well, this may be the true story of how Benny comes to go blind, but I know Little Yid likes Benny so much that he is not going to give Benny the worst of any story he tells about him, and for all anybody knows maybe Benny really goes into the fire to search the old guy. Personally, I do not believe in taking too much stock in any story you hear on Broadway about anything.

But there is no doubt about Blind Benny being blind. His eyelids are tacked down tight over his eyes, and there is no chance that he is faking, because many guys keep close tab on him for years and never catch him peeping once. Furthermore, several guys send Benny to eye specialists at different times to see if they can do anything about his eyes, and all these specialists say he is one of the blindest guys they ever examine. Regret says maybe it is a good thing, at that, because Benny is so smart as a blind guy that the chances are if he can see he will be too smart to live.

He is especially smart when it comes to playing such

games as pinochle. In fact, Benny is about as good a single-handed pinochle player as there is in this town, and there are many first-rate pinochle players in this town, if anybody asks you. Benny punches little holes in the cards so he can tell which is which by feeling of them, and the only way anybody can beat him is to cheat him, and it is considered most discourteous to cheat a blind guy, especially as Benny is always apt to catch a guy at cheating and put up an awful beef.

He is a tall, skinny guy with a thin face, and is by no means bad-looking, while Little Yid is about knee high to a snake, and they look like a father and his little boy as they go along the street with Little Yid hanging onto Blind Benny's arm and giving him the right steer.

Of course it is by no means an uncommon thing on Broadway for citizens to come upon blind guys waiting at a corner for traffic to stop, and for the citizens to steer these blind guys across the street, although if the blind guys have any sense they will keep their dukes on their tin cups while they are being steered, but it is a most unusual proposition in this town for anybody to go steering a blind guy around for fifteen years the way Little Yid steers Blind Benny, as Blind Benny is a guy who takes plenty of steering.

In fact, one time Yid has to be away on business for a week, and he leaves Blind Benny with a committee of guys, and every day one of these guys has to steer Benny around wherever he wishes to go, which is wherever there is anything going on, and Benny wears the whole committee plumb out before Yid gets back, as Benny is certainly a guy who likes to go around and about. Furthermore, he is so unhappy while Yid is away that he becomes a very great nuisance, because it seems that none of the committee can see things as good as Yid for him, or explain them so he can understand them.

Personally, I will not care to have Little Yid do my seeing for me, even if I am blind, because I listen to him telling what he sees to Blind Benny many times, and it seems to me Little Yid is often somewhat cockeyed in his explanations.

Furthermore, I will hate to be explaining things to Blind Benny, because he is always arguing about what is taking place, and giving you his opinions of it, even though he cannot see. In fact, although he cannot see a lick, Blind Benny is freer with his opinions than guys who can see from here to Europe.

It is a very interesting sight to watch Little Yid and Blind Benny at the race track, for they are both great hands for playing the horses and, in fact, Benny is a better handicapper than a lot of guys who have two good eyes and a pair of spectacles to do their handicapping with.

At night they get the form sheet and sit up in their room with Yid reading off the past performances and the time trials, and all this and that, and with Blind Benny doping the horses from what Yid reads, and picking the ones he figures ought to win the next day. They always have a big argument over each horse, and Yid will tell Blind Benny he is daffy to be picking whatever horse it is he picks, and Benny will tell Yid he is out of his mind to think anything else can beat this horse and they will holler and yell at each other for hours.

But they always wind up very friendly, and they always play the horse Benny picks, for Yid has much confidence in Benny's judgment, although he hollers and yells at him more than somewhat when one of his picks loses. They sit up in the grandstand during every race, and Yid will explain to Benny what is doing in the race, and generally he manages to mention that the horse they are betting on is right up there and going easy, even though it may be laying back of the nine ball, for Yid believes in making Blind Benny feel good at all times.

But when a horse they are betting on is really in the running, especially in the stretch, Yid starts to root him home, and Benny roots right along with him as if he can see, and rocks back and forth in his seat, and pounds with his cane, and yells, "Come on with him, jock," the same as anybody with two good eyes.

I am telling you all this about Little Yid and Benny to show you that they are very close friends, indeed. They live together and eat together and argue together, and nobody ever hears of a nicer friendship on Broadway, although naturally some citizens figure for a while that one or the other must have some angle in this friendship, as it is practically uncanny for a friendship to last all these years on Broadway.

Blind Benny has some kind of an income from his people out West who are sorry about him being blind, and Little Yid has a piece of a small factory run by a couple of his brothers over in Hoboken where they make caps such as some citizens wear on their heads, and it seems this factory does very well, and the brothers are willing to send Little Yid his piece without him being around the factory very much, as they do not seem to consider him any boost to a cap factory.

So Yid and Blind Benny have all the money they need to go along, what with making a little scratch now and then on the races, and they never seem to care for any company but their own and are very happy and contented with each other. In all the years they are together, Yid is never known to more than say hello to a doll, and of course Blind Benny cannot see dolls, anyway, which many citizens claim is a great break for Benny, so Yid and Benny are carrying no weight in this respect.

Now one night it seems that Ike Jacobs, the ticket spec, has a pair of Chinee duckets to the opening of a new play by the name of Red Hot Love, a Chinee ducket being a complimentary ducket that is punched full of holes like Chinee money, and which you do not have to pay for, and Ike gives these duckets to Little Yid and Blind Benny, which is considered very large-hearted of Ike, at that.

So when the curtain goes up on Red Hot Love, Yid and Benny are squatted right down in front among many well-known citizens who are all dressed up in evening clothes, because this Red Hot Love has a bunch of swell actors in it, and is expected to be first-class.

Naturally, when the play begins, Yid has to give Blind Benny a little information about what is doing, otherwise Benny cannot appreciate the thing. So Yid starts off in a whisper, but any time Yid starts explaining anything to Benny he always winds up getting excited, and talking so loud you can hear him down at the Battery.

Of course Blind Benny can follow a play as good as anybody if there is plenty of gab on the stage, but he likes to know what actors are doing the gabbing, and what they look like, and what the scenery looks like, and other details that he cannot see, and Little Yid is telling him in such a voice as causes some of the citizens around to say shush-shush. But Little Yid and Blind Benny are accustomed to being shushed in theaters, so they do not pay much attention.

Well, Red Hot Love is one of these problem plays, and neither Little Yid nor Blind Benny can make much of it, although they are no worse off than anybody else around them, at that. But Little Yid tries to explain to Blind Benny what it is all about, and Benny speaks out loud as follows:

"It sounds to me like a rotten play."

"Well," Little Yid says, "maybe the play is not so rotten but the acting is."

There is much shushing from one and all around them, and the actors are giving them the bad eye from the stage, because the actors can hear what they say, and are very indignant, especially over this crack about the acting.

Well, the next thing anybody knows down the aisle come a couple of big guys who put the arm on Little Yid and Blind Benny and give them the old heave-o out of the joint, as you are not supposed to speak out loud in a theater about any bad acting that is going on there, no matter how bad it is.

Anyway, as Little Yid and Blind Benny are being prodded up the aisle by the big guys, Blind Benny states as follows:

"I still claim," he says, "that it sounds like a rotten play."

"Well," Little Yid says, "the acting certainly is."

There is much applause as Yid and Benny are getting the heave-o, and many citizens claim it is because the customers are glad to see them heaved, but afterwards it comes out that what many of the customers are really applauding is the statements by Little Yid and Benny.

Well, Yid and Benny do not mind getting the heave-o so much, as they are heaved out of many better theaters than this in their time, but they are very indignant when the box office refuses to give them back the admission price, although of course their duckets do not cost them anything in the first place and they are a little out of line in trying to collect.

They are standing on the sidewalk saying what an outrage it is when all of a sudden out of the theater pops this doll by the name of Mary Marble, and her face is very red, and she is also very indignant, because it seems that in the second act of the play there are some very coarse cracks let out on the stage, and it seems that Mary Marble is such a doll as believes that cracks of this nature are only fit for married people to hear, and she is by no means married.

Of course Little Yid and Blind Benny do not know at the time that she is Mary Marble, and in fact they do not know her from Adam's off ox as she marches up to them and speaks as follows:

"Gentlemen," she says, "I wish to compliment you on your judgment of the affair inside. I hear what you say as you are getting ejected," she says, "and I wish to state that you are both right. It is a rotten play, and the acting is rotten."

Now off this meeting, what happens but Mary Marble gets to going around with Little Yid and Blind Benny whenever she can spare time from her job, which is managing a little joint on Broadway where they sell stockings such as dolls wear on their legs, except in summer time, although even when they wear these stockings you cannot tell if a doll has anything on her legs unless you pinch them, the stockings that dolls wear nowadays being very thin, indeed. Furthermore, whenever she is with them, it is now Mary Marble who does most of the explaining to Blind Benny of what is going on, because Mary Marble is such a doll as is just naturally bound to do all the explaining necessary when she is around.

When it comes to looks, Mary Marble is practically no dice. In fact, if she is not the homeliest doll on Broadway, I will guarantee she is no worse than a dead heat with the homeliest. She has a large beezer and large feet, and her shape is nothing whatever to speak of, and Regret, the horse player, says they never need to be afraid of entering Mary Marble in a claiming race at any price. But of course Regret is such a guy as will not give you a counterfeit dime for any doll no matter what she looks like.

Mary Marble is maybe twenty-five years old—although Regret says he will lay six to five against her being any better than twenty-eight—and about all she has running for her, any way you take her, is a voice that is soft and gentle and very nice, indeed, except that she is fond of using it more than somewhat.

She comes from a little town over in Pennsylvania, and is pretty well educated, and there is no doubt whatever that she is unusually respectable, because such a looking doll as Mary Marble has no excuse for being anything but respectable on Broadway. In fact, Mary Marble is so respectable that many citizens figure there must be an angle, but it is agreed by one and all that she is perfectly safe with Little Yid and Blind Benny, no matter what.

And now at night instead of always doping the horses, Little Yid and Blind Benny will often sit up in their room talking about nothing much but Mary Marble, and Benny asks Yid a million questions over and over again.

"Tell me, Yid," Blind Benny will say, "what does Mary look like?"

"She is beautiful," Yid always says.

Well, of course, this is practically perjury, and many citizens figure that Yid tells Blind Benny this very large lie because he has an idea Benny wishes to hear only the very best about Mary Marble, although it comes out afterwards that Little Yid thinks Mary Marble is beautiful, at that.

"She is like an angel," he says.

"Yes, yes," Blind Benny says, "tell me more."

And Little Yid keeps on telling him, and if Mary Mar-

ble is only one eighth as good-looking as Yid tells, Zieg-
feld and Georgie White and Earl Carroll will be breaking each other's legs trying to get to her first.

"Well," Blind Benny often says, after Little Yid gets
through telling him about Mary Marble, "she is just
as I picture her to myself, Yid," he says. "I never care
so much about not being able to see until now, and
even now all I wish to see is Mary."

The idea seems to be that Blind Benny is in love with
Mary Marble, and the way Little Yid is always boosting
her it is no wonder. In fact, the chances are a lot of
other citizens will be in love with Mary Marble if they
listen to Yid telling Blind Benny about her, and never
get a gander at her personally.

But Blind Benny does not mention right out that he
is in love with Mary Marble, and it may be that he
does not really know what is eating him, which is often
the case with guys who are in love. All Blind Benny
knows is that he likes to be with Mary Marble and to
listen to her explaining things to him, and, what is more,
Mary Marble seems to like to be with Blind Benny,
and to explain things to him, although as far as this
goes Mary Marble is such a doll as likes to be explaining
things to anybody any time she gets a chance.

Now Little Yid and Blind Benny are still an entry
at all times, even when Mary Marble is with them, but
many citizens see that Little Yid is getting all sorrowed
up, and they figure it is because he feels Blind Benny
is gradually drifting away from him after all these years,
and everybody sympathizes with Little Yid no little,
and there is some talk of getting him another blind guy
to steer around in case Blind Benny finally leaves him
for good.

Then it comes on a Saturday night when Little Yid
says he must go over to Hoboken to see his brothers

about the cap business and, as Mary Marble has to work in the stocking joint on Saturday nights, Little Yid asks Blind Benny to go with him.

Of course Blind Benny does not care two cents about the cap business, but Little Yid explains to him that he knows a Dutchman's in Hoboken where there is some very nice real beer, and if there is one thing Blind Benny likes more than somewhat it is nice real beer, especially as it seems that since they become acquainted with Mary Marble he seldom gets nice real beer, as Mary Marble is a terrible knocker against such matters as nice real beer.

So they start out for Hoboken, and Little Yid sees his brothers about the cap business, and then he takes Blind Benny to a Dutchman's to get the nice real beer, only it turns out that the beer is not real, and by no means nice, being all needled up with alky, and full of headaches, and one thing and another. But of course Little Yid and Blind Benny are not going around complaining about beer even if it is needled, as, after all, needled beer is better than no beer whatever.

They sit around the Dutchman's quite a while, although it turns out that the Dutchman is nothing but a Polack, and then they nab a late ferryboat for home, as Little Yid says he wishes to ride on a ferryboat to get the breeze. As far as Blind Benny is concerned, he does not care how they go as long as he can get back to New York to meet up with Mary Marble when she is through work.

There are not many citizens on the ferryboat with them, because it is getting on toward midnight, and at such an hour anybody who lives in Jersey is home in bed. In fact, there are not over four or five other passengers on the ferryboat with Little Yid and Blind Benny, and these passengers are all dozing on the benches in the smoking-room with their legs stuck out in front of them.

Now if you know anything about a ferryboat you know that they always hook big gates across each end of such a boat to keep automobiles and trucks and citizens and one thing and another from going off these ends into the water when the ferryboat is traveling back and forth, as naturally it will be a great nuisance to other boats in the river to have things falling off the ferryboats and clogging up the stream.

Well, Little Yid is away out on the end of the ferryboat up against the gate enjoying the breeze, and Blind Benny is leaning against the rail just outside the smoking-room door where Little Yid plants him when they get on the boat, and Blind Benny is smoking a big heater that he gets at the Dutchman's and maybe thinking of Mary Marble, when all of a sudden Little Yid yells like this:

"Oh, Benny," he yells, "come here."

Naturally Benny turns and goes in the direction of the voice and Little Yid's voice comes from the stern, and Blind Benny keeps following his beezer in the direction of the voice, expecting to feel Little Yid's hand stopping him any minute, and the next thing he knows he is walking right off the ferryboat into the river.

Of course Blind Benny cannot continue walking after he hits the water, so he sinks at once, making a sound like glug-glug as he goes down. It is in the fall of the year, and the water is by no means warm, so as Benny comes up for air he naturally lets out a loud squawk, but by this time the ferryboat is quite some jumps away from him, and nobody seems to see him, or even hear him.

Now Blind Benny cannot swim a lick, so he sinks again with a glug-glug. He comes up once more, and this time he does not squawk so loud, but he sings out, very distinct, as follows: "Good-by, Pal Yid."

All of a sudden there is quite a splash in the water near the ferryboat, and Little Yid is swimming for Blind Benny so fast the chances are he will make a sucker of Johnny Weissmuller if Johnny happens to be around, for Little Yid is a regular goldfish when it comes to water, although he is not much of a hand for going swimming without provocation.

He has to dive for Blind Benny, for by this time Blind Benny is going down for the third time, and everybody knows that a guy is only allowed three downs when he is drowning. In fact, Blind Benny is almost down where the crabs live before Little Yid can get a fistful of his collar. At first Little Yid's idea is to take Blind Benny by the hair, but he remembers in time that Benny does not have much hair, so he compromises on the collar.

And being a little guy, Yid has quite a job getting Benny to the top and keeping him there. By this time the ferryboat is almost at its dock on the New York side, and nobody on board seems to realize that it is shy a couple of passengers, although of course the ferryboat company is not going to worry about that as it collects the fares in advance. But it is a pretty lucky break for Little Yid and Blind Benny that a tugboat happens along and picks them up, or Yid may be swimming around the North River to this day with Blind Benny by the nape of the neck going glug-glug.

The captain of the tugboat is a kind old guy with whiskers by the name of Deusenberg, and he is very sorry indeed to see them in such a situation, so after he hauls them on board the tugboat, and spreads them out on bunks to let them dry, he throws a couple of slugs of gin into Little Yid and Blind Benny, it being gin of such a nature that they are half sorry they do not go ahead and drown before they meet up with it.

Then the captain unloads them at Forty-second Street
on the New York side, and by this time, between the
water and the gin, Blind Benny is very much fagged
out, indeed, and in bad shape generally, so Little Yid
puts him in a cab and takes him to a hospital.

Well, for several days Blind Benny is no better than
even money to get well, because after they get the water
out of him they still have to contend with the gin, and
Mary Marble is around carrying on quite some, and
saying she does not see how Little Yid can be so careless
as to let Benny walk off the end of a ferryboat when
there are gates to prevent such a thing, or how he can
let Benny drink tugboat gin, and many citizens do not
see either, especially about the gin.

As for Little Yid, he is looking very sad, and is at
the hospital at all times, and finally, one day when Blind
Benny is feeling all right again, Little Yid sits down
beside his bed, and speaks to him as follows:

"Benny," Little Yid says, "I will now make a confession to you, and I will then go away somewhere and
knock myself off. Benny," he says, "I let you fall into
the river on purpose. In fact," Little Yid says, "I unhook
the gate across the passageway and call you, figuring
you will follow the sound of my voice and walk on
off the boat into the water.

"I am very sorry about this," Little Yid says, "but,
Benny," he says, "I love Mary Marble more than some-
what, although I never before mention this to a soul.
Not even to Mary Marble, because," Little Yid says,
"I know she loves you, as you love her. I love her,"
Little Yid says, "from the night we first meet, and this
love winds up by making me a little daffy.

"I get to thinking," Little Yid says, "that with you
out of the way Mary Marble will turn to me and love

me instead. But," he says, starting to shed large tears, "when I hear your voice from the water saying 'Good- by, Pal Yid,' my heart begins to break, and I must jump in after you. So now you know, and I will go away and shoot myself through the head if I can find some- body to lend me a Roscoe, because I am no good."

"Why," Blind Benny says, "Pal Yid, what you tell me about leading me into the river is no news to me. In fact," he says, "I know it the minute I hit the water because, although I am blind, I see many things as I am going down, and I see very plain that you must do this thing on purpose, because I know you are close enough around to grab me if you wish.

"I know, of course," Blind Benny says, "that there is bound to be a gate across the end of the boat because I often feel it before, and in fact I remember hearing them fix this gate when we are leaving Hoboken. So," he says, "I see that you must unhook this gate. I see that for some reason you wish to knock me off, although I do not see the reason, and the chances are I will never see it unless you tell me now, so I do not put up more of a holler and maybe attract the attention of the other guys on the boat. I am willing to let it all go as it lays."

"My goodness," Little Yid says, "this is most surpris- ing to me, indeed. In fact," he says, "I scarcely know what to say, Benny. In fact," he says, "I cannot figure out why you are willing to go without putting up a very large beef."

"Well, Pal Yid," Benny says, reaching out and taking Little Yid by the hand, "I am so fond of you that I figure if my being dead is going to do you any good, I am willing to die, even though I do not know why. Although," Benny says, "it seems to me you can think up a nicer way of scragging me than by drowning, be- cause you know I loathe and despise water. Now then," he says, "as for Mary Marble, if you—"

But Little Yid never lets Blind Benny finish this, because he cuts in and speaks as follows:

"Benny," he says, "if you are willing to die for me, I can certainly afford to give up a doll for you, especially," he says, "as my people tell me only yesterday that if I marry anybody who is not of my religion, which is slightly Jewish, they will chop me off at the pants pocket. You take Mary Marble," he says, "and I will stake you to my blessing, and maybe a wedding present."

So the upshot of the whole business is Mary Marble is now Mrs. Blind Benny, and Blind Benny seems to be very happy, indeed, although some citizens claim the explanations he gets nowadays of whatever is going on are much shorter than when he is with Little Yid, while Little Yid is over in Hoboken in the cap racket with his brothers, and he never sees Blind Benny any more, as Mary Marble still holds the gin against him.

Personally, I always consider Little Yid's conduct in this matter very self-sacrificing, and furthermore I consider him a very great hero for rescuing Blind Benny from the river, and I am saying as much only the other day to Regret, the horse player.

"Yes," Regret says, "it sounds very self-sacrificing, indeed, and maybe Little Yid is a hero, at that, but," Regret says, "many citizens are criticizing him no little for sawing off such a crow as Mary Marble on a poor blind guy."

Earthquake

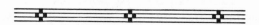

PERSONALLY, I do not care for coppers, but I believe in being courteous to them at all times, so when Johnny Brannigan comes into Mindy's restaurant one Friday evening and sits down in the same booth with me, because there are no other vacant seats in the joint, I give him a huge hello.

Furthermore, I offer him a cigarette and say how pleased I am to see how well he is looking, although as a matter of fact Johnny Brannigan looks very terrible, what with big black circles under his eyes and his face thinner than somewhat.

In fact, Johnny Brannigan looks as if he is sick, and I am secretly hoping that it is something fatal, because the way I figure it there are a great many coppers in this world, and a few less may be a good thing for one and all concerned.

But naturally I do not mention this hope to Johnny Brannigan, as Johnny Brannigan belongs to what is called the gunman squad and is known to carry a blackjack in his pants pocket, and furthermore he is known to boff guys on their noggins with this jack if they get too fresh with him, and for all I know Johnny Brannigan may consider such a hope about his health very fresh indeed.

Now the last time I see Johnny Brannigan before this is in Good Time Charley Bernstein's little joint in Forty-eighth Street with three other coppers, and what Johnny is there for is to put the arm on a guy by the name of Earthquake, who is called Earthquake because he is so fond of shaking things up.

In fact, at the time I am speaking of, Earthquake has this whole town shaken up, what with shooting and stabbing and robbing different citizens, and otherwise misconducting himself, and the law wishes to place Earthquake in the electric chair, as he is considered a great knock to the community.

Now the only reason Brannigan does not put the arm on Earthquake at this time is because Earthquake picks up one of Good Time Charley Bernstein's tables and kisses Johnny Brannigan with same, and furthermore, Earthquake outs with the old equalizer and starts blasting away at the coppers who are with Johnny Brannigan, and he keeps them so busy dodging slugs that they do not have any leisure to put the arm on him, and the next thing anybody knows, Earthquake takes it on the lam out of there.

Well, personally, I also take it on the lam myself, as I do not wish to be around when Johnny Brannigan comes to, as I figure Johnny may be somewhat bewildered and will start boffing people over the noggin with his jack thinking they are all Earthquake, no matter who they are, and I do not see Johnny again until this evening in Mindy's.

But in the meantime I hear rumors that Johnny Brannigan is out of town looking for Earthquake, because
it seems that while misconducting himself Earthquake
severely injures a copper by the name of Mulcahy. In
fact, it seems that Earthquake injures him so severely
that Mulcahy hauls off and dies, and if there is one thing
that is against the law in this town it is injuring a copper
in such a manner. In fact, it is apt to cause great indignation among other coppers.

It is considered very illegal to severely injure any citizen in this town in such a way as to make him haul
off and die, but naturally it is not apt to cause any such
indignation as injuring a copper, as this town has more
citizens to spare than coppers.

Well, sitting there with Johnny Brannigan, I get to
wondering if he ever meets up with Earthquake while
he is looking for him, and if so how he comes out, for
Earthquake is certainly not such a guy as I will care
to meet up with, even if I am a copper.

Earthquake is a guy of maybe six foot three, and
weighing a matter of two hundred and twenty pounds,
and all these pounds are nothing but muscle. Anybody
will tell you that Earthquake is one of the strongest
guys in this town, because it seems he once works in
a foundry and picks up much of his muscle there. In
fact, Earthquake likes to show how strong he is at all
times, and one of his ways of showing this is to grab
a full-sized guy in either duke and hold them straight
up in the air over his head.

Sometimes after he gets tired of holding these guys
over his head, he will throw them plumb away, especially if they are coppers, or maybe knock their noggins
together and leave them with their noggins very sore
indeed. When he is in real good humor, Earthquake
does not think anything of going into a night club and

taking it apart and chucking the pieces out into the street, along with the owner and the waiters and maybe some of the customers, so you can see Earthquake is a very high-spirited guy, and full of fun.

Personally, I do not see why Earthquake does not get a job in a circus as a strong guy, because there is no percentage in wasting all this strength for nothing, but when I mention this idea to Earthquake one time, he says he cannot bear to think of keeping regular hours such as a circus might wish.

Well, Johnny Brannigan does not have anything to say to me at first as we sit there in Mindy's, but by and by he looks at me and speaks as follows:

"You remember Earthquake?" he says. "You remember he is very strong?"

"Strong?" I say to Johnny Brannigan. "Why, there is nobody stronger than Earthquake. Why," I say, "Earthquake is strong enough to hold up a building."

"Yes," Johnny Brannigan says, "what you say is very true. He is strong enough to hold up a building. Yes," he says, "Earthquake is very strong indeed. Now I will tell you about Earthquake."

It is maybe three months after Earthquake knocks off Mulcahy (Johnny Brannigan says) that we get a tip he is in a town by the name of New Orleans, and because I am personally acquainted with him, I am sent there to put the arm on him. But when I get to this New Orleans, I find Earthquake blows out of there and does not leave any forwarding address.

Well, I am unable to get any trace of him for some days, and it looks as if I am on a bust, when I happen to run into a guy by the name of Saul the Soldier, from Greenwich Village. Saul the Soldier winds up in New Orleans following the horse races, and he is very glad indeed to meet a friend from his old home town, and

I am also glad to meet Saul, because I am getting very lonesome in New Orleans. Well, Saul knows New Orleans pretty well, and he takes me around and about, and finally I ask him if he can tell me where Earthquake is, and Saul speaks as follows:

"Why," Saul says, "Earthquake sails away on a ship for Central America not long ago with a lot of guys that are going to join a revolution there. I think," Saul says, "they are going to a place by the name of Nicaragua."

Well, I wire my headquarters and they tell me to go after Earthquake no matter where he is, because it seems the bladders back home are asking what kind of a police force do we have, anyway, and why is somebody not arrested for something.

I sail on a fruit steamer, and finally I get to this Nicaragua, and to a town that is called Managua.

Well, for a week or so I knock around here and there looking for Earthquake, but I cannot find hide or hair of him, and I am commencing to think that Saul the Soldier gives me a bum steer.

It is pretty hot in this town of Managua, and of an afternoon when I get tired of looking for Earthquake, I go to a little park in the center of the town where there are many shade trees. It is a pretty park, although down there they call it a plaza, and across from this plaza there is a big old two-story stone building that seems to be a convent, because I see many nuns and small female kids popping in and out of a door on one side of the building, which seems to be the main entrance.

One afternoon I am sitting in the little plaza when a big guy in sloppy white clothes comes up and sits down on another bench near me, and I am greatly surprised to see that this guy is nobody but Earthquake.

He does not see me at first, and in fact he does not know I am present until I step over to him and out with my jack and knock him bowlegged; because, knowing Earthquake, I know there is no use starting out with him by shaking hands. I do not boff him so very hard, at that, but just hard enough to make him slightly insensible for a minute, while I put the handcuffs on him.

Well, when he opens his eyes, Earthquake looks up at the trees, as if he thinks maybe a coconut drops down and beans him, and it is several minutes before he sees me, and then he leaps up and roars, and acts as if he is greatly displeased. But then he discovers that he is handcuffed, and he sits down again and speaks as follows:

"Hello, copper," Earthquake says. "When do you get in?"

I tell him how long I am there, and how much inconvenience he causes me by not being more prominent, and Earthquake says the fact of the matter is he is out in the jungles with a lot of guys trying to rig up a revolution, but they are so slow getting started they finally exasperate him, and he comes into town.

Well, finally we get to chatting along very pleasant about this and that, and although he is away only a few months, Earthquake is much interested in what is going on in New York and asks me many questions, and I tell him that the liquor around town is getting better.

"Furthermore, Earthquake," I say, "they are holding a nice warm seat for you up at Ossining."

"Well, copper," Earthquake says, "I am sorry I scrag Mulcahy, at that. In fact," he says, "it really is an accident. I do not mean to scrag him. I am aiming at another guy, copper," he says. "In fact," he says, "I am aiming at you."

Now about this time the bench seems to move from

under me, and I find myself sitting on the ground, and the ground also seems to be trying to get from under me, and I hear loud crashing noises here and there, and a great roaring, and at first I think maybe Earthquake takes to shaking things up, when I see him laid out on the ground about fifty feet from me.

I get to my pins, but the ground is still wobbling somewhat and I can scarcely walk over to Earthquake, who is now sitting up very indignant, and when he sees me he says to me like this:

"Personally," he says, "I consider it a very dirty trick for you to boff me again when I am not looking."

Well, I explain to Earthquake that I do not boff him again, and that as near as I can figure out what happens is that we are overtaken by what he is named for, which is an earthquake, and looking around and about, anybody can see that this is very true, as great clouds of dust are rising from piles of stone and timber where fair-sized buildings stand a few minutes before, and guys and dolls are running every which way.

Now I happens to look across at the convent, and I can see that it is something of a wreck and is very likely to be more so any minute, as the walls are teetering this way and that, and mostly they are teetering inward. Furthermore, I can hear much screeching from inside the old building.

Then I notice the door in the side of the building that seems to be the main entrance to the convent is gone, leaving the doorway open, and now I must explain to you about this doorway, as it figures quite some in what later comes off. It is a fairly wide doorway in the beginning with a frame of heavy timber set in the side of the stone building, with a timber arch at the top, and the wall around this doorway seems to be caving in from the top and sides, so that the doorway is now shaped like the letter V upside down, with the timber framework bending, instead of breaking.

As near as I can make out, this doorway is the only entrance to the convent that is not closed up by falling stone and timber, and it is a sure thing that pretty soon this opening will be plugged up, too, so I speak to Earthquake as follows:

"Earthquake," I say, "there are a lot of nuns and kids in this joint over here, and I judge from the screeching going on inside that some of them are very much alive. But," I say, "they will not be alive in a few minutes, because the walls are going to tip over and make jelly of them."

"Why, yes," Earthquake says, taking a peek at the convent, "what you say seems reasonable. Well, copper," he says, "what is to be done in this situation?"

"Well," I say, "I see a chance to snatch a few of them out of there if you will help me. Earthquake," I say, "I understand you are a very strong guy?"

"Strong?" Earthquake says. "Why," he says, "you know I am maybe the strongest guy in the world."

"Earthquake," I say, "you see the doorway yonder? Well, Earthquake, if you are strong enough to hold this doorway apart and keep it from caving in, I will slip in through it and pass out any nuns and kids that may be alive."

"Why," Earthquake says, "this is as bright an idea as I ever hear from a copper. Why," he says, "I will hold this doorway apart until next Pancake Tuesday."

Then Earthquake holds out his dukes and I unlock the cuffs. Then he runs over to the doorway of the convent, and I run after him.

This doorway is now closing in very fast indeed, from the weight of tons of stones pressing against the timber frame, and by the time we get there the letter V upside down is so very narrow from top to bottom that Earthquake has a tough time wedging himself into what little opening is left.

But old Earthquake gets in, facing inward, and once in, he begins pushing against the doorframe on either side of him, and I can see at once how he gets his reputation as a strong guy. The doorway commences to widen, and as it widens Earthquake keeps spraddling his legs apart, so that pretty soon there is quite a space between his legs. His head is bent forward so far his chin is resting on his wishbone, as there is plenty of weight on Earthquake's neck and shoulders, and in fact he reminds me of pictures I see of a guy by the name of Atlas holding up the world.

It is through the opening between his spraddled-out legs that I pop, looking for the nuns and the kids. Most of them are in a big room on the ground floor of the building, and they are all huddled up close together screeching in chorus.

I motion them to follow me, and I lead them back over the wreckage, and along the hall to the spot where Earthquake is holding the doorway apart, and I wish to state at this time he is doing a very nice job of same.

But the weight on Earthquake's shoulders must be getting very hefty indeed, because his shoulders are commencing to stoop under it, and his chin is now almost down to his stomach, and his face is purple.

Now through Earthquake's spraddled-out legs, and into the street outside the convent wall, I push five nuns and fifteen female kids. One old nun refuses to be pushed through Earthquake's legs, and I finally make out from the way she is waving her hands around and about that there are other kids in the convent, and she wishes me to get them, too.

Well, I can see that any more delay is going to be

something of a strain on Earthquake, and maybe a little irritating to him, so I speak to him as follows:

"Earthquake," I say, "you are looking somewhat peaked to me, and plumb tired out. Now then," I say, "if you will step aside, I will hold the doorway apart awhile, and you can go with this old nun and find the rest of the kids."

"Copper," Earthquake says, speaking from off his chest because he cannot get his head up very high, "I can hold this doorway apart with my little fingers if one of them is not sprained, so go ahead and round up the rest."

So I let the old nun lead me back to another part of the building, where I judge she knows there are more kids, and in fact the old nun is right, but it only takes one look to show me there is no use taking these kids out of the place.

Then we go back to Earthquake, and he hears us coming across the rubbish and half raises his head from off his chest and looks at me, and I can see the sweat is dribbling down his kisser and his eyes are bugging out, and anybody can see that he is quite upset. As I get close to him he speaks to me as follows:

"Get her out quick," he says. "Get the old doll out."

So I push the old nun through Earthquake's spraddled-out legs into the open, and I notice there is not as much space between these legs as formerly, so I judge the old mumblety-pegs are giving out. Then I say to Earthquake like this:

"Well, Earthquake," I say, "it is now time for you and me to be going. I will go outside first," I say, "and then you can ease yourself out, and we will look around for a means of getting back to New York, as headquarters will be getting worried."

"Listen, copper," Earthquake says, "I am never going to get out of this spot. If I move an inch forward or an inch backward, down comes this whole shebang. But, copper," he says, "I see before I get in here that it is a hundred to one against me getting out again, so do not think I am trapped without knowing it. The way I look at it," Earthquake says, "it is better than the chair, at that. I can last a few minutes longer," he says, "and you better get outside."

Well, I pop out between Earthquake's spraddled-out legs, because I figure I am better off outside than in, no matter what, and when I am outside I stand there looking at Earthquake and wondering what I can do about him. But I can see that he is right when he tells me that if he moves one way or another the cave-in will come, so there seems to be nothing much I can do.

Then I hear Earthquake calling me, and I step up close enough to hear him speak as follows:

"Copper," he says, "tell Mulcahy's people I am sorry. And do not forget that you owe old Earthquake whatever you figure your life is worth. I do not know yet why I do not carry out my idea of letting go all holds the minute you push the old nun out of here, and taking you with me wherever I am going. Maybe," he says, "I am getting softhearted. Well, good-by, copper," he says.

"Good-by, Earthquake," I say, and I walk away.

"So," Johnny Brannigan says, "now you know about Earthquake."

"Well," I say, "this is indeed a harrowing story, Johnny. But," I say, "if you leave Earthquake holding up anything maybe he is still holding it up, because Earthquake is certainly a very strong guy."

"Yes," Johnny Brannigan says, "he is very strong indeed. But," he says, "as I am walking away another shock hits, and when I get off the ground again and look at the convent, I can see that not even Earthquake is strong enough to stand off this one."

The Old Doll's House

A very romantic story—so romantic that some very romantic people, indeed, are still scratching their noodles over it. They will never get anywhere. Miss Abigail Ardsley has plenty of potatoes. And she is not the sort to talk.

Now it seems that one cold winter night, a party of residents of Brooklyn comes across the Manhattan Bridge in an automobile wishing to pay a call on a guy by the name of Lance McGowan, who is well-known to one and all along Broadway as a coming guy in the business world.

In fact, it is generally conceded that, barring accident, Lance will some day be one of the biggest guys in this country as an importer, and especially as an importer of such merchandise as fine liquors, because he is very bright, and has many good connections throughout the United States and Canada.

Furthermore, Lance McGowan is a nice-looking young guy and he has plenty of ticker, although some citizens say he does not show very sound business judgment in trying to move in on Angie the Ox over in Brooklyn, as Angie the Ox is an importer himself, besides enjoying a splendid trade in other lines, including artichokes and extortion.

Of course Lance McGowan is not interested in artichokes at all, and very little in extortion, but he does not see any reason why he shall not place his imports in a thriving territory such as Brooklyn, especially as his line of merchandise is much superior to anything handled by Angie the Ox.

Anyway, Angie is one of the residents of Brooklyn in the party that wishes to call on Lance McGowan, and besides Angie the party includes a guy by the name of Mockie Max, who is a very prominent character in Brooklyn, and another guy by the name of The Louse Kid, who is not so prominent, but who is considered a very promising young guy in many respects, although personally I think The Louse Kid has a very weak face.

He is supposed to be a wonderful hand with a burlap bag when anybody wishes to put somebody in such a bag, which is considered a great practical joke in Brooklyn, and in fact The Louse Kid has a burlap bag with him on the night in question, and they are figuring on putting Lance McGowan in the bag when they call on him, just for a laugh. Personally, I consider this a very crude form of humor, but then Angie the Ox and the other members of his party are very crude characters, anyway.

Well, it seems they have Lance McGowan pretty well cased, and they know that of an evening along toward 10 o'clock, he nearly always strolls through West Fifty-fourth Street on his way to a certain spot on Park Ave-

nue that is called the Humming Bird Club, which has
a very high-toned clientele, and the reason Lance goes
there is because he has a piece of the joint, and furthermore he loves to show off his shape in a tuxedo to the
swell dolls.

So these residents of Brooklyn drive in their automo-
bile along this route, and as they roll past Lance
McGowan, Angie the Ox and Mockie Max let fly at
Lance with a couple of sawed-offs, while The Louse
Kid holds the burlap bag, figuring for all I know that
Lance will be startled by the sawed-offs and will hop
into the bag like a rabbit.

But Lance is by no means a sucker, and when the
first blast of slugs from the sawed-offs breezes past him
without hitting him, what does he do but hop over a
brick wall alongside him and drop into a yard on the
other side. So Angie the Ox, and Mockie Max and The
Louse Kid get out of their automobile and run up close
to the wall themselves because they commence figuring
that if Lance McGowan starts popping at them from
behind this wall, they will be taking plenty the worst
of it, for of course they cannot figure Lance to be strolling about without being rodded up somewhat.

But Lance is by no means rodded up, because a rod
is apt to create a bump in his shape when he has his
tuxedo on, so the story really begins with Lance
McGowan behind the brick wall, practically defenseless,
and the reason I know this story is because Lance
McGowan tells most of it to me, as Lance knows that
I know his real name is Lancelot, and he feels under
great obligation to me because I never mention the matter publicly.

Now, the brick wall Lance hops over is a wall around
a pretty fair-sized yard, and the yard belongs to an old
two-story stone house, and this house is well known

to one and all in this man's town as a house of great
mystery, and it is pointed out as such by the drivers
of sightseeing busses.

This house belongs to an old doll by the name of
Miss Abigail Ardsley, and anybody who ever reads the
newspapers will tell you that Miss Abigail Ardsley has
so many potatoes that it is really painful to think of,
especially to people who have no potatoes whatever.
In fact, Miss Abigail Ardsley has practically all the potatoes in the world, except maybe a few left over for general circulation.

These potatoes are left to her by her papa, old Waldo
Ardsley, who accumulates same in the early days of this
town by buying corner real estate very cheap before
people realize this real estate will be quite valuable later
on for fruit-juice stands and cigar stores.

It seems that Waldo is a most eccentric old bloke,
and is very strict with his daughter, and will never let
her marry, or even as much as look as if she wishes to
marry, until finally she is so old she does not care a
cuss about marrying, or anything else, and becomes very
eccentric herself.

In fact, Miss Abigail Ardsley becomes so eccentric
that she cuts herself off from everybody, and especially
from a lot of relatives who are wishing to live off of
her, and any time anybody cuts themselves off from
such characters, they are considered very eccentric, indeed, especially by the relatives. She lives in the big
house all alone, except for a couple of old servants, and
it is very seldom that anybody sees her around and about,
and many strange stories are told of her.

Well, no sooner is he in the yard than Lance
McGowan begins looking for a way to get out, and one
way he does not wish to get out is over the wall again,
because he figures Angie the Ox and his sawed-offs are

bound to be waiting for him in Fifty-fourth Street. So Lance looks around to see if there is some way out of the yard in another direction, but it seems there is no such way, and pretty soon he sees the snozzle of a sawed-off come poking over the wall, with the ugly kisser of Angie the Ox behind it, looking for him, and there is Lance McGowan all cornered up in the yard, and not feeling so good, at that.

Then Lance happens to try a door on one side of the house, and the door opens at once and Lance McGowan hastens in to find himself in the living-room of the house. It is a very large living-room with very nice furniture standing around and about, and oil paintings on the walls, and a big old grandfather's clock as high as the ceiling, and statuary here and there. In fact, it is such a nice, comfortable-looking room that Lance McGowan is greatly surprised, as he is expecting to find a regular mystery-house room such as you see in the movies, with cobwebs here and there, and everything all rotted up, and maybe Boris Karloff wandering about making strange noises.

But the only person in this room seems to be a little old doll all dressed in soft white, who is sitting in a low rocking chair by an open fireplace in which a bright fire is going, doing some tatting.

Well, naturally Lance McGowan is somewhat startled by this scene, and he is figuring that the best thing he can do is to guzzle the old doll before she can commence yelling for the gendarmes, when she looks up at him and gives him a soft smile, and speaks to him in a soft voice, as follows:

"Good evening," the old doll says.

Well, Lance cannot think of any reply to make to this at once, as it is certainly not a good evening for him, and he stands there looking at the old doll, somewhat dazed, when she smiles again and tells him to sit down.

So the next thing Lance knows, he is sitting there in a chair in front of the fireplace chewing the fat with the old doll as pleasant as you please, and of course the old doll is nobody but Miss Abigail Ardsley. Furthermore, she does not seem at all alarmed, or even much surprised at seeing Lance in her house, but then Lance is never such a looking guy as is apt to scare old dolls, or young dolls either, especially when he is all slicked up.

Of course Lance knows who Miss Abigail Ardsley is, because he often reads stories in the newspapers about her the same as everybody else, and he always figures such a character must be slightly daffy to cut herself off from everybody when she has all the potatoes in the world, and there is so much fun going on, but he is very courteous to her, because after all he is a guest in her home.

"You are young," the old doll says to Lance McGowan, looking him in the kisser. "It is many years since a young man comes through yonder door. Ah, yes," she says, "so many years."

And with this she lets out a big sigh, and looks so very sad that Lance McGowan's heart is touched.

"Forty-five years now," the old doll says in a low voice, as if she is talking to herself. "So young, so handsome, and so good."

And although Lance is in no mood to listen to reminiscences at this time, the next thing he knows he is hearing a very pathetic love story, because it seems that Miss Abigail Ardsley is once all hotted up over a young guy who is nothing but a clerk in her papa's office.

It seems from what Lance McGowan gathers that there is nothing wrong with the young guy that a million bobs will not cure, but Miss Abigail Ardsley's papa is a mean old waffle, and he will never listen to her having any truck with a poor guy, so they dast not let him know how much they love each other.

But it seems that Miss Abigail Ardsley's ever-loving young guy has plenty of moxie, and every night he comes to see her after her papa goes to the hay, and she lets him in through the same side door Lance McGowan comes through, and they sit by the fire and hold hands, and talk in low tones, and plan what they will do when the young guy makes a scratch.

Then one night it seems Miss Abigail Ardsley's papa has the stomach ache, or some such, and cannot sleep a wink, so he comes wandering downstairs looking for the Jamaica ginger, and catches Miss Abigail Ardsley and her ever-loving guy in a clutch that will win the title for any wrestler that can ever learn it.

Well, this scene is so repulsive to Miss Abigail Ardsley's papa that he is practically speechless for a minute, and then he orders the young guy out of his life in every respect, and tells him never to darken his door again, especially the side door.

But it seems that by this time a great storm is raging outside, and Miss Abigail Ardsley begs and pleads with her papa to let the young guy at least remain until the storm subsides, but between being all sored up at the clutching scene he witnesses, and his stomach ache, Mr. Ardsley is very hard-hearted, indeed, and he makes the young guy take the wind.

The next morning the poor young guy is found at the side door frozen as stiff as a board, because it seems that the storm that is raging is the blizzard of 1888, which is a very famous event in the history of New York, although up to this time Lance McGowan never hears of it before, and does not believe it until he looks the matter up afterwards. It seems from what Miss Abigail Ardsley says that as near as anyone can make out, the young guy must return to the door seeking shelter after wandering about in the storm a while, but of course by this time her papa has the door all bolted up, and nobody hears the young guy.

"And," Miss Abigail Ardsley says to Lance McGowan, after giving him all these details, "I never speak to my papa again as long as he lives, and no other man ever comes in or out of yonder door, or any other door of this house, until your appearance tonight, although," she says, "this side door is never locked in case such a young man comes seeking shelter."

Then she looks at Lance McGowan in such a way that he wonders if Miss Abigail Ardsley hears the sawed-offs going when Angie the Ox and Mockie Max are tossing slugs at him, but he is too polite to ask.

Well, all these old-time memories seem to make Miss Abigail Ardsley feel very tough, and by and by she starts to weep, and if there is one thing Lance McGowan cannot stand, it is a doll weeping, even if she is nothing but an old doll. So he starts in to cheer Miss Abigail Ardsley up, and he pats her on the arm, and says to her like this:

"Why," Lance says, "I am greatly surprised to hear your statement about the doors around here being so little used. Why, Sweetheart," Lance says, "if I know there is a doll as good-looking as you in the neighborhood, and a door unlocked, I will be busting in myself every night. Come, come, come," Lance says, "let us talk things over and maybe have a few laughs, because I may have to stick around here a while. Listen, Sweetheart," he says, "do you happen to have a drink in the joint?"

Well, at this Miss Abigail Ardsley dries her eyes, and

smiles again, and then she pulls a sort of a rope near
her, and in comes a guy who seems about ninety years
old, and who seems greatly surprised to see Lance there.
In fact, he is so surprised that he is practically tottering
when he leaves the room after hearing Miss Abigail
Ardsley tell him to bring some wine and sandwiches.

And the wine he brings is such wine that Lance
McGowan has half a mind to send some of the lads
around afterwards to see if there is any more of it in
the joint, especially when he thinks of the unlocked side
door, because he can sell this kind of wine by the carat.

Well, Lance sits there with Miss Abigail Ardsley sip-
ping wine and eating sandwiches, and all the time he
is telling her stories of one kind and another, some of
which he cleans up a little when he figures they may
be a little too snappy for her, and by and by he has
her laughing quite heartily indeed.

Finally he figures there is no chance of Angie and
his sawed-offs being outside waiting for him, so he says
he guesses he will be going, and Miss Abigail Ardsley
personally sees him to the door, and this time it is the
front door, and as Lance is leaving he thinks of something he once sees a guy do on the stage, and he takes
Miss Abigail Ardsley's hand and raises it to his lips
and gives it a large kiss, all of which is very surprising
to Miss Abigail Ardsley, but more so to Lance McGowan
when he gets to thinking about it afterwards.

Just as he figures, there is no one in sight when he
gets out in the street, so he goes on over to the Humming
Bird Club, where he learns that many citizens are greatly
disturbed by his absence, and are wondering if he is
in The Louse Kid's burlap bag, for by this time it is
pretty well known that Angie the Ox and his fellow
citizens of Brooklyn are around and about.

In fact, somebody tells Lance that Angie is at the

moment over in Good Time Charley's little speak in
West Forty-ninth Street, buying drinks for one and all,
and telling how he makes Lance McGowan hop a brick
wall, which of course sounds most disparaging of Lance.

Well, while Angie is still buying these drinks, and
still speaking of making Lance a brick wall hopper, all
of a sudden the door of Good Time Charley's speak
opens and in comes a guy with a Betsy in his hand
and this guy throws four slugs into Angie the Ox before
anybody can say hello.

Furthermore, the guy throws one slug into Mockie
Max, and one slug into The Louse Kid, who are still
with Angie the Ox, so the next thing anybody knows
there is Angie as dead as a door-nail, and there is Mockie
Max even deader than Angie, and there is The Louse
making a terrible fuss over a slug in his leg, and nobody
can remember what the guy who plugs them looks like,
except a couple of stool pigeons who state that the guy
looks very much like Lance McGowan.

So what happens but early the next morning, Johnny
Brannigan, the plain-clothes copper, puts the arm on
Lance McGowan for plugging Angie the Ox, and
Mockie Max and The Louse Kid, and there is great re-
joicing in copper circles generally because at this time
the newspapers are weighing in the sacks on the coppers
quite some, claiming there is too much lawlessness going
on around and about and asking why somebody is not
arrested for something.

So the collar of Lance McGowan is water on the wheel
of one and all because Lance is so prominent, and anybody will tell you that it looks as if it is a sure thing
that Lance will be very severely punished, and maybe
sent to the electric chair, although he hires Judge Goldstein, who is one of the surest-footed lawyers in this
town, to defend him. But even Judge Goldstein admits

that Lance is in a tough spot, especially as the newspapers are demanding justice, and printing long stories about Lance, and pictures of him, and calling him some very uncouth names.

Finally Lance himself commences to worry about his predicament, although up to this time a little thing like being charged with murder in the first degree never bothers Lance very much. And in fact he will not be bothering very much about this particular charge if he does not find the D.A. very fussy about letting him out on bail. In fact, it is nearly two weeks before he lets Lance out on bail, and all this time Lance is in the sneezer, which is a most mortifying situation to a guy as sensitive as Lance.

Well, by the time Lance's trial comes up, you can get 3 to 1 anywhere that he will be convicted, and the price goes up to 5 when the prosecution gets through with its case, and proves by the stool pigeons that at exactly twelve o'clock on the night of January 5th, Lance McGowan steps into Good Time Charley's little speak and plugs Angie the Ox, Mockie Max and The Louse Kid.

Furthermore, several other witnesses who claim they know Lance McGowan by sight testify that they see Lance in the neighborhood of Good Time Charley's around twelve o'clock, so by the time it comes Judge Goldstein's turn to put on the defense, many citizens are saying that if he can do no more than beat the chair for Lance he will be doing a wonderful job.

Well, it is late in the afternoon when Judge Goldstein gets up and looks all around the courtroom, and without making any opening statement to the jury for the defense as these mouthpieces usually do, he says like this:

"Call Miss Abigail Ardsley," he says.

At first nobody quite realizes just who Judge Goldstein is calling for, although the name sounds familiar to one and all present who read the newspapers, when in comes a little old doll in a black silk dress that almost reaches the floor, and a black bonnet that makes a sort of a frame for her white hair and face.

Afterwards I read in one of the newspapers that she looks like she steps down out of an old-fashioned ivory miniature and that she is practically beautiful, but of course Miss Abigail Ardsley has so many potatoes that no newspaper dast to say she looks like an old chromo.

Anyway, she comes into the courtroom surrounded by so many old guys you will think it must be recess at the Old Men's Home, except they are all dressed up in clawhammer coat tails, and high collars, and afterwards it turns out that they are the biggest lawyers in this town, and they all represent Miss Abigail Ardsley one way or another, and they are present to see that her interests are protected, especially from each other.

Nobody ever sees so much bowing and scraping before in a courtroom. In fact, even the judge bows, and although I am only a spectator I find myself bowing too, because the way I look at it, anybody with as many potatoes as Miss Abigail Ardsley is entitled to a general bowing. When she takes the witness stand, her lawyers grab chairs and move up as close to her as possible, and in the street outside there is practically a riot as word goes around that Miss Abigail Ardsley is in the court, and citizens come running from every which way, hoping to get a peek at the richest old doll in the world.

Well, when all hands finally get settled down a little, Judge Goldstein speaks to Miss Abigail Ardsley as follows:

"Miss Ardsley," he says, "I am going to ask you just two or three questions. Kindly look at this defendant," Judge Goldstein says, pointing at Lance McGowan, and giving Lance the office to stand up. "Do you recognize him?"

Well, the little old doll takes a gander at Lance, and nods her head yes, and Lance gives her a large smile, and Judge Goldstein says:

"Is he a caller in your home on the night of January fifth?" Judge Goldstein asks.

"He is," Miss Abigail Ardsley says.

"Is there a clock in the living-room in which you receive this defendant?" Judge Goldstein says.

"There is," Miss Abigail Ardsley says. "A large clock," she says. "A grandfather's clock."

"Do you happen to notice," Judge Goldstein says, "and do you now recall the hour indicated by this clock when the defendant leaves your home?"

"Yes," Miss Abigail Ardsley says, "I do happen to notice. It is just twelve o'clock by my clock," she says. "Exactly twelve o'clock," she says.

Well, this statement creates a large sensation in the courtroom, because if it is twelve o'clock when Lance McGowan leaves Miss Abigail Ardsley's house in West Fifty-fourth Street, anybody can see that there is no way he can be in Good Time Charley's little speak over five blocks away at the same minute unless he is a magician, and the judge begins peeking over his specs at the coppers in the courtroom very severe, and the cops begin scowling at the stool pigeons, and I am willing to lay plenty of 6 to 5 that the stools will wish they are never born before they hear the last of this matter from the gendarmes.

Furthermore, the guys from the D.A.'s office who are handling the prosecution are looking much embarrassed, and the jurors are muttering to each other, and right away Judge Goldstein says he moves that the case against his client be dismissed, and the judge says he is in favor of the motion, and he also says he thinks it is high time the gendarmes in this town learn to be a little careful who they are arresting for murder, and the guys from the D.A.'s office do not seem to be able to think of anything whatever to say.

So there is Lance as free as anybody, and as he starts to leave the courtroom he stops by Miss Abigail Ardsley, who is still sitting in the witness chair surrounded by her mouthpieces, and he shakes her hand and thanks her, and while I do not hear it myself, somebody tells me afterwards that Miss Abigail Ardsley says to Lance in a low voice, like this:

"I will be expecting you again some night, young man," she says.

"Some night, Sweetheart," Lance says, "at twelve o'clock."

And then he goes on about his business, and Miss Abigail Ardsley goes on about hers, and everybody says it is certainly a wonderful thing that a doll as rich as Miss Abigail Ardsley comes forward in the interests of justice to save a guy like Lance McGowan from a wrong rap.

But of course it is just as well for Lance that Miss Abigail Ardsley does not explain to the court that when she recovers from the shock of the finding of her everloving young guy frozen to death, she stops all the clocks in her house at the hour she sees him last, so for forty-five years it is always twelve o'clock in her house.

Bred for Battle

ONE NIGHT a guy by the name of Bill Corum, who is one of these sport scribes, gives me a Chinee for a fight at Madison Square Garden, a Chinee being a ducket with holes punched in it like old-fashioned Chink money, to show that it is a free ducket, and the reason I am explaining to you how I get this ducket is because I do not wish anybody to think I am ever simple enough to pay out my own potatoes for a ducket to a fight, even if I have any potatoes.

Personally, I will not give you a bad two-bit piece to see a fight anywhere, because the way I look at it, half the time the guys who are supposed to do the fighting go in there and put on the old do-se-do, and I consider this a great fraud upon the public, and I do not believe in encouraging dishonesty.

But of course I never refuse a Chinee to such events, because the way I figure it, what can I lose except my time, and my time is not worth more than a bob a week the way things are. So on the night in question I am standing in the lobby of the Garden with many other citizens, and I am trying to find out if there is any skull-duggery doing in connection with the fight, because any time there is any skullduggery doing I love to know it, as it is something worth knowing in case a guy wishes to get a small wager down.

Well, while I am standing there, somebody comes up behind me and hits me an awful belt on the back, knocking my wind plumb out of me, and making me very indignant indeed. As soon as I get a little of my wind back again, I turn around figuring to put a large blast on the guy who slaps me, but who is it but a guy by the name of Spider McCoy, who is known far and wide as a manager of fighters.

Well, of course I do not put the blast on Spider McCoy, because he is an old friend of mine, and further-more, Spider McCoy is such a guy as is apt to let a left hook go at anybody who puts the blast on him, and I do not believe in getting in trouble, especially with good left-hookers.

So I say hello to Spider, and am willing to let it go at that, but Spider seems glad to see me, and says to me like this:

"Well, well, well, well, well!" Spider says.

"Well," I say to Spider McCoy, "how many wells does it take to make a river?"

"One, if it is big enough," Spider says, so I can see he knows the answer all right. "Listen," he says, "I just think up the greatest proposition I ever think of in my whole life, and who knows but what I can interest you in same."

"Well, Spider," I say, "I do not care to hear any propo-sitions at this time, because it may be a long story, and I wish to step inside and see the impending battle. Anyway," I say, "if it is a proposition involving financial support, I wish to state that I do not have any resources whatever at this time."

"Never mind the battle inside," Spider says. "It is nothing but a tank job, anyway. And as for financial support," Spider says, "this does not require more than a pound note, tops, and I know you have a pound note because I know you put the bite on Overcoat Obie for this amount not an hour ago. Listen," Spider McCoy says, "I know where I can place my hands on the greatest heavyweight prospect in the world to-day, and all I need is the price of car-fare to where he is."

Well, off and on, I know Spider McCoy twenty years, and in all this time I never know him when he is not looking for the greatest heavyweight prospect in the world. And as long as Spider knows I have the pound note, I know there is no use trying to play the duck for him, so I stand there wondering who the stool pigeon can be who informs him of my financial status.

"Listen," Spider says, "I just discover that I am all out of line in the way I am looking for heavyweight prospects in the past. I am always looking for nothing but plenty of size," he says. "Where I make my mistake is not looking for blood lines. Professor D just smartens me up," Spider says.

Well, when he mentions the name of Professor D, I commence taking a little interest, because it is well known to one and all that Professor D is one of the smartest old guys in the world. He is once a professor in a college out in Ohio, but quits this dodge to handicap the horses, and he is a first-rate handicapper, at that. But besides knowing how to handicap the horses, Professor D knows many other things, and is highly respected in all walks of life, especially on Broadway.

"Now then," Spider says, "Professor D calls my attention this afternoon to the fact that when a guy is looking for a race horse, he does not take just any horse that comes along, but he find out if the horse's papa is able to run in his day, and if the horse's mamma can get out of her own way when she is young. Professor D shows me how a guy looks for speed in a horse's breeding away back to its great-great-great-great-grandpa and grandmamma," Spider McCoy says.

"Well," I say, "anybody knows this without asking Professor D. In fact," I say, "you even look up a horse's parents to see if they can mud before betting on a plug to win in heavy going."

"All right," Spider says, "I know all this myself, but I never think much about it before Professor D mentions it. Professor D says if a guy is looking for a hunting dog he does not pick a Pekingese pooch, but he gets a dog that is bred to hunt from away back yonder, and if he is after a game chicken he does not take a Plymouth Rock out of the back yard.

"So then," Spider says, "Professor D wishes to know why, when I am looking for a fighter, I do not look for one who comes of fighting stock. Professor D wishes to know," Spider says, "why I do not look for some guy who is bred to fight, and when I think this over, I can see the professor is right.

"And then all of a sudden," Spider says, "I get the largest idea I ever have in all my life. Do you remember a guy I have about twenty years back by the name of Shamus Mulrooney, the Fighting Harp?" Spider says. "A big, rough, tough heavyweight out of Newark?"

"Yes," I say, "I remember Shamus very well indeed. The last time I see him is the night Pounder Pat O'Shea almost murders him in the old Garden," I say. "I never see a guy with more ticker than Shamus, unless maybe it is Pat."

"Yes," Spider says, "Shamus has plenty of ticker. He is about through the night of the fight you speak of, otherwise Pat will never lay a glove on him. It is not long after this fight that Shamus packs in and goes back to bricklaying in Newark, and it is also about this same time," Spider says, "that he marries Pat O'Shea's sister, Bridget.

"Well, now," Spider says, "I remember they have a boy who must be around nineteen years old now, and if ever a guy is bred to fight it is a boy by Shamus Mulrooney out of Bridget O'Shea, because," Spider says, "Bridget herself can lick half the heavyweights I see around nowadays if she is half as good as she is the last time I see her. So now you have my wonderful idea. We will go to Newark and get this boy and make him heavyweight champion of the world."

"What you state is very interesting indeed, Spider," I say. "But," I say, "how do you know this boy is a heavyweight?"

"Why," Spider says, "how can he be anything else but a heavyweight, what with his papa as big as a house, and his mamma weighing maybe a hundred and seventy pounds in her step-ins? Although of course," Spider says, "I never see Bridget weigh in in such manner.

"But," Spider says, "even if she does carry more weight than I will personally care to spot a doll, Bridget is by no means a pelican when she marries Shamus. In fact," he says, "she is pretty good-looking. I remember their wedding well, because it comes out that Bridget is in love with some other guy at the time, and this guy comes to see the nuptials, and Shamus runs him all the way from Newark to Elizabeth, figuring to break a couple of legs for the guy if he catches him. But," Spider says, "the guy is too speedy for Shamus, who never has much foot anyway."

Well, all that Spider says appeals to me as a very sound business proposition, so the upshot of it is, I give him my pound note to finance his trip to Newark.

Then I do not see Spider McCoy again for a week, but one day he calls me up and tells me to hurry over to the Pioneer gymnasium to see the next heavyweight champion of the world, Thunderbolt Mulrooney.

I am personally somewhat disappointed when I see Thunderbolt Mulrooney, and especially when I find out his first name is Raymond and not Thunderbolt at all, because I am expecting to see a big, fierce guy with red hair and a chest like a barrel, such as Shamus Mulrooney has when he is in his prime. But who do I see but a tall, pale looking young guy with blond hair and thin legs.

Furthermore, he has pale blue eyes, and a far-away look in them, and he speaks in a low voice, which is nothing like the voice of Shamus Mulrooney. But Spider seems satisfied with Thunderbolt, and when I tell him Thunderbolt does not look to me like the next heavyweight champion of the world, Spider says like this:

"Why," he says, "the guy is nothing but a baby, and you must give him time to fill out. He may grow to be bigger than his papa. But you know," Spider says, getting indignant as he thinks about it, "Bridget Mulrooney does not wish to let this guy be the next heavyweight champion of the world. In fact," Spider says, "she kicks up an awful row when I go to get him, and Shamus finally has to speak to her severely. Shamus says he does not know if I can ever make a fighter of this guy because Bridget coddles him until he is nothing but a mushhead, and Shamus says he is sick and tired of seeing the guy sitting around the house doing nothing but reading and playing the zither."

"Does he play the zither yet?" I ask Spider McCoy.

"No," Spider says, "I do not allow my fighters to play zithers. I figure it softens them up. This guy does not play anything at present. He seems to be in a daze most of the time, but of course everything is new to him. He is bound to come out okay, because," Spider says, "he is certainly bred right. I find out from Shamus that all the Mulrooneys are great fighters back in the old country," Spider says, "and furthermore he tells me Bridget's mother once licks four Newark cops who try to stop her from pasting her old man, so," Spider says, "this lad is just naturally steaming with fighting blood."

Well, I drop around to the Pioneer once or twice a week after this, and Spider McCoy is certainly working hard with Thunderbolt Mulrooney. Furthermore, the guy seems to be improving right along, and gets so he can box fairly well and punch the bag, and all this and that, but he always has that far-away look in his eyes, and personally I do not care for fighters with far-away looks.

Finally one day Spider calls me up and tells me he has Thunderbolt Mulrooney matched in a four-round preliminary bout at the St. Nick with a guy by the name of Bubbles Browning, who is fighting almost as far back as the first battle of Bull Run, so I can see Spider is being very careful in matching Thunderbolt. In fact, I congratulate Spider on his carefulness.

"Well," Spider says, "I am taking this match just to give Thunderbolt the feel of the ring. I am taking Bubbles because he is an old friend of mine, and very deserving, and furthermore," Spider says, "he gives me his word he will not hit Thunderbolt very hard and will become unconscious the instant Thunderbolt hits him. You know," Spider says, "you must encourage a young heavyweight, and there is nothing that encourages one so much as knocking somebody unconscious."

Now of course it is nothing for Bubbles to promise not to hit anybody very hard because even when he is a young guy, Bubbles cannot punch his way out of a paper bag, but I am glad to learn that he also promises to become unconscious very soon, as naturally I am greatly interested in Thunderbolt's career, what with owning a piece of him, and having an investment of one pound in him already.

So the night of the fight, I am at the St. Nick very early, and many other citizens are there ahead of me, because by this time Spider McCoy gets plenty of publicity for Thunderbolt by telling the boxing scribes about his wonderful fighting blood lines, and everybody wishes to see a guy who is bred for battle, like Thunderbolt.

I take a guest with me to the fight by the name of Harry the Horse, who comes from Brooklyn, and as I am anxious to help Spider McCoy all I can, as well as to protect my investment in Thunderbolt, I request Harry to call on Bubbles Browning in his dressing room and remind him of his promise about hitting Thunderbolt.

Harry the Horse does this for me, and furthermore he shows Bubbles a large revolver and tells Bubbles that he will be compelled to shoot his ears off if Bubbles forgets his promise, but Bubbles says all this is most unnecessary, as his eyesight is so bad he cannot see to hit anybody, anyway.

Well, I know a party who is a friend of the guy who is going to referee the preliminary bouts, and I am looking for this party to get him to tell the referee to disqualify Bubbles in case it looks as if he is forgetting his promise and is liable to hit Thunderbolt, but before I can locate the party, they are announcing the opening bout, and there is Thunderbolt in the ring looking very far away indeed, with Spider McCoy behind him.

It seems to me I never see a guy who is so pale all over as Thunderbolt Mulrooney, but Spider looks down at me and tips me a large wink, so I can see that everything is as right as rain, especially when Harry the Horse makes motions at Bubbles Browning like a guy firing a large revolver at somebody, and Bubbles smiles, and also winks.

Well, when the bell rings, Spider gives Thunderbolt a shove toward the center, and Thunderbolt comes out with his hands up, but looking more far away than somewhat, and something tells me that Thunderbolt by no means feels the killer instinct such as I love to see in fighters. In fact, something tells me that Thunderbolt is not feeling enthusiastic about this proposition in any way, shape, manner, or form.

Old Bubbles almost falls over his own feet coming out of his corner, and he starts bouncing around making passes at Thunderbolt, and waiting for Thunderbolt to hit him so he can become unconscious. Naturally, Bubbles does not wish to become unconscious without getting hit, as this may look suspicious to the public.

Well, instead of hitting Bubbles, what does Thunderbolt Mulrooney do but turn around and walk over to a neutral corner, and lean over the ropes with his face in his gloves, and bust out crying. Naturally, this is a most surprising incident to one and all, and especially to Bubbles Browning.

The referee walks over to Thunderbolt Mulrooney and tries to turn him around, but Thunderbolt keeps his face in his gloves and sobs so loud that the referee is deeply touched and starts sobbing with him. Between sobs he asks Thunderbolt if he wishes to continue the fight, and Thunderbolt shakes his head, although as a matter of fact no fight whatever starts so far, so the referee declares Bubbles Browning the winner, which is a terrible surprise to Bubbles.

Then the referee puts his arm around Thunderbolt and leads him over to Spider McCoy, who is standing in his corner with a very strange expression on his face. Personally, I consider the entire spectacle so revolting that I go out into the air, and stand around awhile expecting to hear any minute that Spider McCoy is in the hands of the gendarmes on a charge of mayhem.

But it seems that nothing happens, and when Spider finally comes out of the St. Nick, he is only looking sorrowful because he just hears that the promoter declines to pay him the fifty bobs he is supposed to receive for Thunderbolt's services, the promoter claiming that Thunderbolt renders no service.

"Well," Spider says, "I fear this is not the next heavyweight champion of the world after all. There is nothing in Professor D's idea about blood lines as far as fighters are concerned, although," he says, "it may work out all right with horses and dogs, and one thing and another. I am greatly disappointed," Spider says, "but then I am always being disappointed in heavyweights. There is nothing we can do but take this guy back home, because," Spider says, "the last thing I promise Bridget Mulrooney is that I will personally return him to her in case I am not able to make him heavyweight champion, as she is afraid he will get lost if he tries to find his way home alone."

So the next day, Spider McCoy and I take Thunderbolt Mulrooney over to Newark and to his home, which turns out to be a nice little house in a side street with a yard all around and about, and Spider and I are just as well pleased that old Shamus Mulrooney is absent when we arrive, because Spider says that Shamus is just such a guy as will be asking a lot of questions about the fifty bobbos that Thunderbolt does not get.

Well, when we reach the front door of the house, out comes a big, fine-looking doll with red cheeks, all excited, and she takes Thunderbolt in her arms and kisses him, so I know this is Bridget Mulrooney, and I can see she knows what happens, and in fact I afterwards learn that Thunderbolt telephones her the night before.

After a while she pushes Thunderbolt into the house and stands at the door as if she is guarding it against us entering to get him again, which of course is very unnecessary. And all this time Thunderbolt is sobbing no little, although by and by the sobs die away, and from somewhere in the house comes the sound of music I seem to recognize as the music of a zither.

Well, Bridget Mulrooney never says a word to us as she stands in the door, and Spider McCoy keeps staring at her in a way that I consider very rude indeed. I am wondering if he is waiting for a receipt for Thunderbolt, but finally he speaks as follows:

"Bridget," Spider says, "I hope and trust that you will not consider me too fresh, but I wish to learn the name of the guy you are going around with just before you marry Shamus. I remember him well," Spider says, "but I cannot think of his name, and it bothers me not being able to think of names. He is a tall, skinny, stoop-shouldered guy," Spider says, "with a hollow chest and a soft voice, and he loves music."

Well, Bridget Mulrooney stands there in the doorway, staring back at Spider, and it seems to me that the red suddenly fades out of her cheeks, and just then we hear a lot of yelling, and around the corner of the house comes a bunch of five or six kids, who seem to be running from another kid.

This kid is not very big, and is maybe fifteen or sixteen years old, and he has red hair and many freckles, and he seems very mad at the other kids. In fact, when he catches up with them, he starts belting away at them with his fists, and before anybody can as much as say boo, he has three of them on the ground as flat as pancakes, while the others are yelling bloody murder.

Personally, I never see such wonderful punching by a kid, especially with his left hand, and Spider McCoy is also much impressed, and is watching the kid with great interest. Then Bridget Mulrooney runs out and grabs the frecklefaced kid with one hand and smacks him with the other hand and hauls him, squirming and kicking, over to Spider McCoy and says to Spider like this:

"Mr. McCoy," Bridget says, "this is my youngest son, Terence, and though he is not a heavyweight, and will never be a heavyweight, perhaps he will answer your purpose. Suppose you see his father about him sometime," she says, "and hoping you will learn to mind your own business, I wish you a very good day."

Then she takes the kid into the house under her arm and slams the door in our kissers, and there is nothing for us to do but walk away. And as we are walking away, all of a sudden Spider McCoy snaps his fingers as guys will do when they get an unexpected thought, and says like this:

"I remember the guy's name," he says. "It is Cedric Tilbury, and he is a floorwalker in Hamburgher's department store, and," Spider says, "how he can play the zither!"

I see in the papers the other day where Jimmy Johnston, the match maker at the Garden, matches Tearing Terry Mulrooney, the new sensation of the lightweight

division, to fight for the championship, but it seems
from what Spider McCoy tells me that my investment
with him does not cover any fighters in his stable except
maybe heavyweights.

And it also seems that Spider McCoy is not monkeying
with heavyweights since he gets Tearing Terry.

Princess O'Hara

Now of course Princess O'Hara is by no means a regular princess, and in fact she is nothing but a little red-headed doll, with plenty of freckles, from over in Tenth Avenue, and her right name is Maggie, and the only reason she is called Princess O'Hara is as follows:

She is the daughter of King O'Hara, who is hacking along Broadway with one of these old-time victorias for a matter of maybe twenty-five years, and every time King O'Hara gets his pots on, which is practically every night, rain or shine, he is always bragging that he has the royal blood of Ireland in his veins, so somebody starts calling him King, and this is his monicker as long as I can remember, although probably what King O'Hara really has in his veins is about ninety-eight per cent alcohol.

Well, anyway, one night about seven or eight years back, King O'Hara shows up on his stand in front of Mindy's restaurant on Broadway with a spindly-legged little doll about ten years of age on the seat beside him, and he says that this little doll is nobody but his daughter, and he is taking care of her because his old lady is not feeling so good, and right away Last Card Louie, the gambler, reaches up and dukes the little doll and says to her like this:

"If you are the daughter of the King, you must be the princess," Last Card Louie says. "How are you, Princess?"

So from this time on, she is Princess O'Hara and afterwards for several years she often rides around in the early evening with the King, and sometimes when the King has his pots on more than somewhat, she personally drives Goldberg, which is the King's horse, although Goldberg does not really need much driving as he knows his way along Broadway better than anybody. In fact, this Goldberg is a most sagacious old pelter, indeed, and he is called Goldberg by the King in honor of a Jewish friend by the name of Goldberg, who keeps a delicatessen store in Tenth Avenue.

At this time, Princess O'Hara is as homely as a mud fence, and maybe homelier, what with the freckles, and the skinny gambs, and a few buck teeth, and she does not weigh more than sixty pounds, sopping wet, and her red hair is down her back in pigtails, and she giggles if anybody speaks to her, so finally nobody speaks to her much, but old King O'Hara seems to think well of her, at that.

Then by and by she does not seem to be around with the King any more, and when somebody happens to ask about her, the King says his old lady claims the Princess is getting too grown-up to be shagging around Broadway, and that she is now going to public school. So after not seeing her for some years, everybody forgets that King O'Hara has a daughter, and in fact nobody cares a cuss.

Now King O'Hara is a little shriveled-up old guy with a very red beezer, and he is a most familiar spectacle to one and all on Broadway as he drives about with a stovepipe hat tipped so far over to one side of his noggin that it looks as if it is always about to fall off, and in fact the King himself is always tipped so far over to one side that it seems to be a sure thing that he is going to fall off.

The way the King keeps himself on the seat of his victoria is really most surprising, and one time Last Card Louie wins a nice bet off a gambler from St. Louis by the name of Olive Street Oscar, who takes eight to five off of Louie that the King cannot drive them through Central Park without doing a Brodie off the seat. But of course Louie is betting with the best of it, which is the way he always dearly loves to bet, because he often rides through Central Park with King O'Hara, and he knows the King never falls off, no matter how far over he tips.

Personally, I never ride with the King very much, as his victoria is so old I am always afraid the bottom will fall out from under me, and that I will run myself to death trying to keep up, because the King is generally so busy singing Irish-come-all-yeez up on his seat that he is not apt to pay much attention to what his passengers are doing.

There are quite a number of these old victorias left in this town, a victoria being a low-neck, four-wheeled carriage with seats for four or five people, and they are very popular in the summertime with guys and dolls who wish to ride around and about in Central Park taking the air, and especially with guys and dolls who may wish to do a little offhand guzzling while taking the air.

Personally, I consider a taxicab much more convenient and less expensive than an old-fashioned victoria if you wish to get to some place, but of course guys and dolls engaged in a little offhand guzzling never wish to get any place in particular, or at least not soon. So these victorias, which generally stand around the entrances to the Park, do a fair business in the summertime, because it seems that no matter what conditions are, there are always guys and dolls who wish to do a little offhand guzzling.

But King O'Hara stands in front of Mindy's because he has many regular customers among the citizens of Broadway, who do not go in for guzzling so very much, unless a case of guzzling comes up, but who love to ride around in the Park on hot nights just to cool themselves out, although at the time I am now speaking of, things are so tough with one and all along Broadway that King O'Hara has to depend more on strangers for his trade.

Well, what happens one night, but King O'Hara is seen approaching Mindy's, tipping so far over to one side of his seat that Olive Street Oscar, looking to catch even on the bet he loses before, is offering to take six to five off of Last Card Louie that this time the King goes plumb off, and Louie is about to give it to him, when the old King tumbles smack-dab into the street, as dead as last Tuesday, which shows you how lucky Last Card Louie is, because nobody ever figures such a thing to happen to the King, and even Goldberg, the horse, stops and stands looking at him very much surprised, with one hind hoof in the King's stovepipe hat. The doctors state that King O'Hara's heart just naturally hauls off and quits working on him, and afterwards Regret, the horse player, says the chances are the King probably suddenly remembers refusing a drink somewhere.

A few nights later, many citizens are out in front of

Mindy's, and Big Nig, the crap shooter, is saying that things do not look the same around there since King O'Hara puts his checks back in the rack, when all of a sudden up comes a victoria that anybody can see is the King's old rattletrap, especially as it is being pulled by Goldberg.

And who is on the driver's seat, with King O'Hara's bunged-up old stovepipe hat sitting jack-deuce on her noggin but a red-headed doll of maybe eighteen or nineteen with freckles all over her pan, and while it is years since I see her, I can tell at once that she is nobody but Princess O'Hara, even though it seems she changes quite some.

In fact, she is now about as pretty a little doll as anybody will wish to see, even with the freckles, because the buck teeth seem to have disappeared, and the gambs are now filled out very nicely, and so has the rest of her. Furthermore, she has a couple of blue eyes that are most delightful to behold, and a smile like six bits, and all in all, she is a pleasing scene.

Well, naturally, her appearance in this manner causes some comment, and in fact some citizens are disposed to criticize her as being unladylike, until Big Nig, the crap shooter, goes around among them very quietly stating that he will knock their ears down if he hears any more cracks from them, because it seems that Big Nig learns that when old King O'Hara dies, all he leaves in this world besides his widow and six kids is Goldberg, the horse, and the victoria, and Princess O'Hara is the eldest of these kids, and the only one old enough to work, and she can think of nothing better to do than to take up her papa's business where he leaves off.

After one peek at Princess O'Hara, Regret, the horse player, climbs right into the victoria, and tells her to ride him around the Park a couple of times, although

it is well known to one and all that it costs two bobs
per hour to ride in anybody's victoria, and the only
dough Regret has in a month is a pound note that he
just borrows off of Last Card Louie for eating money.
But from this time on, the chances are Regret will
be Princess O'Hara's best customer if he can borrow
any more pound notes, but the competition gets too
keen for him, especially from Last Card Louie, who is
by this time quite a prominent character along Broadway, and in the money, although personally I always
say you can have him, as Last Card Louie is such a
guy as will stoop to very sharp practice, and in fact
he often does not wait to stoop.

He is called Last Card Louie because in his youth
he is a great hand for riding the tubs back and forth
between here and Europe and playing stud poker with
other passengers, and the way he always gets much
strength from the last card is considered quite abnormal,
especially if Last Card Louie is dealing. But of course
Last Card Louie no longer rides the tubs as this occupation is now very old-fashioned, and anyway Louie has
more profitable interests that require his attention, such
as a crap game, and one thing and another.

There is no doubt but what Last Card Louie takes
quite a fancy to Princess O'Hara, but naturally he cannot
spend all his time riding around in a victoria, so other
citizens get a chance to patronize her now and then,
and in fact I once take a ride with Princess O'Hara
myself, and it is a very pleasant experience, indeed, as
she likes to sing while she is driving, just as old King
O'Hara does in his time.

But what Princess O'Hara sings is not Irish-come-
all-yeez but "Kathleen Mavourneen," and "My Wild
Irish Rose," and "Asthore," and other such ditties, and
she has a loud contralto voice, and when she lets it out

while driving through Central Park in the early hours of the morning, the birds in the trees wake up and go tweet-tweet, and the coppers on duty for blocks around stand still with smiles on their kissers, and the citizens who live in the apartment houses along Central Park West and Central Park South come to their windows to listen.

Then one night in October, Princess O'Hara does not show up in front of Mindy's, and there is much speculation among one and all about this absence, and some alarm, when Big Nig, the crap shooter, comes around and says that what happens is that old Goldberg, the horse, is down with colic, or some such, so there is Princess O'Hara without a horse.

Well, this news is received with great sadness by one and all, and there is some talk of taking up a collection to buy Princess O'Hara another horse, but nobody goes very far with this idea because things are so tough with everybody, and while Big Nig mentions that maybe Last Card Louie will be glad to do something large in this matter, nobody cares for this idea, either, as many citizens are displeased with the way Last Card Louie is pitching to Princess O'Hara, because it is well known that Last Card Louie is nothing but a wolf when it comes to young dolls, and anyway about now Regret, the horse player, speaks up as follows:

"Why," Regret says, "it is great foolishness to talk of wasting money buying a horse, even if we have any money to waste, when the barns up at Empire City are packed at this time with crocodiles of all kinds. Let us send a committee up to the track," Regret says, "and borrow a nice horse for Princess O'Hara to use until Goldberg is back on his feet again."

"But," I say to Regret, "suppose nobody wishes to lend us a horse?"

"Why," Regret says, "I do not mean to ask anybody to lend us a horse. I mean let us borrow one without asking anybody. Most of these horse owners are so very touchy that if we go around asking them to lend us a horse to pull a hack, they may figure we are insulting their horses, so let us just get the horse and say nothing whatever."

Well, I state that this sounds to me like stealing, and stealing is something that is by no means upright and honest, and Regret has to admit that it really is similar to stealing, but he says what of it, and as I do not know what of it, I discontinue the argument. Furthermore, Regret says it is clearly understood that we will return any horse we borrow when Goldberg is hale and hearty again, so I can see that after all there is nothing felonious in the idea, or anyway, not much.

But after much discussion, it comes out that nobody along Broadway seems to know anything about stealing a horse. There are citizens who know all about stealing diamond necklaces, or hot stoves, but when it comes to horses, everybody confesses themselves at a loss. It is really amazing the amount of ignorance there is on Broadway about stealing horses.

Then finally Regret has a bright idea. It seems that a rodeo is going on at Madison Square Garden at this time, a rodeo being a sort of wild west show with bucking bronchos, and cowboys, and all this and that, and Regret seems to remember reading when he is a young squirt that stealing horses is a very popular pastime out in the Wild West.

So one evening Regret goes around to the Garden and gets to talking to a cowboy in leather pants with hair on them, and he asks this cowboy, whose name seems to be Laramie Pink, if there are any expert horse stealers connected with the rodeo. Moreover, Regret explains to Laramie Pink just why he wants a good horse stealer, and Pink becomes greatly interested and wishes to know if the loan of a nice bucking broncho, or a first-class cow pony will be of any assistance, and when Regret says he is afraid not, Laramie Pink says like this:

"Well," he says, "of course horse stealing is considered a most antique custom out where I come from, and in fact it is no longer practiced in the best circles, but," he says, "come to think of it, there is a guy with this outfit by the name of Frying Pan Joe, who is too old to do anything now except mind the cattle, but who is said to be an excellent horse stealer out in Colorado in his day. Maybe Frying Pan Joe will be interested in your proposition," Laramie Pink says.

So he hunts up Frying Pan Joe, and Frying Pan Joe turns out to be a little old pappy guy with a chin whisker, and a sad expression, and a wide-brimmed cowboy hat, and when they explain to him that they wish him to steal a horse, Frying Pan Joe seems greatly touched, and his eyes fill up with tears, and he speaks as follows:

"Why," Frying Pan Joe says, "your idea brings back many memories to me. It is a matter of over twenty-five years since I steal a horse, and the last time I do this it gets me three years in the calabozo. Why," he says, "this is really a most unexpected order, and it finds me all out of practice, and with no opportunity to get myself in shape. But," he says, "I will put forth my best efforts on this job for ten dollars, as long as I do not personally have to locate the horse I am to steal. I am not acquainted with the ranges hereabouts, and will not know where to go to find a horse."

So Regret, the horse player, and Big Nig, the crap shooter, and Frying Pan Joe go up to Empire this very same night, and it turns out that stealing a horse is so simple that Regret is sorry he does not make the tenner himself, for all Frying Pan Joe does is to go to the barns where the horses live at Empire, and walk along until he comes to a line of stalls that do not seem to have any watchers around in the shape of stable hands at the moment. Then Frying Pan Joe just steps into a stall and comes out leading a horse, and if anybody sees him, they are bound to figure he has a right to do this, because of course not even Sherlock Holmes is apt to think of anybody stealing a horse around this town.

Well, when Regret gets a good peek at the horse, he sees right away it is not just a horse that Frying Pan Joe steals. It is Gallant Godfrey, one of the greatest handicap horses in this country, and the winner of some of the biggest stakes of the year, and Gallant Godfrey is worth twenty-five G's if he is worth a dime, and when Regret speaks of this, Frying Pan Joe says it is undoubtedly the most valuable single piece of horseflesh he ever steals, although he claims that once when he is stealing horses along the Animas River in Colorado, he steals two hundred horses in one batch that will probably total up more.

They take Gallant Godfrey over to Eleventh Avenue, where Princess O'Hara keeps Goldberg in a little stable that is nothing but a shack, and they leave Gallant Godfrey there alongside old Goldberg, who is groaning and carrying on in a most distressing manner, and then Regret and Big Nig shake hands with Frying Pan Joe and wish him goodby.

So there is Princess O'Hara with Gallant Godfrey hitched up to her victoria the next night, and the chances are it is a good thing for her that Gallant Godfrey is a nice tame old dromedary, and does not mind pulling a victoria at all, and in fact he seems to enjoy it, although he likes to go along at a gallop instead of a slow trot, such as the old skates that pull these victorias usually employ.

And while Princess O'Hara understands that this is a borrowed horse, and is to be returned when Goldberg is well, nobody tells her just what kind of a horse it is, and when she gets Goldberg's harness on Gallant Godfrey, his appearance changes so that not even the official starter is apt to recognize him if they come face to face.

Well, I hear afterwards that there is great consternation around Empire when it comes out that Gallant Godfrey is missing, but they keep it quiet as they figure he just wanders away, and as he is engaged in certain large stakes later on, they do not wish it made public that he is absent from his stall. So they have guys looking for him high and low, but of course nobody thinks to look for a high-class race horse pulling a victoria.

When Princess O'Hara drives the new horse up in front of Mindy's, many citizens are anxious to take the first ride with her, but before anybody has time to think who steps up but Ambrose Hammer, the newspaper scribe who has a foreign-looking young guy with him, and Ambrose states as follows:

"Get in, Georges," Ambrose says. "We will take a spin through the Park and wind up at the Casino."

So away they go, and from this moment begins one of the greatest romances ever heard of on Broadway, for it seems that the foreign-looking young guy that Ambrose Hammer calls Georges takes a wonderful liking to Princess O'Hara right from taw, and the following night I learn from Officer Corbett, the motorcycle cop who is on duty in Central Park, that they pass him with Ambrose Hammer in the back seat of the victoria, but with Georges riding on the driver's seat with Princess O'Hara.

And moreover, Officer Corbett states that Georges is wearing King O'Hara's old stovepipe hat, while Princess O'Hara is singing "Kathleen Mavourneen" in her loud contralto in such a way as nobody ever hears her sing before.

In fact, this is the way they are riding along a little later in the week, and when it is coming on four bells in the morning. But this time, Princess O'Hara is driving north on the street that is called Central Park West because it borders the Park on the west, and the reason she is taking this street is because she comes up Broadway through Columbus Circle into Central Park West, figuring to cross over to Fifth Avenue by way of the transverse at Sixty-sixth Street, a transverse being nothing but a roadway cut through the Park from Central Park West to the Avenue.

There are several of these transverses, and why they do not call them roads, or streets, instead of transverses, I do not know, except maybe it is because transverse sounds more fancy. These transverses are really like tunnels without any roofs, especially the one at Sixty-sixth Street, which is maybe a quarter of a mile long and plenty wide enough for automobiles to pass each other going in different directions, but once a car is in the transverse there is no way it can get out except at one end or the other. There is no such thing as turning off to one side anywhere between Central Park West and the Avenue, because the Sixty-sixth Street transverse is a deep cut with high sides, or walls.

Well, just as Princess O'Hara starts to turn Gallant Godfrey into the transverse, with the foreign-looking young guy beside her on the driver's seat, and Ambrose Hammer back in the cushions, and half asleep, and by no means interested in the conversation that is going on in front of him, a big beer truck comes rolling along Central Park West, going very slow.

And of course there is nothing unusual in the spectacle of a beer truck at this time, as beer is now very legal, but just as this beer truck rolls alongside Princess O'Hara's victoria, a little car with two guys in it pops out of nowhere, and pulls up to the truck, and one of the guys requests the jockey of the beer truck to stop.

Of course Princess O'Hara and her passengers do not know at the time that this is one of the very first cases of heisting a truckload of legal beer that comes off in this country, and that they are really seeing history made, although it all comes out later. It also comes out later that one of the parties committing this historical deed is nobody but a guy by the name of Fats O'Rourke, who is considered one of the leading characters over on the west side, and the reason he is heisting this truckload of beer is by no means a plot against the brewing industry, but because it is worth several C's, and Fats O'Rourke can use several C's very nicely at the moment.

It comes out that the guy with him is a guy by the name of Joe the Blow Fly, but he is really only a fink in every respect, a fink being such a guy as is extra nothing, and many citizens are somewhat surprised when they learn that Fats O'Rourke is going around with finks.

Well, if the jockey of the beer truck does as he is requested without any shilly-shallying, all that will happen is he will lose his beer. But instead of stopping the truck, the jockey tries to keep right on going, and then all of a sudden Fats O'Rourke becomes very impatient and outs with the old thing, and gives it to the jockey, as follows: bang, bang.

By the time Fats O'Rourke lets go, The Fly is up on the seat of the truck and grabs the wheel just as the jockey turns it loose and falls back on the seat, and Fats O'Rourke follows The Fly up there, and then Fats O'Rourke seems to see Princess O'Hara and her customers for the first time, and he also realizes that these parties witness what comes off with the jockey, although otherwise Central Park West is quite deserted, and if anybody in the apartment houses along there hears the shots the chances are they figure it must be nothing but an automobile backfiring.

And in fact The Fly has the beer truck backfiring quite some at this moment as Fats O'Rourke sees Princess O'Hara and her customers, and only somebody who happens to observe the flashes from Fats O'Rourke's duke, or who hears the same buzzes that Princess O'Hara, and the foreign-looking young guy, and Ambrose Hammer hear, can tell that Fats is emptying that old thing at the victoria.

The chances are Fats O'Rourke will not mind anybody witnessing him histing a legal beer truck, and in fact he is apt to welcome their testimony in later years when somebody starts disputing his claim to being the first guy to heist such a truck, but naturally Fats does not wish to have spectators spying on him when he is giving it to somebody, as very often spectators are apt to go around gossiping about these matters, and cause dissension.

So he takes four cracks at Princess O'Hara and her customers, and it is a good thing for them that Fats O'Rourke is never much of a shot. Furthermore, it is a good thing for them that he is now out of ammunition, because of course Fats O'Rourke never figures that it is going to take more than a few shots to heist a legal beer truck, and afterwards there is little criticism of Fats' judgment, as everybody realizes that it is a most unprecedented situation.

Well, by now, Princess O'Hara is swinging Gallant Godfrey into the transverse, because she comes to the conclusion that it is no time to be loitering in this neigh-

borhood, and she is no sooner inside the walls of the
transverse than she knows this is the very worst place
she can go, as she hears a rumble behind her, and when
she peeks back over her shoulder she sees the beer truck
coming lickity-split, and what is more, it is coming right
at the victoria.

Now Princess O'Hara is no chump, and she can see
that the truck is not coming right at the victoria by
accident, when there is plenty of room for it to pass,
so she figures that the best thing to do is not to let
the truck catch up with the victoria if she can help it,
and this is very sound reasoning, indeed, because Joe
the Blow Fly afterwards says that what Fats O'Rourke
requests him to do is to sideswipe the victoria with the
truck and squash it against the side of the transverse,
Fats O'Rourke's idea being to keep Princess O'Hara and
her customers from speaking of the transaction with
the jockey of the truck.

Well, Princess O'Hara stands up in her seat, and tells
Gallant Godfrey to giddap, and Gallant Godfrey is gid-
dapping very nicely, indeed, when she looks back and
sees the truck right at the rear wheel of the victoria,
and coming like a bat out of what-is-this. So she grabs
up her whip and gives Gallant Godfrey a good smack
across the vestibule, and it seems that if there is one
thing Gallant Godfrey hates and despises it is a whip.
He makes a lunge that pulls the victoria clear of the
truck, just as The Fly drives it up alongside the victoria
and is bearing over for the squash, with Fats O'Rourke
yelling directions at him, and from this lunge, Gallant
Godfrey settles down to running.

While this is going on, the foreign-looking young guy
is standing up on the driver's seat of the victoria beside
Princess O'Hara, whooping and laughing, as he probably figures it is just a nice, friendly little race. But Prin-

cess O'Hara is not laughing, and neither is Ambrose Hammer.

Now inside the next hundred yards, Joe the Blow Fly gets the truck up alongside again and this time it looks as if they are gone goslings when Princess O'Hara gives Gallant Godfrey another smack with the whip, and the chances are Gallant Godfrey comes to the conclusion that Westrope is working on him in a stretch run, as he turns on such a burst of speed that he almost runs right out of his collar and leaves the truck behind by anyway a length and a half.

And it seems that just as Gallant Godfrey turns on, Fats O'Rourke personally reaches over and gives the steering wheel of the beer truck a good twist, figuring that the squashing is now a cinch, and the next thing anybody knows the truck goes smack-dab into the wall with a loud kuh-boom, and turns over all mussed up, with beer kegs bouncing around very briskly, and some of them popping open and letting the legal beer leak out.

In the meantime, Gallant Godfrey goes tearing out of the transverse into Fifth Avenue and across Fifth Avenue so fast that the wheels of Princess O'Hara's victoria are scarcely touching the ground, and a copper who sees him go past afterwards states that what Gallant Godfrey is really doing is flying, but personally I always consider this an exaggeration.

Anyway, Gallant Godfrey goes two blocks beyond Fifth Avenue before Princess O'Hara can get him to whoa-up, and there is still plenty of run in him, although by this time Princess O'Hara is plumb worn out, and Ambrose Hammer is greatly fatigued, and only the foreign-looking young guy seems to find any enjoyment in the experience, although he is not so jolly when he learns that the coppers take two dead guys out of the truck, along with Joe the Blow Fly, who lives just long enough to relate the story.

Fats O'Rourke is smothered to death under a stack of kegs of legal beer, which many citizens consider a most gruesome finish, indeed, but what kills the jockey of the truck is the bullet in his heart, so the smash-up of the truck does not make any difference to him one way or the other, although of course if he lives, the chances are his employers will take him to task for losing the beer.

I learn most of the details of the race through the transverse from Ambrose Hammer, and I also learn from Ambrose that Princess O'Hara and the foreign-looking young guy are suffering from the worst case of love that Ambrose ever witnesses, and Ambrose Hammer witnesses some tough cases of love in his day. Furthermore, Ambrose says they are not only in love but are planning to get themselves married up as quickly as possible.

"Well," I say, "I hope and trust this young guy is all right, because Princess O'Hara deserves the best. In fact," I say, "a prince is none too good for her."

"Well," Ambrose says, "a prince is exactly what she is getting. I do not suppose you can borrow much on it in a hock shop in these times, but the title of Prince Georges Latour is highly respected over in France, although," he says, "I understand the proud old family does not have as many potatoes as formerly. But he is a nice young guy, at that, and anyway, what is money compared to love?"

Naturally, I do not know the answer to this, and neither does Ambrose Hammer, but the very same day I run into Princess O'Hara and the foreign-looking young guy on Broadway, and I can see the old love light shining so brightly in their eyes that I get to thinking that maybe money does not mean so much alongside of love, at that, although personally, I will take a chance on the money.

I stop and say hello to Princess O'Hara, and ask her how things are going with her, and she says they are going first class.

"In fact," she says, "it is a beautiful world in every respect. Georges and I are going to be married in a few days now, and are going to Paris, France, to live. At first I fear we will have a long wait, because of course I cannot leave my mamma and the rest of the children unprovided for. But," Princess O'Hara says, "what happens but Regret sells my horse to Last Card Louie for a thousand dollars, so everything is all right.

"Of course," Princess O'Hara says, "buying my horse is nothing but an act of great kindness on the part of Last Card Louie as my horse is by no means worth a thousand dollars, but I suppose Louie does it out of his old friendship for my papa. I must confess," she says, "that I have a wrong impression of Louie, because the last time I see him I slap his face thinking he is trying to get fresh with me. Now I realize it is probably only his paternal interest in me, and I am very sorry."

Well, I know Last Card Louie is such a guy as will give you a glass of milk for a nice cow, and I am greatly alarmed by Princess O'Hara's statement about the sale, for I figure Regret must sell Gallant Godfrey, not remembering that he is only a borrowed horse and must be returned in good order, so I look Regret up at once and mention my fears, but he laughs and speaks to me as follows:

"Do not worry," he says. "What happens is that Last Card Louie comes around last night and hands me a G note and says to me like this: 'Buy Princess O'Hara's horse off of her for me, and you can keep all under this G that you get it for.'

"Well," Regret says, "of course I know that old Last Card is thinking of Gallant Godfrey, and forgets that the only horse that Princess O'Hara really owns is Goldberg, and the reason he is thinking of Gallant Godfrey is because he learns last night about us borrowing the horse for her. But as long as Last Card Louie refers just to her horse, and does not mention any names, I do not see that it is up to me to go into any details with him. So I get him a bill of sale for Princess O'Hara's horse, and I am waiting ever since to hear what he says when he goes to collect the horse and finds it is nothing but old Goldberg."

"Well," I say to Regret, "it all sounds most confusing to me, because what good is Gallant Godfrey to Last Card Louie when he is only a borrowed horse, and is apt to be recognized anywhere except when he is hitched to a victoria? And I am sure Last Card Louie is not going into the victoria business."

"Oh," Regret says, "this is easy. Last Card Louie undoubtedly sees the same ad in the paper that the rest of us see, offering a reward of ten G's for the return of Gallant Godfrey and no questions asked, but of course Last Card Louie has no way of knowing that Big Nig is taking Gallant Godfrey home long before Louie comes around and buys Princess O'Hara's horse."

Well, this is about all there is to tell, except that a couple of weeks later I hear that Ambrose Hammer is in the Clinic Hospital very ill, and I drop around to see him because I am very fond of Ambrose Hammer no matter if he is a newspaper scribe.

He is sitting up in bed in a nice private room, and he has on blue silk pajamas with his monogram embroidered over his heart, and there is a large vase of roses on the table beside him, and a nice-looking nurse holding his hand, and I can see that Ambrose Hammer is not doing bad, although he smiles very feebly at me when I come in.

Naturally I ask Ambrose Hammer what ails him, and after he takes a sip of water out of a glass that the nice-looking nurse holds up to his lips, Ambrose sighs, and in a very weak voice he states as follows:

"Well," Ambrose says, "one night I get to thinking about what will happen to us in the transverse if we have old Goldberg hitched to Princess O'Hara's victoria instead of one of the fastest race horses in the world, and I am so overcome by the thought that I have what my doctor claims is a nervous breakdown. I feel terrible," Ambrose says.

Money from Home

It comes on a pleasant morning in the city of Baltimore, Md., and a number of citizens are standing in front of the Cornflower Hotel in Calvert Street, speaking of this and that, and one thing and another, and especially of the horse races that are to take place in the afternoon at Pimlico, because these citizens are all deeply interested in horse races, and in fact they are not interested in much of anything else in this world.

Among these citizens is The Seldom Seen Kid, who is called The Seldom Seen because he is seldom seen after anything comes off that anybody may wish to see him about, as he has a most retiring disposition, although he can talk a blue streak whenever talking becomes really necessary. He is a young guy of maybe twenty-five years of age, and he always chucks a good front, and has a kind face that causes people to trust him implicitly.

Then there is Hot Horse Herbie, who is called Hot Horse Herbie because he generally knows about some horse that is supposed to be hotter than a base-burner, a hot horse being a horse that is all heated up to win a horse race, although sometimes Hot Horse Herbie's hot horses turn out to be as cold as a landlord's heart. And there is also Big Reds, who is known to one and all as an excellent handicapper if his figures are working right.

Now these are highly respected characters, and if you ask them what they do, they will tell you that they are turf advisers, a turf adviser being a party who advises the public about horse races, and their services are sometimes quite valuable, even if the coppers at the racetracks do say that turf advisers are nothing but touts, and are always jerking them around, and sometimes going so far as to bar them off the tracks altogether, which is a grave injustice, as it deprives many worthy citizens of a chance to earn a livelihood.

In fact, the attitude of these coppers is so odious toward turf advisers that there is some talk of organizing a National Turf Advisers' Association, for mutual protection, and bringing the names of the coppers up at the meetings and booing them for ten minutes each.

There is another guy standing in front of the Cornflower Hotel with The Seldom Seen Kid and Hot Horse Herbie and Big Reds, and this guy is a little, dark complected, slippery-looking guy by the name of Philly the Weeper, and he is called by this name because he is always weeping about something, no matter what. In fact, Philly the Weeper is such a guy as will go around with a loaf of bread under his arm weeping because he is hungry.

He is generally regarded as a most unscrupulous sort of guy, and in fact some people claim Philly the Weeper is downright dishonest, and ordinarily The Seldom Seen Kid, and Hot Horse Herbie and Big Reds do not associate with parties of this caliber, but of course they cannot keep Philly the Weeper from standing around in front of the Cornflower Hotel with them, because he resides there the same as they do.

In fact, Philly the Weeper is responsible at this time for The Seldom Seen Kid and Hot Horse Herbie and Big Reds being able to continue residing in the Cornflower, as conditions are very bad with them, what with so few of the public being willing to take their advice about the horse races, and the advice turning out the wrong way even when the public takes it, and they are all in the hotel stakes, and the chances are the management will be putting hickeys in their keyholes if it is not for Philly the Weeper okaying them.

The reason Philly the Weeper is able to okay them is because a musical show by the name of "P's and Q's" is trying out in Baltimore, and Philly the Weeper's fiancée, Miss Lola Ledare, is a prominent member of the chorus, and the company is stopping at the Cornflower Hotel, and Philly the Weeper lets on that he has something to do with them being there, so he stands first-class with the hotel management, which does not think to ask anybody connected with the "P's and Q's" company about the matter.

If the hotel management does ask, the chances are it will find out that the company regards Philly the Weeper as a wrong gee, the same as everybody else, although it thinks well of his fiancée, Miss Lola Ledare, who is one of these large, wholesome blondes, and by no means bad-looking, if you like them blonde. She is Philly the Weeper's fiancée for several years, but nobody holds this against her, as it is well known to one and all that love is something that cannot be explained, and, anyway, Miss Lola Ledare does not seem to let it bother her very much.

She is such a doll as enjoys going around and about, being young, and full of vitality, as well as blonde, and if Philly the Weeper is too busy, or does not have enough dough to take her around and about, Miss Lola Ledare always seems able to find somebody else who has a little leisure time on their hands for such a purpose, and if Philly the Weeper does not like it, he can lump it, and usually he lumps it, for Miss Lola Ledare can be very, very firm when it comes to going around and about.

In fact, Philly the Weeper is telling The Seldom Seen Kid and Hot Horse Herbie and Big Reds, the very morning in question, about Miss Lola Ledare and nine other members of the "P's and Q's" company being around and about the night before with an English guy who checks in at the Cornflower early in the evening, and who is in action in the matter of going around and about before anybody can say Jack Robinson.

"He is a young guy," Philly the Weeper says, "and from what Lola tells me, he is a very fast guy with a dollar. His name is the Honorable Bertie Searles, and he has a valet, and enough luggage to sink a barge. Lola says he takes quite a fancy to her, but," Philly the Weeper says, "every guy Lola meets takes quite a fancy to her, to hear her tell it."

Well, nobody is much interested in the adventures of Miss Lola Ledare, or any of the other members of the "P's and Q's" company, but when Philly the Weeper mentions the name of the English guy, The Seldom Seen Kid, who is reading the sport page of the *News*, looks up and speaks as follows:

"Why," he says, "there is a story about the Honorable Searles right here in this paper. He is the greatest amateur steeplechase rider in England, and he is over here to ride his own horse, Trafalgar, in some of our steeplechase races, including the Gold Vase at Belmont next week. It says here they are giving a fox hunt and a big dinner in his honor to-day at the Oriole Hunts Club."

Then he hands the *News* to Philly the Weeper, and Philly the Weeper reads the story himself, and says like this:

"Well," he says, "from what Lola tells me of the guy's condition when they get him back to the hotel about six bells this A.M., they will have to take him to the Oriole Hunts Club unconscious. He may be a great hand at kicking them over the sticks, but I judge he is also quite a rum-pot."

"Anyway," Hot Horse Herbie says, "he is wasting his time riding anything in the Gold Vase. Personally," he says, "I do not care for amateur steeplechase riders, because I meet up with several in my time who have more larceny in them than San Quentin. They call them gentlemen riders, but many of them cannot even spell gentleman. I will take Follow You and that ziggaboo jock of his in the Gold Vase for mine against any horse and any amateur rider in the world, including Marsh Preston's Sweep Forward."

"Yes," Big Reds says, "if there is any jumper alive that can lick Follow You, with the coon up, I will stand on my head in front of Mindy's restaurant on Broadway for twenty-four hours hand running, and I do not like standing on my head. Any time they go to the post," Big Reds says, "they are just the same as money from home."

Well, of course it is well known to one and all that what Hot Horse Herbie and Big Reds say about Follow You in the Gold Vase is very true, because this Follow You is a Maryland horse that is a wonderful jumper, and furthermore he is a very popular horse because he is owned by a young Maryland doll by the name of

Miss Phyllis Richie, who comes of an old family on the Eastern Shore.

It is such an old family as once has plenty of dough, and many great race horses, but by the time the family gets down to Miss Phyllis Richie, the dough is all gone, and about all that is left is a house with a leaky roof on the Tred Avon River, and this horse, Follow You, and a coon by the name of Roy Snakes, who always rides the horse, and everybody in Maryland knows that Follow You supports Miss Phyllis Richie and her mother and the house with the leaky roof by winning jumping races here and there.

In fact, all this is quite a famous story of the Maryland turf, and nobody is violating any secrets or poking their nose into private family affairs in speaking of it, and any time Follow You walks out on a race-track in Maryland with Roy Snakes on his back in the red and white colors of the Richie stable, the band always plays "My Maryland," and the whole State of Maryland gets up and yells.

Well, anyway, jumping races do not interest such characters as The Seldom Seen Kid and Hot Horse Herbie and Big Reds, or even Philly the Weeper, very much, so they get to talking about something else, when all of a sudden down the street comes a spectacle that is considered most surprising.

It consists of a young guy who is dressed up in a costume such as is worn by fox hunters when they are out chasing foxes, including a pink coat, and tight pants, and boots, and a peaked cap, and moreover, the guy is carrying a whip in one hand, and a horn in the other, and every now and then he puts this horn to his mouth and goes ta-ta-tee-ta-ta-tee-ta-dah.

But this is not as surprising as the fact that behind the guy are maybe a dozen dogs of one kind and another, such as a dachshund, a Boston bull terrier, a Scottie, a couple of fox hounds, and a lot of just plain every-day dogs, and they are yipping, and making quite a fuss about the guy in the costume, and the reason is that between ta-ta-dees he tucks his horn under one arm and reaches into a side pocket of his pink coat, and takes out some little brown crackers, which he chucks to the dogs.

Well, the first idea anybody is bound to have about a guy going around in such an outfit baiting dogs to follow him, is that he is slightly daffy, and this is the idea The Seldom Seen Kid, and Hot Horse Herbie, and Big Reds, and Philly the Weeper have as they watch the guy, until he turns around to chide a dog that is nibbling at the seat of his tight pants, and they see that the guy has a sign on his back that reads as follows:

"BARKER'S DOG CRULLERS"

Then of course they know the guy is only up to an advertising dodge, and Hot Horse Herbie laughs right out loud, and says like this:

"Well," Herbie says, "I will certainly have to be in tough shape to take such a job as this, especially for a guy like old Barker. I know him well," Herbie says. "He has a factory down here on Lombard Street, and he likes to play the horses now and then, but he is the toughest, meanest old guy in Maryland, and will just as soon bat your brains out as not. In fact, he is thinking some of batting my brains out one day at Laurel last year when I lay him on the wrong horse. But," Herbie says, "they tell me he makes a wonderful dog cruller, at that, and he is certainly a great hand for advertising."

By this time, the young guy in the fox hunter's costume is in front of the hotel with his dogs, and nothing will do but The Seldom Seen Kid must stop him, and speak to him.

"Hello," The Seldom Seen Kid says, "where is your horse?"

Well, the young guy seems greatly surprised at being accosted in this manner by a stranger, and he looks at The Seldom Seen Kid for quite a spell, as if he is trying to figure out where he sees him before, and finally he says like this:

"Why," the young guy says, "it is very strange that you ask me such a question, as I not only do not have a horse, but I hate horses. I am afraid of horses since infancy. In fact," he says, "one reason I leave my home town is because my father wishes me to give up my musical career and drive the delivery wagon for his grocery-store, although he knows how I loathe and despise horses."

Now, of course, The Seldom Seen Kid is only joking when he asks the young guy about his horse, and does not expect to get all this information, but the young guy seems so friendly, and so innocent, that The Seldom Seen Kid keeps talking to him, although the dogs bother the young guy quite some, while he is standing there, by trying to climb up his legs, and he has to keep feeding them the little brown crackers out of his pocket, and it seems that these crackers are Barker's Dog Crullers, and Hot Horse Herbie personally tries several and pronounces them most nutritious.

The young guy says his name is Eddie Yokum, and he comes from a town in Delaware that is called Milburn, and another reason he comes to Baltimore besides wishing to avoid contact with horses is that he reads in a paper that the "P's and Q's" company is there, and he wishes to get a position with the show, because it seems that back in Milburn he is considered quite an excellent singer, and he takes a star part in the Elks'

minstrel show in the winter of 1933, and even his mother
says it will be a sin and a shame to waste such talent
on a delivery wagon, especially by a guy who can
scarcely bear the sight of a horse.

Well, Eddie Yokum then starts telling The Seldom
Seen Kid all about the Elks' minstrel show, and how
he gives imitations of Eddie Cantor and Al Jolson in
black face; and in fact he gives these imitations for The
Seldom Seen right then and there, and both are exactly
alike, except of course Eddie Yokum is not in black face,
and The Seldom Seen Kid confesses the imitations are
really wonderful, and Eddie Yokum says he thinks so,
too, especially when you consider he never even sees
Eddie Cantor or Al Jolson.

He offers to render a song by the name of "Silver
Threads Among the Gold," which it seems is the song
he renders in the Elks' minstrels in Milburn, while imitating Eddie Cantor and Al Jolson, but Hot Horse Herbie and Big Reds tell The Seldom Seen Kid that this
will be going too far, and he agrees with them, although
Eddie Yokum seems greatly disappointed.

He is a very nice-looking young guy, with big round
eyes, and a pleasant smile, but he is so innocent that
it is really surprising to think he can walk around Baltimore, Md., safe and sound, even made up as a fox hunter.

Well, it seems that when Eddie Yokum arrives in Baltimore, Md., from Milburn, he goes around to the theater
where the "P's and Q's" company is playing to see about
getting a position with the show, but nobody wishes
to listen to him, and in fact the stage doorman finally
speaks very crossly to Eddie, and tells him that if he
does not desire a bust in the beezer, he will go away
from there. So Eddie goes away, as he does not desire
a bust in the beezer.

By and by he has a great wish to eat food, and as
he is now all out of money, there is nothing for him

to do but go to work, so he gets this job with Barker's Dog Crullers, and here he is.

"But," Eddie Yokum says, "I hesitate at taking it at first because I judge from the wardrobe that a horse goes with it, but Mr. Barker says if I think he is going to throw in a horse after spending a lot of money on this outfit, I am out of my head, and in fact Mr. Barker tells me not to walk fast, so as not to wear out these boots too soon. I am commencing to suspect that Mr. Barker is a trifle near."

By this time, no one except The Seldom Seen Kid is paying much attention to Eddie Yokum, as anybody can see that he is inclined to be somewhat gabby, and quite a bore, and anyway there cannot possibly be any percentage in talking to such a guy.

Hot Horse Herbie and Big Reds are chatting with each other, and Philly the Weeper is reading the paper, while Eddie Yokum goes right along doing a barber, and the dogs are still climbing up his legs after the Barker's Dog Crullers, when all of a sudden Philly the Weeper looks at the dogs, and speaks to Eddie Yokum in a most severe tone of voice, as follows:

"See here, young fellow," Philly says, "where do you get the two fox hounds you have with you? I just notice them, and I will thank you to answer me promptly, and without quibbling."

Well, it seems from what Eddie Yokum says that he does not get the fox hounds anywhere in particular, but that they just up and follow him as he goes along the street. He explains that the Boston bull, the dachshund, and the Scottie are what you might call stooges, because they belong to Mr. Barker personally, and Eddie has to see that they get back to the factory with him every day, but all the other dogs are strays that join out with him here and there on account of the crullers and he shoos them away when his day's work is done.

"To tell the truth," Eddie Yokum says, "I am always somewhat embarrassed to have so many dogs following me, but Mr. Barker sometimes trails me in person, and if I do not have a goodly throng of dogs in my wake eagerly partaking of Barker's Dog Crullers, he is apt to become very peevish. But," Eddie says, "I consider these fox hounds a great feather in my cap, because they are so appropriate to my costume, and I am sure that Mr. Barker will be much pleased when he sees them. In fact, he may raise my salary, which will be very pleasant, indeed."

"Well," Philly the Weeper says, "your story sounds very fishy to me. These fox hounds undoubtedly belong to my old friend, Mr. Prendergast, and how am I to know that you do not steal them from his country place? In fact, now that I look at you closely, I can see that you are such a guy as is apt to sneeze a dog any time, and for two cents I will call a cop and give you in charge."

He is gazing at Eddie Yokum most severely, and at this crack about his friend Mr. Prendergast, and a country place, The Seldom Seen Kid reaches over and takes the newspaper out of Philly the Weeper's hands, because he knows Philly has no friend by the name of Mr. Prendergast, and that even if he does have such a friend, Mr. Prendergast has no more country place than a jaybird, but he can see that Philly has something on his mind, and right away The Seldom Seen Kid raps to what it is, because there in the paper in black type is an advertisement that reads as follows:

> "LOST, STRAYED, OR STOLEN: TWO LIVER-AND-WHITE FOX
> HOUNDS ANSWERING TO THE NAMES OF NIP AND TUCK.
> $200 REWARD AND NO QUESTIONS ASKED IF RETURNED TO THE
> ORIOLE HUNTS CLUB."

·Hot Horse Herbie and Big Reds read the advertisement over The Seldom Seen Kid's shoulder, and each makes a lunge at a fox hound, Hot Horse Herbie grabbing one around the neck, and Big Reds snaring the other by the hind legs; and this unexpected action causes some astonishment and alarm among the other dogs, and also frightens Eddie Yokum no little, especially as The Seldom Seen Kid joins Philly the Weeper in gazing at Eddie very severely, and The Seldom Seen Kid speaks as follows:

"Yes," he says, "this is a most suspicious case. There is only one thing to do with a party who stoops so low as to steal a dog, and especially two dogs, and that is to clap him in the clink."

Now of course The Seldom Seen Kid has no idea whatever of clapping anybody in the clink, because as a matter of fact he is greatly opposed to clinks, and if he has his way about it, they will all be torn down and thrown away, but he figures that it is just as well to toss a good scare into Eddie Yokum and get rid of him before Eddie discovers what this interest in the fox hounds is all about, as The Seldom Seen Kid feels that if there is any reward money to be cut up, it is best not to spread it around any more than is necessary.

Well, by this time, Eddie Yokum has a very good scare in him, indeed, and he is backing away an inch or two at a time from The Seldom Seen Kid and Philly the Weeper, while Hot Horse Herbie and Big Reds are struggling with the fox hounds, and just about holding their own, when who comes walking up very briskly but a plainclothes copper by the name of Detective Wilbert Schmalz, because it seems that the manager of the Cornflower Hotel gets sick and tired of the dogs out in front of his joint, and telephones to the nearest station-house and wishes to know if there is no justice.

So the station-house gets hold of Detective Wilbert Schmalz and tells him to see about this proposition; and here he is, and naturally Detective Schmalz can see by Eddie Yokum's costume and by the dogs around him that he is undoubtedly very unlawful, and as he comes walking up, Detective Schmalz speaks to Eddie Yokum as follows:

"Come with me," he says. "You are under arrest."

Now what Eddie Yokum thinks he is under arrest for is stealing the fox hounds, and by the time Detective Schmalz gets close to him, Eddie Yokum is near one of the two entrances to the Cornflower Hotel that open on Calvert Street, and both of these entrances have revolving doors.

So all of a sudden, Eddie Yokum makes a jump into one of these entrances, and at the same time Detective Schmalz makes a grab for him, as Detective Schmalz can see by Eddie Yokum's attempt to escape that he is undoubtedly a very great malefactor, but all Detective Schmalz gets is the sign off Eddie's back that reads "Barker's Dog Crullers."

Then Detective Schmalz finds himself tangled up in the revolving door with the dachshund, which is trying to follow Eddie Yokum, and crying in a way that will break your heart, while Eddie is dashing out the other entrance, and there is great confusion all around and about, with Hot Horse Herbie and Big Reds using language to the fox hounds that is by no means fit for publication.

In fact, there is so much confusion that very few people notice that as Eddie Yokum pops out the other entrance and heads for the middle of the street where he will have plenty of racing room, a big, shiny town car with a chauffeur and a footman pulls up at the curb in front of the hotel, and the footman leaps off the seat and yanks open the door of the car right under Eddie Yokum's nose, and the next thing anybody knows, Eddie is inside the town car, and the car is tearing down the street.

Afterwards Eddie Yokum remembers hearing the footman mumble something about being sorry, they are late, but Eddie is too bewildered by his strange experience, and too happy to escape the law, to think of much of anything else for a while, and it does not come to him that he must be mistaken for somebody else until the town car is rolling up the driveway of the Oriole Hunts Club, a few miles out of Baltimore, and he sees a raft of guys and dolls strolling around and about, with the guys dressed up as fox hunters, just the same way he is.

Now, of course the guy Eddie Yokum is mistaken for is nobody but the Honorable Bertie Searles, who at this time is pounding his ear back in the Cornflower Hotel, and the chances are glad of it, but nobody can scarcely blame the chauffeur and the footman for the mistake when they see a guy dressed up as a fox hunter come bouncing out of a hotel, where they are sent to pick up an English gentleman rider, because anybody is apt to look like an Englishman, and a gentleman, too, if they are dressed up as a fox hunter.

Naturally, Eddie Yokum knows that a mistake is going on the minute he gets out of the car and finds himself surrounded by guys and dolls all calling him the Honorable Bertie Searles, and he realizes that there is nothing for him to do but to explain and apologize, and get away from there as quick as he can, and the chances are he will do this at once, as Eddie Yokum is really an honest, upright young guy, but before he can say a word, what does he see on the clubhouse veranda in riding clothes but the most beautiful doll he ever claps eyes on in his whole life.

In fact, this doll is so beautiful that Eddie Yokum is practically tongue-tied at once, and when she is introduced to him as Miss Phyllis Richie, he does not care what happens if he can only hang around here a little while, for this is undoubtedly love at first sight as far as Eddie Yokum is concerned, and Miss Phyllis Richie is by no means displeased with him, either, although she remarks that he is the first Englishman she ever sees who does not have an English accent.

So Eddie Yokum says to himself he will just keep his trap closed until the real Honorable Bertie Searles bobs up, or somebody who knows the real Honorable Bertie Searles comes around, and enjoy the sunshine of Miss Phyllis Richie's smile as long as possible; and to show you what a break he gets, it seems that nobody in the club ever sees the Honorable Bertie Searles in person, and they are all too busy getting the fox hunt in his honor going to bother to ask Eddie any questions that he cannot answer yes or no.

Anyway, Eddie Yokum keeps so close to Miss Phyllis Richie that nobody has much chance to talk to her, although a tall young guy with a little mustache and a mean look keeps trying, and Miss Phyllis Richie explains that this guy is nobody but Mr. Marshall Preston, who is as great an amateur rider in America as the Honorable Bertie Searles himself is in England.

Furthermore, she explains that Mr. Marshall Preston is the owner of a horse by the name of Sweep Forward, that is the only horse in this country that figures a chance to beat her horse, Follow You, in the Gold Vase, unless maybe the Honorable Bertie Searles' horse, Trafalgar, is an extra-good horse.

Then she commences asking Eddie Yokum about his horse, Trafalgar, and of course Eddie not only does not know he has such a horse, but he hates just even talking about horses, and he has quite a time switching the conversation, because Miss Phyllis Richie seems bound and determined to talk about horses, and especially her horse.

"I am only sorry," Miss Phyllis Richie says, "that it is not possible to let you ride Follow You over a course, just so you can see what a wonderful horse he is, but," she says, "it is a well-known peculiarity of his that he will not permit any one to ride him except a colored boy, not even myself. In fact, several times we try to put white riders on Follow You, and he half kills them. It is most unfortunate, because you will really appreciate him."

Well, naturally Eddie Yokum does not consider this unfortunate by any means, as the last thing in the world he wishes to do is to ride a horse, but of course he does not mention the matter to Miss Phyllis Richie, as he can see that a guy who does not wish to ride horses is not apt to get to first base with her.

What bothers Eddie Yokum more than somewhat, however, is the way this Mr. Marshall Preston keeps scowling at him, and finally he asks Miss Phyllis Richie if she can figure out what is eating the guy, and Miss Phyllis Richie laughs heartily, and says like this:

"Oh," she says, "Mr. Marshall Preston seems to have an idea that he loves me, and wishes to marry me. He hates anybody that comes near me. He hates my poor horse, Follow You, because he thinks if it is not for Follow You coming along and winning enough money to support us, I will have to marry him out of sheer poverty.

"But," Miss Phyllis Richie says, "I do not love Mr.

Marshall Preston, and I will never marry except for love, and while things are not so good with us right now, everything will be all right after Follow You wins the Gold Vase, because it is a $25,000 stake. But no matter what happens, I do not think I will ever marry Mr. Marshall Preston, as he is very wild in his ways, and is unkind to horses."

Well, this last is really a boost for Mr. Marshall Preston with Eddie Yokum, but naturally he does not so state to Miss Phyllis Richie, and in fact he says that now he takes a second peek at Mr. Marshall Preston he can see that he may be a wrong gee in more ways than one, and that Miss Phyllis Richie is quite right in playing the chill for such a guy.

Now there is a great commotion about the premises, with guys coming up leading horses, and a big pack of fox hounds yapping around, and it seems that the fox hunt in honor of the Honorable Bertie Searles is ready to start, and Eddie Yokum is greatly horrified when he realizes that he is expected to take part in the fox hunt, and ride a horse, and in fact Miss Phyllis Richie tells him they pick out the very finest horse in the club stables for him to ride, although she says she is afraid it will not compare to the horses he is accustomed to riding in England.

Well, at this, Eddie Yokum is greatly nonplused, and he figures that here is the blow-off sure enough, especially as a guy who seems to be a groom comes up leading a tall, fierce-looking horse, and hands Eddie the bridle-reins. But Eddie cannot think of words in which to put his confession, so when nobody seems to be noticing him, he walks off by himself toward the club stables, and naturally the horse follows him, because Eddie has hold of the reins.

Now the presence of this horse at his heels is very

disquieting to Eddie Yokum, so when he gets behind
the stables which shut him off from the sight of the
crowd, Eddie looks around for something to tie the horse
to, and finally drops the reins over the handle of a motorcycle that is leaning up against a wall, this motorcycle
being there for the grooms to run errands on to and
from the city.

Well, it seems that in the excitement over getting the
fox hunt started, nobody misses Eddie Yokum at first,
and away goes the crowd on their horses with the
hounds yapping quite some, while Eddie is standing
there behind the stables thinking of how to break the
news about himself to one and all, and especially to
Miss Phyllis Richie.

Then Eddie Yokum happens to look up, and who does
he see coming up the driveway in such a direction that
they cannot miss seeing him if he remains where he
is, but Philly the Weeper and Hot Horse Herbie, leading
a pair of hounds, which are undoubtedly the fox hounds
they get from Eddie Yokum, and which they are now
delivering to claim the reward.

Naturally, the sight of these parties is most distasteful
to Eddie Yokum, because all he can think of is that in
addition to everything else, he will now be denounced
as a dog thief, and Eddie can scarcely bear to have Miss
Phyllis Richie see him in such a light, so he grabs up
the motorcycle, and starts it going, and leaps in the
saddle, and away he sprints down a country lane in
the opposite direction from the driveway, for if there
is one thing Eddie Yokum can do, it is ride a motorcycle.

He forgets about the horse being hooked to the motorcycle, and of course the poor horse has to follow him,
and every time Eddie Yokum looks around, there is the
horse, and Eddie gets the idea that maybe the horse is
chasing him, so he gives the motorcycle plenty of gas,

and makes it zing. But it is very bumpy going along the country lane, and Eddie cannot lose the horse, and, besides, Eddie is personally becoming very tired, so finally he pulls up to take a rest.

By this time, the horse has enough lather on him to shave the House of David, and seems about ready to drop dead, and Eddie Yokum will not care a cuss if he does, as Eddie is sick and tired of the horse, although the horse is really not to blame for anything whatever.

Anyway, Eddie Yokum is lying stretched out on the ground taking a rest, when he hears the fox hounds barking away off, but coming closer right along, and he figures the fox hunters will also be moving in his direction, and as he does not wish to ever again be seen by Miss Phyllis Richie after ducking the hunt, he unhooks the horse from the motorcycle, and gives it a good kick in the vestibule, and tells it to go on about its business, and then he crawls in under a big brush-heap beside the lane, dragging the motorcycle in after him.

Well, what is under the brush-heap but a little bitsy fox, all tuckered out, and very much alarmed, and this little bitsy fox seems glad to see such a kind and sympathetic face as Eddie Yokum possesses, and it crawls into Eddie Yokum's lap, and roosts there shivering and shaking, and the next thing Eddie knows the brush-heap is surrounded by fox hounds, who are very anxious to get at the little bitsy fox, and maybe at Eddie Yokum, too, but Eddie remembers that he has some of Barker's Dog Crullers still left in his pocket, and he cools the hounds out no little by feeding them these appetizers.

By and by the fox hunters come up, following the hounds, and they are greatly surprised when Eddie Yokum comes crawling out from under the brush-heap with the little bitsy fox in his arms, especially as they meet up with Eddie's horse all covered with perspiration, and figure he must just finish a terrible run, because of course they do not know about the motorcycle hidden under the brush-heap.

They are all the more surprised when Eddie Yokum tells them that he does not believe in killing foxes, and that he always personally catches them with his bare hands after the dogs locate them, but Eddie feels rewarded when Miss Phyllis Richie smiles at him, and says he is the most humane guy she ever meets, especially when Eddie says his horse is too tired for him to ride him home, and insists on walking, carrying the little bitsy fox.

Well, Eddie is commencing to wonder again how he can confess what an impostor he is, and get away from this company, but the more he looks at Miss Phyllis Richie, the more he hates to do it, especially as she is talking about what a wonderful time they will have at the dinner in his honor later on in the evening, as it seems that this is to be a very fine affair, indeed, and Harry Richman and several other stars of the "P's and Q's" company are expected to be present to entertain, and Eddie Yokum can see where he may be missing a great opportunity to come in contact with such parties.

But by the time he gets back to the clubhouse, Eddie's mind is pretty well made up to get himself out of this predicament, no matter what, especially as the clubhouse doorman calls him aside, and says to him like this:

"Mr. Searles," the doorman says, "a most obnoxious character is here just a little while ago claiming he is you. Yes, sir," the doorman says, "he has the gall to claim he is the Honorable Bertie Searles, and he is slightly under the influence, and has several dolls with him, including a very savage blonde. Of course we know he is not you, and so we throw him out.

"He is very cheerful about it, at that, Mr. Searles," the doorman says. "He says it does not strike him as a very lively place, anyway, and that he is having more fun where he is. But the savage blonde is inclined to make much of the matter. In fact, she tries to bite me. It is a very strange world, Mr. Searles."

Well, Eddie Yokum figures right away that this must be the guy they mistake him for, and he also figures that the guy is a sure thing to be coming back sooner or later, and as it is now coming on dusk, Eddie starts easing himself down the driveway, although they tell him there is a nice room ready for him at the club where he can clean up and take a rest before dinner; but he does not get very far down the driveway, when who steps out of some bushes but Philly the Weeper, who speaks as follows:

"Well, well, well," Philly the Weeper says. "I know my eyes do not deceive me when I see you sprinting away on a motorcycle, but," he says, "imagine my astonishment when I describe you to the doorman, and he tells me you are the Honorable Bertie Searles. Why, you can knock me over with the eighth pole, I am so surprised, because of course I know you are nothing but a dog thief, and I am waiting around here for hours to get an explanation from you for such goings on."

Naturally, Philly the Weeper does not mention that he already has Hot Horse Herbie collect two C's from the club secretary for returning the hounds, and that he sends Herbie on back to Baltimore, for Philly the Weeper has a nose like a beagle, and he smells something here the minute he sees Eddie Yokum going away on the motorcycle, and he keeps himself in the background while Hot Horse Herbie is collecting the dough, although Philly does not neglect to take the two C's off of Herbie afterwards, for safe-keeping.

Of course, Philly the Weeper has no idea Eddie Yokum is trying to run away entirely on the motorcycle, or he will not be hanging around waiting for him to come back, but there Eddie is, and Philly the Weeper gets the whole story out of him in no time, because Eddie figures the best thing for him to do is to throw himself on the mercy of Philly the Weeper as far as the stolen dogs are concerned.

Well, Philly the Weeper is greatly interested and amused at Eddie's story of how he is mistaken for the Honorable Bertie Searles, and has to go fox hunting, and of his sudden and great love for Miss Phyllis Richie; but when Eddie gets down to telling him about how he is now trying to slip away from the scene, Philly the Weeper becomes very severe again, and speaks as follows:

"No, no," Philly says, "you are not to go away, at all. You are to remain here at the club for the dinner in your honor to-night, and, moreover, you are to take me into the club with you as your valet, because," Philly says, "I wish to play a joke on certain members of this organization, including my old friend, Mr. Prendergast, who will undoubtedly be present. If you will do this for me, I will forget about you stealing Mr. Prendergast's fox hounds, although he is inclined to be very drastic about the matter."

Now, of course if Eddie Yokum is such a guy as does a little serious thinking now and then, the chances are he will see that there is something unusual about all this, but Eddie is not only very innocent, but by this time he is greatly confused, and all he can think of to say to Philly the Weeper is that he is afraid the real Honorable Bertie Searles will come back and expose him.

"You need not worry about this," Philly the Weeper

says. "I am present in ambush when the Honorable Bertie Searles and his party, including my fiancée, Miss Lola Ledare, are given the bum's rush out of here a short time ago, and as they depart I hear him promising to give Lola and her friends a big party downtown tonight after the show to reimburse them for the churlish treatment they received here. Remember," Philly says, "you will not only be rounding yourself up for stealing Mr. Prendergast's dogs, but you will be able to be with the doll you love so dearly all evening."

So the upshot of it all is, Eddie Yokum goes back to the club, taking Philly the Weeper with him and explaining that Philly is his valet; and one thing about it, Philly makes Eddie more important than somewhat, at that, which is a good thing, as some of the members are commencing to wonder about Eddie, especially Mr. Marshall Preston, who is all burned up at the way Eddie is pitching to Miss Phyllis Richie.

Now, the reason Philly the Weeper wishes to get inside the clubhouse is not to play any jokes on anybody, as he says, especially on his friend Mr. Prendergast, because in the first place he has no friend named Mr. Prendergast, and in the second place, Philly the Weeper has no friends by any names whatever. The reason he wishes to get inside the clubhouse is to collect any little odds and ends of jewelry that he may find lying about the premises later on, for collecting articles of this kind is really one of Philly the Weeper's regular occupations, though naturally he does not mention it to Eddie Yokum.

As a matter of fact, he is of quite some service to Eddie Yokum when they go to the room that is assigned to Eddie, as he coaches Eddie in the way a guy shall act at dinner, and in talking to such a doll as Miss Phyllis Richie, and he also fixes Eddie's clothes up for him a little, as the dinner is to be in fox hunting costume, which is a good thing for Eddie, as he does not have any other costume.

The only argument they have is about the little bitsy fox, which Eddie Yokum is still carrying around with him, and which he wishes to keep with him at all times, as he is now very fond of the little creature, but Philly the Weeper convinces him that it is better to turn it loose, and let it return to its native haunts, and when Eddie does same the little bitsy fox creates a riot in the club kennels when it goes streaking past them headed for the woods.

Well, Eddie Yokum is a very hospitable soul, and he wishes Philly the Weeper to attend the dinner with him, but Philly says no, a valet is supposed to be a sort of hired hand, and does not go in for social functions with his boss, so Eddie goes down to dinner alone, leaving Philly the Weeper in the room, and Eddie is greatly delighted to find Miss Phyllis Richie is waiting for him to escort her in, and for the next couple of hours he is in a sort of trance, and cannot remember that he is not the Honorable Bertie Searles, but only Eddie Yokum, of Milburn, Del.

All he can remember is that he hauls off and tells Miss Phyllis Richie that he is in love with her, and she says she loves him right back, and the only trouble with this conversation is that Mr. Marshall Preston accidentally overhears it, and is so unhappy he can scarcely think, because it is only a couple of hours before that Mr. Marshall Preston asks Miss Phyllis Richie to please marry him.

Mr. Marshall Preston is so unhappy that he goes out to the bar before dinner is over and has a few drinks, and then he goes upstairs to a room he is occupying for the evening, just in time to catch Philly the Weeper collecting a job lot of trinkets in the room to add to a bundle he already collects from other rooms.

Naturally, this unexpected intrusion is most embarrassing to Philly the Weeper, especially as Mr. Marshall Preston recognizes him as the Honorable Bertie Searles' valet, and it is perhaps just as well for Mr. Marshall Preston that Philly the Weeper is not rodded up at this time, as Philly never cares to be embarrassed. But Mr. Marshall Preston turns out to be very broad-minded, and instead of making a scene over finding Philly the Weeper at his collecting, he speaks to Philly as follows:

"Sit down," he says. "Sit down, and let us talk this over. What is there about this party who calls himself the Honorable Bertie Searles that causes me to wonder, and what is your real connection with him, and why does your face seem so familiar to me? Tell me your tale, and tell me true," Mr. Marshall Preston says, "or shall I call the gendarmes?"

Well, Philly the Weeper can see that Mr. Marshall Preston is no sucker, so he tells him that the Honorable Bertie Searles at the club is 100 per cent phoney, because he is nobody but Eddie Yokum, and he explains how he gets there, and that the real Honorable Bertie Searles is downtown enjoying himself with members of the "P's and Q's" company.

"And," Philly says, "the reason my face seems familiar to you may be because I am around the race-tracks quite often, although I never have much truck with the steeplechasers."

Now, Mr. Marshall Preston listens to all this with great interest, and when Philly the Weeper gets through, Mr. Marshall Preston sits there quiet for awhile, as if he is studying something out, and finally he says like this:

"I will call up the Honorable Bertie Searles, and we

will have him come here and expose this impostor,"
he says. "It will be a good lesson to Miss Phyllis Richie
for taking up with such a character without first finding
out something about him. But in the meantime," he
says, "let us continue talking while I make up my mind
about handing you over to the cops."

They continue talking until Mr. Marshall Preston
forgets about calling the Honorable Bertie Searles until
an hour later, and then he may just as well save himself
the trouble, for at the moment he is telephoning, the
Honorable Bertie Searles is on his way to the Oriole
Hunts Club with Miss Lola Ledare, and a taxi-load of
other blondes, and a few brunettes, because right in the
middle of a nice party, some of the blondes remember they are due at the club to help Harry Richman
put on a number, and the Honorable Bertie Searles says
he will go along and demand an explanation from the
club for his treatment earlier in the day, although the
Honorable Bertie Searles says he does not really care
a whoop, as he is treated worse in better clubs.

Well, while all this is happening, the dinner is going
along very nicely, and it is a gala scene, to be sure,
what with the decorations, and music, and all, and Eddie
Yokum is in more of a trance than ever over Miss Phyllis
Richie, when all of a sudden an old phflug by the name
of Mrs. Abernathy comes running into the dining-hall
letting out a squawk that she is robbed. It seems that
she leaves a purse containing some dough, and other
valuables, with her wraps in the dolls' dressing-room
upstairs, and when she goes up there to powder her
nose, or some such, she finds somebody knocks off her
poke.

Now, this causes other dolls to remember leaving their
leathers laying around upstairs, and some of them investigate at once, and find they are clipped, too, and pres-

ently guys who occupy rooms in the club are also letting out bleats and it becomes apparent that some thievery is going on around and about, and the club manager telephones for the police, because the beefs are commencing to be most upsetting.

Well, naturally Eddie Yokum is paying little attention to this commotion, because he is too greatly interested in Miss Phyllis Richie, but all of a sudden a bunch of coppers walk into the room, and who is among them but Detective Wilbert Schmalz, and the minute Eddie sees him, he becomes alarmed, as he is afraid Detective Schmalz may recognize him and put the arm on him for stealing the fox hounds, even though this matter is now supposed to be rounded up with Philly the Weeper.

So Eddie Yokum excuses himself to Miss Phyllis Richie and steps in back of a stand of potted plants, where he will not be conspicuous, and about this time he hears a familiar voice asking what is the trouble here, and why are all the coppers present, and somebody speaks up and says:

"Why, we are robbed."

Then Eddie Yokum hears the familiar voice again, which he recognizes as the voice of Mr. Barker, who makes the dog crullers, and it is quite a loud voice, at that, and very unpleasant, and in fact it is such a loud voice that it causes Eddie Yokum to tremble in his topboots, for Mr. Barker states as follows:

"You are robbed?" he says. "Well, think of me, and how I am robbed, too. I am robbed of my hunting clothes, and I have to appear here at a hunts dinner for the first time in all the years I am a member of this club, the way you see me. If they do not happen to have sense enough to find their way home, I will also be robbed of Adolph, my dachshund, and Boggie, my Boston, and McTavish, my Scottie. But," Mr. Barker says, "if it takes me the rest of my life, I will find the young squirt who runs off with my hunting clothes and choke the tongue out of his head."

Well, at this, Eddie Yokum peeks around the potted plants, and he sees Mr. Barker standing nearby in a dinner jacket, and apparently very angry, indeed, and this is quite a situation for Eddie Yokum, because he is between Detective Schmalz, who may wish to put the arm on him, and Mr. Barker, who wishes to choke the tongue out of his head, and as if this is not enough, there is now a great commotion at the front door, with dolls squealing, and guys yelling, and Eddie Yokum hears somebody say that a guy is out there claiming he is the Honorable Bertie Searles, and trying to fight his way in.

The racket is so great it attracts everybody's attention, and Eddie Yokum sees his chance and slips away quietly, popping into the first door he comes to, and this door leads down a stairway into the furnace-room, so Eddie hides himself behind a furnace for awhile.

In the meantime, there is much excitement upstairs, as it seems that the Honorable Bertie Searles finally battles his way inside against great odds, and is identified by all the members of the "P's and Q's" company who are with him, including Harry Richman and the other stars, as the guy he claims he is, and he is demanding apologies from everybody connected with the club, while a search is going on for the phoney Honorable Bertie Searles.

Finally, Detective Schmalz, who joins the search, frisks the room that Eddie occupies, and finds a couple of missing purses, now empty, and everybody is saying that there is no doubt Eddie is not only an impostor, but that he and his valet are thieves; although Mr. Marshall Preston puts in here, and says he does not think the valet is a party to the crime, as he personally sees the valet leaving the premises some time before the robbery can possibly take place.

So then everybody agrees that Eddie must be a lone hand criminal, and Miss Phyllis Richie is so mortified she gets her wraps and goes out on the veranda, especially after somebody describes Eddie Yokum, and Mr. Barker says he is surely the guy who cops his hunting costume, and Detective Schmalz, who listens in on the description, states that he is positive the guy is a much wanted dog snatcher.

Mr. Marshall Preston goes out on the veranda and tries to console Miss Phyllis Richie, and in fact he tells her that it is now time for her to make up her mind to marry him and find safety from adventurers such as Eddie Yokum, but Miss Phyllis Richie gives him a very short answer, and there are undoubtedly large tears in her eyes as she speaks, and anybody can see that she is feeling very downhearted, so Mr. Marshall Preston leaves her to her sorrow.

Well, pretty soon the entertainment goes into action, and the real Honorable Bertie Searles becomes the guest of honor in place of Eddie Yokum, and everybody forgets the unpleasant incidents of the evening, because the Honorable Bertie Searles is full of life and spirits and does not center his attention on any one doll, as Eddie does when he is guest of honor, but scatters his shots around and about, although it is plain to be seen that the Honorable Bertie Searles cares for Miss Lola Ledare more than somewhat, even if she does keep wishing to go back and fight the doorman all over again.

Meantime, Eddie Yokum is down in the furnace-room, and how to get out and away from the club without being observed becomes something of a problem, as Eddie is still in the fox-hunting costume, and such a costume is bound to attract attention at all times, and, furthermore, the only entrance to the furnace-room seems to be the room through which Eddie comes in the first place.

Well, Eddie sits there behind the furnace thinking things over, and he can hear the music and the laughter upstairs, and he is wishing he is back in Milburn, Del., where he has a home, and friends; and thinking of Milburn, Del., reminds Eddie of the time he blacks up his face and gives imitations of Al Jolson and Eddie Cantor; and thinking of this gives him a brand-new idea.

This idea is to black up his face right there and walk out to safety, because Eddie figures that anybody who sees him is bound to take him as an employee of the furnace-room, so he peeks into the furnace, and finds a lot of soot, and he makes his face blacker than a yard up a chimney.

Moreover, Eddie gets another break when he finds a suit of blue overalls left by some guy who works in the furnace-room, and also an old cap, and when he sneaks out the door a little later, he is nothing but a boogie, as far as anybody can see, and not a very clean boogie, at that, and the chances are he will be out of the club and gone in two minutes, if he does not happen to run into the Honorable Bertie Searles, who is teetering around looking for Miss Lola Ledare, who is absent from the scene longer than the Honorable Bertie Searles thinks is necessary.

As a matter of fact, Miss Lola Ledare is at this time off in a corner with Mr. Barker, giving Mr. Barker quite a canvass one way and another, for Miss Lola Ledare is a doll who believes in scattering her play, but of course this has nothing to do with the story.

Well, when he runs into Eddie Yokum, naturally the Honorable Bertie Searles thinks Eddie is really a colored

guy, and right away the Honorable Bertie Searles gets
a big idea, as guys who are rummed up a little always
do. The Honorable Bertie Searles says that so far the
entertainment in his honor lacks the old Southern touch
he is led to believe he will find in such spots as Baltimore,
Md., especially by colored parties, and he considers Eddie a great capture, and insists on leading him out on
the floor where the entertainment is going on, and presenting him to the crowd as a bit of real Southern
atmosphere.

Naturally, Eddie Yokum is somewhat embarrassed,
and alarmed, because he is afraid he will be recognized
by somebody, but no one gives him a tumble for who
he is, and everybody laughs heartily at what they consider the Honorable Bertie Searles' humor. Then the
Honorable Bertie Searles says his protégé will now sing,
and there is nothing for Eddie Yokum to do but sing,
so he goes into "Silver Threads Among the Gold," and
the orchestra picks him up nicely, and accompanies his
singing.

Ordinarily, Eddie will be very glad to sing before
such an audience, and even now he has a notion to give
them Al Jolson and Eddie Cantor, then he commences
thinking of what will happen to him if he is recognized,
and he gets so alarmed he sings a little flat.

As he is singing, Eddie Yokum makes sure of the direction of the front entrance to the club, and he keeps
edging in this direction as his song comes to a close,
so it seems very natural when he finishes to bow himself
off in an aisle leading to the entrance; only Eddie keeps
right on going out the entrance, and he is on the veranda,
and flying, when who does he run into but Miss Phyllis
Richie.

Well, at the sight of Miss Phyllis Richie, Eddie Yokum
forgets he is all sooted up, and looks like a smudge,

and in fact all he can think of is how much he loves Miss Phyllis Richie, and he rushes up to her and speaks as follows:

"Darling," Eddie Yokum says, "I am in a bit of a hurry right now, and do not have time to explain matters, but do not believe anything you hear about me, because it is by no means true; and, anyway," Eddie says, "I adore you."

Naturally, Miss Phyllis Richie thinks at first that Eddie is a real jig, and she is somewhat startled for a moment, but then she recognizes his voice, and she becomes very indignant, indeed.

"Why," Miss Phyllis Richie says, "you impostor! You cad! You liar! Why," she says, "you dog stealer! You common burglar! If you do not get away from here at once, I will call Mr. Marshall Preston and he will thrash you within an inch of your life, and turn you over to the police!"

And with this, she hauls off and biffs Eddie Yokum a hard slap in the kisser, and then she bursts out crying, and there is nothing for Eddie Yokum to do but to continue on his way, because he hears the Honorable Bertie Searles yelling for him, and he does not desire any further complications at this time.

All Eddie Yokum wishes to do is to go away somewhere and sit down and rest, and get his nerves composed again, as he is feeling greatly fatigued; and the first thing he does is to go to his rooming-house and wash himself up, and put on his best suit of clothes, which he brings with him from Milburn, Del., and then he starts thinking things over, and what he especially thinks over is why Miss Phyllis Richie calls him a common burglar, for of course Eddie Yokum does not know he is suspected of prowling the Oriole Hunts Club, although he knows it the next morning when he reads

all about the robbery in the paper, and also about how
the coppers are looking for a guy who impersonates the
Honorable Bertie Searles to get into the club for the
purpose of committing the crime.

Well, this is a very great shock to Eddie Yokum, and
he can see at once why he stands like a broken leg with
Miss Phyllis Richie. Moreover, he can see that there is
just one guy who can state that he does not get into
the club to commit any crimes, and this guy is nobody
but Philly the Weeper, so Eddie figures the thing for
him to do is to find Philly the Weeper, and get him to
straighten this matter out, although of course if Eddie
is well acquainted with Philly the Weeper he will know
that getting Philly to straighten anything out is just
the same thing as asking a gimlet to straighten out.

But Eddie Yokum has great faith in human nature
and honesty, so the next morning he goes around in
front of the Cornflower Hotel looking for Philly the
Weeper; but Philly is by no means there, although The
Seldom Seen Kid and Hot Horse Herbie and Big Reds
are present; and at first none of them recognize Eddie
without his fox hunter's costume until he asks The Seldom Seen Kid where Philly is, and The Seldom Seen
Kid says like this:

"Well," he says, "if you can tell us, we will be greatly
obliged, for we are seeking him ourselves to cut his ears
off unless he kicks in with our share of a small score
we make on some dogs. Yes," The Seldom Seen Kid
says, "we will just love to see Philly the Weeper, but
the 'P's and Q's' company goes to New York this morning, and the chances are he goes there, too, because he
never gets far away from his fiancée, Miss Lola Ledare,
for fear he will starve to death. But we will catch up
with him sooner or later."

Then The Seldom Seen Kid seems to remember Eddie

Yokum's face, and he starts to laugh, because the last time he sees Eddie Yokum it is a very humorous spectacle, to be sure; but Eddie Yokum does not see anything to laugh about, and he starts in telling The Seldom Seen Kid and Hot Horse Herbie and Big Reds how Philly the Weeper makes him take him into the club as his valet, and what happens, and how he wishes to find Philly to prove his innocence; and Hot Horse Herbie is especially horrified, and states as follows:

"Why," he says, "I ought to know this fink has something on his mind that spells larceny when he tells me he is going to stick around out there at the club awhile and sends me back to town. But," Herbie says, "it does not occur to me it is anything more serious than maybe stealing a couple of dogs over again to collect another award. There is no doubt but what he prowls the joint and leaves this poor guy to take the fall."

"Philly the Weeper is a wrong gee," The Seldom Seen Kid says. "I know he is a wrong gee because he means to defraud us of our end of the two C's he gets yesterday, but I never figure he is wrong enough to do such a trick as he does to this guy here. It is really most preposterous. Well," The Seldom Seen Kid says, "the races are over here tomorrow and the best thing for you to do is to go with us and see if we can find Philly the Weeper. Anyway," he says, "if you stick around here you will be picked up and placed in the sneezer, and it is very, very difficult to get out of a Baltimore sneezer, once you are in."

So this is how Eddie Yokum comes to be in New York and around Mindy's restaurant on Broadway the next week with The Seldom Seen Kid, and Hot Horse Herbie, and Big Reds, and also with other prominent turf advisers, and followers of the sport of kings, for Mindy's restaurant is a great resort for such characters.

But although he looks high and low, Eddie Yokum does not see hide or hair of Philly the Weeper, and neither does The Seldom Seen Kid and Hot Horse Herbie and Big Reds, although his fiancée, Miss Lola Ledare, is around in different spots nearly every night with the Honorable Bertie Searles, and the price against the Honorable Bertie Searles' horse, Trafalgar, in the Gold Vase Steeplechase goes up by the minute, and some bookmakers will give you as good as 10 to 1 that the Honorable Bertie cannot even sit on a horse Saturday, let alone ride one.

Most of the conversation around Mindy's at this time is about the Gold Vase Steeplechase, but it is conceded by one and all that it is a set-up for Miss Phyllis Richie's Follow You, and every time Eddie Yokum hears her name he has a pain in his heart, because he even forgets to think of Philly the Weeper when he is thinking of Miss Phyllis Richie.

What with being around with parties interested in horse racing, Eddie Yokum takes to reading the sport pages quite some, and when it comes on the day before the Gold Vase, he reads about Miss Phyllis Richie arriving at the Savoy-Plaza with a party of friends from all over Maryland to see the race, and he hangs around in front of the hotel for three hours just to get a peek at her, although he is somewhat discouraged when he sees Miss Phyllis Richie with Mr. Marshall Preston.

In the evening, he hears the citizens around Mindy's speaking of Mr. Marshall Preston's horse, Sweep Forward, and of other horses, but the conversation makes no impression on Eddie Yokum, because he does not know anything about racing, and in fact he never sees a race, because he hates horses so much, but there is so much excitement over the Gold Vase that finally he feels a desire to see this race, and he asks The Seldom

Seen Kid and Hot Horse Herbie and Big Reds if they will take him with them the next day.

Well, they say they will, although they will much rather take somebody that has something, because the truth of the matter is, they are getting a little tired of Eddie Yokum, as he is strictly a non-producer at this time, and they have to sustain him as he goes along, and the only reason they do this is they feel sorry for him, and The Seldom Seen Kid and Hot Horse Herbie and Big Reds are noted for their kind hearts.

The Seldom Seen Kid is especially sorry for Eddie Yokum, because he knows of Eddie's love for Miss Phyllis Richie, as Eddie confides same to The Seldom Seen Kid one evening, and as The Seldom Seen often carries the old torch himself, he knows how it feels.

But he is wishing Eddie Yokum will get a job and forget Miss Phyllis Richie, as The Seldom Seen Kid regards it as a hopeless passion, especially as he reads in a paper that Miss Phyllis Richie is planning to go abroad with a party that will include Mr. Marshall Preston immediately after the race for the Gold Vase, although The Seldom Seen Kid does not show this item to Eddie Yokum.

Well, the day of the Gold Vase Steeplechase is always a great day at Belmont Park, as it brings together all the greatest steeplechasers in the country, and the best riders, including gentleman jocks and professionals, and the finest society crowd, and Eddie Yokum is quite bewildered by what he sees and hears as he wanders around and about, although he cannot help a feeling of loathing that all this is over horses.

He looks around for Miss Phyllis Richie, and asks The Seldom Seen Kid where she is apt to be at such a place as a race-track, and The Seldom Seen says the chances are she will be out under the trees behind the

grandstand where the horses are walked around and
saddled not long before the big race, to take a peek at
her horse, and furthermore, The Seldom Seen Kid says:

"I only wish you are on speaking terms with her, at
that," he says. "There is a rumor that Miss Phyllis Richie's nigger jockey, Roy Snakes, is off on a bender,
or something to this effect. Anyway, they say he is missing, and if they cannot find him, or get another jig jock,
they will have to scratch Follow You, because no white
guy alive can ride Follow You in a race.

"Now," The Seldom Seen Kid goes on, "I hear there
is not another coon steeplechaser in these parts just now,
and if you can find out if Roy Snakes is really absent,
I can get a fair price on Sweep Forward. With Follow
You out, he is a triple-plated pipe. It will really be quite
a favor to me, and some of my customers if you can
secure this information for me before the rush
sets in."

Well, Eddie Yokum does not understand what this
is all about, but he does get the idea that Miss Phyllis
Richie may be in some sort of predicament, so he goes
out under the trees behind the grandstand, and waits
around there awhile, and sure enough he finally sees
Miss Phyllis Richie standing under a tree around which
an old guy by the name of Ike is leading a big chestnut
horse, and there is a large ring of guys and dolls around
the tree looking at the horse, and furthermore he sees
that Miss Phyllis Richie's eyes are all red and swollen
as if she is weeping.

Now at this spectacle, Eddie Yokum's heart goes out
to Miss Phyllis Richie, and he will walk right up to
her as bold as a lion if he is not afraid of the horse, so
he waits awhile longer, and pretty soon Miss Phyllis
Richie leaves the group and goes across the grass to
the jockey-house, and what Miss Phyllis Richie is going

to the jockey-house for is to ask if Roy Snakes shows up, or if they find another darky jockey for her.

But it seems the answer is no both ways, and Miss Phyllis Richie is turning away looking most despondent when Eddie Yokum steps up to her and speaks to her as follows:

"Miss Richie," Eddie says, "if there is anything I can do to help you out in this situation, kindly so state. I know you despise me," he says, "but I will gladly lay down my life for you."

Well, at this, Miss Phyllis Richie stops and gazes at him awhile, and there is great sarcasm in her voice when she finally says:

"Why, the last time I see you, you are colored. It is a pity you are not the same way now, or you might take Roy Snakes' place in this race. Good-day to you, Mr. Burglar, or I will call a Pinkerton."

She turns away, and goes back to where the old guy is walking the horse around, and Eddie Yokum follows her at a distance, but gets up in time to hear her telling Ike it is no use waiting on Roy Snakes, or anybody else, and to go ahead and declare Follow You out of the Gold Vase Steeplechase.

Then she disappears in the crowd, but Eddie Yokum can see that she is very sad, and he is sad himself, and he gets to talking to Ike, and he asks him what about a guy blacking himself up and fooling Follow You into thinking he is a smoke, and Ike says it is undoubtedly a great idea.

"In fact," Ike says, "if I am younger, I will do it myself, just to save Miss Phyllis Richie, because I hear if she does not win this stake, she is going to marry Mr. Marshall Preston, and this is a sad fate for a young doll, to be sure. Between you and me, Mr. Marshall Preston is far from being all right."

Well, at this news, Eddie Yokum becomes greatly agitated, and he tells Ike to get him some cork, and he will ride Follow You, and old Ike is so delighted that he does not bother to ask Eddie Yokum if he is a good rider. He leaves Follow You in charge of a stable boy, and takes Eddie Yokum over to the secretary's office and announces him as a gentleman jockey from Delaware, who is willing to help Miss Phyllis Richie out of her predicament about a jockey, and when they suggest that Eddie Yokum seems to be as white as any of the other white guys who try to ride Follow You and fail, and Ike says Eddie is going to ride blackface, there is quite a looking up of the rules.

But there is nothing in the rules against such a thing, although an old guy in the office with a big white mouser says it seems quite irregular, and that he does not recall a similar case in fifty years of experience. However, he says the office is willing to establish a precedent in the case of such a great horse as Follow You, though he cannot figure what on earth becomes of Roy Snakes, or why the only other two colored steeplechase jockeys in the East, Washington and Lincoln, find it necessary to go to Aiken two days before this race.

He is still muttering about the matter when Ike takes Eddie Yokum to the jockey-house, and then Ike sends in to Frank Stevens' bar in the clubhouse and buys several bottles of liquor to get corks for Eddie to burn and black up with, although Ike personally drinks all the liquor himself.

Well, all the time Eddie Yokum is blacking up, he is saying every prayer he knows that Roy Snakes, or one of the other dinge jockeys appears to ride Follow You, but no such thing happens, and by and by Eddie is out in the Richie colors, and is as black as anything, and maybe blacker, and while Follow You gives him quite a snuffing over when Eddie approaches him, the horse seems satisfied he is dealing with a smoke, and afterwards some people claim this is a knock to the way Eddie smells.

No one will ever know what Eddie Yokum suffers when he is hoisted up on Follow You, and there is considerable criticism of his riding technique, as he does not seem to be sure which is the front end and which is the back end of a horse.

But by this time, Eddie is determined to go through with this proposition if he gets killed, and it looks as if he will, at that, although it does not look as if he will get killed any sooner than the Honorable Bertie Searles, who arrives at the course slightly mulled, and who insists on practicing a few tricks he once observes at a rodeo in England, when the horses are going to the post, because the Honorable Bertie Searles thinks Miss Lola Ledare is in the grandstand watching him, and he warns her to be sure and take note of his fancy riding.

Now, the Honorable Bertie Searles is riding along next to Eddie Yokum, and he seems such a good-natured sort of guy that Eddie figures it may not be a bad idea to get a little advice from him, so he asks the Honorable Bertie Searles what are the rules of such a race, and what is the best thing for a guy who does not know much about it to do; and while the Honorable Bertie Searles is somewhat surprised at the question, especially from a smudge rider, he answers as follows:

"Why," he says, "all you do is to try and keep going. If you fall off your horse, do not worry, but just get back on again, and take the jump all over and keep going, unless your neck is broken. Personally, I generally let my horse, Trafalgar, do the thinking for me in a race, because Trafalgar is quite a thinker, and maybe your horse is a thinker, too. But," he says, "keep going."

The most astonished guy around at seeing Eddie Yokum on Follow You is undoubtedly Mr. Marshall Preston, who is riding his horse Sweep Forward, but he is no more astonished than Miss Phyllis Richie, who is sitting in a box in the grandstand with a party of friends from Baltimore, Md., and who is still weeping, thinking her horse is out of the race.

She stops weeping when she sees her colors on the track, and looks at the jockey-board to see who is riding her horse, but the name E. Yokum on the board means nothing to her, as she never hears Eddie's real name before, and she does not recognize him at first, and figures he is some new colored jockey old Ike digs up at the last minute.

The horse players on the lawn and the bookies under the stand are also somewhat astonished, because there nobody ever hears of E. Yokum before, either, except maybe The Seldom Seen Kid, and Hot Horse Herbie, and Big Reds, and even they do not know Eddie in his make-up until they run down to the rail to watch the post parade, and Eddie Yokum tips them a large wink, although the reason Eddie tips them this wink is to squeeze a large tear out of his eye, because Eddie is so alarmed he is half crying, and only love sustains him in the saddle.

Well, when The Seldom Seen Kid and Hot Horse Herbie and Big Reds see who is on Follow You, and see Eddie's wink, they figure that there must be something very special doing in this race, and they start running around everywhere, hoping they may be able to raise a few bobs to bet on Follow You, but of course nobody is going to let them have a few bobs for any purpose, and they are greatly discouraged about the matter, when who do they run into but Miss Lola Ledare,

who is not in the grandstand at all, as the Honorable
Bertie Searles thinks, but is standing on the edge of
the betting ring with some large coarse banknotes in
her hand.

Naturally, when they see Miss Lola Ledare in posses-
sion of funds, they are greatly interested, and they sur-
round her and ask her what seems to be troubling her,
and Miss Lola Ledare speaks freely to them, as she is
not aware of any coolness between them and her fiancé,
Philly the Weeper, and what she speaks is as follows:

"Why," she says, "they do not allow ladies in the betting ring, and I am waiting here for some one to come
along and bet this money for me on Sweep Forward,
so your arrival is most timely. The bet is for Philly.
He raises this money on some old family heirlooms that
I never know he possesses, and he requests me to place
it for him. Personally," she says, "I think the Honorable
Bertie Searles will win the race on Trafalgar, because
he tells me so himself, and I have half a notion to bet
some of the money on him, only I am afraid of what
Philly will say if Trafalgar does not come in."

Well, The Seldom Seen Kid takes the dough out of
Miss Lola Ledare's hand, and says to her like this:

"Lola," he says, "it will be a privilege and a pleasure
for me to do Philly the service of betting this money
for him—and by the way, where is Philly?"

"Why," Lola says, "he asks me not to mention to anybody that he is present, but I know he will not mind
you knowing. He is sitting away up in one corner of
the grandstand all by himself. To tell the truth, Philly
has become somewhat solitary of late, and I am commencing to get somewhat displeased with him, because
I like sociable guys, like the Honorable Bertie Searles."

Well, The Seldom Seen Kid is somewhat surprised
to find that he takes ten large C's off of Miss Lola Ledare,

because he does not know there is this much money in the world, and he hurries into the ring and bets it all on Follow You and gets 6 to 5 for the money, as Follow You is favorite, even with somebody by the name of E. Yokum up, which shows what the public thinks of the horse, although with Roy Snakes riding, the price will be 7 to 10.

There is a ton of money for Sweep Forward at the last minute, and some very, very smart guys are betting on him, and furthermore there is a rumor that Sweep Forward has help in the race, which is a way of saying that some of the others will be trying to assist Sweep Forward to win, and there is also a rumor that Follow You is a stiff in the race, and this is why Roy Snakes is not riding; but one thing about a race-track, you can always hear anything, and the public sticks to Follow You, no matter what.

There are ten other horses in the Gold Vase, and there is money for all of them, including Trafalgar, although Trafalgar is 15 to 1, as nobody seems to care for the way the Honorable Bertie Searles is riding the horse going to the post, what with the Honorable Bertie Searles doing hand-stands in the saddle, and otherwise carrying on.

Now the Gold Vase Steeplechase is a race of about three miles, or about two and a half times around the course, and the horses have to make about nineteen jumps over hedges and a water jump, and everybody that knows about these matters will tell you that this is the toughest race in this country, especially with a big field of starters, and many things can happen in the race, including death. In fact, a steeplechase rider is regarded as a very poor risk, indeed, by all insurance companies, although it is perhaps just as well that Eddie Yokum does not know this as he goes to the post.

But Eddie is smart enough to remember what the Honorable Bertie Searles tells him about letting the horse do the thinking, and it happens that Follow You is quite a thinker, indeed, and very experienced, so when the starter tells them to come on, Eddie just hangs onto Follow You's mane and lets him do as he feels best, and Follow You feels that it is best to go right to the front.

At least Eddie Yokum hangs onto Follow You's mane until the horse hits the first jump, when Mr. Marshall Preston, on Sweep Forward, comes out of the pack with a rush, and yells look out, and Eddie is looking out as Follow You jumps with Sweep Forward, and Eddie lets go the mane so he can look out better, and the next thing Eddie knows he is on the grass, and the rest of the field is going past him, and Follow You is standing there looking greatly surprised.

Well, there is a groan from the grandstand, for here is the public choice apparently out of the race before it really starts, but Eddie suddenly remembers what the Honorable Bertie Searles tells him about keeping going, and taking all the jumps, so he gets on his feet, and backs Follow You up against the fence and climbs on him and sends him at the jump again, and this time Eddie does not forget to hang onto the horse's mane.

But all this takes up some time, and the rest of the field is anyway half a mile ahead, but three horses go down at the second jump, and two more at the third, and at both these jumps, Eddie Yokum falls off Follow You as the horse is jumping, and the public is commencing to marvel about Follow You making every jump twice, and wondering if it is a handicap he is giving the others, or what.

Sweep Forward is out in front going easy, and fencing like a bird, with Mr. Marshall Preston looking very graceful in the saddle, and who is laying right close to him all the time but the Honorable Bertie Searles, on Trafalgar. The rest are strung out all along the course, and it looks like a parade more than anything else.

Well, the real tough jump on the course is the water jump in front of the grandstand, and they take this jump twice during the race, and the first time Eddie Yokum falls off Follow You into the water he is so long coming up that many customers think maybe he is drowned, and most of them hope he is, at that.

But one thing about Follow You, he never runs away when he loses his rider, but stands perfectly still until Eddie is on his back again, although Follow You is commencing to look very pained, especially when it appears to be a sure thing that he will be lapped by Sweep Forward and Trafalgar, anyway, before the race is over.

However, other horses keep going down at the various jumps, and at the end of the second mile, only Sweep Forward and Trafalgar, and a horse that is called Great Shakes, with a professional jockey by the name of Smithers, up, and Follow You are left in the race, although of course you cannot say Follow You is really in the race because he is now almost a full mile to the rear, and Miss Phyllis Richie faints three different times in the grandstand, once out of dismay, and twice out of vexation.

It seems that Miss Phyllis Richie does not recognize Eddie Yokum even yet, but she can see that the guy on her horse does not have any great knack for riding, and she is annoyed no little, especially as everybody on the premises is now uniting in a Bronx cheer for Follow You and his jockey.

The way Eddie Yokum is riding Follow You when he is not falling off is really something remarkable, as he is all over the horse, and sometimes halfway under him, and when the Honorable Bertie Searles sees this exhibition, he gets sored up, because he figures Eddie is trying to show him up as a trick rider, although of course Eddie has no such idea whatever.

Now Trafalgar is never more than two lengths off Sweep Forward at any stage of the race, and anybody can see that the Honorable Bertie Searles has a great horse under him, and in fact it looks as if he can go to the front whenever he is ready, and when Great Shakes falls with Smithers at about the fourteenth jump, it is strictly a two-horse race, because by this time Eddie Yokum is in the water jump again, and, anyway, Follow You is getting pretty much fagged out, because the way the race figures, Follow You does twice as much work as any of the other horses, and he is carrying top weight of 175 pounds, at that, counting Eddie's 150 and the lead in his saddle slots.

In fact, Follow You is so fagged out that he is just able to jog along, and the jumps in the last mile are as tough for him as they are for Eddie, and in fact once when Eddie is stretched out on the grass after a jump, it looks as if Follow You wishes to lay down beside him.

Well, in the meantime, Mr. Marshall Preston on Sweep Forward and the Honorable Bertie Searles on Trafalgar, are tearing for the last jump neck and neck, because the Honorable Bertie Searles now makes his serious challenge, and the crowd is up and yelling and nobody even thinks of Eddie Yokum and Follow You plugging along away back yonder, except maybe Miss Phyllis Richie.

Sweep Forward and Trafalgar take off for the final jump just like a team, and as Trafalgar jumps, Mr. Marshall Preston gives him a smack across the nose with his riding bat, which upsets Trafalgar no little, and in fact causes him to stumble and fall as he clears the jump, but not before the Honorable Bertie Searles can reach out almost in mid-air and tweak Mr. Marshall Preston's saddle pad in such a way that Sweep Forward falls, too, because naturally the Honorable Bertie Searles is slightly irked by Mr. Marshall Preston playing such a dirty trick on Trafalgar.

Well, Mr. Marshall Preston lets out a loud cry as Sweep Forward falls, because Mr. Marshall Preston finds himself pinned down under the horse with a broken leg, and he is in great pain at once, and while the Honorable Bertie Searles is not hurt, Trafalgar gets up and runs off so fast there is no chance that the Honorable Bertie Searles can catch him, and by and by along the course comes Eddie Yokum on Follow You, the only horse left in the race, with one jump to go.

Well, the Honorable Bertie Searles runs up the course, somewhat excited, and begins coaching Eddie Yokum, telling him to take it easy, and to bear a little to the left going over the jump to keep from landing on Mr. Marshall Preston and Sweep Forward, and Eddie tries to do as he is told, but Follow You is now a mighty weary horse, and for the first time in years he falls taking a hurdle, and Eddie finds himself on the turf alongside Mr. Marshall Preston, who stops groaning long enough to look at Eddie Yokum in great surprise, and to speak to him as follows:

"I am dying," Mr. Marshall Preston says. "Tell Miss Phyllis Richie that with my last breath I ask her forgiveness for getting Philly the Weeper to slug her jockey, Roy Snakes, and put him out of business. She will find him in Harlem. Tell her I am also sorry I put Washington and Lincoln, the only other jig jocks around, under contract and send them away, but it is necessary for me to win this stake and enough in bets to pay my wife in South Dakota some back alimony I owe her."

And with this, Mr. Marshall Preston closes his eyes and starts groaning again, and Eddie Yokum remembers about the race, especially as the Honorable Bertie Searles is calling on him to get up, and be a man, and keep going, so Eddie gets up and starts looking around for Follow You, but Follow You is now standing with his head hanging down, and when Eddie climbs on him again, Follow You does not seem inclined for any further action, especially in the way of making another jump.

Well, here is a predicament, to be sure, and as Eddie has no previous experience with balky horses, he scarcely knows what to do, especially as Follow You will not respond to kind words, or to kicks in the stomach, which are advised by the Honorable Bertie Searles, and in fact what does Follow You do but sit down there in the middle of the course, and Eddie slides right off his tail.

Then Eddie runs around in front of Follow you to argue with him face to face, and maybe give him a good yanking by the head, and for the first time since the race starts, Follow You gets a good look at who is riding him, and it seems that between the perspiration that is running down Eddie's face from his efforts, and falling into the water jump a couple of times, he is now no longer a boogie, but mostly white, and Follow You is not only startled but greatly insulted.

He starts scrambling to his feet at once, and Eddie Yokum is just barely able to climb back on the horse by his mane before Follow You starts running, taking the last jump again in wonderful shape, and then tearing on down the home stretch to finish inside the time limit as the winner of the race, and all that keeps Follow You from continuing on around the course again is the fact that Eddie falls off of him plumb exhausted.

Well, the excitement over this is very great, as Follow You's victory saves the public's money, and they take Follow You to the judge's stand, and put a blanket of roses on him, and Eddie Yokum is also there, holding himself up by leaning against old Ike, when Miss Phyllis Richie comes running up and starts kissing the rest of the burnt cork off of Eddie's face right in front of everybody, and speaking to him as follows:

"Oh," she says, "I recognize you when you come out of the water jump the last time, and I say to myself, then and there, I know he will win, because I remember your wonderful ride at the fox hunt. I love you," she says.

Naturally, Eddie Yokum tells Miss Phyllis Richie that her love is reciprocated, and he does not mention to her that the ride she speaks of at the fox hunt is negotiated on a motorcycle, because at this time there is further excitement, as it seems The Seldom Seen Kid and Hot Horse Herbie and Big Reds find Philly the Weeper up in the grandstand, and take him out back and give him quite a going over for beating them out of their end of the reward money he collects for the fox hounds, and also remove from his person a batch of pawn-tickets for the jewelry and other valuables he collects at the Oriole Hunts Club and converts into cash to bet on Sweep Forward.

Philly the Weeper says Mr. Marshall Preston permits him to keep the jewelry on condition he leaves a few articles in Eddie Yokum's room, after making a business deal with Philly the Weeper to take care of Roy Snakes in return for Mr. Marshall Preston's kindness in not turning him over to the police when he finds him collecting the knickknacks.

"Mr. Marshall Preston is a hard guy," Philly the Weeper says. "He tells me he starts out making love to Miss Phyllis Richie only with the idea of conning her into withdrawing Follow You from this race, so he can put over a big betting coup. But her having to have a ziggaboo jock makes it easier for him. But only a very hard guy will attempt to use love for such a base purpose," Philly the Weeper says. "Can you imagine me trifling with the love of Miss Lola Ledare in such a fashion?"

But Miss Lola Ledare says she is not going to give such a scalawag as Philly the Weeper a chance to trifle with her love any more, anyway, as she is much fonder of the Honorable Bertie Searles; and The Seldom Seen Kid turns the pawn-tickets he takes off Philly the Weeper over to Eddie Yokum, along with ten C's to remove the articles from hock, although he does not mention the sum of money he wins on Follow You with the ten C's.

It comes out that Mr. Marshall Preston is not too badly hurt, after all, so everybody is happy all the way around; but naturally Eddie Yokum is happiest of all, and he is standing around after the races mentioning his happiness to Miss Phyllis Richie, when all of a sudden he is seen to turn quite pale, and out of a clear sky, and as tired as he is, he starts running, and a large guy is observed running after him.

It is some hours before Miss Phyllis Richie sees Eddie Yokum to kiss him again, and to inquire why he seems to be trying to avoid one of her oldest and dearest Baltimore friends, Mr. Barker.